Love

Lockdown

Elle Rease

Cover Design: Rudelle Oosthuysen

ISBN 978-1-990901-56-0

Prologue

Asha Dewali was blessed with a good life: she'll never complain about or deny it. It was a fact. She couldn't change it. Frankly, she didn't want to.

Well, not really. There were many perks to being the eldest daughter of the Dewali family, with only one minor setback.

But that might not even matter. She was probably making a mountain out of a molehill, as usual, and this stress could be pointless. She should take deep breaths, find her centre and focus on the matters at hand. Why worry about something that might not be in the cards?

She attempted to snap out of her morbid musings, applauding when the next model appeared at the start of the runway. She loved the way that dress clung to the woman's size zero frame, creating the illusion of curves. Once Asha got around to setting the fashion world alight with her bold ideas, she was going to make sure that she only used curvier models. The hype the media made over skinny women made her sick to her stomach.

Never mind that she *was* one of those skinny women. Just… never mind.

"That'll look great on you," Marietta remarked with a warm smile. "You've got the length."

"Thank you for not saying I'll look like a praying mantis, wearing that," Asha teased. "Did you see the silk on the previous piece? I thought I was going to die. It was so beautiful!"

"I love Fashion Week," Marietta agreed. "Thanks for inviting me along."

"Are you kidding? You're my best friend." Her green eyes were distracted by the next gown that sashayed down the runway. "Oh wow, I've tried that style myself, but I couldn't get it to look so effortless."

"You shouldn't be so hard on yourself. Your collection had people on their feet."

Asha smiled grimly. "I'm nowhere near the Valentinos of the world."

"But you're getting there." Mariette nudged her in the ribs with her elbow. "Come on, relax. You've been uptight the last couple of weeks. Is everything okay at home?"

"Oh, yeah. Amazing."

"Your cool, British demeanour doesn't fool me, Asha Dewali. Spit it out already!"

"Can we talk about it later? I don't want to think about it right now."

"Sure, but I'm holding you to it."

Asha was granted about five minutes of silence, and

she cherished every second. Her attention remained glued to the creations on the ramp. Whenever it wavered, she forced it back to more interesting waters. She clapped along with everyone else, and smiled whenever she noticed the paparazzi. She was not going to think about that other thing, no way. So what if she's turned twenty-five? It didn't mean anything.

She sipped on her bottle of still water, trying to ease the knot of worry that clutched her gut in a death grip. She briefly closed her eyes to give her rising panic a moment to bow down to her will. By the time the designer walked down the ramp to receive a standing ovation, Asha felt more like herself.

Because of her surname, the designer stepped off the stage and made his way to Asha.

"Great job in Paris," he said, giving her a kiss on each cheek. "Looks like I'll have to watch my back from now on."

"Thank you." Asha gave him a polite smile. Everyone knew the fashion industry was cutthroat. Designers, photographers and supermodels hid behind white smirks, bright enough to give the sun a run for its money, but they were never real. "This is an incredible collection. I can't wait to own a few pieces!"

He placed his hand over his heart. "Darling, that's such a compliment, coming from you. I hope I see you at the after party!" And off he went to socialize with another big name.

"Well, I can't say that ever gets old," Asha muttered.

"It doesn't matter, Ash. We've got bigger fish to fry. After party, here we come!" Marietta cheered.

"Hopefully, we'll bump into a bunch of hot actors again. I could do with an A-list shag."

"Then an actor is probably not your best bet, unless you're looking for someone high maintenance," Asha commented, picking her bag up and allowing her best friend to drag her through the crowd, towards the exit.

"Oh my gosh, look!" Marietta pointed to a group of men. "Aren't they the Sarantos brothers?"

Her anxiety, now as familiar to her as her reflection, claimed her mind for a couple of seconds while she stared at the young Greek men. "Yes, it looks like them."

"Man, that Konstantinos can warm my bed any day."

"Is sex all you ever think about?"

Marietta glanced over her shoulder at Asha, laughing. "Of course! Wouldn't you, if you could have him?"

"He's not my type," Asha said truthfully. "Come on, let's get out of here. I think daddy sent a car to collect us."

"Your dad is the best. You're so lucky, Ash."

Oh yes, you have no idea how lucky I am, Asha thought demurely. She shook her head firmly. *I'm not going to start thinking like that. I have a good life. I'll never go hungry; our companies are successful; and that other thing will never, ever happen to me.*

Those last couple of words sounded more like a question as they echoed in her head. She prayed that she was right.

* * * * *

"SO, YOU SAY *this* is the perfect place to pick up chicks?" Loikanos asked his brother in Greek.

Konstantinos grinned while they were being ushered to the awaiting cars, responding: "Wait until you see the women at the after party."

"No wonder father never allowed me to come here." The twenty-three-year-old couldn't seem to pull his gaze away from the women that surrounded them. "And no wonder he's always so mad at you when you get back from Fashion Week."

That comment made Konstantinos' facial expression smooth out. "Yes, he always finds a way to remind me of my responsibilities. He forgets that I'm a grown man. I can do what I want."

"Keep telling yourself that," Loikanos laughed, slapping his older brother on the back. "I thought you'd be glad to take over from father. That way, you get to make more money, buy bigger houses, and drive faster cars."

"I do that anyway," Konstantinos said. He got into the awaiting BMW X6 first, waiting for his brother to join him before he went on. "My trust fund is big enough to sustain me for a very, very long time."

"I can't wait to turn twenty-five. I want my money, too."

"Patience, brother. In the meantime, let me pay for your drinks." Konstantinos quirked a smile. "I can assure you, you'll get lucky tonight."

Loikanos lifted a shoulder in nonchalance. "I mean, I'll have to see if I get along with anyone first."

Konstantinos' phone beeped, alerting him that he had

a message. He unlocked his screen, raising an eyebrow once he saw the picture his previous conquest had sent him. "Look at this," he murmured, handing his phone to his brother.

Loikanos' eyes went wide. "Do you always get this? She's completely topless!"

"Only if I leave without saying goodbye. Take notes, brother. Women don't like to be reminded that you can have anyone you want, whenever you want, wherever you want… Or however, in fact. They'll do anything to make you go back to them." Konstantinos made sure he had his brother's attention. "Don't, under any circumstances, think that they want *you*. Sure, you were blessed with the finest Sarantos DNA—"

"Not unlike you."

"That's not the point. You could look like an oil painting, or like dog shit, and they'll still want you. Do you know why?"

"We're billionaires."

"Exactly." Konstantinos took his phone back. "Never be fooled. That's what father always tells me."

"So, you've never been in love?"

Konstantinos looked away, remembering the tumultuous relationship of a few years ago. No one else in his family knew the details, although they'd met her. He'd mentioned a few things to his brother, but Loikanos seemingly couldn't recall Konstantinos' heartbreak. Everything had been perfect, until… *No, don't go there*, he reminded himself. *Save face.*

His answering laugh sounded forced to his own ears. "Don't be ridiculous. I've never known a woman long enough to love her. Except for mama, of course."

"That's hardly the same thing." Loikanos gazed up at the tall skyscrapers of New York City. "I'd be concerned if you were in love with mama."

"I would be, too. That's luckily not the case."

"I've been in love before."

Konstantinos snorted. "Please, tell me how you forgot to think with the head that's on your shoulders."

"No need to be sarcastic, brother. We were both in high school. I would've done anything for her, but she moved to Spain with her family."

"It was the best thing that could've happened to you."

"Sceptic."

"Yes, and proud of it."

"That could change in a matter of seconds, you know."

Konstantinos turned back to his window as the car slowed down, watching the crowd that was gathered outside the venue of the after party. "Let's hope that never happens."

* * * * *

"Thank you for coming, ladies and gentlemen. I know how busy your schedules are. I won't take up too much of your time."

Smiling faces greeted Denise Lemont. One merely had to glance at the *Forbes' Richest* list to know that she had ten of the most successful individuals in the room. Luckily, this did nothing to intimidate her. As the moderator, she was the person in charge of this negotiation. She's done research into these families and their descendants to be as informed as humanly possible. She couldn't afford to be caught off-guard, especially since her ex-husband had completely blindsided her a few months ago.

Tonight, she couldn't let her feelings show, and she wouldn't allow herself to become emotionally involved.

She didn't fail to notice that these couples were happy and still in love, even after decades of marriage. She knew there was a method to their madness, and felt proud that they'd chosen *her* for this task again. After the work she did three years earlier, the proof of her success was in the pudding, so to speak.

"Let's get started. I assume you've all had a chance to catch up on business?" She nodded, pleased, when they inclined their heads in acknowledgement. "My timing's impeccable, then." She consulted her notes. "Tonight, we will discuss the recent birthdays of the Dewali and Sarantos' children, as well as the impact this has on the rest of our business here." She turned to the Indian couple across from her. "Mr. Dewali? You have the floor."

"Sukesh," he corrected her gently, his British accent as alluring as his green eyes. He glanced at his wife. "Yes, our Asha is twenty-five now. She is currently the managing director of Dewali Fashions, though she has dreams of becoming a respected designer in her own right. She is educated and ambitious. We're very proud that she's being considered for this merger."

"Thank you, Sukesh," Denise said. "I've looked through her file, and you're lucky to have a daughter like her. She is smart and capable." Her eyes found the couple sitting to the left of Sukesh. "Mr. Sarantos?"

The Greek man cleared his throat. If the frown lines on his forehead were any indication, he hardly cracked a genuine smile. "Konstantinos is not as ambitious as Miss Dewali, sadly," he admitted in heavily accented English. "We do believe, however, that the right partnership will encourage him to be."

"Konstantinos means well," his wife Kolina added. "He needs someone to bring his business mind forward, to make him think of the bigger picture. He will be a great asset, once he commits his vision to something he cares about."

"He is also highly educated, with a degree in civil engineering," Nikos Sarantos assured everyone.

"Are you happy with this arrangement, Sukesh?" Denise asked, raising an eyebrow. "Mrs. Dewali?"

"Asha is more than capable to make Konstantinos the person his parents long for him to be," Anushka replied. "She's a smart woman. We would never suggest something that'll harm the Sarantos family in any way. Our families have always been supportive of each other's enterprises."

"I'm particularly looking forward to this union," Mr. Borgstrom commented.

"It will be interesting to see how well the fashion and motor industries collide with oil and property, yes," his wife agreed.

The Dewali couple smiled their appreciation for the sentiment.

"We hope that your daughter will be able to change

our son," Kolina said. "He has been lost for quite some time, and it will be refreshing to see how he matures during their relationship. We agree to this proposition."

Denise raised both her eyebrows. "Mr. and Mrs. Dewali?"

"Yes," they chorused.

"Alright." Denise swiped her finger across the screen of her tablet device. "As per the rules of engagement, Asha and Konstantinos will be sent to the Dewali penthouse suite in London, for exactly one calendar month. When would you like for this to occur?"

"As quickly as possible," Nikos grumbled. "The sooner Konstantinos gets his arse into gear, the better for us all."

"It looks like we can intervene within a week." Denise highlighted two items in her notes. "Both Asha and Konstantinos are scheduled to fly home via London in the next couple of days. They can be intercepted and taken to the penthouse."

"How are we going to withhold them from using their mobile phones?" Sukesh asked.

Denise gave him a reassuring smile. "We have handled this before." She nodded in the direction of the Shiau and Orloff couples. "Jun and Yerik are incredibly happy together. Please, Mr. Dewali, let me worry about the details."

"I have no doubt you've got everything under control, Miss Lemont," Anushka said.

Sukesh rose, holding his hand out to Nikos. "Always a pleasure, Nik."

"I look forward to calling you family soon," Nikos

muttered. He didn't look very excited, unsmiling as he was.

"Ladies and gentlemen, I believe that concludes our business for today." Denise pushed her chair out and got to her feet, shaking their hands one by one. "We are excited to see the Sarantos and Dewali families merge, in more than just the business sense. Let's make the wedding of the decade happen!"

CHAPTER 1

"I CAN'T WAIT to get home," Asha told her siblings as they boarded one of the Dewalis' the private jets. "This has been fun, but I miss India."

"You are such a weirdo," Kash mumbled. "No one who's *from* India actually wants to go back."

"Kashinath Dewali!" She folded her arms over her chest and gave him a good glare. "That's where our headquarters are—our bread and butter—or have you forgotten?"

"You're the only one who really cares about that," her brother reminded her. "You're the one that's being prepped to run Dewali Enterprises, as if it was yours to begin with."

"Seeing as you don't take it seriously, I have to."

"I hope you exclude me in that generalization," Farida mumbled. "I want to get into cars, but daddy won't let me."

"That's because you're a girl."

Asha bit her lip as she stared at her sister, the youngest Dewali sibling. "I'm afraid he has a point. Daddy prefers that you work with me in Fashions."

"Sometimes I wonder why our family is so backwards," Farida sighed. "It's not like this is the Middle Ages! Girls can design cars!"

You have no idea how backwards we really are.

Asha wished she was still her sister's age. That way, she wouldn't have known half of the things currently occupying space in her brain. Then again, she wouldn't change a thing. She was luckier than billions of others. She might be worried about her duties to her family, but she could also be wrong about it. Everything will work out the way she planned.

It had to.

"I hate flying from New York to London." Kash made himself comfortable on his seat, strapping in. "I can't believe the two of you dragged me all the way over here to watch women—who are in dire need of a decent meal, by the way—parade up and down a runway."

"They were half-naked," Farida said, frowning. "I thought men loved that."

"Sure, when they're in our beds. Not in front of a thousand other people."

"Men," Asha muttered. She picked up the latest edition of *Vogue* and began flipping through the pages, waiting for one of the pilots to announce their departure. "I doubt I'll ever truly understand them."

"It's pretty simple, Ash: men love sex, whether they're gay or straight. Those of us who are straight, love having it with women. Big surprise there, right?"

"And that's all there is to life? Sex?"

"Not everyone's as uptight as you." Kash rolled his eyes when she flipped him off. "Sure, we like fast cars and big mansions like everyone else, and we'll work to get it if we have to, but *sex* is what it's all about. It makes life worth living."

Asha thought of Praven and her back stiffened. Why was the male species so focused on fulfilling their carnal pleasures?

"Is that why you're on page six again?" Farida handed him the newspaper she was reading. "It says there that you couldn't keep your affection for… Hmm, what was her name?"

"I honestly can't remember. I had so much to drink." He squinted at the text in front of him. "What's wrong with kissing a woman in public?"

"That's not the problem, though, is it? You were groping each other like a bunch of horny teens, Kash! Couldn't you wait to get to your hotel room?"

"I don't think we made it to my hotel room," he said with a self-satisfied smirk. "As far as I can recall, we did it in the bathrooms."

Asha clicked her tongue. "So unsanitary."

"God, I hope you get a boyfriend soon, 'cause your attitude is getting old."

"What attitude?" she asked, taken aback.

"When was the last time you loosened up? You and Praven broke up *ages* ago, Ash! Get over it already! Move on!"

"It's got nothing to do with him. When you start

working, instead of dicking around, you'll know the true meaning of 'stress'."

"Excuses, excuses. Honestly, you say 'dicking around' like it's a bad thing."

"There's no reasoning with you, is there?"

He gave her his signature grin. "Oh, come on! You love that we're this close."

"Yeah, we're not like other families," Farida agreed. "I'm glad I get to be one of those girls who can call her brother and sister for advice on romance."

"If you're calling your *sister* for that, then you should have your head examined," Kash snorted. "What does Ash know of romance?"

"I know that 'romance' has nothing to do with 'dicking around'," Asha supplied.

"When was the last time you went on a date?"

She was immensely glad when the plane started moving. Now, she only had to hold out for another couple of hours, and then she'll finally be rid of her siblings. Hopefully, her brother will get bored with his investigation into her private life. "I don't need to go on dates. I'm not planning on doing anything with anyone. I'm too busy."

"It's going to catch up with you at some point, that's all I'm saying."

"It's so easy for a man to judge, isn't it?"

Farida watched the argument as if she was viewing a tennis match, barely holding back her giggles. "You guys are so funny."

"Ash, you don't have to be in a relationship with someone to have fun," Kash continued, chucking the newspaper aside so he could give her his full attention. "You can get someone on the side."

Asha's stared at him in surprise, mouth gaping open.

He sent his gaze to the ceiling. "Right, for a second I forgot who I was talking to. Seriously, was Praven the only man you've ever slept with?"

Farida gasped. "You're not a virgin anymore?"

"I swear to God, if you don't stop talking right now, I'll bash your face in," Asha warned her idiot brother.

Kash held his arms up in surrender. "What, was it a state secret?"

"Do you want to scar your sister for life?"

"You're not a virgin anymore?" Farida repeated, eyeing her sister.

Asha rubbed her temples and closed her eyes. "No, I'm not. But I've only slept with Praven."

"You didn't tell me! And then you preach me about staying a virgin—"

"Wait, *you're* still a virgin?" Kash interrupted, seeming simultaneously flabbergasted and disgusted.

"That's beside the point!" Asha glared at her younger sister. "Do as I say, not as I do. As for *you*, Kashinath Dewali, shut your yap or I'll do it for you!"

"You know she's serious when she starts rhyming," Kash said, nudging Farida in the ribs with a smile. "Next, she'll start foaming at the mouth."

Farida hid a giggle behind her hand.

"I'm done talking to both of you." Asha plugged her earphones into her iPod, covering her ears as the plane took off. She was about to press play when she heard her brother say something that had her sighing.

"You know you're not supposed to use any electronic devices for the first and last ten minutes of a flight."

Damn it, she took rules seriously. She stuffed her iPod into her bag and turned to her window, watching New York disappear as they ascended. She couldn't wait to get to India: her homeland always made her relax. She loved her brother and sister to bits, but could only tolerate their presence in small doses.

"What's the big deal, Kash? I've been told that I should stay a virgin until my wedding night."

Kash snorted. "You literally *just* said that we don't live in the Middle Ages anymore, sis. Besides, how are you going to know what you like on your wedding night if you don't practice until then?"

"But don't guys like knowing they're the first?" Farida hedged.

"It's actually terrifying," he admitted. "Girls have this idea in their heads that it's meant to be special, so when a guy finds out you're still a virgin, they want to run in the opposite direction. They don't want you falling in love with them just because they were your first, and they also don't want to hurt you… And first times hurt for a girl."

"But what if you're *with* someone? What if you've been dating for months?"

"I suppose it could be different then, but it's still scary. All I'm saying is, a guy feels more comfortable knowing you know what's going to happen next."

Asha zoned out, preferring to stay impartial to their debate, lest it push her blood pressure over the edge again. His comments were already driving her up the wall. Was that really how men thought? Could that be why Praven had said all those horrible things to her while they'd been together?

Don't go there, Asha!

She couldn't stop it. One by one, their memories flitted through her mind, good and bad, tormenting her with a past she wished she could forget. Will she ever recover from his abrupt dismissal? Better yet, will she ever trust another man enough to move on and try again?

The seatbelt light switched off, followed by a brief announcement informing them that they were free to roam the cabin. Asha got up and strode to the lavatory, ignoring the inquiring looks her siblings sent her. Her back ramrod straight to feign control, she closed herself in the cubicle and rested against the door, facing the mirror.

The woman on the other side seemed tense and sad and, to some extent, like a total stranger. Asha remembered a happy-go-lucky version of herself, but that felt like a long time ago.

She moved forward, closer to the stranger, to open a tap and splash her face with water. The cool temperature soothed her frayed nerves. She remained like that—eyes shut and head hovering over the basin—for a few seconds, breathing through her panic.

You've got this. You're Asha Dewali, heir to a billion-dollar fortune. Nothing should frighten you.

With her internal pep-talk done, she dried her face, combed her fingers through her waist-length dark hair, and exited the lavatory. Kash and Farida were watching a movie together, oblivious that Asha had resurfaced. She reached for her portfolio and took her seat, getting ready to finish a design she'd started that morning.

She found herself staring out the window more often than not, watching the dark blue ocean and spattering of clouds. Everything felt... *off*, somehow, and she couldn't seem to concentrate for long.

This was unlike her. She's always been commended for her ability to focus but, ever since her twenty-fifth birthday, she couldn't even meditate. She was too consumed by thoughts of her future; too worried that she was going to be sold to the highest bidder, like some kind of prized cow.

Stop thinking about it, she chided herself. *You know you attract what you fear. It might not be you. There are other billionaire families out there. Any one of them could've been chosen. Maybe no one will be chosen this time, 'cause everyone's realized that it's no longer necessary, and that there are better ways to go about business mergers!*

She managed to squeeze two designs out of her brain before the swirling descent to Heathrow started. She had a smile on her face once they got low enough to make out London's landmarks. She had good memories of England, since she had grown up here. She'd gone to the most prestigious schools, and made friends with the richest and most well-known families in the UK.

And then, of course, there was Praven.

They'd been together for seven years. Why they weren't married with children by now, or why he'd really bailed before putting a ring on her finger, only he would know. It's been ten months since they broke up, but it was still a mystery. Sometimes she felt relieved, which made no sense.

It's true what they say: one never forgets one's first love.

"Ladies and gent, we are on final approach. Kindly fasten your seatbelts."

Asha followed the instructions of the flight attendant, absently noting her brother and sister doing the same. The plane touched down smoothly and quickly proceeded to the private section of the airport, where it parked in a hangar.

Kash had his phone on before the door opened. "Hmm, dad wants to see all of us before you go to India, Ash."

She frowned, checking her own phone and reading the same message. Her father was obsessed with broadcasting texts, instead of sending individual ones. "I wonder what about."

"I guess we won't know until we see him. He says he's sent a car for us."

"You can't say that you won't enjoy the break before you go back to India," Farida added. "Maybe you could stay here for a couple of days? We could go shopping!"

Asha pulled a face, but couldn't deny that Farida's offer was tempting. "Fine, but let's go see what daddy wants, first."

She went to the cockpit to inform the pilots of the change in plans, and followed her siblings out of the plane. They headed to the idling Maybach and she thanked the driver, who was holding the door for them.

There were two black SUV's waiting behind them, presumably filled with bodyguards.

Asha was about to slide onto the backseat when an exclamation from Pierce, the head of their security, had her blinking in shock.

"Ah, damn!" His eyes were on his phone. "My battery just died."

"Do you have a charger?"

He shook his head sadly. "Miss Dewali, may I use yours?"

She hesitated for a second, loathe to part with her phone. Then she felt guilty for second-guessing him. Didn't her security team work long enough hours, away from their families, to justify being treated like humans? She shouldn't act like a spoilt socialite!

"It must be urgent," she replied, handing it over. "You look like you need a holiday, Pierce."

He smiled grimly. "I'll be sure to mention that to your father, Miss Dewali. Thank you."

He shut the door after she got comfortable. Kash and Farida's phones beeped at the same time, and they compared texts. Asha leaned her head back, closing her eyes. She could feel the early onset of two days' worth of jetlag already.

"Ooh, Emily's at Harrods!" Farida turned to Pierce. "Can you drop me off there?"

"Of course, Miss Dewali."

"I'm definitely coming along. Emily is damn fine," Kash said.

"Dad wants to see *all of us*," Asha reminded them. "We should get that out the way first."

"It's only twelve," Farida whined. "We can meet up with daddy for dinner! Besides, you look like you need a nap."

Asha wasn't going to argue that. "Kash, you shouldn't ruin Farida's fun. You know Emily doesn't like you."

He narrowed his eyes. "Of course she does!"

"If you stopped hitting on her, she might give you the time of day."

"Yeah, she knows what you're like, Kash," Farida added.

"Well, I can change." Kashinath folded his arms over his chest. "For a while."

Asha burst out laughing. "I would pay to see that."

"I'm going along," he said firmly.

"Okay," Asha muttered, shrugging. "Don't say I didn't warn you."

She gazed out the window. It was raining lightly, which caused major traffic jams on the way to Harrods. A small smile played at the corners of her mouth as she watched the people of London go about their day. Sometimes, she fantasized about being a regular, middle-class person, yet she couldn't relate completely because her life was vastly different.

Before she knew it, the car pulled over at Harrods. She waved her siblings off, who were at each other's throats about some idiotic topic once again, and wondered how they could have such boundless energy after a long-haul flight.

Maybe she was getting old.

The motion of the car, coupled with no one around to keep her company, caused her to nod off on the way to her parents' apartment. When she regained consciousness, she was on the couch in her parents' penthouse suite. Had Pierce carried her from the car?

She frowned, running a hand through her hair. She walked to the kitchen to get a bottle of still water. "Mum? Daddy? Are you here already?" she called, making her way through the large rooms. It was deathly quiet. "Probably still on their way," she muttered. She searched her handbag for her phone. "Where did I put it?"

With a start, she remembered that she'd given it to Pierce. He must've forgotten to return it. She strolled to the study, intent on giving Marietta a call. Her heart skipped a beat once she realized that there wasn't a phone on either her mother or father's desks.

Maybe this was all just a horrible dream, and she'll wake up on the couch again, yet she couldn't shake the feeling that something was amiss. She wasn't sure if she wanted to find out what.

CHAPTER 2

"AH, LONDON," KONSTANTINOS declared when he got out of the plane. His good mood was met by rainy weather. He laughed at the sight of the droplets outside the hangar. "How I've missed you!"

"Speak for yourself." Loikanos joined his side with a sigh. "This place sucks. Why aren't we going home?"

"Apparently, father wants to meet with us first." Konstantinos strode to the awaiting car, grateful that he wouldn't have to walk through Heathrow airport like an average Joe. There were perks to being rich. "I'm preparing myself for another session of disgruntled disappointment and absolutely no smiles from his side."

"I'm glad I have a brother who gets into trouble all the time. That way, father doesn't pay attention to *me*."

He smirked as he got comfortable on the backseat of the Range Rover. "Enjoy it while it lasts."

Loikanos' phone rang, prompting Konstantinos to

pat his pockets in search of his own. He frowned and opened the window, getting the attention of one of his bodyguards. "I think I left my phone on the plane."

The man inclined his head. "I'll go get it for you, Mr. Sarantos."

"Thank you." He glanced at his younger brother, trying to get the gist of the conversation.

"You don't say? Uh-huh. Really? Right now? *Today?*" Loikanos' dark gaze darted over the hangar. "That's really interesting. Oh, sure. Sure, I'll come over. Jeez, have some faith! Of course I won't do that." There was a long pause, in which he looked ready to murder whoever was speaking to him. "Look, I know I'm an idiot half of the time, but you should know that... Yeah, so stop telling me to... Uh-huh. I get it, okay? See you soon."

Konstantinos raised an eyebrow. "What was that about?"

"One of my old school friends," his brother muttered, putting his phone in his pocket. "He wants to meet up for drinks."

"Right now?"

"Yes, and I probably shouldn't keep him waiting. You don't know how he gets. Are you going to be okay by yourself?"

"Are you kidding me?"

Loikanos laughed, mock-punching his brother on the shoulder. "Look after yourself. I'll give you a call." He checked to make sure he had his wallet. "I'll take another car. Give my apologies to father, will you?"

"Sure, 'cause he needs another reason to be mad at

me!" Konstantinos shouted, but his brother was already rushing to the other side of the hangar, where there was another convoy of cars. Konstantinos shook his head with a chuckle. "Disaster in the making, that one."

"Sir?"

He waved his driver's question away. The driver took that to mean that Konstantinos was ready to get out of here, and promptly started the engine. "Wait! I left my phone in the plane."

"Christopher is busy getting it," the man said, stepping down on the accelerator. "He'll bring it to your father's offices."

"That's not the point," Konstantinos mumbled under his breath. He dug in the seat pockets, happy to find a car magazine, even though it was one he's already scanned through once before. He flipped the pages slowly, keeping his attention on the photographs and articles.

He hated sitting around with nothing to do. He has always been a busybody, constantly yearning for the next big adventure. He'd driven his parents insane as a child, running off with a new group of friends every other day. Frankly, if he were honest with himself, nothing has really changed now that he was in his mid-twenties.

When a yawn crept up on him, he frowned. He hadn't realized, until this very moment, how exhausted he was. He'd made it his personal mission to show his brother a good time in New York, so he had performed at a higher rate than usual. Loikanos was an idealist about love and the opposite sex, and a part of Konstantinos wanted to show his brother how disillusioned he appeared whenever he rambled on about finding "The One".

Konstantinos stifled a yawn, his eyelids drooping. Maybe it won't be so bad to have a quick nap…

He must've nodded off, because the car had stopped by the time he woke up again. The door was being held open and, without waiting to see where he was going, he made a dash through the rain for the building they were parked in front of. One of his bodyguards had called the elevator, cracking a smile as Konstantinos stepped inside.

"Top floor, eh?" he asked conversationally, annoyed when his bodyguard didn't respond. He watched the numbers count up and grinned once the lift stopped at the penthouse suite. "Wouldn't expect anything less."

He walked into the apartment, looking around at the decorations in confusion. It had a definite Indian vibe. He turned back to the elevator to ask his bodyguard what was going on, but there was no one there. That was weird. Was this his father's attempt at a prank?

"Hello?" he called in Greek. "Is anyone here?"

There was no response.

"Okay then," he muttered, deciding to explore. He found a bowl of fruit in the beautiful yet simplistic kitchen, grabbing an apple as he made his way to where he presumed a living room was. A smile blossomed on his face once he saw the massive TV, his eyes automatically finding the hidden surround sound speakers. He bit into the apple and reached for the remote.

Whatever this place was, at least he'll be entertained while he waited for his father to show up.

"What're *you* doing here?"

He glanced over his shoulder. His eyebrows pulled together. "Asha Dewali? Are you here to see my father?"

The Indian heiress crossed her arms and tilted her head to the side, regarding him silently. She was wearing olive green chinos and a white formal shirt, the sleeves rolled up to her elbows. Her feet were bare, indicating that she had made herself at home.

Konstantinos mimicked her stance, trying to figure out what's going on. "Seriously, why are you here?"

Her mouth parted on a gasp, as if something lifechanging has dawned on her. "Oh my God," she breathed. Her knees must've been weak, because she took a seat on the arm of one of the chairs, staring at him with wide eyes. "No!"

Has he summed her up incorrectly? Was she actually mentally disturbed?

He shifted on his feet. "Asha, does my father have business with you, as well?"

She burst into a fit of laughter, tears streaming down her face while she clutched at her stomach. It looked like she *was* insane.

"What's going on?" He had this sinking feeling, one he couldn't really explain or find the origin of. It wasn't helping that she couldn't speak. "Asha!"

"*Think*, Konstantinos!" she urged him, wheezing as she wiped the wet tracks from her cheeks.

"About *what*?"

"Oh my God, you honestly don't know?" She lifted the edge of her shirt to dab at her eyes, exposing her toned stomach. "Wow, you're more self-absorbed than I realized! And to think…" She trailed off when another batch of hysterical giggles overtook her. "To think we'll be spending the rest of our lives together! *Ha!*"

"Spending the rest of…" His eyes widened as the meaning of her words struck home. Surely, she didn't mean… "You can't be serious! That's a myth!"

"Is it really?" She shook her head, looking like she was at a loss. "I knew I shouldn't have worried about this, and paid it absolutely no attention. It's like I manifested my worst fears! If that isn't proof of the law of attraction, then I don't know what is!"

"No, it's a myth!" he insisted. He ran his fingers through his hair and glanced around, anxious for the moment when a camera crew will jump out of nowhere to show them this was a sick joke. "Families can't arrange marriages anymore! We live in the twenty-first century, for God's sake!"

"Doesn't seem like any of that matters when you've got a big bank balance." Her eyes had a faraway look in them. "This must be a sick dream."

He felt as helpless as she was, and had no clue what to say.

She closed her eyes. "Who am I kidding?"

"Well, I don't have to stay for this," he declared, heading back to the elevator. "I can leave, and neither of us will have to go through with this."

"Excellent idea!" She was instantly at his side. "They

can't keep us here." She pressed the button. It didn't light up. "What the heck?"

He did the same, wondering if there was an electrical error of sorts. "Where are the stairs?"

"Oh, this way."

He followed her to a polished black door and fiddled with the handle. "Locked. Where's the key?"

"Uh, I have no idea, but it should be where we keep the other keys."

He trailed behind her, his stomach dropping to his shoes. Something didn't feel right. "I'll see if I can get a hold of the lobby," he told her once he spotted the intercom. "Find those keys."

"Okay."

The screen was blank, indicating that the cameras have been disconnected. He pressed the small white button. "Hello? Is anyone there?"

Silence.

"This isn't funny," he persisted. "We need to get out of the penthouse suite. Is there something wrong with the elevator?"

There was no sign of life.

He swore under his breath and turned on his heel, coming up with ways to get out of here. His hope plummeted when Asha returned, looking mortified. That was never a good sign.

"I can't find any keys. Like, any at all."

"No one's answering," he said, pointing at the intercom.

"What if this isn't a joke?" She bit her lip, her green eyes filling with tears. This time, it wasn't because she was laughing. The seriousness of their situation was overwhelming. "What if they're really expecting us to go through with this?"

He didn't have an answer to that question.

"I can't..." She set her jaw and clenched her hands into fists. "I can't marry *you*!"

He immediately took offense, bristling at the accusatory tone she was using, as if he disgusted her. "*I* can't marry *you*! You're the most anal-retentive person I've ever known."

"I was thinking about the more obvious reason, like how we don't even know each other that well!" she snapped. "I am *not* anal, you jerk!"

He cocked an eyebrow. "That's not what I've heard."

"Oh, you want to go *there*, do you? As if you're one to talk! You don't take anything seriously!"

"I think it's time you get off your high horse, lady," he warned.

"What if I like the view from here?" She took a few deep breaths to calm herself. "If this is real," she went on, motioning to their surroundings, "then we'll be stuck here for a while. In fact, they're probably already announcing our..." Suddenly, as if possessed, she stalked back to the living room.

Feeling as if his life was falling to pieces, he went after her. He watched as she flipped to a celebrity news channel, frown deepening once she turned up the volume.

"...received word that Asha Dewali and Konstantinos Sarantos will be getting married in six weeks," the female presenter was saying, one of those have-I-got-news-for-*you* kind of smiles on her face. "They've recently returned from New York's Fashion Week, where the hot Greek billionaire is rumoured to have proposed."

His blood was boiling in anger. He was expected to marry Asha in *six weeks*? How deranged was his family?

"The nuptials might come as a surprise to most, but sources tell us that they have been inseparable since Dewali's split from her long-term boyfriend, Praven Kahn, earlier this year."

Photographs of Asha and Konstantinos were being cycled through on the screen. Notably, none of them had the two in frame together. Surely people could see this was fake news?

"Their union will no doubt be a huge benefit to the booming businesses of the Dewali and Sarantos families—"

Asha turned the TV off, raising her hands to her head in apparent horror. "This can't be happening to me."

"Where did they get this information? Who are their so-called 'sources', anyway?"

"If you don't know by now that most of the stories on the news are exactly that, then you're dumber than I've been led to believe."

"I have an engineering degree, lady!"

"Congratulations. Did you buy it?"

He took a step back, fuming at her insinuation. "I'm not marrying you."

"Then we're in agreement." She slowly turned to him. Her face would've been pretty, if it wasn't so completely deadpan. "We'll wait it out in here, since we don't have much of a choice, but we'll wash our hands of each other once those doors open. We'll break off the engagement and never, *ever* see each other again."

"Agreed," he confirmed, holding his hand out. "They can't force us to get married."

She briefly shook his hand. "If you'll excuse me, I think I need to sleep. It's been a long day."

"Great idea. Where's the master bedroom?"

She gave him an annoyed look. "This isn't *your* apartment. You're not getting the master suite."

"Seeing as *I'm* the one being affected by this latest development in my father's asinine plan, I think it's only fair."

"Like hell!"

He watched her storm off into the hallway and shook his head. What on earth had his parents been thinking, pairing him off with *her*?

Choosing to get comfortable on the couch, he punched the pillow under his head and stared at the ceiling. He'll move into the master bedroom and kick her out later. He was too tired now, and needed energy if he was going to survive the next couple of days.

* * * * *

"THEY DON'T LOOK too happy about this," Anushka commented.

"Were any of us?" Sukesh reminded her. "I wanted to throttle you at first."

Nikos's gaze was on the TV screen, where Konstantinos was drifting off to sleep. "I do not feel comfortable watching them like this."

"It's for their own safety, in case of an emergency. As you saw, they're locked in there. Besides, there are only cameras in the main living areas," Anushka soothed. "A team will be watching over them 24/7 to ensure they're okay."

"But why can't we hear them?" he insisted.

"I think that's best," Kolina answered, giving her husband's hand a squeeze. "They're clearly not pleased with what we've done."

Denise entered the room and smiled at the two sets of parents. "Is everything alright?"

"We're just setting Nikos' mind at ease," Sukesh informed her.

"Yes, this is different from your lockdown, isn't it?" the French woman murmured, eyes fixed to the screen. "Back then, there wasn't all of this technology to contend with." She gave them a comforting look. "I assure you that we will do our best not to infringe on their privacy. This method worked well with Jun and Yerik."

"We know," Kolina said as she bumped her shoulder to her husband's. "Everything will be fine. Konstantinos will come to his senses." She leered at the Dewalis. "Although it seems like Asha is just as difficult as he is."

"That is exactly what he needs," Denise insisted gently. "They were paired off for a reason."

Nikos inclined his head reluctantly. "It did not work when we tried to make him understand the importance of our business, it's true."

His wife seemed pleased that he was coming around. "Besides, Asha is far too beautiful to escape his notice for long."

Sukesh laughed. "Thank you, I think."

"This is a good match." Kolina nodded to herself. "They might not see it yet, but we do."

Denise clicked her fingers, prompting a server to pour everyone another glass of champagne. "We'll be checking in with them to make sure they have everything they need. The fridge is fully stocked and there are recipe books on the shelf. Asha can learn to cook in no time."

Kolina's eyebrows shot up. "Asha does not know how to cook?"

"She's been more focused on the academic and professional aspects of her life than anything else," Sukesh explained.

"Is that why her relationship with Praven Kahn failed?" Nikos queried.

The Dewalis narrowed their gazes.

Denise stepped in to keep the peace. "No, Praven Kahn left her for another woman."

"She better learn to cook, or Konstantinos will do the same."

The Dewalis exchanged worried and somewhat incredulous glances, relaxing when Kolina and Nikos started laughing. The two conversed in Greek before switching back to English.

"Then again, it might be the wake-up call that Konstantinos needs," Kolina said, still chuckling to herself. "He has a habit of comparing women to each other. If Asha is different from the rest of them, she might capture his heart the way I did Nikos'."

"Good, then it's settled." Denise raised her glass. "To Asha and Konstantinos!"

"To Asha and Konstantinos!" they echoed.

CHAPTER 3

TO HIS EXTREME irritation, he was still on the couch in the Dewalis' apartment when he woke up two hours later. Clearly, this wasn't a bad dream so, unfortunately, he wouldn't be able to spend the next couple of weeks in bed, wishing his life away.

He reached for the television remote, hoping for a good show to occupy his time. A quick glance at the floor-to-ceiling windows showed him that it was—unsurprisingly—still raining in London. The clock on the screen informed him that it was about nine o'clock. Normally, he would've been preparing to hit the clubs with a bunch of his mates to drink and hook up with random women.

Now, however, he wasn't going to get any action for the foreseeable future. What was he going to do with his free time?

After about half an hour of a *Boston Legal* rerun, he sighed from boredom. He got up and explored the rest of the apartment, surprised to find that it had two storeys. A hallway led to a study, gym and massive library, and had a staircase right at the end. He ascended to the next floor, peeking into the first of four bedrooms. He recalled that Asha has a brother and sister, so it made sense that there would be a room for each.

She wasn't asleep in the master bedroom, but in one that could've qualified as the main one by the sheer size of it. She was curled up on a King-size canopy bed. The decorations were predominantly red, white and black.

He rolled his eyes. Did she have to be such a cliché? What was it with fashion designers, anyway? They created such extravagant clothes, and yet they were incredibly predictable at home.

Konstantinos went to the master bedroom, for interest's sake. It contained a mahogany four-poster bed—with two suitcases on it—and neutral fabrics. He nodded, impressed, at the large TV built into the opposite wall. There was a sitting area in front of the windows that could be used as a place to work.

Wait a minute…

He stepped up to the bed, stunned to realize the luggage belonged to him. Who'd put it here? *When* had they brought it up here?

Striding to the large walk-in closet, his jaw dropped. He instantly recognized a bunch of his hoodies and, upon closer inspection, saw that the rest of the clothes folded in the wardrobe also belonged to him. He could've sworn he'd left it all behind in his three-bedroom villa at his family's mansion in Greece! What on earth was it doing *here?*

Did they honestly think that he was going to move here, indefinitely? To be with *Asha?*

"This is insane," he grumbled in his native tongue, grabbing sweatpants from one of the suitcases and putting it on, along with a new pair of socks and trainers. He might as well exercise, mostly to see if he could exhaust himself enough to get another couple of hours of sleep.

The gym contained the latest equipment and gadgets, including high-end surround sound speakers. He connected his phone via Bluetooth, selected his favourite playlist, and started stretching to loosen up his muscles, all the while eyeing his reflection in the mirror wall to his right. He liked what he saw. His biggest hope was that he wouldn't end up like his father: constantly annoyed and completely out of shape.

He turned the volume up and climbed on the rowing machine. His adrenaline was pumping. He hummed along to an Usher song, although he would've preferred listen to it in a nightclub.

For the first time, it looked like money couldn't buy everything.

When he was a teenager, he'd heard the rumours, of course. There were currently five families worldwide that had thrown their lots in together, owning assets of unimaginable worth all around the world: Sarantos, Dewali, Borgstrom, Shiau and Orloff. The net worth of each family was estimated at over forty billion dollars. Traditionally, on their offspring's twenty-fifth birthdays, a union was arranged by way of a merger:

both in the business and marital sense.

His parents had been married in a similar fashion, thirty years ago, although at that time the families that ran the world hadn't taken business mergers to the international stage yet. Globalisation hadn't been as prominent as it was today.

A few years ago, Jun Shiau had married Yerik Orloff, though Konstantinos had thought they'd met coincidentally, seeing as they'd hung out in the same circles. They had seemed so happy on their wedding day; not at all like a couple who had been forced to be together. Their marriage had secured the merger between the Orloff and Shiau businesses, and the net worth of the resulting new company was mind-boggling.

He was now convinced that their marriage had been arranged. It appeared as if they were still going strong, though he couldn't see why, given that the basis of their relationship had been built on what their *families* wanted. They didn't even share the same culture, traditions and family values!

This whole situation was messed up. He was going to have a couple of words to say to his parents once he got out of here.

Twenty-five minutes in, he got off the rowing machine and patted his face dry with a towel. Kanye West was currently singing his hit, *Love Lockdown*, which caused Konstantinos to burst into hysterical laughter. Talk about a coincidence!

He wondered if his parents—and Asha's, for that matter—knew what they were doing, because they were coming across as lunatics who were interfering with the natural progression of their children's lives.

Asha walked into the gym, dressed in black sweatpants and a bright pink top. Her hair was pulled into a high ponytail. She looked as irritated as he felt. "You couldn't be any louder, could you?" she muttered in her posh British accent, turning the volume down. "I was sleeping."

"I figured the gym's soundproof," he shrugged. He rolled his eyes when she glared at him. "I couldn't sleep, okay? I don't really sleep that much."

"Fabulous. I'm stuck in here with an insomniac."

"Are you usually this snippy?"

She went to a closet, getting out a yoga mat. "It's hard to think of the positive things in my life when I have to listen to Eminem shouting about how much he hates his ex-wife."

He lifted a shoulder again. "That's not my problem. I like Eminem."

"Makes sense. Like him, you refuse to grow up."

"Aren't you a ray of sunshine?"

She ignored that, starting with mountain pose. "Do you own a shirt?"

"I own several, actually. I just don't like wearing them when I work out." He made his way to the treadmill, choosing a sloping marathon mode for thirty minutes. His feet quickly found a rhythm he was comfortable with. "Thought that's obvious."

"If you spent half your time in the office, instead of focussing on your physical appearance like the self-centred jerk you are rumoured to be, then you'll probably be a very successful man."

"If you spent half your time getting laid, instead of focussing on anal things like businesses that run themselves by now, then you'll probably be a much nicer woman."

"I am nice!"

"I have yet to discover whether that's wishful thinking, or the truth. Also, I think you're supposed to be *calming down* with yoga, not getting more worked up."

"Oh, I'm getting worked up, am I?"

"Do we really have to talk to each other?" he grumbled.

"You are such a jerk. I can't believe all those rumours are true."

"They're not." He glanced at her. "You've already made your mind up about me, and I'm not in the mood to change it. I doubt that I'll be in that mood by the time we get out of here."

"Are you saying my mind can't be changed? That I'm too set in my ways to give people second chances?"

"No, *you* said that. Do you like looking for things that don't exist? Maybe you should start a hunt for bigfoot. You'll probably be successful with that, although you'll come across as a bit nuttier than you are now."

"I'm *not* crazy!" she yelled, her hands pressing together in front of her chest. She slowly switched to tree pose. "That's a nasty thing to say."

"'Nah-stee'," he mocked, chuckling. "You really have a stick up your ass, Miss Fancy-pants."

She glared at him. "Why aren't you out of breath? I was hoping you'd quit yapping by now."

He raised an eyebrow, giving her a half-grin. "Have you seen my body at all? I'm incredibly fit."

"And vain, apparently."

"I'm blessed with good genes."

"I don't think I've ever met anyone so self-centred before."

"I think you have." He saw her frown and elaborated: "I hear Praven Kahn's got a big ego, especially lately. How *is* he, by the way?"

She stayed silent for a couple of minutes. "We don't talk about our personal lives."

"Then don't get personal with your comments." His muscles were burning now that the treadmill was giving him more resistance, imitating the way he would've run uphill. "I have a thick layer of skin, but you have sharp nails."

She went from tree pose to another, finally looking like she was calming down. If he'd known how grumpy she would get about being woken from a deep sleep, he wouldn't have been so loud. Despite what she thought, he wasn't an inconsiderate asshole.

Konstantinos found his eyes wandering over to her every now and again. With that constant frown gone from her face, her true beauty was shining through. She might not have the best personality, but she was definitely the type of woman he'd look at twice in a club or restaurant. She wasn't any fun, though, so she wouldn't have kept his attention for long in the real world.

He shook his head with a sigh, glancing at the treadmill's timer.

His parents clearly had no clue about what kind of woman made him tick. If they'd consulted him about this asinine plan, he would've steered them in the right direction. He'd never fall for the likes of Asha Dewali. First of all, he didn't believe in love. He had a good time with a woman for two weeks or so, and then he moved on. Secondly, he's always pictured himself settling down with someone French…

Fifty years from now.

He's tried being in a committed relationship. It hadn't worked out. Obviously, it wasn't meant for him.

Having completed his treadmill challenge, he made his way to the weights section. His stomach growled while he bench-pressed fifty-five kilograms. He couldn't remember the last time he's eaten. Lunch, maybe? Hopefully Asha was making herself useful in the kitchen. He'd love to have a big homecooked meal.

Konstantinos emerged from the gym an hour later, drenched in sweat, and walked to the kitchen. He was dismayed to find that no pots on the stove and nothing in the oven.

"Asha! Where's dinner?" he called.

"You're crazy if you think I'm going to cook for you!" she shouted from somewhere on the lower level of the apartment.

He frowned. "You're Indian! That's not very hospitable of you!"

"Being Indian has nothing to do with it!"

"What am I supposed to eat?" he asked as he went foraging in the pantry.

"Not my problem!"

Sighing deeply, he retrieved three tins of tuna. He took feta cheese, tomatoes, onions, green peppers and eggs out of the fridge, deciding to make a quick salad. It took ten minutes for the eggs to boil, giving him enough time to wolf down another two apples. He mixed all the ingredients together in a large bowl, grabbed a fork from one of the drawers, and walked to the living room.

"Ugh, tuna?" Asha asked as he sat down on the couch next to her. She had a large sketchpad propped up on her legs, which were curled under her.

"What about it?"

"It stinks."

"Well, I need a lot of protein if I want to keep this up," he said, absently patting his eight-pack stomach.

"You smell like sweat."

"That's what happens when you exercise for two hours straight." He pulled a face at the program on the television. "*Mrs. Eastwood & Company*? Really?"

Her shoulders went up as she turned her attention back to the drawing in front of her. "I like Dina Eastwood."

"You're busy with something else." He fished for the remote. "You don't mind if I change the channel, do you?"

"Go watch in your room."

"I guess everyone thought it would be better for me to get the master bedroom, after all," he gloated. He switched to a movie channel, sighing with pleasure once he saw that *Iron Man 2* had just started on one of the movie channels. "This is the life."

"What do you mean, everyone?"

"All of my things were in the master bedroom. You can't have it."

She stared at the screen for a moment, her mouth twitching into a smile when Robert Downey Jr. gave one of his infamous one-liners. "I put your things there."

He narrowed his eyes at her. "What?"

"I figured I was being a bitch. I took your bags over."

"Did you put my stuff in the closet, as well?"

"What? No." She frowned at him. "You have things in the closet?"

"Yeah. There are a bunch of suits, too."

"Why would there be suits in your closet? We can't go out."

"I wondered the exact same thing."

"This whole thing is so stupid," she said, tapping her pencil on the sketchpad. "I'm never going to fall for someone like you. You're not my type. Not even close."

"Right back at you, princess."

She gave him an irritated look.

"Hmm, you're right. 'Princess' isn't right."

"Thank you!"

He smiled broadly. "It's more like 'ice princess', anyway."

"You're impossible." She got up, heading for the hallway. "I can't work here."

"Finally, she gets the hint!" he shouted after her, finishing his tuna salad. He got comfortable on the couch. He'll take a shower after the movie. He could stomach the smell of his own sweat and wasn't as disgusted by it as Asha seemed to be.

CHAPTER 4

ASHA SAT DOWN at her mother's desk in the study with a sigh, positioning her sketchpad carefully. She was shit out of luck where inspiration was concerned, and being in this abandoned apartment with the World's Most Arrogant Bachelor was not helping things along.

She stared at the computer screen in front of her, momentarily distracted. She'd really wanted to watch that episode of *Mrs. Eastwood & Company*, even though she's seen it before. Of all the shows created for the *E! Entertainment* channel, she enjoyed that one the most. There was something about Carmel-by-the-Sea…

"Hold up," she muttered to herself, switching the computer on. What if she could still read her emails, or update her Twitter status? They might've taken her phone, but that didn't mean that she couldn't communicate with the outside world anymore!

Excitement pulsed through her as she typed her password into the dialogue box. She opened her email application. "Yes!" she whispered under her breath once it showed the number of items in her inbox. She wouldn't have had emails if the internet in the apartment was disabled.

She saw a whole thread from Marietta. She opened the first one.

From: Marietta Angelotti
To: Asha Dewali
Subject: Fashion Week

Hi girl!

I just wanted to say thanks for taking me with you to Fashion Week. I had an absolute blast! It was so much fun to catch up again. We really should see each other more often. I'm not that busy at work, and daddy doesn't mind me travelling. I think he likes when I'm not in his face, actually...

You seemed distracted, though, and I'm worried about you. Everything OK? You're not still thinking about Praven, are you?

Let me know when you're home. M.

Asha smiled, pressing the instant-reply button on the keyboard. Nothing happened. She hovered the mouse's cursor over the reply option on the screen, but it was greyed out, meaning that she couldn't use it. She pouted for a moment, trying every possible shortcut to send an email, but couldn't find anything.

It seemed as if this particular form of exchange will

only be one way.

"Okay, let's see what else is going on out there," she muttered, clicking on the next email Marietta had sent.

From: Marietta Angelotti
To: Asha Dewali
Subject: Holy Cow!

Okay, seriously! There are some crazy rumours about you! Are you home yet? I tried your cell, but it was off. You've got to call me, OK? As soon as you get this! M.

Asha wracked her brain, trying to remember when she'd arrived in London. It had been a little before six. By the time Marietta had phoned, Asha must've given her mobile to Pierce. Had he switched it off?

Ugh, that means he was in on it! Asha thought miserably. *He must've been under orders to somehow get my phone out of my possession.*

What did it matter, anyway? She was already here, on lockdown, with Konstantinos Sarantos. Nothing could get worse than that, although not being able to chat to her best friend was a close second.

She clicked on Marietta's reply to her own email, which had a different subject.

From: Marietta Angelotti
To: Asha Dewali
Subject: OMG WTF?!?!?!?!

Either you've seriously been holding out on me, or

something's going on! The news said you're getting
married to none other than KONSTANTINOS
SARANTOS!!!!!!!

What the hell, Ash?!!?!?! You didn't even sit together
at Fashion Week! When were you going to tell me???
You pretended like you hardly knew the guy!!!

Seriously, CALL ME RIGHT NOW!!!!

She winced, knowing that Marietta only used capital
letters when she was having a hard time coming to grips
with things. She wished that she could respond, now
more than ever, but it didn't look like she'd be able to
set Marietta's mind at ease.

The Italian girl had had a psychological break once, in
her late-teens, and had lashed out at everyone she
loved—Asha included—during that time. Asha hoped
that her best friend would remain strong through this,
or that her family would reach out to Marietta before
history repeated itself.

She scrolled past the emails bearing the subject
"Congratulations" without opening them. Those
people clearly didn't know her. The only person whose
opinion mattered was Marietta. She clicked on the next
email.

From: Marietta Angelotti
To: Asha Dewali
Subject: RE: OMG WTF?!?!?!?!

OK, so I just got off the phone with your mom, and she
tells me that you're with Konstantinos for a

*ROMANTIC RENDEZVOUS!?!?!! What the hell,
Ash? Why didn't you tell me?*

   Wait, I have a few questions, actually:

·   *How long have you been dating?*

·   *Why on earth haven't you said anything?*

·   *How did he propose? You went out with ME most
      nights. I know you, girl, and you don't like staying
      up late! When did all of this happen???*

·   *Everybody mentions 'sources'. Who the hell are
      they if you COULDN'T EVEN TELL
      YOUR BEST FRIEND THAT YOU ARE
      WITH KONSTANTINOS
      SARANTOS?!?!?!?!!!!*

·   *Don't you trust me? It's like I don't know you.
      We've been friends for more than ten years!*

·   *Why aren't you responding to any of my emails or
      texts? Your mom said that you decided not to take
      your phone with you, which is super weird by the
      way! Like, use your iPad!*

   *I really hope I hear from you soon, 'cause I'm
GOING OUT OF MY MIND. Are you like his
sex-slave now? You're totally doing the nasty, aren't you?
OMG!! You're so lucky! He is HOT!!!! M.*

   PS: call me!

She sighed deeply, closing the email application. She
swivelled the chair around a couple of times, wondering
what she should do. Asha hated that her best friend was
questioning her integrity and their friendship. Had her
parents taken any of this into consideration before

shaking hands with the Sarantos family?

Letting out another deep breath, she opened Google and searched for "Asha Dewali & Konstantinos Sarantos".

She was surprised to see that, hardly five hours after the announcement of their engagement had been made public, there were over a million hits. Her eyebrows rose as she scanned the first twenty results. They were all from celebrity bloggers, and they were probably raking in tons of cash simply by mentioning the "star-crossed love affair", the non-official title to describe her so-called relationship with her so-called fiancé.

She groaned, palming her forehead softly. People were stupid! How could they believe any of this if it hadn't come straight from the horse's mouth?

She clicked on link after link, hoping that she'd be able to comment on the blogs, but even that feature was disabled. She logged into her Facebook account, but could only view other people's news. Not even the *like* function worked. Twitter, Instagram, and every damn other social networking site she'd signed up for, had similar results.

This was a nightmare!

She opened iTunes, plugged a set of earphones in and pressed *play* on her favourite album. She searched for "latest trends in fashion" on Google Images. If only she could find something to inspire her, she wouldn't focus this much energy on her hopeless situation. She's never been the kind of woman that sat around waiting for her life to change. She made things happen. That's who she's always been, and who she'll continue to be, if her parents allowed it.

Before long, her fingers typed "Indian wedding dress ideas". She pulled a face at the colourful designs in front of her. She was born in India, sure, but she's never been pressured to conform to tradition, present situation excluded.

She wouldn't mind if her guests wore deep purples, blues and greens to her wedding, but she's always wanted to get married in a silver or gold Western-style gown.

"Oh my God, what are you doing? You're not getting married," she chided herself, closing the internet browser and sitting with her head in her hands. "You shouldn't be encouraging this disaster, Asha Dewali. You're not getting married to that… inconsiderate asshole."

That didn't mean that she couldn't start planning for her wedding to the man of her dreams, though. Struck with a sudden bout of enthusiasm, she opened her sketchpad and sharpened her pencil. She leaned her chin on her left hand while her right traced a female figure. She had a smile on her face as the dress began taking shape.

CHAPTER 5

"SO, ASHA'S EXPECTED to marry this guy?"

Anushka frowned at her son's choice of words, shaking out her napkin before placing it on her lap. They were at a trendy restaurant in London to have lunch. "We don't 'expect' her to do anything, but they will get married."

"Same thing." Kashinath rolled his eyes. "How can you be sure she'll even go through with it? He's not her type."

"It's worked for us in the past, and it'll continue to work for us in future."

"I'm glad I'm not the first born," Farida mumbled under her breath. "I'd hate to be stuck with someone I don't really like."

"Agreed," her brother said.

"They may not get along now..." Sukesh trailed off, thanking the waiter who brought their meals. "That's not to say they won't like each other eventually."

Kashinath stared at his parents in disbelief. "Have you met the two of them at all? They'll *never* get along. They're too different. I know it's sometimes a good thing—that whole 'opposites attract' thing—but not in this case. Asha needs someone stable, someone like Praven."

"Well, Praven didn't ask her to marry him," Sukesh argued tightly. He was still upset that Praven Kahn had shattered his daughter's dreams of a happily ever after, especially after they'd spent seven years together. "If he had, she wouldn't be in this position."

"Konstantine, or whatever his name is, would've been better suited to the Mia Borgstrom," Farida said. "She parties all the time, too."

"This isn't just about making the perfect love connection," Anushka reminded them. "It's a business partnership, as much as it is a marriage."

"Well, it's a bad risk for Asha. Konstantin*os*," Kashinath said, giving his sister a look, "is a bad bet. What's he done for the Sarantos' business? Absolutely nothing, except waste their money."

"The same could be said about you," Sukesh commented dryly.

Kashinath closed his mouth, busying himself with his breakfast instead. He should never have raised this topic. It's clear that there was no talking sense into his parents.

"I hope you know what you're doing. We're living in the twenty-first century, for crying out loud." Farida shook her head. "I feel sad for Ash. We're hardly traditional, and yet she's being forced into a marriage she didn't ask for."

"She's not being forced…" Anushka sighed as her children sent their gazes heavenwards. "Okay, so she didn't exactly have a choice in all of this, but it's going to be good for the family, and it'll be good for *her*. This tradition has been standing for nearly a hundred years. We're just bringing it to a new level to secure the futures of all parties involved."

"It's not benefiting the Borgstrom family," Kashinath pointed out.

"Not yet, but maybe one of Asha's children will marry one of the Mia's."

Farida choked on her orange juice, looking grateful when her brother smacked her back a couple of times. "Babies? You actually think she'll have Konstananos' *babies*?"

"Kon-stan-ti-nos!" Kash exclaimed. "Honestly, it's not that complicated!"

"I'm sure their marriage will come to a point where they will want to have a baby, yes," Sukesh said, ignoring his son's outburst.

"Ha! You obviously don't know Ash."

"Yeah, if you think for a second that—"

"Enough," Anushka interrupted before her children could start another debate. "We came here to talk about the wedding, not to express concern over things that don't matter."

"Where are Nikos and Kolina, then?" Farida asked. "Shouldn't they be here?"

"They're on their way, but we wanted to speak with you in private first." Sukesh took a deep breath. "It's going to be a huge wedding. Farida, you'll have to liaise with Marietta regarding the bridesmaids' dresses. The bachelor and bachelorette parties will be held as soon as Asha and Konstantinos are out of the apartment. Everything has to be ready."

"We only have a month," Anushka added.

"I hate to ask an obvious question, but shouldn't this wedding and everything to do with it carry Asha's stamp of approval?" Kashinath enquired. "Or are we doing *everything* behind her back these days?"

Anushka smiled. "Asha's busy designing her wedding dress. We're working around what she's got planned."

There was a long silence while Farida and Kashinath considered that. Then, gearing up for another argument if the look on his face was anything to go by, Kashinath asked: "How do *you* know?"

"Yeah, I thought her phone was confiscated," Farida said.

Husband and wife exchanged glances. "We have our sources," Anushka mumbled.

"Oh my God!" Kashinath's eyes stretched wide. "You're having them monitored?"

Farida dropped her fork. "Using the security cameras in the penthouse apartment?"

"How could you *do* that? She's your daughter! What if she decides to get frisky with him? It's not like he's unattractive—"

"Keep your voice down, Kash," Sukesh reprimanded his son. "Do you want the whole world to know what's going on in our private lives?"

"Maybe, yeah! Are you afraid that some hippie tree-hugging organization will draw up a petition for everyone to sign so you'll release Asha from this social obligation? What are we, trapped in the 1950s?"

"I'm warning you, Kash. This doesn't concern anyone else."

Kashinath was relentless. "She never consented to any of this! You're violating her rights as a human being!"

"You are such a drama queen," Anushka sniffed. "This is a private matter. It doesn't concern anyone, least of all the rest of the human populace. We know what we're doing. We've done it for generations, and it's always ended up well. Your father and I love each other, despite the fact that we didn't know each other before we got married."

"That was almost thirty years ago! Everything was different then."

"This will work," Sukesh insisted. "It worked for Jun and Yerik, and it'll work for Asha and Konstantinos."

Kashinath shook his head grimly. "I hope, for your sake, that you're right. This is ridiculous. I feel so sorry for Ash."

"It's kind of romantic, though, if I'm honest," Farida said with a giggle. "I mean, they're so different. It'll be interesting to see what they work out. Can I get a copy of the security tapes?" Her brother looked at her, horrified, making her laugh again. "What? It's *real* reality TV. Like *The Bachelor*, but better."

"You're unbelievable, all of you." He sighed deeply. "But I know when I'm outnumbered, and I'm starving, so I'll stop talking now."

"There must be a God," Anushka teased. "We've got so much to discuss about the wedding. It'll be better if you use your ears instead of your mouth."

CHAPTER 6

ASHA WOKE UP groggily, her back aching. She squinted at her surroundings, miffed to find that she'd fallen asleep with her head on the desk, especially since she'd drooled over her sketch. She rubbed her eyes, straightening in the chair. She was not ready for the day.

For curiosity's sake, she checked her emails, ignoring those that bore false congratulations to her engagement. There was another one from Marietta, which she promptly opened.

From: Marietta Angelotti
To: Asha Dewali
Subject: Good Morning Mrs. Sarantos-in-the-making

Hi, girl!
I'm meeting your family for lunch tomorrow. They're flying me in, said they want to talk about the wedding

details. I've got a few notes from what you told me when you were convinced that Praven was The One, but things change. I mean, you don't still want an ice cream cake at your wedding, right?

I wish you'd talk to me. Why are you so quiet? I'm not used to it. Stop banging, if that's what you're doing. I know he's HOT, but I need my BFF back, OK?

Love, M.

"I wish I could talk to you," Asha mumbled sadly, "but I'm currently in solitary confinement, like I've committed some sort of heinous crime since the last time I saw you. Visiting hours only start a few weeks from now, and… Oh God, now I'm talking to myself. Bad Asha!"

She got up, flinching from the effect her uncomfortable sleeping position had on her body. She traced a finger over the drawing, carefully avoiding the spots of dried saliva, and smiled. The dress spectacular. It's such a shame she wouldn't be wearing it for years to come. She didn't even have a boyfriend, for heaven's sake.

But you have a fiancé, how weird is that?

She checked the time on the computer, and swore under her breath once she saw it was nearing ten o'clock in the morning. Her mouth was dry so, with a slight limp, she walked to the kitchen. She frowned once she saw the stacks of dishes in the sink. It looked like Konstantinos had an incredible appetite for food, without the accompanying affinity for cleaning.

She made herself a cup of cappuccino with cream.

She sipped on it as she moved through the apartment, in search of her it's-never-going-to-happen future husband. She found him in the master bedroom, eyes glued to the television screen while he furiously worked the buttons on the gaming console controller. She raised an eyebrow at a plate and empty pack of crisps, two cups and three glasses, on the nightstand.

"Thank you, I'd love breakfast," she remarked.

"Oh, you're up," he said, barely sparing her a glance. "How'd you sleep?"

She narrowed her eyes. "Wait, you knew where I was sleeping and didn't do a thing to, I dunno, wake me up so I can move to my bedroom?"

"What're you talking about? You disappeared, I watched TV, got bored, tried to sleep, that didn't work, so then I started playing…" He trailed off, executing another couple of seconds' worth of button-pushing. "Playing Xbox," he went on, "and now, here you are! Awake!"

"I fell asleep at my desk."

"I had no idea where you were."

"Whatever. Are you going to clean up the kitchen?"

"Why would I want to do that?" He seemed truly confused by her question, as if she'd suggested that Santa Clause was Chinese.

"*I'm* not doing it," she told him. "You made that mess, so you clean it up. It's simple, really."

"Give me five minutes."

She counted backwards from ten. "You sound like Kash when you say that."

"Your brother?"

"Yes."

"Sounds like my kind of guy."

As much as she hated to admit it, she did. "You'll probably get along with him. He's like the Indian version of you."

Konstantinos raised an eyebrow. "And what would that be?"

"You know," she shrugged. "An irresponsible man-baby that doesn't have a care in the world and keeps hooking up with random women?"

"Do you read everything the tabloids tell you? It doesn't sound like you make up your own mind about people."

Her mouth popped open. "Have you ever done anything to prove the tabloids wrong?"

He thought about that, the tip of his tongue squashed between his lips as he fought off a demented demon on the television screen. "I guess, when you put it that way, you have a point."

"How can you stand it?"

"Stand what?" he asked absentmindedly. His attention was fixed on his game.

"Being a ladies' man. Doesn't it get lonely?"

"See, this is the problem with females." He exclaimed a curse in Greek. "Argh!" Looking upset, he threw the controller aside, raked his fingers through his dark brown hair—which had golden hues that she suspected weren't natural—before turning his gaze to her again. "Where was I?"

She finished her cappuccino. "You were telling me that females have problems."

"Right, right, and it's true! You all assume—"

"Like the theory, that has been proven, of you being a ladies' man?"

He frowned. "No, that I'm doing it because I'm lonely. I'm not. I like having a good time with women. That's it. End of story."

"And you have no desire whatsoever to change that?"

"Nope, I'm pretty happy." He reached for the controller. "Are you done asking me questions about my personal life? I thought we agreed we weren't going to do that, or are you ready to tell me about Praven Kahn?"

"Ugh, pass," she muttered, heading for the door. "Just make sure you clean up after yourself, 'cause *I'm* not going to!"

"And then you wonder why no one will marry you, even if they're forced to spend a month in confinement with you!" he yelled after her.

She pretended that she hadn't heard, but his comment made the hand that was carrying her empty cup jerk involuntarily. She knew she wasn't really "wife" material: her cooking skills were limited to scrambled eggs, toast, and instant macaroni cheese. She's never done a day of laundry. She knew how to pack a dishwasher, but didn't particularly enjoy doing so.

She mainly spent her time working on designs and trying to make Dewali Enterprises even more profitable than it already was.

"Breakfast," she mumbled to herself. She opened the pantry door. It was stocked with her favourite snacks and food, though there were brands that she wasn't familiar with. She assumed those items were for Konstantinos' enjoyment. "If he doesn't eat all of it in his first day here, that is." She realized she was talking to herself again and shook her head. "Not cool, Asha."

She grabbed two cereal bars, a bunch of grapes and a banana and walked back to the study, where she was hoping to duplicate her sketch of that wedding dress: drool-free, this time.

CHAPTER 7

MAN, HE WAS going to lose his mind.

It's only been one day since he figured out he won't be able to leave this damned penthouse suite, but he couldn't stand playing Xbox or watching movies anymore. As a child, he'd been diagnosed with ADHD. His parents hadn't wanted to put him on medication at the time, preferring to find other ways to channel his energy and keep him occupied. He had done exceptionally well in athletics. In fact, that's when he had first started paying attention to his physique.

Stuck in this apartment, he couldn't even go to a track or swimming pool to do a couple of laps. He was under house arrest with minimum entertainment, ADD, and insomnia. A magical combination for someone who couldn't stand being in the same place for extended periods of time.

He switched the Xbox off and chucked the controller aside, lying down on the bed and rubbing his eyes.

Maybe he should take sleeping tablets at night. That way, he'll kill about eight hours every day. Add the two hours he spent exercising, and he only had to worry about fourteen measly hours—per day!—during which he had to keep himself busy with… something.

It was useless. He was going to be certifiably insane by the time he got out.

He looked at the trash and dirty dishes he's accumulated, sighed, and got them all together. He headed to the kitchen to dispose of the empty packets. Then he turned to the dishwasher and tried to figure out how it worked. Did it need a detergent or something? Where on earth would they keep that?

It took him twenty minutes to get the thing started—with a strange white-and-blue block as soap, the packaging of which insisted it could kick any stain's ass—and he looked at it as it started its cycle, arms crossed over his chest and proud that he could do something by himself. Who needed help?

That feeling lasted for five seconds, at most.

"Over it," he muttered, walking upstairs to the bathroom to take a quick shower. He started unpacking the two suitcases of clothing, shaking his head at the number of items now contained in the closet. It would last well past the day of his wedding, but he wasn't planning on going through with it, anyway.

He got dressed in his favourite pair of loose-fitting jeans. It hung so low that the band of his Calvin Klein underwear showed. He was too lazy to put a belt or shirt on. Even though it must be freezing in London, the temperature was being regulated in the apartment.

He could wear a Speedo if he felt like it.

He took a step to go back downstairs, then froze as something dawned on him.

He went to the walk-in closet opposite his, which he assumed belonged to Asha. His eyes widened and his mouth popped open as he saw rows and rows of high-heeled shoes, dresses and corporate wear, T-shirts and jeans. He turned away before he did something stupid, like burn everything. Their families were completely deranged!

He meandered back to the kitchen to grab an apple, then took off in search of company. Since Asha was the only one he could talk to, he'll have to take what he could get. She was in the study, engrossed by whatever she was drawing, and oblivious that he's joined her.

His gaze swept over the room. The decorations were modern, but impersonal. He couldn't see one family portrait anywhere.

Maybe that's because they want you to add your *photos,* a voice informed him, causing him to shudder.

He made himself comfortable at the unoccupied desk, putting his feet on it while he chewed his apple. The blank computer screen stared at him. He wiggled the mouse, surprised when it came to life. How long has she known that they could access the internet without telling him? If she's been talking to the outside world, he was going to be mightily pissed off.

Five minutes later, he swore under his breath. Nothing worked: Skype, Facebook, his emails, Instagram, Twitter... They might as well be technology from the distant future for the good they were doing him in the present. Some of his friends have contacted him about the engagement but, no matter how much he tried, he couldn't tell them that it wasn't going ahead. He glanced at Asha, who was still pouring over her sketch, and deduced that she's experienced similar issues. That's probably why she never mentioned that they had one-way internet.

He studied her for a moment.

Her dark brown, silky long hair was loose today, pulled over one shoulder, and her light green eyes intently studied her drawing. He wondered if she knew that she pushed her bottom lip out when she was concentrating. Her skin was golden and healthy, looking warm… He shook himself. To top things off, it seemed he was going to suffer from a lighter version of Stockholm Syndrome, too. His life couldn't get any worse.

The silence was killing him.

Konstantinos cleared his throat. "What're you working on?"

She jumped slightly and looked up. "You scared me. How long have you been sitting there?"

"Probably about ten, fifteen minutes," he replied, amused. "I didn't know you get so caught up in your own world that you don't notice anything else."

"That tends to happen when I get into things." She shrugged apologetically, then her eyes narrowed. "Seriously, you're a billionaire! Don't you own *one* shirt?"

"This is comfortable. Why does it bother you?"

Her gaze dropped back to her sketch. "It doesn't."

Yeah right, was what he wanted to say. "So, how long is it going to take you before you get as bored as I am?"

"Even though I can't communicate with anyone other than you, I can still do my work." She gestured to the sketchpad and computer on her desk. "I'll check our company's financial reports. I can still log into our database. And I'll work on my designs."

He rolled his eyes. "So diligent."

"Maybe you should do the same. From what I've heard, you're not exactly involved in your father's businesses."

"There's a reason for that." He finished his apple and threw the core in the direction of the bin, punching the air in triumph when it went in. "I don't think my father *wants* me involved. I'm much better off as the—"

"Troublemaking playboy, doesn't-take-anything-seriously Konstantinos Sarantos?" she supplied, her pencil sliding over the sketch.

"Did you know that your accent prevents you from pronouncing my name properly?"

"Maybe you should've stayed in Greece, since that's the only place where they pronounce your name properly. Would've prevented us from being stuck in this apartment, too."

"I see you haven't stopped with the insults."

"You started it."

"Well, you're not exactly forthcoming with conversational topics."

"That's because *I'm working,*" she said through a clenched jaw.

"Do you ever have fun?"

She was silent for a long time, pretending to be intrigued by her drawing even though her eyes have grown distant. "No," she responded finally, in a voice that was hardly above a whisper.

"I figured. Here you are, presented with the perfect opportunity to take a month's vacation, and yet you spend your time working. Is that why Praven left you?"

"He didn't…" She shook her head. "Why is my relationship with Praven so important to you?"

"Unlike me, you've only had one romantic interest. Since there's nothing better to do, I might as well get to know you."

"You're really forward, aren't you?"

"Is there any other way to be?"

"I doubt that you can remember half of the women you've slept with, so the point to your conversation is moot."

He tilted his head to the side, allowing that. "You're right: I can't remember half of them."

"And you're not ashamed of it?"

"Why should I be? All of my dalliances were consensual and mutually satisfying." He fought against a smile once he saw how worked up she was getting over his lifestyle. "That's right, I said *mutually* satisfying. Do you have a problem with that?"

"No."

"Interesting," he said to himself. There was clearly something that riled her up regarding sex. He wondered why. Even when she was calm, her body was tense. Her posture was so rigid that he doubted she knew how to let go. "What are your friends saying about the engagement?"

"My so-called friends are all congratulating me," she muttered. "Marietta, on the other hand, can't believe it. She's very hurt."

"Best friend?"

"She is."

"Women can get quite dramatic over nothing."

"You sure have a low opinion of us."

He chuckled. "I don't. I respect women, but they make everything more complicated than it should be. Like what's-her-face, your friend—"

"Marietta."

"Whatever. She's upset because she thinks you've lived a secret life, but since when should we tell someone else what's going on in our private lives if we don't want to?"

"You make a good point, but you seem to forget that this 'secret life' I supposedly have is based on a lie."

"You say po-tay-to, I say poh-tah-toe."

"Absolutely no one says poh-tah-toe."

He linked his fingers behind his head, shifting in the chair until he got comfortable. "The whole point is moot, since we won't be getting married. She will be upset for a while, but I think she'll be angrier with your parents than you when she finds out the truth." He gave her a look. "None of this is our fault, Asha. Our families have a distorted view on romance, and they expect a new generation to be okay with that. I'm not, and you're not. Unfortunately, our relationships with friends will suffer, since human beings always find a way to turn themselves into a victim."

She stared at him. "I can't say I'm surprised by that attitude, coming from a man that doesn't take responsibility for anything or anyone."

"And how do you know I don't?"

"Your actions speak louder than words."

He kept quiet, though he had plenty he'd like to clear up. It didn't matter what she thought. It was certainly of no consequence that he's been a model older brother to Loikanos, and that he's made it his personal duty to let Loikanos get the credit for everything. Konstantinos cared for his family, even though he didn't care for their values and traditions. He loved his mother and, although his relationship with his old man was complicated, he had nothing but respect for him. He was Greek, after all.

"And I take it you're measuring my actions against the media's portrayal of me?" he asked lightly.

"There has to be truth to the rumours."

"In that case, Praven broke up with you because you were no longer interesting enough in bed." When she blinked at him, shocked, he shrugged. "*People*. They had a four-page feature on your relationship, and there were many 'sources' that claimed things weren't terribly exciting, sexually."

"Okay, seriously: why do you keep bringing up my love life?"

"Let's just say I've always wondered if there was truth to the rumours and leave it at that." His mouth tilted up mockingly. "Isn't that what you're doing, every time you ask about *my* personal life, or make a remark about my lifestyle?"

"You should've been a lawyer or PR person, 'cause you're really good at deflecting."

He inclined his head, grinning. "Thank you."

"I didn't mean it as a compliment."

"I'm taking it as one, anyway. I have freedom of choice, after all." He grimaced, thinking about his current situation. "Well, on the best of days, I do."

"Do you take that freedom seriously?"

"Where's the fun in doing that?"

She cracked a smile, her green eyes twinkling. "I didn't think so."

"You know, if you weren't so opinionated about every person you meet, you might have a decent sense of humour."

"I'll have you know that I have an excellent sense of humour."

"Really? Prove it."

"And how would I do that, assuming that I want to prove myself to you?"

"We both know you do." He motioned for her to join him at his desk, while he opened Google. "I'll type in the names of people you've no doubt met, select an interesting picture, and you have to say the first thing that comes to mind."

She looked apprehensive. "Why?"

"It'll be fun. Come on, then." He smiled as she made her way over. She sat on the edge of the desk, taking a sip of water from the bottle that had kept her company while she'd been sketching. He typed in the name of a famous actor, adding a couple of phrases to modify his search. He found the picture he was looking for and turned to her. "Well?"

"First of all, I've only met him once."

"Give it your best shot."

She had tears in her eyes from holding back her giggles. "That face totally says, 'I have a turd in my mouth and I'm afraid you'll see it'."

He glanced at the picture and started chuckling. The actor's jaw was clenched while he peered into the lens of the camera, probably intending to look sexy and manly, but it didn't work so well now that Asha has given her five cents' worth. "Okay, next one," he said, taking about ten seconds to select a bad image of a famous supermodel.

"You're making this really easy. She's totally wishing she'd bleached her bum-hole."

He threw his head back and guffawed loudly. "Bum-hole? Seriously? Who says that? Besides you, I mean."

"I was doing it for comedic effect," Asha informed him. "My turn!" She leaned forward to type on the keyboard, clicking a couple of times before straightening again, victory in her eyes. "Give it your best shot."

"But she's my favourite actress," he argued. His eyes were glued to the unflattering picture of his celebrity crush. "And she's a mother now."

"Oh, come on! It's not like she'll ever know."

"She's thinking that she should've worn Spanx."

"I'm only laughing because you know what Spanx are."

He gave her a look. "Have you ever worn it?"

"Just when I wear satin. No one looks good in skin-tight satin. Ooh, I know, I'm going to get snacks while you try to stump me. Would you like a soda?"

"Please," he replied, taking her challenge to heart. By the time she came back with a pack of chewy candies, crisps and two Cokes, he'd already lined up about eight pictures. He nearly choked on some of the comments she made. He was amazed to see that she was finally beginning to relax.

She sat cross-legged on the desk while she flung her opinions around like she was presenting a *Roast* on *Comedy Central*. She proved that she had a very dry sense of humour, one he quite enjoyed, since it meant that he needed a certain level of intelligence understand her. He wasn't sure if she'd developed her style intentionally, or if it was coincidental.

"Wow, we've been in here for an hour," he remarked, wiping tears from his eyes and giving the screen a last look before closing the browser window. "After all the junk I've eaten, I really need to hit the gym."

Asha stretched her arms. "I'll join you. Can you show me how to do weight-lifting?" When he raised his eyebrows, she pushed her hair behind her ears self-consciously. "I've always wanted stronger arms and legs but, being Indian, I'm not exactly built for that."

"Let's see what we can do," he suggested, leading the way out of the study. "Prepare to work out like you've never worked out before."

Chapter 8

Loikanos peered at the woman making her way across the street towards him, comparing her to the image on his iPad's screen. Certain that it was the same person, he locked the device and left it on the backseat. "I'll be right back," he told Christopher, his driver, as he exited the vehicle.

It would be considered weird that he was following a random stranger, but he had to see her up close, to determine whether she was the devious matchmaker he imagined her to be. His brother was currently locked in an apartment with Asha Dewali because of *her*, after all, and although he's promised his parents he wouldn't interfere, he had to make sure Konstantinos' heart was in the right hands.

His brother was his best friend. Loikanos would do anything for that man.

The woman ducked into a Starbucks, leaving him with no option but to do the same. He kept his gaze on her, ignoring the thrill that her features caused. She was older than him—unsurprising, since he was in his early twenties and she was the CEO of her own company—but, physically, the most beautiful woman he's ever seen.

Loikanos, unlike his older brother, was a sucker for love. He believed he'll know his future wife the second he made eye contact with her. He watched her place an order, pay for it and then, as if realizing someone was staring at her, she turned to gaze at him.

He lost his breath.

Her blonde hair was in a bun, exposing her face entirely. Loikanos was happy about that, since it meant he could openly admire her high cheekbones, pink lips, straight nose and big, blue eyes. Her hourglass figure was tucked away in a white knee-length pencil skirt, which revealed her strong calves, and loose-fitting turquoise blouse that did wonders for her complexion. She was clutching a laptop bag in one hand.

At the same time, he saw her dressed in a white wedding gown, her hair framing her face in loose tendrils, and understood that she was the woman of his dreams.

She flinched at the look he was giving her, collected her order and marched outside.

Inhaling, he forgot about his planned ambush and trailed behind her, determined to make her his.

* * * * *

DENISE LEMONT LOOKED to her left and her right

before crossing the street, phone clutched to her ear. "And you say that they have no idea there are people cleaning the apartment at night, Jacob?"

"No, they have no idea," her assistant confirmed. "It's difficult, since Mr. Sarantos suffers from insomnia, but we get it done when he retreats for the evening."

"I'm glad to hear it." She spotted a Starbucks and made a beeline for it, craving a double espresso like nobody's business. A cinnamon dolce latte with extra cream wouldn't hurt, either, but she was watching her figure. "Anything else you wanted to talk to me about?"

"That's it for now."

"Nothing exciting is happening over there? They're not in love yet?"

Jacob chuckled. "It doesn't seem that way. Then again, it's only been three days."

"*Mon Dieu*, I really hope I'm not losing my touch," she muttered, getting in line while her eyes scanned the menu. "*Merci*, Jacob. I appreciate the update."

"You should stop worrying so much, Denise. It'll work."

"Need I remind you that Jun threw herself at Yerik after two days together?"

"That situation was different. They were already hanging in the same social circles. In fact, I still think they hooked up before lockdown."

One corner of her mouth quirked up at the word. Though this was a part of her business that only occurred sporadically, she loved bringing people together. Then she frowned, the rest of his sentence sinking in. "I really hope this works, Jacob. I'm under a lot of pressure."

"You've never failed before. Everything will work out. You should have a slice of black forest cake. You deserve it after that nasty settlement."

She sighed deeply, moving forward in the queue. "That's where you're wrong, *chéri*. Now that I'm divorced and over thirty, I'm going to need to stay very thin to keep up with the younger generation." Not that she wanted to be with a younger man, per se, but the more youthful her appearance, the better her chances at love. It was the sad way society had been set up. "I'll be in the office tomorrow morning, okay? We need to go over a couple of things. We've got venues from all over begging us to use them, but we have to make sure to choose the perfect one."

"Got it. I'll see you then, boss."

She hung up and stuffed her phone in a side pocket of her laptop bag. For some reason, that simple move was more of a struggle than usual. It held so many things—her MacBook air, an iPad, notepad, a small case that contained three pens and one pencil, her wallet, a small make-up kit, a bunch of keys, extra underwear and pantyhose—that she had to shake it around a couple of times before there was space for her phone. She came up with a couple of creative French curses during the process, especially once she remembered that she had to get money out for her order.

Some days, she felt like curling into a tiny little ball and crying until the world ended. Today was one of those days.

She breathed slowly, counted backwards from ten—getting seven and five messed up for some reason—while her hand dove into her bag to retrieve her wallet. By the time she was finished, the cashier was looking at her expectantly. She realized that she's been holding them up for nearly three minutes.

"*Mes excuses,*" she said automatically. With a great sigh, she remembered she wasn't in France, but in London, where they hated the French. If this Starbucks incident was anything to go on, the next couple of weeks were going to be terrible. As a result, she was going to treat herself to feel up to it. Screw her diet! "Pardon. A double espresso and cinnamon dolce latte, please. Extra cream."

The cashier rung up the order and told her the amount she owed.

She handed banknotes over and waited for change, getting out of the way of the other patrons in the shop. It felt as if someone was boring holes into the back of her head, and she assumed it's someone affected by her general uselessness today. She glanced behind her and cringed.

One of the most beautiful men she's ever seen had his eyes on her, curiosity in his brown gaze. He wasn't much taller than her but, then again, she was wearing five-inch heels. A thorough head-to-toe perusal informed her that he was much too young for her, even though he was dressed maturely in cream-colored, double-pleated linen pants and a matching jacket, with a dark blue button-up shirt. His hair reminded her of her favourite dark chocolate and covering his ears; his skin was naturally tanned.

"Miss? Your order's ready."

Well, how about that? Apparently, she still looked like a *mademoiselle*, even though she was nearing her thirty-fifth birthday. She was grateful for the interruption. There she was, shamelessly ogling that poor young man, who looked like he hailed from… Greece…

With a start, she grabbed her order, recognizing Konstantinos' brother. For her to even think about his hands all over her was dirty and wrong. Now that she was divorced and had to consider dating again, she wasn't willing to do so with a man younger than thirty.

She headed for the door, cursing rush hour. She pushed through the crowd, apologizing profusely. People in London were pissed off on the best of days, and today was not the best of days, as she was quickly starting to realize.

"Hey, wait!" a deep voice called behind her.

She figured that they must be seeking the attention of someone else. She breathed with relief as she stepped outside, even if she was now standing in the middle of an equally busy sidewalk. She drank her espresso in one big gulp, disposed of the empty cup, and began sipping on her latte.

Ah, bliss.

A feeling that, despite her mental protests, intensified when Loikanos Sarantos took hold of her elbow and swung her around.

He grinned boyishly. "You're in a hurry!"

She knew that he was Greek, but his accent made him

sound American. She wondered if he'd gone to school in the US. "I-I have to get back to work," she stammered.

"I'll walk you."

"Uh, that is quite alright, thank you."

"Great," he said, purposely misinterpreting her statement and falling into step with her. "What's your name?"

His charm affected her instantly. She found her mouth responding before she gave it permission to. "Denise."

"I'm Louis." She raised an eyebrow, which made him laugh. "Okay, okay, my name's actually Loikanos, but Louis is easier for most people to remember. Are you French?"

"What gave it away? My accent?"

"No, the unforgiving way in which you are clutching that latte," he teased. "It looks like you're ready to decapitate it, à la French Revolution."

She burst out laughing.

"Maybe you're not French, after all. You're not offended?"

"I'm too old to be offended."

His hand rested on the small of her back, steering her away from the entrance of the Underground and towards a black Mercedes AMG. "Old? You?" He gave her a quick glance and shook his head. "You're what, twenty-seven?"

Two compliments in the space of ten minutes? She'll take it! "Thank you, but I really should get going."

"You've mentioned that." He opened the back door

of the car for her. "We'll drive you. Saves you the trouble of waiting for a train."

"The Tube will be faster. I've got to go to the other side of town."

He shrugged. "No problem."

She realized she wasn't going to win and, at that exact moment, the light drizzle turned to pouring rain. "You don't have to tell me twice," she muttered, ducking to slide onto the backseat.

"And yet, that's exactly what I had to do," he remarked as he joined her side. He looked at her with that dimply, impish grin. "So, why don't you tell Christopher where you want to go so he can focus on driving while I get to know you?"

Her mouth popped open at his confident question. She stared at him, forgetting the topic of conversation.

His gaze dropped from her eyes to her mouth. His tongue flicked out to lick his top lip, effectively drawing her attention there.

She noticed that she was holding her breath. What was it about this young man?

Without warning, he pulled her closer for a long, thorough kiss. Her grip on the latte slackened. She felt very uncomfortable, what with her big bag pressed between her left side and arm, and yet she would stare an army of lunatics in the face if it meant that Loikanos kept his mouth where it was. How did a twenty-three-year-old know how to kiss like this? Not even her ex-husband could arouse her this quickly, and it was a well-known fact that Remi Lemont was a womanizing bastard, so it's not like he didn't have enough practice.

"Uh, sir?"

Loikanos pulled away, his eyes twinkling. He seemed embarrassed. "I'm so sorry, Denise, I didn't mean to do that."

"You didn't?"

He gave her a half-smile, ruffling his already mussed-up hair. "You know what I mean."

"Where to?" Christopher asked from the driver's seat.

Denise patted her forehead for a moment, collecting her thoughts. "Kew Gardens," she said shakily, her lips tingling from the kiss.

"You weren't kidding," the young Greek remarked as the car started moving into traffic. "That's going to take a while."

"I never kid," she said. "Loikanos—"

"Please don't," he interrupted. "Don't say anything unless it's positive, or you'll leave me heartbroken."

Her own heart was banging against her ribcage in the rhythm that she wanted him to... *No, Denise! What are you thinking?* "What I meant to say, *chéri*, is that you don't know who I am."

"So, tell me." He leaned back, smiling. Their knees were touching, sending little sparks up and down her spine. "We've got at least forty minutes available to share intimate details about our private lives."

She gulped down the remainder of her latte, then held the empty cup awkwardly. Loikanos took it from her hands and placed it in a holder. She glanced at him, nervous. Here she was: the person who was facilitating the arranged marriage between his brother and Asha Dewali, and he had no idea!

"Do you make a habit of picking up women in Starbucks?" she asked, finding her voice.

He shrugged nonchalantly. "Only if they consent."

Oh, he might be young, too young, but it seemed he was like exactly her ex-husband. Didn't she ever learn? She had to get out of this car before she fell into the same trap again. "And we're all interchangeable?"

"Not exactly," he responded, his eyes boring into hers. "Some are different. Do you make a habit of allowing men to pick you up in Starbucks?"

She laughed softly, shaking her head. "Being recently divorced? *Non.*"

"How is it possible that you are divorced? You're too young to be married."

Somehow, she didn't want to tell him her real age. This might not be anything more than a drive with an attractive, albeit younger, man. She didn't want to spoil it. "These things happen, I guess."

"You left him?"

She grimaced, gazing out of the window instead. "*Non.*"

"How could he leave you? You're a beautiful woman, Denise."

"He wasn't satisfied with just one," she said with a lightness that she didn't feel. There was no doubt that was still grieving her failed relationship.

"Well, he was foolish," he assured her, placing his finger under her chin to turn her head his way. "I could never leave you."

Her heart beat painfully against her rib cage. *Keep it light!* She rolled her eyes. "Have you even had a serious relationship before?"

"Yes," he said, surprising her.

"When you were in diapers?"

"Something like that." He took her hand in his, turning it over and placing a soft kiss in the middle of her palm. "We were together for two years."

Time seemed to freeze as his lips moved to her wrist, seeking her pulse. It's like all of her nerve-endings were now focused on that part of her. She couldn't hear the rain beating down on the roof of the car, the endless honking of late-afternoon traffic, or the radio that was keeping the driver company. Her eyes were trained on Loikanos' head as it kept dipping over her arm, his lips inching to the fold of her elbow.

She couldn't breathe properly.

"Approaching Kew Gardens," the driver informed them, his voice like a crack of thunder through the hazy fog of her mind. "Where to, miss?"

Third compliment! She was having a good day, after all, especially if Loikanos kept massaging her upper arm like that… She cleared her throat and gave Christopher directions to her home. It was a couple of streets away from the botanical gardens but, all too soon, the Mercedes pulled into her short driveway.

She couldn't drag her eyes away from Loikanos, who was staring back at her with the same intensity.

Heat pulsed through her body. She felt as if she was being set alight. She wasn't sure if she felt this way because she was getting sexual attention from a man for the first time since her ex had filed for divorce, or because there was something else going on between them.

"You still don't know who I am," she informed him softly.

"Does it really matter?"

To hell with it. Sure, it's not ethical for her to screw one of her most rewarding clients' sons, but no one had to know, right? Besides, it'll only be this one time.

She reached for the door handle. "Are you coming inside?"

A slow, lazy smile flitted over his face. "You can count on it."

Chapter 9

ASHA GROANED AS she woke up, wondering what she'd been thinking to exercise with Konstantinos. He was going to kill her. Her muscles weren't used to his kind of routine!

"Stupid," she muttered, slowly getting out of the bed. She flinched at the tight muscles in her calves and whimpered as she waddled to the bathroom to start her early-morning routine. She had to have her head examined.

It was quite nice to see him in his element.

She gazed at her reflection. Where had that thought come from? Sure, Konstantinos had an incredible body, but it wasn't as if she was appreciating it in *that* way! It was just... nice to look at. That's all.

"Totally."

Fifteen minutes later—mostly due to her aching body—she made her way downstairs to the kitchen. She was starving, which was unusual. She normally didn't eat in the morning and, instead, had a cup of coffee to get her day going.

"Morning, sleepyhead," Konstantinos greeted once she crossed the threshold. "How are you feeling?"

"Like death." Double-checking the time, she frowned. "Why are you up already?"

"Can't sleep, remember?" He gestured to the stove, which he was manning. "Are you having French toast with me?"

"That'll be nice, thanks."

"You need to work on your vocabulary," he chuckled.

She kept her mouth shut and shuffled to the espresso machine, not wanting to admit that "nice" was about the only adjective she ever used. Her family constantly mocked her for it. "Coffee?"

"Nah, if I had caffeine, I'd be in an even better mood. Something tells me that would be more unbearable for you."

"I'm not really a morning person."

"Then why do you get up this early? No, wait, don't tell me!" He grinned broadly. "To work?"

She nodded begrudgingly.

"We're on holiday, remember? You get to sleep in."

"Old habits die hard."

He shook his head and finished up. "Well, breakfast is served." He loaded their plates and handed one over. "Hopefully you'll answer me this time: *how are you feeling?*"

"Sore," she confessed, eyeing the two slices on her plate. "Where'd you learn how to cook?"

"My mother." He added savoury confectionaries to

his French toast. "I knew you'd be broken today. Didn't I warn you towards the end? But damn, you're stubborn, and a part of me was curious to see how far you'd push it."

Glaring at him, she poured honey over hers. "I wasn't going to give in first."

"Asha, I hate to break this to you, but you can't compete with me." He smacked his rock-hard abs. "I'm years ahead of you."

"Maybe physically."

He burst out laughing. "There she is! Welcome back, Dewali."

She quirked a smile, moving to the breakfast nook, mostly because it was closer than the dining room. "I'm awake now, that's for sure."

"So, what are we doing today?" When she opened her mouth to respond, he hurriedly warned: "If you're about to tell me 'work', I'm taking your toast." He nodded as she remained quiet. "That's what I thought. What else would you like to do?"

She considered that, taking a bite of food. Wow, his mother must've taught him well! "I don't know," she hedged, "read?"

He sighed deeply. "Wrong answer, try again."

"Well, what do *you* want to do?"

"Other than get the hell out of here?" he teased. "We could play Xbox."

"I've never played." He stared at her in shock. "What? I'm not a guy."

"You don't have to be a guy to play Xbox, I'll have you know." He wolfed down the rest of his meal and pushed his plate aside. "Today's goal is finding Asha's favourite game."

She groaned. "Are you *sure* I can't read instead? You'll have more fun without me."

"It's day five of this," he reminded her, motioning to the apartment. "You're the only company I've got. I'm getting tired of doing things alone."

"You're always torturing me," she bitched. Then she realized he wasn't wearing a shirt, as usual. "Could you cover up? You're giving me serious envy because I'll never look like that."

He threw his head back and cackled loudly. "That's a good thing, Asha, 'cause I'm a man."

"You're not going to let this go, are you?"

"Nope."

"Fine," she mumbled as she took her last bite. "Let's go, Sarantos."

He led the way to the living room, which also had an Xbox gaming console, and turned it on. He insisted that she create her own avatar before they started. She enjoyed styling it, ignoring his jibes at her fashion designer antics.

"Thank God, that only took half an hour," he said sarcastically once she completed that task. "Okay, what do you feel like? Space ships, medieval fighting, or a car race?"

She sent him a lost look.

"Process of elimination it is. Let's start with this."

Three hours later, despite herself, she was having fun. Konstantinos had brought over bowls of snacks at some point and seemed to regret teaching her the ropes, seeing as she was kicking his ass. They pushed each other playfully, made funny comments to see who would laugh first, and cursed at the screen whenever the game beat them.

They were acting like they've been friends for years.

She helped him with lunch—although, for the most part, she simply stood watching him make it—and they sat around the table, sharing stories from their childhood. They returned to the living room afterwards, ready to tackle the next challenge their chosen game presented them with.

Asha couldn't quite believe it, yet felt that tense muscle in her neck relax, all the same. When the light began dimming, she realized that they'd been in front of the TV the whole day.

"I think that's enough," she sighed happily, relinquishing her controller. "It's after eight!"

"Good job, Dewali," he cheered. He pressed a few buttons and the Xbox shut down. "I'm proud of you. I thought for sure that you were going to quit around lunch time."

She smiled. "This was fun."

"I'm just glad you didn't say 'nice'."

"Shut up," she giggled, shoving his shoulder.

He stared at her, slowly losing his smile. He turned away. "We'll have to figure out what to do tomorrow. Do you think you can take doing nothing productive, two days in a row?"

She bit her lip and shook her head. "No, sorry. I really want to get back to it. Does that make me a boring person?"

"I suppose it makes you dedicated."

"I feel like I'll miss out on something if I don't. Like, somehow, someone *else* will bring my ideas to life and I'll have missed my chance to take the world by storm."

The corners of his mouth tilted up. "That's why you'll be a great success, but don't forget to take a breather every once in a while."

"Thank you for the reminder." She toyed with her ponytail, eyeing him speculatively. He genuinely seemed bummed that she was going to do her own thing tomorrow, and she felt bad that she wasn't the most entertaining inmate. This must be a lonely experience for someone that didn't like his own company. "Would I make up for it if we watched a movie tonight?"

"Yeah," he answered brightly. He gave her the remote. "Choose something good. I'll make some popcorn."

Bearing his tastes in mind, she chose the latest *Die Hard* film. She was surprised that she enjoyed it as much as he did. She caved when he requested they watch one more before going to bed, but nodded off halfway through, dreaming of Konstantinos as Bruce Willis, saving her from imminent peril.

She surfaced from that fictitious world, frowning when she noticed that she was in his arms. She looked around. "Where are you taking me?"

"To bed, silly," he chuckled, his chest vibrating against her side. He entered her room. "You passed out."

"Oh."

He lay her down gently and helped her with the covers. "Goodnight, Asha."

"Goodnight," she smiled as she gave his hand a squeeze. "Thank you." She promptly dipped back into unconsciousness, and didn't hear if he said anything back.

CHAPTER 10

"THANKS FOR COMING, Marietta. This is such a busy time and I know that Asha appreciates your effort."

She inclined her head and sat down opposite Farida. "Have you spoken to her recently?"

"Not exactly," the youngest Dewali responded carefully. "I get updates from mom and dad."

"I'm glad she's talking to someone, at least," Marietta said lightly, perusing the menu and pretending as if she wasn't wounded by her best friend's dismissal. "I've been waiting for her to make contact."

Farida looked away. "It's... difficult to explain, but they're basically spending as much time together in preparation for the wedding. They haven't been very open about their relationship until now."

"You don't say!"

"I know this must be hard. You two have been close since high school."

"I'm just surprised she's been able to hide this from

me." Marietta motioned for the waiter. "I thought we talked about everything, especially when it comes to boys. Well, mostly because *I'm* the only one who talks about boys."

"This situation is… complicated." Farida folder her hands on the table with a small smile. "Anyway, the reason I called: we need to start planning the bachelorette party. You know Ash best. What kind of games do you think she'll enjoy?"

The waiter appeared at their side. "Ladies, what can I get you?"

They made their order and, once the waiter left, Marietta fixed Farida with a firm stare. "Asha doesn't want the cliché bachelorette party with cliché games. She made that much clear to me in the past. She also doesn't want her fiancé doing anything wild."

Farida's brows furrowed. "I didn't know that."

"She'll prefer something that includes her and Konstantinos." Marietta felt strange saying that name in the same context as Asha's. Heck, she still wasn't used to the engagement. "Something like both of them attending the same event will work. There could be various entertainers, ranging from music to dance to comedy?"

"That *does* sound like her!" Farida exclaimed excitedly. "She couldn't stop talking about that burlesque show you took her to a few months ago! Maybe we should arrange something like that?"

Marietta contemplated it. "Yes, I believe that's classy enough for her. What're Konstantinos' friends like? Will they cause trouble?"

"I don't actually know," Farida replied, biting down on the corner of her lip. "As far as I'm aware, Loikanos is his best friend. His brother," she added when Marietta frowned.

"Oh." Marietta paused for a moment. "What *do* we know about him?"

Farida seemed nervous. "Well, that he used to be a playboy and—"

"Which brings me to my next question," Marietta interrupted. "*When did this happen?*"

"I really wish I could answer that."

"None of this makes any sense to me." Marietta raked her fingers through her brown hair. The edge of hysteria was worming its way into her calm demeanour. She fought it as best she could, yet she had the sense that her friendship with Asha was built on a huge lie. It didn't sit well with her. "I don't know what to believe."

"She'll be back soon to answer all the questions you have," Farida soother, reaching across the table to squeeze Marietta's hand. "Right now, we have to be there for her and make sure everything is perfect."

Marietta put a firm handle on her anxiety by filling her lungs with oxygen. "You're right. Let's do this."

CHAPTER 11

KONSTANTINOS FROWNED AT his brother's email.

From: Loikanos Sarantos
To: Konstantinos Sarantos
Subject: Hooking Up

Hi, bro. I know you can't respond to this, but that's okay. I kind of prefer it this way. Knowing you, you'll have a couple of snarky comments to make once you read this. I met a woman and HOLY SMOKES do I like her! She's sexy as hell, and French (I know how much you wanted to marry a French woman, fifty years from now, ha ha, beat you to it :-)) and funny and kind and sweet. I can't believe her husband left her for another woman. Yup, that's right: she's divorced. Can you imagine dad's reaction? Ha ha ha! I really like her, though. We've been spending the past five days together. She's The One, man. I love her. Anyway, this one-sided

conversation has been fun, but I've got to go please my
woman now. I suggest you do the same: Asha's sexy, in
her own way. Peace!

There were so many things wrong with what he's just
read, Konstantinos didn't know where to begin. It
sucked that he couldn't reply, 'cause he sure had a
mouthful to say to his little brother. Loikanos has only
known the woman—divorced, no less—five days, and
he thought he loved her? What the hell was Loikanos
thinking? Not even to mention his absurd comment
about Asha!

Sure, things were much more bearable between the
two of them lately, but that didn't mean that
Konstantinos was suddenly romantically interested in
her. She wasn't as uptight as she'd been at first, thanks
to him insisting that she unwind more often, yet—

"Did you get a stupid email, too?"

He glanced up at the woman in question. "Yes, my
brother's hopelessly in love someone he's only known
a couple of days."

"Damn, that's rough, but very sweet in a way."

"How about yours?"

"Marietta," Asha responded slowly. "She's sending
me pictures of the bridesmaids' dresses and asking
rhetorical questions about whether I want a burlesque
show at our engagement party."

"I'm assuming it's rhetorical for two reasons."

She quirked a smile. "You bet. One, you and I are
never getting married; and two, I can't answer her. I
thought she'd get the picture by now, but she can be

dim sometimes."

He chuckled. "And you're supposed to be her best friend?"

"Ugh, I can't believe I said that. I think I'm going mad from being in this damn apartment." She sighed and rubbed her eyes. "I was supposed to be in India by now. Obviously, I'm not."

And I was supposed to be adding notches to my bedpost, he thought grimly. "Nine days down."

"One step closer to us *not* getting married," she agreed, sending him a small smile.

He returned her smile, thinking that Loikanos might have a point: Asha *was* sexy. She wore comfortable clothing that fitted her slight frame perfectly. She hasn't really bothered with make-up, but she didn't need it. Her skin had a natural glow, thanks to her genes, and her eyes always sparkled, even when she was annoyed or angry.

The same eyes now glanced at his bare chest, as they always seemed to do. He fought a smirk.

"Damn it!" she exclaimed, pushing her chair back. "That's *it!* You're going to wear a shirt, right now."

"But I don't want to."

"Well, you're going to."

"You can't make me." He stood up and walked to her. "What is it that makes you so uncomfortable?"

Her gaze drifted from his collarbones to his stomach. She swallowed deeply. "It's ridiculous how ripped you are. I mean, you have an eight-pack. I've always thought that a *six*-pack was a bit too much, but this…"

He raised an eyebrow once she trailed off. "I worked

hard to get my body this way."

"It's just not fair," she mumbled, reaching out to touch the definition in his stomach. "I mean, I've been trying to keep up with your exercise regime, but you're on a whole other level, and I don't have any muscle memory."

"Yeah, I think you should stick to yoga." He attempted to ignore the tingling sensation her fingers caused on his skin. What was that about? "There's nothing wrong with your body, anyway."

"Seriously?" She seemed enamoured by his stomach. She traced the ridges of his muscles with the fingers of both hands. "This can't be normal. This is the type of thing you see in *Men's Health* or soft porn."

He barked a laugh. "You watch soft porn?"

"You know what I mean."

"I don't, actually. You're Asha Dewali: the woman who walks around like she's got a stick up her butt, and you watch soft porn?"

"Okay fine, you have a point," she answered, reluctantly pulling away from him. "I only watched it once, and it was completely by accident. I didn't know what it was until..." She tucked her hair behind her ears. "Cup of coffee?"

"You look like you need something stronger than that. What made you realize you were watching soft porn?"

She hesitated. "Let's get that 'something stronger' you were talking about, first."

He burst out laughing, leading the way to the bar. "Fair enough. I'm going to take a wild guess and say you don't drink whiskey?"

"Ugh, no." She nudged him away from the fridge, which was fully stocked with alcohol of all varieties. She pushed her bottom lip out as she concentrated on the labels in front of her. "I don't think they did any of this for me."

"That's because you're not the wild child. Come on, I'll teach you how to drink tequila."

"I don't know," she said, sounding less than thrilled.

"You'll like it, I promise. You just need to be broken in gently." He pointed to the barstools. "Go on, take a seat. I'll fix you something. Do you like cocktails?"

"Sure."

He smiled at the bottles of orange juice and grenadine he found in the fridge, choosing to pour them both a Tequila Sunrise. There was a jar of decorative cherries as well, and he spent a couple of seconds theatrically adding it their drinks, happy that he got a giggle for his trouble. He added a straw and pushed it to her.

She took a tentative sip. "This has tequila in it?"

"Yup."

"But it tastes so yum!"

He grinned. "Yup."

"I wish I had a camera. You're drinking a semi-pink cocktail. I think that deducts a serious amount of man points."

"I'm so secure in my masculinity, not even that threat makes me worry." He watched her drain about half of the glass, then got back to the matters at hand. "What made you realize you were watching soft porn?"

She shifted self-consciously while she chewed on a

cherry. "Well, one night I was flipping through the channels—"

"Wait, how old were you?"

"Uhm, fifteen or sixteen."

"Continue."

"Thank you, your majesty," she mocked. "I was looking for a movie to watch, and I settled on this one because of the title—though, for the life of me, I can't remember it now—and things looked pretty normal in the beginning. Then there was this scene with a bath…" She avoided his eyes. "One woman was sitting on the edge, and the other was *in* the bath, her face, uh…"

He started laughing. "Oral sex? You feel this uncomfortable because of soft porn *oral sex*?"

"It was very strange to watch that."

"It would make me hot." He perked up. "I know! We should totally watch a gritty porno."

"We will definitely *not* do that," she argued. "It's gross."

"How do you know? You've never tried it before."

She was exasperated, he could tell. He had that effect on her. "I'm not drunk enough for that, and I don't think I ever will be!"

"We could fix that. Finish your drink." She raised her eyebrows, but he smiled innocently. "Time to take the training wheels off this particular ride, and teach you how to drink *tequila*. You heard me," he added when she simply sat there, staring at him.

"I swear, if any of this gets out to the real world, I'm going to be really upset." She removed the straw and emptied her glass, wincing. "How much did you put in there?"

"Hardly any," he chuckled in response. He got two shot glasses, sliced up a lemon and pulled a salt shaker nearer. He filled the glasses and demonstrated what she had to do with the salt. "Okay, lick it off."

"I've seen this in movies."

"I can't believe you've never had tequila before, but I'll let it go. Lick." Konstantinos followed suit, throwing back the shot and finishing it off with a bite of lemon. He grinned at her facial expression. "The first time is always the most horrible. It gets better, I swear."

"I'm drinking, and it's not even seven o'clock in the evening."

"Just remember the horrible emails we're getting at all times of the day, and you'll stop worrying about the time of day. Another?" She nodded bravely, making him smile. He refilled their glasses. "Good girl."

She swallowed it down. "You lied. It's not getting better."

"Lemon," he reminded her.

"Right." She squeezed the lemon's juice into her mouth and licked her fingers. "So, have you ever watched porn that disgusted you?"

The question took him off guard. He thought about it while he filled their glasses for a third time. "Yeah, I guess I've seen one or two that I wish I hadn't."

"What were they about?"

He noticed that she didn't need prompting anymore, but he didn't want to make her feel like she was drinking alone, so he went through the whole ritual with her before answering. "I remember one of them distinctly. It was an S&M type of thing, and two guys were doing a woman at the same time." He laughed at her frown. "One of them was using the back door."

"Right." She didn't seem as disturbed by that visual as he'd thought she would. "So it wasn't the bondage that freaked you out?"

"Sure, in a way. Another round?"

"Why not? My parents aren't here to stop me."

Konstantinos peeked at her while he poured. "How're you feeling?"

"Slightly tipsy, to be honest. I normally stop way before this point in the evening, but hey, I'm having fun."

He didn't know why it pleased him to hear her say that. "Good, me too. Why don't we take it to the next level and do this without salt and lemon?"

"I was wondering when we'll stop, 'cause my teeth feel funny." She clinked her glass to his before draining it. She kept the rim of the glass on her lower lip, her tongue snaking inside to get the last couple of drops. "Why does bondage freak you out?"

He blinked, having been distracted by her tongue. "Uhm, I don't know."

"Is it because you don't want to be tied down to anyone, not even physically?" she asked, putting the glass down and tapping it with a fingertip.

Because I had a bad experience once.

He shuddered at the memory and tilted the tequila bottle to fill her glass. "Something along those lines."

She waited for him to do the same to his own, before

raising it to her mouth. She didn't even pull faces anymore. "I think it could be fun." She giggled. "Wow, I can't believe I just said that aloud. But I think it works for people who live in their heads, you know? People who always want control of everything can find it hard to relax in the bedroom. If you're tied down, it's like turning tables."

"Are you sure?" he questioned when she motioned for another round.

"Are you scared?" she countered.

"Of course not." His head was getting woozy and he was a seasoned drinker. He could only imagine how *she* must be feeling. Her eyelids were getting droopy. "And I get what you're saying, but I don't know if I'll ever be okay to let someone tie me up."

At least, not again.

"Ah, trust issues." She drunkenly lifted a finger to the ceiling. "I knew it! Who was the woman that ruined you?"

Memories of his past were fuzzy, partly due to the alcohol. He's suppressed that incident, for the most part. "There has to be someone, right? No one is born like this… We all start out in life being very trusting and trustworthy."

"Big words, good job. And yeah, I guess you're right. I can't remember the last time I fully gave someone my trust, without any guarantee that things were going to work out."

"Praven?" He was curious to know why they broke up after seven years. Heaven knew he's never had a relationship last that long. Besides, if they hadn't called it quits, he wouldn't be in this apartment right now, getting drunk with his so-called fiancée.

"Another shot first."

He obeyed, feeling like he was going to need it, too. His knees were getting weak. He plopped down on the barstool next to her, his right hand clutching the nearly-empty tequila bottle. "What happened?"

She sighed. She toyed with her empty glass for a while. Then, turning her glossy gaze to his, she took a deep breath. "He said I was shit in bed."

That was not what he expected. Since when do gossip magazines get it right? "No one's shit in bed."

"Apparently, I am," she said in a dramatic whisper, swaying slightly. "We were together for five years when we started having sex. Two years after that, he couldn't take it anymore. I'm a shitty lover. He was my first everything, but *I* was the disappointment."

"Your first everything?" he echoed, taken aback. "You mean he was your first kiss, too?" She nodded, and he whistled. "Well, were you *his* first?"

"You know, I'm not really sure. I mean, we started dating in our last year of high school, but he had other girlfriends before me." She tapped her chin. "Looking back on it, I'm starting to think he had girlfriends *while* we were dating. If he had sex before he dated me, surely he wouldn't wait five years before he could score with me. Right?"

Talk about a sensitive subject. Konstantinos coughed while he thought of how to respond. "I don't know Praven that well, so I can't answer on his behalf." He shook his head, frowning deeply. "But no one's *shit* in bed. Were those his exact words?"

"Yes."

"Jeez, no wonder you've got a stick up your butt. I mean, there are many women who let their insecurities get in the way, but I've never regretted bedding a woman."

"But you're a man."

"So is Praven."

She propped her elbow on the counter, resting her chin on her hand. She seemed to have forgotten that fact. "Right."

"I can't believe he said that to you. Contrary to popular belief, I haven't enjoyed all of my sexual experiences, but I've never insulted any woman I've slept with."

"But you're Greek. Don't you *have* to respect women, or something?"

"I'd like to think that's true for all cultures."

"Hmm. I think I'd like another drink now."

"Only if you insist."

"I do," she said firmly.

He had another round with her, watching her carefully. He had a feeling she's never told anyone the real reason for her breakup, even if the tabloids had guessed correctly. She seemed so lost in her own mind, probably reliving the nightmare of being told she's a bad lover, that a sense of determination flowed through him. When he looked back on it later, he wouldn't be certain whether his next move had been due the alcohol or a desire to make her feel better.

He turned to her. "Kiss me."

She blinked a couple of times, confused. "I beg your pardon?"

"You know, when you're drunk, you sound Irish." He chuckled to himself. "Come on, kiss me. I want to see if you know how to kiss properly. Maybe that's your problem."

"Then I had a sucky teacher."

"That's not a word," he informed her. "I'd like to help."

She let out a long breath. "Fine, let's do this, then." She leaned forward, putting her hands on his shoulders, and smashed their lips together.

He couldn't help it: he started laughing once she opened his mouth with hers. He pushed her back and tried to get a hold of himself. "Okay, first of all, there's a difference between *kissing* and *charging*."

Asha frowned. "I thought men liked aggressive kissing."

"Again, there's a difference between *kissing* and *charging*. It's not a turn-on if you stick your tongue in my mouth and just hold it there, especially if it's that stiff." He touched the side of her face when tears formed in her eyes, smiling in reassurance. "Don't worry, I'll teach you, but first I need to ask you a question. Did you enjoy it when Praven kissed you?"

She was silent for a while, processing that. "No, actually."

"That's what I thought. Let's change your experience." He slid his fingers into her silky hair and pulled her closer. "Feel what I do, and fall in when you're ready, okay?"

"Okay," she replied, rolling her eyes.

He let his mouth softly flit over hers, thinking how deliciously plump her lips were. He gently sucked on the top one, feeling her mouth parting on a gasp. He didn't close his eyes, since he never kissed with his eyes shut, and neither did she. She stared at him in astonishment as he kept at it. Then, when he was about to give up and tell her he couldn't help her, she threw her arms around his neck, pushing her hips between his legs as she slid off her barstool.

This time, when she pushed her tongue into his mouth, it was to search for his, to prod it into a kiss that had his loins tightening instantly. He gave her what she wanted, coiling his tongue around hers, opening her mouth wider to give him more access. He wanted to absorb her taste.

"When's the last time you shaved?" she breathed, barely lifting her mouth from his before going in for another toe-curling kiss.

He only replied once he got a chance. "Two days ago. Does it hurt?"

"No." She moaned when his hands went down to her petite, rounded behind. "I like it."

She had such a small bone structure. His hands felt huge on her ass: he loved how it made him feel. It was as if he was a bear protecting a baby deer. Probably not the type of analogy he should make while locking lips with an attractive woman, but...

"Oh my God," she murmured. She stepped away from him, breathing harshly and touching her swollen lips. Her chin was red from the grazing she'd received, courtesy of his stubble. "I didn't know kissing could be like that."

His chest was heaving. "You're a fast learner."

"We probably shouldn't do that again."

"Probably not."

"I should go to bed. Goodnight, Konstantinos."

"Goodnight, Asha."

He regretted their decision the minute she disappeared into the hallway, although that baffled him further. He should be glad that things hadn't gone any further! Sure, they were becoming fast friends, but they weren't going to go through with any of this once they were released from the confines of this penthouse apartment.

"This is a nightmare," he muttered, running his fingers through his hair before he walked to the master bedroom. He paused at her door, which was shut, and rested his hand on it. He longed to talk to her about what's occurred, if only to find out if he was the only one shaken.

He felt like he'll never be turned on like that by another woman. That made even less sense.

It took him an hour to fall asleep, tossing and turning as he was, but he welcomed the black void on the other side.

CHAPTER 12

ASHA FELT LIKE a total cliché when she woke up the next day with a splitting headache. How many times has she read books and magazine articles that explained that overindulging in alcohol lead to hangovers? Obviously, she'll have to read a few more before the message stuck.

She groaned, rubbing her forehead. The digital alarm clock on her bedside table informed her that it was nine in the morning. Flashes of the previous night dropped into her brain, one by one. She touched her chin with a frown that quickly turned into raised eyebrows.

Good God, had she seriously kissed Konstantinos?

"My life couldn't get any worse," she muttered. She carefully got out of bed, the pounding behind her eyes close to breaking point. Deciding to get cleaned up, she went into the en-suite bathroom and took a long, soothing shower. The condensation made her want to vomit, but she clamped her mouth shut and forced her insides to behave. She brushed her teeth, dressed in loose-fitting clothing and headed downstairs.

She heard music playing in the gym and would've rolled her eyes if her head didn't hurt so much. It's typical that Konstantinos didn't have a hangover. *She* was the one suffering because she's never had tequila before. It was unfair.

She was hungry, but one look at most of the items in the fridge made her stomach roll and heave. She pushed two slices of rye bread into the toaster. She remembered reading somewhere that a great hangover cure was something dry.

"Good morning."

She gave him a good glare. "How come you get to exercise like there's nothing wrong with you? Shirtless, no less."

"There isn't anything wrong with me," he answered, shrugging while he patted his forehead dry with a small towel. He raised an eyebrow at the toaster. "You're going to need more than that if you want to feel better."

"I don't think I can stomach more."

"Trust me."

"I did that last night, and look where it got me."

He rolled his eyes, instantly making her envious since she couldn't do the same. "You asked for more, remember? I was only doing what you asked." He moved to the fridge, taking out a carton of eggs, milk, mushrooms, tomatoes, green peppers, onions and cheese. "It's time you learnt how to cook 'cause honestly, I can't take doing this by myself anymore."

"I know how to cook," she said stubbornly.

"Oh, really? Then why have *I* been doing all the cooking?"

His brown eyes were lit with challenge and she didn't have the energy to argue. "Fine, I can't cook."

"I knew it!" he cheered. "Come on, help me chop this up."

"What're you making?"

"Omelettes."

She placed a hand in front of her mouth, shaking her head. "Eggs…"

"Believe me, it'll make you feel better."

"I'll take your word for it." She took the ripe tomatoes and retrieved a sharp knife from a drawer. She couldn't remember ever slicing up anything before. Okay, she was clearly a spoiled rich girl. It couldn't hurt to try, right?

Konstantinos peeked over her shoulder. "If you could make them thinner, that would be great."

"Yes, Chef," she mocked.

"How else are you going to learn?"

"By watching you?"

"You've been doing that for more than a week."

"Well, not always. You do your thing, and I do mine."

"Well, that was until—" He cut himself off with a cough. "If you could hurry up, that'd be great. I need to get these things in the pan. Start with the onions first, since they take longer to fry."

Annoyed by his bossy tone, she chopped up an onion. Her eyes burned and she felt like she could choke. She wiped her tears away. "Argh, this is so irritating! Why am *I* the one crying when I could be behind the stove?"

"You don't even know how to switch it on."

"Whatever, of course I do."

"You probably won't be any good at it. I know what I'm doing. You're my apprentice."

She looked at the toast, which had popped out ages ago, with longing. "Do I really have to eat all of this?"

"It'll make you feel better," he reminded her. He watched her handiwork again. "Those onions will do. Bring them over here."

She lifted the chopping board and turned to the stove, once again aware that he wasn't wearing a shirt. Honestly, for a billionaire, he sure didn't act like one. Her free hand went up to her mouth while he transferred the chopped onions from the board to a pan. She remembered that kiss and how it had made her blood sizzle, much like the sound of onions meeting hot oil.

"How, uh, is your chin feeling?" he asked, pulling her back to the present.

She tensed. "What do you mean?"

"I know my stubble isn't exactly the softer kind."

"I'm fine," she insisted. She was close to him, too close. She could feel his body heat and smell his sweat. It was a lot sexier than it sounded, so she stepped away and put distance between them, carrying on with her duties without visual reminders of that kiss they'd shared.

Her toes curled whenever she thought about it.

They were silent for the next couple of minutes while he added the other ingredients to his mixture. She watched him manoeuvre around the kitchen like it was second nature, trying not to smile at how comfortable he seemed. Thirty years ago, their roles would've been reversed. She quite enjoyed the fact that a man was making her breakfast.

"Okay, yours is up first," he said, sprinkling cheese over the ingredients before closing the omelette. "Bring me a plate."

She took two down from the overhead cupboard behind her, handing one of them over. He expertly slid the omelette from the pan to the plate, giving it back to her. "Thanks," she said. "I'll sit here and wait for you to finish."

"Don't let that get cold, though." He gave her a knife and fork. "You can start eating."

"I hope you're right about this," she mumbled, taking a bite and chewing cautiously. When she swallowed, she half expected her stomach to protest. It didn't. "Hmm, this is really good."

"I told you."

Halfway through her omelette, she poured them both a glass of fruit juice. He wasn't finished at the stove, even though he's already wolfed down one omelette. She found it amusing that he had such a big appetite, thinking how fitting it was that he could always afford to feed himself.

"About Praven."

She flinched. "We're back to that, are we?"

"Not directly." He glanced at her. "His reason for leaving is crap and you're much better off without him. The person you spend the rest of your life with should be willing to address issues in the relationship and look for a solution *with* you."

"Since when are you a relationship expert?"

"Since I've had so much free time on my hands that I can't do anything but watch *Dr. Phil*," he teased. He lost the smile when she giggled. "I'm serious, though. You deserve better than Praven Kahn."

"Blessing in disguise, then?"

"Something like that."

Asha critically observed him for a long time. She couldn't deny that she'd felt something during that kiss last night. Who had initiated it? It was all blurry, but she was definitely the one who had wanted more, which was exactly why she'd stopped. It couldn't mean that she was falling in love with him, could it? He totally wasn't her type. While they've been stuck in here, he hasn't even considered looking at his tasks and responsibilities at his family's company. Instead, he's kept busy with things that weren't important. In her opinion, at least.

She packed her dirty dishes away, absently noticing that the fridge and pantry were always stocked. How was that possible if they didn't go shopping for food? Did that mean that someone was coming *in*?

"I'm thinking of taking a look at those designs my father emailed me," Konstantinos informed her, unknowingly breaking her out of her train of thought. "Actually, no. I'm *going* to have a look. I've got an engineering degree: I might as well put it to good use."

She gaped at him. Here she was, thinking that he wasn't her kind of man, and then he said something like that. "That's great. I'm sure he'll appreciate it."

"I've got nothing better to do."

His body language told her what he wouldn't, though: he was excited to do this, to make his mark and play his part. When he got this way, he reminded her of a little boy.

She fought a smile, crossing her arms over her chest. "Thanks for breakfast. I feel much better."

"Good." He nodded to himself, making sure the stove was switched off. He turned to her. "Things are cool between us, right? I mean, after last night."

"Things are fine," she assured him. "Thanks for showing me the difference between… Well, you know. It was nice."

"Nice?" He laughed softly. "For someone who was raised with English as a first language, that's all you can come up with? *Nice?*"

"I don't have to inflate an ego that's already the size of Jupiter."

"Oh, I don't know." He waggled his eyebrows. "The sun's still bigger. I'm aiming to blow up my ego to its proportions."

"Uh-huh." She turned on her heel, biting her bottom lip to keep from giggling like a schoolgirl. What was wrong with her? "I've got work to do. I'll be in the study."

She felt giddy and nearly floated all the way to her desk. Oh God, her worst nightmare was coming true: she really *did* like him. A lot.

Why did a kiss change everything?

CHAPTER 13

HALFWAY ACROSS THE city, Denise was wondering the same thing.

"They kissed?" she asked.

Jacob nodded. "But that was all."

"That's still progress." She checked her calendar. "We've got less than three weeks left. Whatever they're doing, they better keep it up."

"Everything's going to be fine." He eyed her for a long time. "You've been different these past couple of days. Anything you'd like to share?"

Oh, sure, she'll go right ahead and tell him about her affair with Loikanos Sarantos. It wouldn't have any repercussions whatsoever, and it certainly wouldn't bring her work ethic and responsibilities to her clients into question, either.

She could tell Jacob that the rumours were true: sleeping with a younger man when you're heading for your forties was nothing short of breath-taking. She could confide that Loikanos made her feel like they were setting her sheets alight, in the most literal sense; how one heated glance from him made her rip off her clothes and beg him to take her; how a mere look at his youthful, tanned and athletic body made parts of her clench, parts that haven't done so in years.

She could go on to say that it wasn't just physical, either. How much she liked it whenever Loikanos laughed, or shared a childhood memory with her; how much she basked in the fact that he seemed genuinely interested in her own upbringing; how he texted her when she least expected it and brightened her day.

Pass.

"*Non, chéri,*" she answered, clearing her throat and tucking her blonde hair behind her ears. She briefly closed her eyes, remembering how Loikanos had complimented her when she'd first taken her hair out of its usual professional bun. As a result, she no longer wore it up.

She was such a fool! Where was this even going?

"I'm loving the new hairstyle. It brings out those blue eyes of yours."

"Can we get back to work?" She tapped on her iPad's screen. "We've got an appointment with Anushka Dewali and Kolina Sarantos coming up." *And then I'll have to pretend like I'm not having intercourse with the latter's youngest son.* "They want to discuss the flowers and decorations at the venue. Have you received confirmation on the guest list from The Orangery?"

Jacob nodded. "The Palace has agreed that everyone's welcome, though they have a lot of rules regarding alcohol and flowers."

"That's fine," Denise said, waving the comment away with a well-manicured hand. "We can work within those rules, since neither of the in-laws really wants anyone drinking at the reception. Are we doing the rehearsal dinner there, as well?"

"Yes, they've cleared their schedule for us. They were giving me a hard time until I told them whose wedding it was."

"The power of a name." She shook her head, her thoughts wandering to a certain twenty-three-year-old billionaire. Oh God, she was turning into such a *Madame Cougouar.* "Alright, draw up a list of the possible combinations regarding food and drink. They couldn't have selected cultures that are more conflicting than the Greeks and Indians, could they?"

"Luckily, neither of the families looks like they're overly traditional."

"Any updates on Asha's wedding dress?"

"I've got the final design here." He flipped through his file, taking a page out of it and handing it over. "This is a photo of her sketch. It looks like she wants gold."

Denise took in the plain, sleeveless gown with a mermaid tail, a smile touching the corners of her mouth. "It's simple but elegant and would do wonders for her colouring. Asha Dewali is a wise woman. I can't wait for her next collection to hit the runways in Paris." She pouted as she thought of Konstantinos. "The groom should wear cream or beige, with a golden undercoat and tie. I'll swing the idea by the ladies later this afternoon."

"Perhaps she'll design something for him, too."

Denise considered that. "Yes, I think you're right. Keep an eye on it."

"Anything else?"

"If they're kissing, then I think we're ready for the rings. Send three sets: one gold with emeralds and diamonds, one platinum with tanzanite, and one with…" She pouted, thinking. "Hmm, citrine. It's going to be interesting to see which one Konstantinos will choose for Asha."

Jacob was furiously taking notes. "Cartier or Bvlgari?"

"Contact both? Oh, Harry Winston! And Graff. Make it happen. Give them seven days to send us their most exclusive pieces. I'd like those rings in the apartment a week before Asha and Konstantinos are scheduled to come out. That's all for now, *merci* Jacob."

He inclined his head with a slight smile. "Whatever's going on in your life, keep at it. It's working wonders for your complexion."

She was blushing by the time he shut her office's door, leaving her with her own thoughts. She could smell Loikanos' Hugo Boss Orange aftershave as if he was right next to her. She closed her eyes to get her ducks in a row. She was at work: she shouldn't be thinking about her private life.

Her cell phone beeped. It was in her hand before she could think to grab it, her heart beating wildly once she saw she had a new email from Loikanos. She turned to her laptop, opening her email application to read it on a bigger screen.

From: Loikanos Sarantos
To: Denise Lemont
Subject: Dinner Date

Good morning, mon amour. It feels like days since I've seen you. I still can't believe you went to the office, when I expressly told you not to get out of bed or you'll regret it ;-). My only hope is that you are, indeed, regretting it. I shouldn't have let you go, but I'll leave you with the option of making it up to me tonight. I have reservations. Reply if you're interested, and I'll give you the details. Sincerely yours, Loikanos.

This was ridiculous! He was twelve years younger than her! Sure, she had some friends who have dallied with young men, but it was different now that the shoe was on *her* foot. Feeling this giddy couldn't be a good sign, either. If she didn't nip it in the bud, she'll end up falling for him, and where would that lead?

Nowhere, that's where. She'll be heartbroken, he'll get pouty for having lost a lover. She would've violated the trust of her clients and end up losing her job.

She shouldn't reply. He's giving her the perfect opportunity to back out with no hard feelings.

Her fingers were typing her eager response, her brain realizing too late that she'd hit "Send" before it could kick in and stop her.

Whoops.

She'll have to worry about the fallout some other time.

CHAPTER 14

IT TOOK A while for his brain, which was used to partying, fun and sex, to think about engineering. His eyes scanned the construction plans of a new hotel in Dubai, narrowing every time his creativity hit a wall. He couldn't be that rusty, could he? It's been two years since his graduation, for crying out loud. He had to get a grip.

That was very hard to do when Asha Dewali was sitting at her desk, on the other side of the room, with her lower lip jutted out, the way it always did when she was concentrating. Her lips reminded him of the kiss that never should've happened.

He shifted in his seat, clearing his throat and pulling his notepad closer. He might love technology, but he preferred writing things down, especially when he had to make impossible calculations. His pen scribbled a couple of notes down: things that bothered him about the design. Maybe a building like that could work in a place that wasn't hit with vicious storms twice a year but, unless they changed the structural beams of the building, they were going to can this whole thing.

What was it about Dubai, anyway? They always built bigger, more obscenely shaped structures. What happened to the good old days, when the Empire State Building had been an architectural triumph and engineering masterpiece?

Okay, there was no need to get angry at the latest trends. He could do this.

It wasn't setting his mind at ease knowing that his father has chosen him as the head of the project. He had no idea where this was coming from, but Nikos Sarantos' sudden confidence in his son's abilities was baffling on about five different levels. To make matters worse, he's been invited to a board meeting less than a month from now to discuss the feasibility of this building's construction. How was anyone going to take him seriously, knowing he's never worked a day in his life?

"How're you getting on over there?"

He spared Asha a look. "It's going."

She stretched her arms and leaned back on her chair. "What're you working on? Can I see it?"

"A new hotel in Dubai. Construction is scheduled to start in six months' time," he answered dryly. "And I, Konstantinos Sarantos, 'must make sure it happens', according to my father."

"Sounds cool." She made her way over to him. "Do you mind?"

He shook his head, handing her the frontal view of the building.

"Ooh, it's pretty!" she exclaimed, tracing the printout with a finger. She pointed to the base of the building. "Are those alternate energy methods?"

"Yeah, what they're trying to do is integrate solar panels between the windows, while still making it appear like a glass structure. It makes sense, since Dubai gets a lot of sun every year. The base of every floor will have the best solar technology that currently exists." He chuckled to himself. "They're pushing the envelope. There's another building that has three massive fans to generate power from the high-speed winds they get."

"I think I saw a program about that one on Discovery. At least this won't really affect the structure of the building, right? The one with the fans had to have springs or something installed to make sure there would be no damage every time the wind acts up."

"Springs," he echoed, shaking his head with a laugh. "I guess you can call it that. And although this doesn't affect the structure, it does affect the building's appearance. In Dubai, appearance is everything."

"That's a laugh, considering that I'm not allowed to wear miniskirts in certain areas." She tilted her head to the side. "You know, I kind of like that there'll be this silver line running through every floor. I mean, it's hardly a third of the size of one story, and it reminds me of those lines in trees that shows us how old they are."

"Hmm, I didn't think of that."

"That's 'cause you're the technical brain, and I'm the creative one," she teased, playfully bumping her hip to his shoulder. Her eyes dipped down to his chest. "Seriously, Teeny! Can't you just wear a damn shirt every once in a while?"

"Whoa, whoa, whoa! *What* did you call me?"

"Teeny."

He stared at her, stunned.

She seemed disturbed by his silence. Clearing her throat, she explained: "Your name is such a mouthful—"

"But it's my name, the one you should use."

"—and it's not like I can yell 'Konstantinos!' if I need you, 'cause it's too long—"

"You just did, and it sounded fine."

"—so I figured I should give you a nickname," she finished, ignoring his protests. "'Nos' doesn't work for me, and I mulled over 'Tanti' for a while, but it sounds too weird. In the end, I settled on 'Teeny'."

"I don't like it."

She grinned at him. "You don't have to like it."

"If you haven't noticed, I'm taller than you," he said, rising to his full height.

"By, like, a few inches."

He gestured to his ripped body. "I'm bigger than you."

"What's your point, Mr. I'm-too-sexy-for-my-shirt?"

"I am definitely not going to be called 'Teeny', since that means small, and *nothing* about me is small."

Her mouth popped open. "Your ego is bigger than I thought."

"If you knew that before you gave me this stupid nickname, shouldn't you have known better?"

"It's called irony, Teeny. Get over it."

"It's not. Besides, if that's how you feel, I'm calling you Bigfoot." That had the desired effect: she glared at him. He crossed his arms over his broad chest and gave her a smirk. "That's right. *Bigfoot.*"

"That's never going to fly."

"Until you stop with Teeny, you're now officially known as Bigfoot Dewali."

"I never back down from a challenge first," she warned him. "You hate 'Teeny' as much as I hate 'Bigfoot'!"

He shrugged. "I'm going to love pushing your buttons more, Bigfoot."

She let out a cry of frustration. "How do you get so many women to sleep with you when you're such an obnoxious ass?"

"Do you really want to know?"

"I asked!"

"Like this," he murmured, pulling her into his arms and kissing her. He started, as before, by softly playing with her lips. She froze in his arms with wide eyes, but that all changed once he slipped his tongue into her mouth.

She sighed softly and locked her hands behind his neck, stepping up to him so he could feel her heat against his stomach and chest.

When she reacted this way, he lost all control. With other women, he could have a gentle make-out session until their clothes came off, at the very least. He didn't understand why Asha made him respond differently. He cupped her face in his hands, trapping her between his body and the edge of the desk. He felt the nail of one of her fingers tenderly scrape down his spine, making him shiver. And then she wondered why he didn't like to wear shirts at home?

She shifted to sit on the desk, her legs wrapping around his waist. He tugged at her oversized T-shirt, wanting to feel her skin on his fingertips. The kiss intensified until he thought he was going to combust. He could hardly get enough air into his lungs. It's been nearly two weeks since he's had sex. He was on fire for her.

Later, he wouldn't be able to explain how he'd managed to pull away from her. One second he was contemplating taking her, right there on the desk; the next he was on the other side of the room, staring at her with eyes that could see through her clothes.

"We said we weren't going to do that again," he murmured huskily, hooking his thumbs through the front belt loops on his jeans, mostly to use his hands to cover what she was doing to him.

It didn't help: her eyes travelled down to his crotch. She bit her bottom lip once she saw. "You started it."

He was happy to hear that she wasn't unaffected by him. "I did, but we really shouldn't do that again."

"Hmm," came her noncommittal response.

"I'm going to…" He raked his fingers through his hair, heading for the door. "Take a cold shower."

He couldn't be sure, but as he exited the room, he thought he heard her say: "Damn."

Chapter 15

Asha had to be admitted to a psychiatric institution. Seriously, it's a good thing that he'd stopped, that he had gone off to do God-knows-what, and that they weren't making out in the study anymore. It was a very, very good thing.

Then why did it feel like the opposite?

She carefully avoided Konstantinos after that, trying to get her ducks in a row. Would she have fallen for him under normal circumstances? Would she have felt this way if they'd hung out together in the real world, with the distractions of everyday life? Better yet, would she have been able to hog his attention for more than a couple of days while the rest of the women in the world surrounded them?

Wait a minute… Did she admit she's fallen for him? That was impossible! Sure, they got along, but that's because they *had* to. He was the only person she could talk to and, when he wasn't being a total self-absorbed douche, she enjoyed his company. None of that meant that she was developing romantic interest in him.

Yes, his kisses made her want to do all sorts of devilish things with him, but every woman must feel that way once she's locked lips with him. Asha was simply proving, once again, that he was a playboy.

"Ugh," she muttered, braiding her damp hair. It was obvious that he needed to work on himself if he ever wanted to be taken seriously in life. She hated being a part of other people's learning curves. Why couldn't they figure their lives out by themselves? Why did she want to get involved with Konstantinos and his ego?

She ignored the little voice in her head that told her that maybe, just maybe, *she* had to learn from this experience, too. She'd been fine before he came along, and she'll be fine once she got out of here.

She thought about her life outside these walls, grimacing. Retrospectively, she realized how unhappy she's been. She never used to go out, she didn't drink alcohol, and she never approached men. Currently, she was throwing herself at a womanizing idiot, every chance she got. She should never have picked up that first glass of tequila. It had opened a can of worms that shouldn't have seen the light of day.

Unsurprisingly, it was difficult to avoid contact with Konstantinos, especially since he was taking such a great interest in that Dubai construction project. She was filled with inspiration, having already completed five designs for her next collection, meaning she was always at her desk in the study when he worked at his. When he wasn't doing that, he was in the gym for two hours a day, or playing Xbox, or watching movies.

Oh, and eating. The man was always hungry.

Speaking of, she had to get food in her stomach or she was going to pass out. She fastened her braid, dismissed the idea that she should wear make-up, and headed downstairs to the kitchen. She felt like having a slice of chocolate cake, though she doubted there was any.

She passed him in the living room, but pretended as if she didn't see him. They haven't spoken in a day and it was killing her, yet she couldn't afford a rerun of the incident in the study until she was sure that what she felt for him didn't solely exist because of their confinement. Besides, she didn't even know if he's as shaken as she was. He could've already forgotten.

A quick inspection of the kitchen confirmed her suspicions: if she truly wanted chocolate cake, she was going to have to make it from scratch. She pushed her bottom lip out while she thought, her eyes scanning the small bookcase of recipes. Should she risk it?

"Why not?" she mumbled to herself, reaching for one with the title *Cookies, Cakes & Other Delicacies*. She paged to the index, searching for chocolate cake, before flipping to the appropriate page. The ingredients might as well have been in Greek. She had no idea what most of them were.

She opened the pantry to match the list in the book to the labels of the items on the shelves, and spent four minutes looking for the equipment she'll need. Whoever designed this kitchen had to be smacked on the head: it wasn't very user-friendly. No wonder the private chef always appeared to be disgruntled when cooking dinner for the Dewali family.

"Preheat oven to 180 degrees Celsius," she quoted softly, tapping the page with a finger. She turned to the oven and blinked a couple of times. It was a top-of-the-range stainless steel one, and it had three different compartments. Which one should she use?

"Can I help?"

She jumped in fright, glancing at him rather angrily once her breathing was back to normal. "I'm sure I can figure it out."

He strolled to the open recipe book. "Cake, huh? You're going to want to use the largest compartment," he said, pointing.

"I knew that."

"Sure you did." He'd actually donned a shirt today, though it clung to his upper body like a second skin. He leaned against the counter, watching her. "I'm assuming you also know that you'll have to lower the temperature to 150 degrees if you're using that compartment?"

Who was she trying to fool? She had no idea what she was doing. "Why?"

"Well, even though it's smaller than a conventional oven—like the ones that ninety-five percent of the general population use—the size means it'll heat up quicker."

She eyed him suspiciously. "You make cakes?"

"I pay attention when my mom feels like *baking* a cake, and I help out sometimes. I have a similar oven in my home in Greece." He cocked an eyebrow. "Do you need any help?"

"Sure," she answered, sighing deeply. "No harm in that, right?"

"So cynical. Come on, I'll show you how to use this mixer."

She found it amusing that someone like Konstantinos Sarantos, world-renowned lady-killer, knew his way around the kitchen. Then again, she assumed that it could be part of his repertoire of tricks to get women into bed. She wondered how many times he's seduced them over a home-cooked meal, then decided that she really didn't want to know.

She was *not* jealous.

"Why cake?" he enquired as he poured the batter into two round pans.

"I have a craving for it." She took a bite of a banana. "I've learnt by now to listen to what my body wants. If it's asking for tons of sugar and fat, then so be it."

He chuckled. "Women are always worried about their figures."

"Says the man who's only ever had sex with skinny women."

"Were you there when I had sex with them?"

"Of course not."

"Then you can't comment, can you?"

She opened her mouth to protest, then clamped it shut. "Okay, you have a point, but I'm *assuming* you've always had sex with skinny women."

"I've had sex with skinny women, yes." He handed her the two pans to put into the oven. "I've *enjoyed* sex more when the woman had a bit more meat on her bones, though."

She set the timer and gave him a look. "You're saying that you like sleeping with plump women?"

"Yes, if they're not too self-conscious about their bodies."

"I don't understand that. Explain."

"How can I put this?" He thought for a while, helping her load the dishwasher before dragging the ingredients for the cake's icing closer. "Sex is never pleasurable if the woman doesn't think she's sexy. You'd think that, if I've got a boner, that would be proof enough that I'm attracted to her, but you won't believe how annoying it is when someone keeps asking if she's doing something wrong or if she looks ugly. I like for sex to be instinctual, instead of instructional."

"I bet you've never had someone tell you you're a sucky lover."

"That really shouldn't be a word." He laughed again. "And I haven't always been good. I had to learn to interpret the intricacies of a woman's body correctly."

"But no one's ever *told* you that—"

"I've received criticism too, Bigfoot," he said, giving her a wink. "I didn't let that rule my future, though. I'm always willing to learn new things."

That stung. "Sex isn't as important to others, as it is to you."

"When sex isn't important to others, it's because they've never enjoyed it before. It's one of the best recreational activities I can think of."

"You know, if you apply all of this energy to your work, Teeny, you'll be a very successful man."

He smiled. "That's what I'm trying to do. Now, will you help with the icing? If I recall correctly, *you* wanted to bake a cake."

She moved to his side and started adding ingredients to the mixing bowl. "Are you figuring anything out about that building?"

"I've started a list of issues that I have to raise with my father once I get out of here, but it's going well so far. I get the feeling I won't always enjoy what I'm doing, but I think it's time that I take my role seriously."

"Hardly two weeks in and you're already a changed man."

"I won't go that far, but there's always room for improvement." He grinned at her, his dark brown eyes sparkling. "In *every* aspect of your life."

"Why does it sound like I should read into that?"

"No reason. You don't have to do anything. You have a choice. Now, are you going to be okay on your own? You won't burn the place down?"

"I think I can handle it from here, thanks," she responded with an eye roll.

"When the timer goes off, open the oven door but keep everything inside to cool off for thirty minutes or so. Then you'll be able to apply the icing."

"I prefer reading the recipe book for that piece of information, simply because it doesn't talk."

"You have to admit that I've been a giant help," he said, dipping his finger into the bowl of icing to taste it. "Wow, that's delicious. Here, you try."

His finger hovered in front of her lips and, without thinking, she took it into her mouth, gently sucking the creamy deliciousness off. She closed her eyes in bliss and moaned softly. "Wow, you're right! And *I* made that! Incredible!" When she glanced at him, his eyes had darkened. "What?"

He cleared his throat, eyeing his finger curiously. "Nothing. I'll be in the study."

She only understood what had happened once she was alone in the kitchen. How stupid could she possibly get? Sucking his finger? *Really?* Especially after the two kisses they've shared? She really needed more life experience, or she'll be in his bed by the end of the month.

And that couldn't happen.

* * * * *

HIS FINGER WAS still tingling. He tried his best to ignore it *and* the remembered vision of her full lips folding around it. He wished he could've taken a snapshot of her face: eyes closed, mouth pouting… Then again, it didn't look like he'll easily forget.

Why did he keep putting himself in this damn situation? He had to avoid physical contact with her if he wanted to stay sane.

Luckily, he received an email from his brother at that moment. He welcomed the distraction.

From: Loikanos Sarantos
To: Konstantinos Sarantos
Subject: Marriage

Yo, bro! How're you getting on with Asha? I realize you can't answer, but I asked anyway, 'cause I don't want to come across as a SOB who doesn't give a crap about his brother's happiness. Seeing as I'm your best man at the wedding, will you be my best man? I'm seriously going to ask this woman to marry me. Not right now, because she seems to be under the impression that we don't belong together, but I know she digs me. I'm already looking at rings. I wish you were here, man, I could really use your advice. You've been with an older woman before, right? You'd know what advice to give. Anyway, I'm taking Denise out for dinner tonight (again :-)). Maybe you should do the same! Obviously, you can't come out to London for dinner, but do the whole candle-lit thing over there. Wear a tux. Cheers!

Konstantinos hated how his brother never wrote in separated paragraphs, though it wasn't that surprising. Face-to-face, Loikanos was like an excited Labrador puppy and, if given half the chance, he could speak continuously without stopping for breath.

What was this about Denise being older? How much older? Man, he wished he could reply. As if Loikanos' previous suggestions weren't bad enough... Have dinner with Asha? They did that every single night. What difference would a couple of candles and a tuxedo make?

"He's such an idiot sometimes," he muttered under his breath, shaking his head. And yet, he was starting to wonder if it was a good idea. They could pretend that they're going somewhere special, dress up, and have fun. Well, maybe not *that* much fun, seeing as he'll have to cook. She had to get up to speed with that ASAP, because he was running out of ideas.

He craved sushi. It was one of the dishes he had no idea how to prepare. Unlike Asha's, his cravings will have to go—

He sat up straight, frowning. He's noticed that someone kept bringing new groceries to the apartment, but he never really thought about what that meant until now. There had to be some form of surveillance system in place, to let them know when the coast was clear. He glanced around the room, but couldn't find any indication that there were cameras.

Well, if the Dewalis were anything like the Sarantos family, the cameras wouldn't be out in the open.

He grabbed his notepad and a thick permanent marker, writing a couple of big letters and numbers on the page: SUSHI 19:00. Holding it in front of him as if he was a driver at Heathrow Airport, he walked to the living room. He turned this way and that, feeling like a moron. Then, figuring that this was a stupid notion, he tore the page from the notepad and walked to the elevator, sliding it under the door.

"How're things looking here?" he asked, entering the kitchen.

Asha looked up from where she was putting icing on the cake. "Great, don't you think? I mean, it's the first time I've ever baked, but nothing burnt."

"Not bad at all. Looks great."

"Now that it's done, I don't really want to eat it anymore." She smiled shyly. "It's so pretty, and I made it all by…" She trailed off, avoiding eye contact. "I mean, you helped, but I made it."

He burst out laughing. "I'll take what I can get. What's for dinner, Chef Bigfoot?"

She rolled her eyes. "I'm not making dinner. I've already made dessert."

"Well, what if we have some fun for dinner?"

"Fun?" She gave him a dry look. "We can't go out."

"I think I just ordered sushi."

"I love sushi!"

"I figured."

"Wait, what do you mean you ordered sushi?"

He opened the fridge door and took out a cup of yoghurt. "Haven't you wondered how we keep getting new supplies? I mean, a two-litre bottle of milk hardly lasts a day with me around."

"Nothing lasts long with you around."

"I think someone sneaks in here every other night when we're otherwise occupied to replace all of the stuff we've used." He finished the yoghurt and threw away the empty container. "I showed them my order."

"What do you mean?"

"I wrote it down on paper, paraded around in the apartment like a lunatic, and slid it into the elevator."

"The security cameras! Of course!" Her eyes widened. "Uhm, that means that whoever's watching has seen us kiss. Twice."

He cleared his throat uncomfortably. "It also means that I'll get sushi, tonight at seven. Why don't we focus on the positives?"

"This is so embarrassing! What if my family has been

watching?"

"I'll be very disappointed if my in-laws turn out to be peeping toms."

"They are *not* your in-laws! And don't for one second think that they're the only ones watching."

He thought about his parents and shook his head. "My father has more important things to do than to keep track of my life." The second those words were out, he realized her point. Nikos Sarantos has tried, from day one, to get Konstantinos to pull his socks up. "Whatever. Look, let's get dressed up and have a good time, okay? I literally can't wait for that sushi to arrive."

"I hope for your part it does. You don't look like the kind of guy that deals well with disappointment."

He rolled his eyes. "I'm not half that bad." He rummaged in the pantry for a pack of biscuits and made a cup of coffee. "So, we have a deal? We'll pretend like we're at some hot-shot sushi spot in London?"

"Deal. Does that mean I have to wear make-up?"

"Absolutely." He grinned, taking his snack to the living room. "Be ready by seven!"

CHAPTER 16

"CAN WE SEND The Orangery our menu?" Denise asked, pinching her phone between her left ear and shoulder.

"Yes," Anushka Dewali replied. "I've discussed this with Kolina, in depth. We are finally in agreement."

Denise had to stop herself from laughing. She remembered how difficult Kolina had been during their appointment yesterday. "I'm happy to hear it, *Madame* Dewali. Hopefully that is an omen of the good things to come."

"Is everything going according to plan with Asha and Konstantinos?"

"It seems as though they have made a connection." Denise glanced up when Jacob peeked into her office, motioning for him to come in. He handed a page over and she quickly scanned the couple of sentences. She smiled. "In fact, *Madame*, I can confirm that they're having a sushi date tonight."

"That's wonderful news! I knew Asha would come out of her shell eventually."

"The formula never fails, *Madame* Dewali."

"I can't thank you enough, Denise. Let me know if you need anything else from us."

She smiled. "I will. Have a good day, *Madame.*"

"You too!"

Hanging up, she looked at Jacob. "When did this request come through?"

"About half an hour ago."

"Is it a trap? Maybe they're trying to find a new way out."

"I don't think it's a trap. There will be more than enough time for us to set up the dining room without them noticing. I don't have reason to believe that they have thought about leaving since the first day they arrived."

"Thank you for the reassurance, *chéri*," she said. She brought her iPad to life, opening the file she'd created, which contained a list of Konstantinos' interests, likes and dislikes. "This is going to be a very large order. He is quite the sushi connoisseur."

Jacob took out a notepad. "Let's hear it."

Denise pouted thoughtfully. "Alright, let me see… Four salmon and four tuna sashimi, two crab stick hand rolls, eight pieces of prawn California rolls, four rainbow rolls, six salmon roses, and two battleships. He'll have a bottle of Pinot Gris. Chocolate mousse for dessert."

"Asha baked a cake, so I doubt that dessert will be necessary."

"Very well," she said, struggling to hide her surprise. "Now, Asha's order is simpler: four salmon fashion sandwiches with cream cheese, three salmon roses, four salmon maki, and one salmon nigiri. Do they still have passion fruit cordials and lemonade?"

"Yes."

"Then she should be sorted for drinks. If they're eating at seven o'clock sharp, then I expect their order to be ready and waiting before that. Use the silverware in the apartment, with matching lids."

"Got it."

"You've got your afternoon cut out for you. Nothing but the best, Jacob, do you hear?"

He inclined his head with a smile. "I'm on it."

She checked the time, letting out a sigh when she saw it was past three already. The closer they got to the day Asha and Konstantinos were going to leave the penthouse suite, the more stressful her working environment became, especially since she was romantically involved with—

Her phone rang, shaking her out of her thoughts. "Hello?"

"Hello, beautiful."

She positively melted at the sound of his voice. "How are you?"

"I'm great now that I'm talking to you," Loikanos responded, a smile in his voice. "You sound strained, *mon amour*. Is everything okay?"

"Just busy at work."

"Can you spare a couple of hours tonight? I'd like to take you out."

She frowned. He wanted to go out? Normally, he came over to her house to make love to her as many times as was humanly possible. The stiff muscles in her legs were a constant reminder of her new lifestyle.

"Out?"

"Yes, out." He chuckled. "Or are you only using me for my body, *mademoiselle?*"

"I'm not a *mademoiselle*," she reminded him, blushing. "And I didn't say I'm using you, either."

"Then let me take you out, *mon amour*. I'll wine and dine you and, by the end of the evening, I swear I will satisfy every desire you may have."

She caught her top lip between her teeth. "Where are we going?"

"I'm taking that as a yes and not telling you anything else. Be ready at seven. I'll pick you up."

"Alright."

"Oh, Denise?" His tone of voice had gone from cheerful to downright sexy, making her shiver.

"Yes?"

"Wear your turquoise underwear again."

She closed her gaping mouth as he hung up, locking her knees together. She couldn't deny it anymore. She might not have known him for long, but Loikanos was beginning to make a big impact on her life. She would have to do something, soon, to put a stop to their doomed relationship.

Right after she saw what trick he had up his sleeve for this evening, naturally.

CHAPTER 17

ASHA FELT RIDICULOUS while she blow-dried her long hair. What was she doing, getting all dressed up for a date? A date with Konstantinos, no less! Clearly, she was getting stir crazy.

She applied her make-up, putting emphasis on her eyes by way of several layers of mascara. She didn't like colour on her lips, but chose a soft pink shade that wouldn't clash with her light green mini dress, made of layers of silk and chiffon. She'd retrieved it from the walk-in closet in the master bedroom while Konstantinos had been in the gym. She didn't want to spend too much thought on why most of her clothes were there.

She dug in her drawer for the right accessories, deciding on a thin gold necklace that hung past her cleavage, a few rings, and teardrop earrings. She slipped her feet into high-heeled sandals and took one last, long look in the full-length mirror. She had three minutes to go until crunch time. Why was she nervous?

Taking deep, steadying breaths, she walked out of her room. She half expected to meet him in the hallway that led to the staircase, but he was nowhere to be seen. She assumed that he was already downstairs. Her heels clicked all the way to the dining room and she felt cheerful and... beautiful, even though she wasn't actually going *out* for dinner.

Her mouth popped open once she stepped into the room. Not because of the beautifully decorated table, or the many lit candles. Her surprise was also not due a bunch of stunning red roses. No, it had to do with Konstantinos being a no-show.

"Unbelievable," she said with a soft laugh, claiming the head of the table. "Why am I shocked? He's never on time. Why would he be? He's a womanizing idiot. I thought we've established this, Asha Dewali?" She rolled her eyes. "And now you're talking to yourself again. Classic. Why don't you go throw yourself off the building?"

She was about to peek under the silver covers of the platter when he showed up. She met his gaze and gave him a good glare.

"You're early," he commented. She had to admit, he looked sexy as sin in his gunmetal-coloured chinos and a burgundy button-up shirt. His dark hair was slicked back. Normally it made men look like good-for-nothing gangster wannabes, but he had such a strong jawline that it was criminal for him to draw attention away from it. "You're in my spot."

"The early bird catches the worm," she said

flippantly.

"And then suffers from indigestion for the remainder of the day," he countered, hovering next to her. He looked down at her with a small smile playing at the corners of his lips and crossed his arms over his chest. "Come on, Bigfoot."

"Oh, you think you're going to intimidate me into moving when I don't want to?"

"I know I am. I can stand here all night."

She was determined to put him in his place, but it was awkward when he simply remained there, staring at her. With a great sigh, she rose, ready to mouth him off for being late *and* a douche, in that order. Her words tumbled back down her throat as he pulled the chair to his left out, like a gentleman.

"Didn't expect that, did you?"

She sat down, a slight frown on her forehead at his chivalry. She didn't really know what to say.

"Sorry for being late. I assumed that you were one of those women who'll only decide to show up half an hour after the agreed time." He uncorked the bottle of white wine and poured them both a glass. "Looking back on it, I'm not sure why I made that particular deduction, but we're here now, so let's get on with it. To our date," he toasted, holding his wine glass up.

She gave him a helpless look. "I don't drink wine."

"You do tonight. It'll go very well with the sushi, trust me."

"Fine. To our date." She clinked her glass to his before taking a little sip. She pulled a face. "That's so dry!"

"You get used to it, just like tequila."

"I obviously don't have a high tolerance for alcohol."

He chuckled. "Want to hear a secret? No one does." He lifted the cover from the large platter, giving a soft moan of approval. "This is the life. I knew it would work! I should remember this for future reference."

Her eyes widened at the sight of the mountain of sushi in front of them. "We're only two people."

"I eat for three, remember? Ah man, I've got sashimi! There is a God."

She took her set of designer chopsticks, watching him as he loaded his plate with sushi. "How can you eat sashimi? It's raw fish without any rice to draw one's attention away from that fact."

"It's divine, though I guess it's a bit of an acquired taste—"

At that moment, she remembered something she'd read years ago in an issue of *Cosmopolitan*: men that loved seafood, loved giving oral sex. She had no idea why it made a jolt of electricity zap through her body, kick-starting her heart into a fast gallop.

He was still talking, oblivious to her mental processing. "—and after that, I was sold. I always start with sashimi. Aren't you going to take some? I'm assuming the fashion sandwiches are yours."

"Hmm." She loaded her plate with a couple of pieces and took another sip of wine. She felt incredibly hot, and was thankful that she didn't have pale skin. Her genetic heritage hid blushes.

"*Bon appétit,*" he announced cheerfully, dunking a piece of sashimi into soya sauce and taking a bite. He let out another moan, his eyes closing briefly. "Wow, this is five-star sushi. Whoever set this dinner up needs a raise."

"That good, huh?" She giggled nervously, tentatively biting her fashion sandwich. The cream cheese filling was a delicious addition. She sipped on her wine, aware that he kept glancing at her. After a while, she couldn't take it anymore. "What?"

"You look really pretty tonight, Asha."

She stopped breathing as his eyes locked on hers. "Thank you, so do you."

"Word of advice: never call a man 'pretty' or 'Teeny'."

"I've done both, and I'm still here," she laughed. For the first time, she was glad that he had such an accommodating personality. She went from being awkward to extremely comfortable in the space of two seconds. "I think I'm going to keep at it. Holy crap, that's a lot of wasabi!"

He grinned boyishly, stuffing his face with another bite of sashimi. "I don't mind the burn."

"Obviously not."

"You don't add any accessories?"

"Nope. I did in the beginning, but I like sushi the way it is these days. Sometimes I'll use a bit of soya…" She trailed off. She was babbling! Since when was she like this?

"You're a salmon rose fan, too?"

"Oh, but of course! It's like an orgasm in your mouth."

He threw his head back and barked a laugh. "No, an *orgasm* in your mouth is like an orgasm in your mouth."

"That doesn't make any sense."

"Of course it does, or have you never given someone a blowjob before?"

Yup, she would've been blushing if she were white. Thank God for small miracles. How was it that, minutes ago, she'd been thinking about that oral sex article, and now he was raising the subject? The word "coincidence" didn't quite cut it. It was eerie.

"Uh, no comment."

He stared at her in unabashed surprise. "You never gave Praven a blowjob?"

"I tried once, but I wasn't very good at it, or so I was told," she mumbled in response. She purposefully filled her mouth with a salmon rose to prevent her from saying anything more embarrassing than that.

Unfortunately, Konstantinos wasn't letting the subject go. "And he never went down on you?"

"I never really saw the point in it."

"You never…" He shook his head in disbelief. "It can be more pleasurable than sex itself, if done right."

"To men, sure, but don't women need penetration?"

"Who said a man can't penetrate a woman during oral?"

He probably didn't do it on purpose but, as she was about to ask him what the hell he was talking about, his tongue snaked out to catch the long string of sashimi. She watched, in awe, as it led the raw piece of tuna into his mouth before cutting it in half with his teeth. It's a good thing her chopsticks were made of metal, or she would've snapped them. As it was, she felt like she was sitting in a puddle.

"We always end up talking about this." She was horrified to hear that her voice sounded hoarse. She reached for her wine again. "Why do you suppose that is?"

He shrugged. "Sexual frustration?"

"It's been months for me."

"I don't know how you do it," he said honestly, shaking his head.

"I don't have a penis?"

"I know a lot of women that don't share your sentiments."

"Sluts," she muttered under her breath.

He picked up on the word, anyway. "*Au contraire*! I think it's great. Women shouldn't feel inhibited, and they deserve pleasure as much as men do."

"You mean you've never looked a woman and thought, 'she is such a slut'?"

"Not really," he answered. "My definition of a slut is someone who screws someone else when she's already in a relationship."

"I guess that makes sense."

"You know, I'm still stuck on the fact that you've only been with one man. It blows my mind, and not in a sexy way. You were a virgin into your twenties!" He was already almost halfway through his dinner. The man had an appetite that boggled the brain. "That's almost unheard of in recent years."

"Yeah well, I'm letting my freak flag fly," she said with mock cheer.

"I didn't mean to insult you, I'm just genuinely surprised. You're a beautiful woman, Asha. I can't believe some guy didn't try to steal your virtue years ago." He waggled his eyebrows at her with a grin. "Then again, you've never had someone perform oral sex on you, so you're practically still a virgin. There's hope for you yet!"

"Do you take anything seriously?"

"Not really."

"It's unbelievable." She finished half of her wine. "I wish I could be more like you."

"I regret to inform you of this, Bigfoot Dewali, but you're already a little like me." He topped her glass up with a chuckle. "You never drank tequila before you were stuck in this hellhole with me."

It had to be the wine. There was no logical reason why, without the encouragement of alcohol, she'd announce: "I hate to say this to someone who definitely does not need more compliments than he's already heard in his life, but this place isn't as much of a hellhole as I initially anticipated."

He stared at her for a long time, as if he was trying to see that she was telling the truth. Then he smiled, his gaze shifting to his plate. "I feel the same way."

Her heart was banging like a bongo drum. Were they discussing their feelings? And why did she care if they were? They had agreed not to get married by the time they stepped out of this apartment. For them to develop emotions for each other that would contradict their intentions… She couldn't even imagine what a big catastrophe that would be.

"Do you make a habit of overanalysing things?"

She blinked, snapping out of her trance and forcing

her attention back on her food. "What're you talking about?"

"Don't deny it. I can basically see the cogs turning."

"It's my hidden talent."

"It's not as hidden as you've been led to believe," he teased, bumping his elbow against hers.

She giggled, loosening up a little. "Kash always tells me that I'm too serious for my own good."

"Your brother?"

"Yes."

"Funny: my brother tells me the exact opposite." He looked pleased when she laughed. "I don't know what it is about younger brothers, but they pretend like they know it all."

"They *do*! My sister isn't nearly half that bad."

"How old is she?"

"Nineteen." She smiled, thinking about Farida. "She's a sweetie pie, though she's probably driving boys mad."

"Nothing at all like her big sister, then."

She rolled her eyes. "I most definitely do *not* drive boys mad."

"Perhaps not boys, but men must fall all over themselves."

"How would I know? I couldn't even kiss properly until you came along, so why would I know how to interpret the signals that men send me?"

"I never said you kiss properly now." She raised one eyebrow, making him laugh. "In fact, I'd go so far as to say that there is a lot of room for improvement. You definitely need more lessons. Tons, in fact."

"You're such an ass sometimes."

"'Aah-s'," he mocked with a chuckle. "Your accent is so funny."

"I think the correct statement would be: 'your accent is so British'."

"By the way, what I said back there, about room for improvement?" He waited for her to nod, turning in his chair to face her. "That was a signal."

She felt like she was staring at a snake. Was he admitting that he'd been flirting with her? "What do you mean?"

"I'm telling you that I was sending you a 'signal', as you say. Your interpretation of it is still in question."

She pushed her plate aside. "Are you saying that you're—"

"Interested in you?" He drummed his fingers on the edge of the table for a while, eyes on hers. "I am, yes, though I'm not quite sure why yet."

She couldn't look away from him.

"How about you, Asha?"

"I'm… attracted to you, but I don't know if it's because we're stuck here, or if it would've happened naturally in a more public environment."

"Probably not. We don't hang out in the same circles, and I would never have got to know you if not for all of this."

"That's exactly my point. We'll be over this once we hit the outside world."

He rested his right ankle on his left knee and looked at it thoughtfully. "How sure are you of that? I mean, maybe our parents aren't completely crazy. Maybe this all *works*, you know? The same thing happened to my mother and father, and they seem happy."

"I can't work on 'maybe'. I'm not the sort of girl who commits on 'maybe'."

"But you're a fashion designer. You have to occasionally take risks, or your work won't be front and centre on a Paris or New York runway."

"The repercussions of a fashion mistake—"

"Are minimal compared to those of the heart, I realize that, but you can't be afraid of life, Asha. Don't let Praven ruin you."

She felt close to tears, but not because of her memories of Praven. He was right: by deciding to remove herself from the playing field, she was missing out on all the action. Was this truly what she wanted to see when she looked back on her life one day?

"What're you suggesting?"

He smiled at her. "I'm not really sure, but why not see where this is going? If, by the end of our time together, you feel like you don't want to continue seeing me, then so be it."

"I can't believe I'm considering this."

"There's something you should know, though."

She eyed his grin suspiciously. "What?"

"Since you're my fiancée, I'm not going to sleep with you until we're married."

Never, in a thousand years, would she have expected that from Konstantinos Sarantos, of all people. "Then what're we going to do to pass the time?" she blurted out.

He guffawed loudly. "People shouldn't have sex to pass the time, Bigfoot. And we're still getting to know each other."

She bit down on the insides of her cheeks to stop herself from smiling like an idiot. It didn't work. "My, my, Teeny! Are you telling me you want to, dare I say it, *date* first?"

"Something like that, though this is all I have to offer," he responded, gesturing to their surroundings. "For all intents and purposes, I can't afford to take you on a holiday to Switzerland or the South of France, to an ice-skating rick, to dinner or even to watch a movie. I'm waiting for my ship to come in."

Giggling, she got up to sit on his lap, putting her arms around his neck. "Are you implying that I'm only interested in you for your money?"

"Rumour has it that you want to merge my family's company with yours, actually." He pushed her hair behind her ears, shifting so she was more comfortable.

Sudden courage flowed through her veins, but she wasn't going to blame it on the wine anymore. "I guess I'll have to refrain from admitting to that until I see how big your ship is." She moved her bum on his crotch in a suggestive manner.

He had a twinkle in his eyes. His one hand dropped to her leg while the other touched the curve of her waist, his thumb stroking her ribs over the thin material of her dress. "Size of my ship aside… How receptive is your harbour?"

Was it normal to get turned on by words? "I'm not really certain. My harbour hasn't seen many ships on the horizon."

He sat up straighter to capture her lips with his. She

accepted him instantly, moaning as his tongue started rubbing the side of hers. She chose this moment to play with his mouth, raking her fingers through his hair. His hold on her tightened, and something was hardening against her bum. She changed her position to straddle him instead.

He tasted like sushi and spicy wine and heat. She nearly squirmed with delight when his hands shifted down to cup her backside. Why did that one action turn her body to jelly? Was she doing the same to him?

"I'm starting to wonder whether being chaste until our wedding night is such a good idea," he murmured.

"Is the room for improvement growing smaller?"

"Slowly but surely, but I don't like to overinflate a woman's ego."

She laughed softly. "You don't have to worry about doing that. Did you shave especially for this occasion? I'm not feeling any scraping on my skin."

"You sound disappointed."

"Little bit," she admitted. "It's probably not good for me, but it feels nice."

He rolled his eyes dramatically. "Honestly, woman! Is that the only word you have in your vocabulary to describe things? 'Nice'?"

"Does 'hot' work for you?"

"It's better."

"How about 'sexy'?"

"Hmm, I like the sound of that. Do you think it'll only feel 'sexy' on your cheeks, or on other parts of your body, too?"

She closed her eyes as she mulled over that one,

licking her lips. "It'll probably feel better everywhere else."

"Asha, stop teasing me," he pleaded softly, clenching his jaw. "I'm struggling to hold back as it is, and the look on your face isn't helping."

"You mean I turn you on?"

"Very much so."

She smiled slightly. "I'm not used to turning someone on."

"I'm not used to holding back."

"Fair enough." She got off his lap a bit unwillingly. "Would you like dessert? There are still a few pieces of cake left."

"I'd love a piece. Race you there."

She burst into girly giggles as she rushed to the kitchen, but he swept her up into his arms before she made it all the way. She marvelled in his strength, his arms around her waist, her back pressed to his chest. It felt so good, so right!

"Don't think you've won," he whispered in her ear. "I let you get a head-start because you're wearing incredibly sexy heels."

"Many more where these came from."

He let her stand, turning her around and touching her hair softly. "I've got my work cut out for me, don't I?"

She beamed at him. Yes, he did. If he wanted to be the cause of her giddiness, then so be it! He'll simply have to pay the price tenfold.

CHAPTER 18

"AH, THAT DRESS is finally starting to look tailored to your body, Marietta," Anushka said appraisingly. "Do you feel comfortable?"

Marietta was staring at her reflection in the mirror melancholically. She was always the bridesmaid and never the bride, though she couldn't understand why. She was an attractive woman that liked to have a good time. Who wouldn't want to put a ring on it?

Her dress was white with a gold belt around her waist, flaring out over her hips in ripples of chiffon, in a Grecian goddess style. Since Asha was getting married in gold, everyone else had to wear white, but this gown was more reminiscent of a wedding dress than Asha's.

Marietta had a strong desire to get walk down the aisle as a bride. She'd always assumed that Asha would have to play bridesmaid to *her* nuptials first. Things weren't going according to plan.

Her life was falling apart.

Snap out of it!

She cleared her throat. "It's very comfortable, Mrs. Dewali." Her morbid thoughts have been multiplying of late. She didn't quite know what to make of them. "It's a good thing there will be heating at the venue, or I would've frozen to death, though."

Farida laughed, stepping out of her dressing cubicle wearing a similar dress. "I agree! It's been snowing non-stop. Typical of Ash, trying to make miracles happen in the middle of winter."

Marietta forced her smile. She still hasn't really forgiven her best friend for keeping the engagement a secret. Konstantinos Sarantos, of all people! Asha had never seemed interested in him and, besides, he wasn't her type. Everyone knew that he slept around like his sole mission in life was to contract as many STDs as possible.

The other bridesmaids joined them to gush over the wedding. The dresses were designed in a way that suited their different body types. They all looked stunning and excited, making a knot of jealousy twist in Marietta's stomach. They had probably known about the engagement but she, Asha's so-called *best friend*, had had no idea until the announcement was made. Life was so unfair!

She wasn't exactly sure why she was furious. It wasn't something she could control. She kept thinking back to when their friendship had started, and how close they've been ever since. From day one, Asha had made

Marietta feel like she truly cared. Marietta had trusted the Indian heiress with her deepest, darkest secrets...

And now Asha was getting married to that hot piece of meat, instead of some loser like Praven Kahn!

Whoa. Was *that* what this was about? Was she jealous of the man Asha was getting married to? Was that more pertinent than Asha's betrayal itself?

Her eyes found her reflection again. What she saw there was completely foreign to her. There was something in her gaze that simultaneously scared the crap out of, and fascinated, her. She flipped through her vocabulary to put to words what she was experiencing, and an unexpected one surfaced.

Vengeance. The woman in the mirror wanted vengeance.

CHAPTER 19

KONSTANTINOS FELT BETTER than he has in years, which was silly.

Why should one woman change his life instantly, and so completely? He's been with many: uptight ones, laidback ones, creepy ones and money-hungry ones, but they've never changed his life on such a grand, permanent basis. Not enough to make him look forward to his wedding.

He normally only wanted their bodies, anyway, but it's like Asha has taken a hold of his heart, a hold that she wasn't intending on letting go.

How could a couple of days shift his perspective, especially when he considered that he would never have dated her otherwise? They were being forced into this situation by their families. If they'd bumped into each other in public, he wouldn't have found her chilly attitude charming, and he certainly wouldn't have wanted to find out *why* she acted the way she does. He never would've known that she could be as passionate as most of the women he's bedded, or that she would inspire him to be more creative than usual.

Then again, should he be focusing on what would've happened in the outside world, when they were forming such a tight bond in this apartment?

"You better be thinking about ways to make that building sparkle like a diamond."

He blinked a couple of times to clear his thoughts. His gaze found hers, on the opposite end of the couch they were laying on. Their knees were up: hers, to rest her large sketchpad against; and his, to be comfortable while he read a book about the challenges of solar power in large structures.

"Nope, you're thinking about what we agreed neither of us would be thinking about," she sighed, putting her sketchpad on the coffee table and giving him a look. "Not cool, Teeny."

"You're in an awfully good mood today," he teased. He chucked the book aside and sat up, eyeing her with a grin. "It doesn't make any sense, since you complained about your period this morning."

"Well, men have it *really* easy. Bastards."

"'Bah-stahds'," he mocked.

"Yes, that's exactly what you are."

"I thought I was your fiancé."

She fought her smile. "Allegedly."

"And I thought you were busy designing my outfit for our wedding," he murmured, reaching for her sketchpad. He laughed when she slapped his hand away. "Oh, come on! I'm allowed to see it, aren't I? I'm going to have to wear it."

"If you want to get married to me, you'll definitely be wearing it," she warned. She pulled the sketchpad out of his reach as he tried to get a grip on it again. "You can do better than that."

"Let me see it, Bigfoot, or I'll bring out the big guns."

"Big guns, huh? I'd love to see you try. You've never seen me when I'm PMS-ing."

He grabbed her ankles and pulled her onto his lap in one smooth move. "So far, you've been a tame little kitty cat while you're PMS-ing."

"I should pick up some weight so you can't push me around anymore," she commented, resting her hands on his bare chest. She sighed theatrically. "I've completely given up on the shirt debate."

"First of all, I can bench-press more than you weigh—"

"Oh no, you can't."

He raised his eyebrows. "Are you challenging me, Bigfoot?"

"Yes," she replied boldly.

He gave her a lazy kiss and shifted her off him, going to the carpet to lie down on his back. He gestured for her to come over. "I'll prove it to you."

"'Me, Tarzan! You, Jane'?" she quoted.

"Something like that, now get your skinny ass over here!"

She pursed her lips, but walked to him. "You know, it's not a good idea to make your future wife feel like… Whoa! What're you—"

He'd put one hand on her thigh and pulled on her clothes with the other, making her fall into his grip and easily holding her above his chest. "You're so light," he commented as he pushed her up, before bringing her back down to his torso. "What's not a good idea?"

"I thought you said you preferred plump women."

"I said I prefer women who don't have any issues with their bodies."

"Okay, okay! You've made your point! Please, put me down!"

He chuckled, slowly bringing her down and turning her to lay, stomach-to-stomach, on top of him. "And that last move was something I learnt in ballet," was out of his mouth before he could stop it. He hoped that she would let it go.

He should've known better.

"Ballet? Excuse me?" she asked, stunned. "You, Konstantinos Sarantos, took ballet?"

"Only for a couple of years," he admitted. "The physics behind it really—"

"Nah-ah!" she interrupted with a giggle. "Oh my God, my future husband took ballet? You *have* to wear tights to the wedding!"

He held her firmly when she wanted to jump off, planning to distract her from the subject of conversation. "Never," he whispered on her lips, urging them into action. By God, he'll never tire of kissing her, not as long as he lived. There was something about her that was different to anyone he's known before.

She relaxed against him, her fingers in his hair as she

began kissing him back. Her legs slipped past his hips to straddle him. She sat up and took him with her. She moaned as his arms locked around her waist.

"No, this isn't going to work," she gasped, pulling away. "You're not going to take my mind off of you being a ballerina!"

"We're called 'danseurs'."

"Po-tay-toe, poh-tah-toe. Come on, time to get you in tights!"

"Asha, you can't kiss me like that and then insist I wear tights."

"*You* kissed *me*," she reminded him, "because you wanted to distract me!" She gave him a swift kiss on the mouth and stood up, holding her hand out to him. "Please, *please*! I want to see you in tights!"

He allowed her to help him to his feet. "Are you secretly a lesbian?"

"Considering that you get my panties wet by kissing me like that?" Her eyes widened as soon as the words were out. She slapped a hand over her mouth. "Oh my God! I didn't just say that!"

He grinned. "Yes, you did." She backed away at the predatory look in his eyes, not seeing that there was a wall behind her, and he stalked towards her. "Am I really that good at it, Miss Dewali?" he murmured, leaning down to trail kisses from her neck to her collarbone.

She shuddered when his hands caged her in against the wall. "I didn't mean to say that," she breathed.

"But you did, so now I want to know if it's true." He pressed his hips to hers. "Do I make your panties wet?"

Her hands slid to his butt, giving it an encouraging squeeze. "You know you do, Teeny."

He chuckled, lifting his gaze to hers. "Just to prove how drastically my life is changing, that nickname isn't killing the mood."

"How about the thought of you in tights?"

"Asha, the only thing tights would do is show you how prominent my bulge can get when you're around."

Her green eyes widened fractionally. "You said we can't sleep together before we get hitched."

"I know." He tilted her chin up and kissed her softly. "That doesn't mean I can't turn you on, does it?"

"You've already proven you can." She had a teasing glint in her eyes, one eyebrow raising. "Does that mean I make you hard, Mr. Sarantos?"

He took a deep breath, grinding his crotch against hers. "You tell me."

"I hate your stupid rule of not having sex before the wedding!"

"And *I* hate your stupid period," he complained right back.

She burst out laughing. "Okay fine, I'll let the tights-issue go… for now."

"Say forever, and we might have a deal."

"No friggin' way am I letting it go forever! Ooh, do you have pictures? I need proof!"

"I'm going to need something seriously embarrassing from your past to get out of this one."

"Well, I wasn't very fashionable back then."

"Nope, that's not going to cut it."

"Then you'll have to be happy with my dismal

attempts at being a girlfriend."

"I've forgotten all about that," he admitted. "I'm starting to think that your ex was smoking his socks for letting you go." His one hand slipped under the loose-fitting shirt she was wearing, cupping one of her full breasts. "You're a firecracker."

She bit down on her bottom lip. "And you're the male equivalent of a cock-tease!"

He realized that he was touching bare flesh, not warmed silky material as he'd initially thought, and tensed as he raised his gaze to hers. "Why aren't you wearing a bra?"

She swallowed at the searing look he gave her and raised her chin. "I didn't feel like it."

He tried to think about the things that normally made his arousal fly out the window—sick people in hospitals, the smell of manure, airplanes in the sky, a thunderstorm—but they weren't working. Usually, after imagining doctors operating on a hit-and-run victim, he was so out of the mood that it took his lover half an hour to get him hard again.

None of this applied while Asha Dewali's soft, warm breast was in his hand, and the rest of her body was sandwiched between him and the wall.

"Teeny?" Her voice was hardly above a whisper. "What's wrong?"

Primal instincts were screaming at him to ravish her right here, against the wall. They wanted it, anyway. It's not like he would be doing it against her will...

Not until we're married.

The muscles of his arms and shoulders bulged with the effort of keeping his restraint. Slowly, he dropped his hand. He closed his eyes, took a deep breath—a mistake, he realized, since it only made him more aware of her scent—and backed away five steps.

"I really need a cold shower," he muttered, turning on his heel and marching out of the living room. He didn't mean to make her feel like he was angry, but how was he supposed to act like he wasn't affected by her presence?

He didn't even bother trying to answer that question. A more important one raised its head: if their relationship didn't work out, how was he ever going to lust after other women when Asha has made him experience desire on a whole new level?

CHAPTER 20

DENISE GROANED TIREDLY at her phone's insistent ringing, rolling over on her stomach and reaching for it on her nightstand. She was dazed and confused, and forgot to answer in English. "*Que?*"

"I hope that means you're happy to hear from me," Jacob chuckled.

She blinked in the dimly lit room. "I'm sorry, *chéri*. What time is it?"

"You asking that question validates my suspicion that you took the day off for a good reason. It's nearly twelve o'clock."

"In the evening?"

Jacob laughed again. "No."

"What's going on?"

"I need you to phone Bvlgari yourself. They're giving me such grief about the rings, even though I dropped the Sarantos and Dewali names, and gave them everything they needed regarding design and sizes."

"It's that new manager, isn't it? He's been difficult ever since he jumped out of the closet."

"I think you mean, *came* out of the closet."

"Yes," she mumbled. The warm, male body beside her turned around, spooning her. She felt like she had fog in her head when he kissed her bare shoulder. "Was there anything else, *chéri?*"

"Uh, yes." Jacob cleared his throat. Never a good sign. "There's no easy way to say this, but your ex-husband phoned. He wants to go for lunch."

She froze. "What?"

"He says the two of you need to have a serious discussion, but he wouldn't say what about."

"Tell him I'm busy."

"I will do that, if he phones again."

"*Merci*, darling," she said, her body losing its frigidity once a young—albeit expertly seductive—hand slid over her waist, down her stomach, to the spot between her legs that was getting more exercise these days than what could surely be considered normal. "I'll see you tomorrow."

"You bet!"

She hung up and turned in Loikanos' embrace. She could barely keep her eyes open. "Haven't you had enough?"

"Of you?" He shifted to be on top of her, framing her face with his big hands. "The day I get enough of you, *mon amour*, is the day hell freezes over."

"You're starting to make me feel like this isn't just about sex," she said, her voice shaky. She held her breath while she waited for his answer, not sure what she wanted it to be. At the back of her mind, she prayed that she hasn't destroyed the chance to keep seeing him.

He kissed her softly. "It's not. I fell in love with you the second I first saw you."

"But how can you—"

"Unless you're about to say that you love me too, I don't want to hear it."

"But I'm thirty-five!"

"Yes, you are."

"And *you're* barely legal!"

"I'm twenty-three, not thirteen." He grinned broadly, a twinkle in his dark eyes. "Denise, why are you fighting this?"

"You don't want to be tied down to an old maid like me so early in your life," she replied, tears pricking her eyes. She couldn't help but think she was the biggest idiot known to womankind. All she would accomplish by speaking this way, was to push him right out of her life when she didn't really want him to go in the first place.

"How do you know?" He got off her and sat up, crossing his legs. The sheet pulled away at his movement, giving her a glimpse of the male organ that has given her an unimaginable amount of pleasure in the last couple of weeks. "I'm not like my brother, Denise. I believe in love at first sight and happily ever after. I've always been a hopeless romantic, and I think we make connections with other people regardless of the circumstances or, in our case, ages."

She swallowed, suddenly wide awake. Were they fighting? She was too used to Remi's sarcasm and incessant shouting: she wasn't sure how young folk handled disagreements. She realized, quite abruptly, that she didn't want to make Loikanos unhappy.

She was in love with him.

"*Mon cher*, there are certain things that you don't know about me." She hesitated. "If you knew, you wouldn't like me very much." He surprised her by throwing his head back and guffawing loudly. "What's so funny?"

"Give me some credit, Denise," he chuckled. "I may be young, but I'm not stupid. I know what you do for a living, and it doesn't bother me in the slightest. You're bringing families together and helping people fall in love." He raked his fingers through his hair. It was getting longer, making him look like a male supermodel. He belonged on a billboard somewhere, not in her bed... "My brother never would have become serious about someone in any other way. I've always knew he would have to be forced to see that love isn't so bad. I'm in your corner, hoping this union works. In fact, your job is why I introduced myself to you. I wanted to make sure he was in good hands."

She stared at him. All the reasons why she was afraid to love him have dissolved. She's always known he was mature, but *this*... This was intimidating and exciting, at the same time.

"Now, if you want to stop what we're doing because you're only interested in the sex, then tell me," he said seriously, his face guarded. "If that's all that you want with me, I can't make you change your mind."

She threw her arms around his neck and held him close to her, laughing softly. She was so relieved! "I think you just confirmed why I'm in love with you, *mon cher*," she whispered.

He kissed her neck, running his fingers through her long hair. "Does that mean we can date? Hold hands in public? Make each other dinner?"

"Yes, and it also means that you have unlimited access to my body." She pulled away and grinned at him. "I'll try not to use the headache-excuse too often."

"You make me happy, Denise."

"Oh, *mon cher*, you make *me* happy," she murmured, pushing him on his back and straddling his lap. "I think it's time that I reward your patience, Loikanos."

"I love the way you say my name. Your accent makes me sound like some sort of delicacy."

"Well, you taste divine," she grinned.

He laughed and rolled his eyes at her. "Touché." Slowly, his facial expression became neutral. He touched her hair. "Please don't meet with your ex. I have a bad feeling about that."

"How'd you know about it?"

"Your phone's volume is set very loud. I didn't mean to eavesdrop." He took a deep breath. "I think he wants you back, Denise."

She blinked in surprise. "Remi and I are over."

"Alright, I'll accept that." He pulled her face down to kiss her frown away. "Now, about that reward…"

Chapter 21

THE DAYS WERE beginning to roll into one, but Asha didn't find herself giving a damn. She was too happy getting to know Konstantinos. As unbelievable as it sounded, she was falling harder than before.

She looked up from her portfolio when he made a hissing noise, as if calling a cat. She giggled at the naughty look on his face. He was sitting behind his own desk, feet perched on top of it, completely shirtless. Honestly, she's never seen a man so ripped in real life and now, apparently, she was getting married to him.

There must be a God.

"Can I see my outfit?" he queried for the third time since joining her in the study.

She pouted. "Why is it important to you?"

"As far as I recall, it's *my* wedding, too. Besides, I want to make sure that you're not going to choose baby-shit yellow or powder blue."

"Ah damn, I was so sure you'd look good in candyfloss pink."

His eyes widened fractionally, but then he saw that she was teasing. "That's it, Bigfoot. I'm coming over, and you're showing me what I'm getting married in."

She couldn't ignore how excited it made her to see him stride to her side of the room, so she didn't really blame herself for nearly drooling at the sight of him. If he noticed, he didn't say anything. She still found it amazing that she could turn him on, too.

She's never felt this feminine in her life.

"Let's see what you've got for me," he said, sitting on the edge of her desk.

"Okay, but if you don't like it—"

"I'm sure I will. Come on, Bigfoot."

Even though it was the most stupid nickname in the history of the world, she secretly loved it. It's not the kind of thing that he would've called any of his previous women, and she certainly didn't want to end up like them: discarded, never to have his arms around them again.

"I'm nervous," she admitted. Flipping to the page she'd dedicated solely to Konstantinos' hotness, she said: "There it is."

"Thank God it's not a cliché black tuxedo."

She eyed him. "I'm a fashion designer. Do you really think that I'll let you get married in a black tux?"

"I guess I forgot who I was dealing with, for a second." He turned the sketch, his dark brown eyes scanning it with real interest. "White, huh? I take it you won't be in white?"

"Well, I'm not exactly a virgin."

"Neither am I."

"Like your nickname, I thought it'd be funny and ironic," she teased.

"I like the gold waistcoat and tie, but I'm *not* wearing gold shoes."

She burst out laughing. "Spoilsport."

"Do you know anything else about the wedding?"

"Nope, but I'm sure we can Google it." She stretched her arms above her head. "I kind of like that I don't have to worry about any of the details. From what I've heard, planning a wedding is stressful."

He shifted, turning to the screen. "Let's Google it, then. I'd like to know what I'm getting myself into."

"Apart from me, you mean?" she asked, fluttering her lashes at him. She loved how his eyes always seemed to darken, like they did now.

"Your innuendos are going to get you into trouble, fiancée."

"Ooh, are you going to tie me to the bed?"

"Maybe I should."

She had no idea why that thought made her clamp her thighs together. Why was she getting turned on by that? Was there something wrong with her for thinking bondage was extremely sexy?

Letting out a long breath, she avoided eye contact when she, as nonchalantly as she could muster, asked: "Oh, is it something you've done before?"

"Yes, but I was the one tied to the bed."

Whoa.

She suddenly had a vision of Konstantinos, the incredibly masculine and powerful man that was going to bound to her in holy matrimony, with his arms spread wide, his hands cuffed to bedposts, completely at her mercy. She could do anything to him, absolutely anything she wanted...

"Asha? Are you okay?"

She shook out of her fantasy, feeling her cheeks heat up and mentally thanking her genetics for blessing her with blush-free skin. "Yeah, I'm fine," she said huskily. She cleared her throat and turned to her keyboard. "Okay, so I'm going to Google our wedding. Yeah."

"What's wrong? You seem distracted."

"I got lost in my thoughts, that's all. Ooh, look! Apparently, the reception is going to be at The Orangery."

"And the ceremony?"

She sighed deeply. "Westminster Abbey."

"That place gives me the creeps," he told her, leaning in to read the window she'd opened on the computer screen. "There are, like, twenty or so tombs in there."

"I didn't even know that we could get married there." She clicked on a couple of links, eventually winding up at Westminster Abbey's *Frequently Asked Questions* page. "See? It says here that only the Royal family, some or other Bath members and people who live in the Abbey's precinct are allowed."

"Didn't Jun and Yerik get married there, too?"

"Yeah, so whoever's organizing this has Royal connections." That fact sunk into her brain. She was silent for a while. "This is serious."

"Oh, you didn't think it was?" He chuckled, tilting her chin up so she could look at him. "Asha, we're getting *married*."

She rubbed her temples and got to her feet. "Because you want to get laid."

"No, actually. I'm looking forward to all of this," he said, gesturing to the space between them. "I want to spend the rest of my life getting to know you. You keep me on my toes. You're not a pushover; you're a strong and independent woman. I can't imagine being with anyone else."

"Wow, whenever I thought about someone getting cold

feet, I assumed it would be *you*."

He laughed again. "So did I, to be honest."

"I don't know why, but all of this," she said, pointing to the computer screen, "just made it real to me. I mean, we're going to be living together—"

"We already are. There's nothing that'll surprise me anymore."

She was losing steam. "Okay, you're right. But this is *real!* We're getting married in less than a month, going off on honeymoon, and then we'll be dealing with mergers and all sorts of other things…" She closed her eyes at the horror her life has become. "We're going to start hating each other, I just know it."

"Asha, you're freaking out. It's normal to feel this way, but everything will be okay."

She gave him a look. "You only believe that because you don't take anything seriously."

"I don't take *most things* seriously." He stared at her. "When I make a commitment to someone or something, I stick to it, no matter what. I need to know that you're willing to do the same. We're not signing any prenups, and I don't believe in divorce or annulment."

"Neither do I."

"When we say 'I do', it's going to be until death do us part. Are you willing to live with that?"

She stepped up to him, burying her face in his bare chest. His arms pulled her closer. "When did you turn into my favourite fantasy?" she groaned theatrically.

"Right about the time you turned into mine," he responded, nibbling on her earlobe. "Are you ready to see this through with me?"

"Until death do we part?"

"Until death do we part," he confirmed.

She sighed happily and kissed his collarbone. "I do."

CHAPTER 22

"THE RINGS HAVE arrived!"

Denise jumped in her seat, flushing when she noticed that she wasn't alone in her office. "I'm glad that asshole of a man got the hint," she muttered. She gestured for Jacob to come in. "Let me see them."

Her assistant strode to her desk and opened the large case that contained three dark purple, velvet boxes. She lifted the lid of each one, her smile widening at the sight of the rings.

For a split-second, she imagined Loikanos dropping to one knee and proposing. She knew she would say yes, even though their love affair was only three weeks old. She's never felt this way about anyone before, and she wouldn't mind spending the rest of her life getting to know him.

Besides, wasn't this exactly what she was forcing—*encouraging*, she reminded herself—Asha and Konstantinos to do?

"Any girl would be thrilled to have a tanzanite ring," she murmured, touching the platinum creation fondly. "I get the feeling it's between the emeralds and the citrine, though. Asha might be a billionaire heiress, but she's actually simplistic in her style."

"I'm not so sure," Jacob argued with a smile. "Women go gaga for bling."

"We'll see, *chéri.*" She dragged her iPad closer, opening her organizer. "We'll have to get those into a place that only Konstantinos accesses. The gym, perhaps?"

He shook his head. "He's still sleeping in the master bedroom, so I'll put it in his underwear drawer or something."

"Good thinking…" She trailed off with a frown. "Wait, they're not sleeping together?"

"All the condoms are accounted for. From the look of things, Konstantinos wants them to wait until they're married."

She nearly fell off her chair. "Konstantinos Sarantos? The same man who chases skirts on a regular basis?"

"The same man who *used to* chase skirts on a regular basis," Jacob corrected.

"Wow, I guess people can change."

"It certainly seems that way. Have you confirmed the private jet for their honeymoon yet? Maui seems like the best option."

She raised an eyebrow, grinning. "I don't know, *chéri*, have I?"

He burst out laughing and took a seat opposite her. "Come now, Denise. You have to tell me who this man is!"

"What man?"

"Don't play dumb. I've known you for years and I've never seen you this happy. You wear your hair down—something you never did while married to Remi—and you're always smiling and glowing."

"You make me sound as if I used to be an awful woman to work for."

"You were never awful," Jacob soothed. "You were just unhappy. But that's no longer the case, so out with it!"

She bit down on her tongue, giving him a serious look. She didn't want to give anyone the identity of her lover until Loikanos has informed his parents of their relationship, but that didn't mean she couldn't at least give Jacob the abridged version.

"He's twelve years younger than me," she admitted.

Her assistant whistled. "Good for you, *Madame*."

"Oh, shush!" She blushed happily. "We met about three weeks ago, and we've been seeing each other every night since. He's really amazing, *chéri*. I love him."

"I didn't doubt that for a second. When do I get to meet him?"

"Soon," she replied honestly. Last night, Loikanos had asked her to be his date to Asha's big day. "We're going to the wedding together."

"Is this true love? Sounds that way."

"It feels like—"

"Denise?"

They both looked up at the man hovering in the doorway, and her heart dropped to her feet. She couldn't deal with this, not after having such a tender conversation with her assistant. Why couldn't he leave her alone?

Remi addressed her in French, probably to cut Jacob out of the conversation. "I called for you, my love, and asked to have lunch. Why didn't you agree?"

Denise had to grip the armrests of her chair to fight against the condescending tone he was using. Flashbacks of her marriage momentarily paralyzed her. She remembered how their fights always started... She would accuse him of cheating, and he would use this wounded voice to tell her that she had it all wrong, even when she provided him with concrete evidence. And then, on the occasions she chose to press the matter, he would transform from a charming man into a hurtful monster.

"We're divorced, Remi," she answered in English, for Jacob's benefit as well as her own, should she be pushed to report this. "We have nothing to say to each other."

"How can you say that, darling? I have missed you since we've been—"

"Save it!" Wow, standing up to him was really taking a lot of energy. She kept thinking about Loikanos and how confident he made her feel. This gave her the strength to get rid of her ex-husband for good. "I don't want to see you, or I would've asked Jacob to arrange a lunch date. Now, get out of my office before I call security."

The familiar frustrated rage momentarily burned in Remi's eyes, but then he hid it behind a placating smile.

"I see it will take more than one appearance to convince you that I am a changed man. I won't stop trying. Have a good day."

Her body went limp as he disappeared from view. She was trembling, feeling faint. She's always loathed confronting Remi.

Jacob rested a hand on her shoulder. "I think you should phone that hunk of yours. He'll make you feel better."

"I'm sorry you had to see that."

"Denise, don't apologize." Jacob headed to the door with the ring boxes and turned to smile at her. "I'll get the this into the apartment. Oh, and I'll inform security not to allow Remi in the building again. Phone your hunk."

She wiped the back of her hand over her clammy forehead and took deep breaths, picking her phone up and dialling Loikanos' number. He usually didn't keep her waiting for long before answering. Luckily, today wasn't any different.

"Hello, beautiful."

He sounded distracted. "Am I bothering you? I could call—"

"Calm down, *mon amour.* Breathe." He waited for her to comply. "What's the matter?"

"Remi was here."

There was a short silence. "What did he want?"

"He wants to go for lunch. He was trying his best to be charming."

"I told you, didn't I? He wants you back."

"I don't understand why!" she exclaimed, wiping her

tears away. "He left me for another woman! What can he possibly want from me?"

"You are beautiful, smart and successful. What man wouldn't want you?"

She started relaxing. There was something about Loikanos that made tranquillity settle over her. She loved him for it. "I've never stood up to him before. I told him to get out and that I don't want to see him."

"And how did that feel, *mon amour*?" Loikanos asked, chuckling.

"Well, now that I look back on it, I feel pretty good. But it was scary."

"It will get better."

"Am I interrupting something?"

"Don't worry about it," he said dismissively. "I was in a meeting, but they'll wait for me. Are you alright now?"

She smiled. "Yes, thanks to you. You must really love me if you're willing to aggravate your colleagues for me."

"You know it." She could almost hear him grin. "And you phoned me in a moment of crisis, so that must mean you love me, too."

"I do," she whispered.

"What time do you finish work today? I'm taking you out."

"Probably around four-thirty. Is it going to be a surprise?"

"Would you expect anything less?"

Giggling, she shook her head and wished that he was here with her. "No, I wouldn't. So, are you collecting me from my house?"

"Yes, at seven. Wear something sexy, something that shows off your long legs."

"Then you must keep the top buttons of your shirt undone, so I can see a bit of your chest. You know I go weak at the knees for your chest, *mon cher.*"

He chuckled. It was a rich, seductive sound that reached through the airwaves to send a shiver down her spine. "I will do what I can to please you, *mon amour.* See you later."

CHAPTER 23

KONSTANTINOS STEPPED OUT of the shower and grabbed a towel to dry himself. There was a raging snowstorm outside and he was secretly thankful that he couldn't leave the apartment. Sure, he missed interacting with other people, but England wasn't the best place to spend winter. He much preferred the Caribbean.

He walked to his closet to get fresh underwear, pausing once he saw three unfamiliar velvety boxes stuffed between his socks. He kneeled and opened each one.

At first, he was startled to see how meticulously this arranged marriage was being executed. It felt like he was a contestant on *Big Brother*. How did they know that he was ready to present Asha with a ring? Could they hear their intimate conversations, see the way he stared at her, and witness their passion for each other?

If he thought about it for too long, it would start

freaking him out all over again.

But then, as soon as his eyes locked on the golden band that was decorated with glittering emeralds and diamonds, a vision of Asha's face floated in front of him. It reminded him of her eyes, and of how emotionally mature they've become together.

See all the options first, before you make a choice.

He immediately dismissed the tanzanite creation—in what world would he give her something that appeared to be so cold, when she was anything but an ice princess?—and picked up a strange, golden stone in a platinum ring. He liked how the two colours offset each other. He especially liked that the gem was similar to the glow of Asha's skin. Closing his eyes, he could feel his fingers tingling at the memory of how smooth she felt.

Konstantinos knew which one he was going to use to formally ask her to marry him. Now, he simply had to wait for the right moment.

He dressed in jeans and a V-neck T-shirt, pocketed the dark purple box and made his way downstairs to the kitchen. Along the way, a warm, low light in the living room grabbed his attention, and he made a beeline for it.

"What's this?" he asked, leaning on a wall and crossing his arms over his chest.

Asha was in the middle of the room, lighting a bunch of tiny candles. She wore cut-off denim shorts that displayed her slim legs and a loose-fitting, light green top with short sleeves. Her hair was braided over one shoulder, and he noticed silver studs in her earlobes.

She straightened when he spoke and glanced over her shoulder. "I have a surprise for you," she smiled.

"What kind of surprise?"

"Well, you got us sushi, so I decided to make my own order. You need a break from cooking." She pulled a cloth, which was draped over the coffee table, off to reveal stacks of white boxes and a bottle of red wine. "Ta-da!"

He burst out laughing. "You have all the restaurants in the world at your disposal, and you ordered Chinese?"

"I've been craving egg-fried rice for days," she replied. She sat down on the carpet and motioned for him to join her. "Come over here, or I'll eat all of this by myself."

"I will pay good money to see that." He sauntered to her and carefully sank down to the floor, making sure that the ring box didn't poke out and ruin the surprise. "You have the appetite of a baby bird."

"Baby birds are constantly hungry."

"Smartass," he teased. "You know what I mean."

She handed him a pair of chopsticks and opened one of the boxes for herself. "I do, but I like it when you are forced to clarify."

"I'm convinced you're a sadist." He dug in with gusto, loving her choice of cuisine despite his earlier remarks.

"In all honesty—and I'm only saying this because you're my fiancé and we're supposed to share everything—when you told me about being tied to a bed, I kind of liked the idea," she finished in a rush, before pouring them both a glass of wine.

He fought a smile. Not only did she enjoy a glass of red with him lately, but she freely spoke about her desires, too. He loved watching her confidence blossom, and knowing that it was partly due to him. She made him want to be responsible, after all, so it seemed like a fair trade.

"You'd like to tie me up?"

"I don't know what's wrong with me!" she exclaimed.

"There's nothing wrong with kinky sex." He gave her a grin that would normally turn the opposite sex into jelly, happy when he saw that she wasn't unaffected by his charm. "In fact, I highly recommend it… But I won't be the one tied down in this scenario."

She opened her mouth to retort, thought about it, and chewed on a mouthful of egg-fried rice.

"You're not objecting?"

"No, as long as the restraints don't chafe my wrists."

He raised an eyebrow. "Who said anything about wrists?"

Asha's hold on the chopsticks faltered. "What else would you…" She trailed off as realization struck. Her eyes went wide and he could almost see the wheels turning in her brain. "So, my feet? Why don't I mind the sound of that?"

He shifted. He was getting turned on, and his jeans weren't helping. His imagination ran wild. Asha, tied to the bed by her hands and feet while he slowly licked his way over every inch of her skin… He cleared his throat to drag his thoughts back to the present.

"I was merely saying it to see where your limits are," he said slowly. "I mean, we're going to be together for

the rest of our lives. We'll have to keep the flame alive."
He got an idea, smiling broadly. "What's your number
one fantasy?"

She gulped down half of her wine before responding.
"Well, most recently I really want you at my mercy."

And his mind wandered down *that* particular
avenue... He reeled it back in before things got out of
hand. "Before you met me, I meant."

"Oh, you know," she said, shrugging. "The usual.
Mile-high club, in an elevator, blindfolded—"

"Wait a minute, you've never done any of that?" He
stared in surprise when she shook her head. "Did
Praven want to be on top all the time?"

Her gaze dropped to her food. "Something like that."

"I'm going to have so much fun with you, I can barely
restrain myself."

"Nothing too kinky, right? I mean, I don't want to
wear disgusting masks or something."

"Nor would I want you to hide your face." The
thought of doing that made him frown. "We won't do
anything you're not comfortable with, Bigfoot."

"Deal," she said, smiling at the nickname, as she often
did. "Anyway, how's your dinner? I can't help but
notice you've already moved on to box number two."

"You still sound like you're surprised by the amount
of food I consume."

"Do you blame me?" She pointed to the empty box
he'd just put down. "That's jumbo-sized, and you're
not full yet."

"Don't worry, I won't make you pick up the tab when
we eventually go out on real dates," he teased.

"That's very good to know. You could bankrupt me."
She got more comfortable, stretching one of her legs until it touched his. He adored that. "How're things going with the building?"

"Despite the list of issues, I still think it's feasible. I'd like to see it in Dubai's skyline, especially around sunset."

She winked at him. "Look at you, all grown up!"

"It's all your fault, yeah."

"We're even, especially since I'm considering kinky stuff in the bedroom."

He nodded in agreement. "You're also not as uptight anymore. Do I have something to do with that?"

She giggled and looked away. "I don't know what you're talking about."

"It's too early in our relationship to start keeping secrets, don't you think?"

"Nothing like a bit of mystery to keep a man on his toes. A characteristic that, according to you, is one of my best."

"That's true, Bigfoot. You have the memory of an elephant."

"And you better not forget—" She broke off when the lights and electronic devices in the room lost power. "Well," she remarked dryly, "it's a good thing I lit these candles. Do you think it's the entire building, or just our floor?"

He rose to his feet and walked to the big windows. "Uh, it looks like it's the whole block."

"You're kidding me! In the middle of a snowstorm?"

"Maybe they have a problem with one of the

substations."

She sighed heavily. "I guess I should get blankets. Now that the heating is turned off, it's going to get cold."

"If it's not too much trouble," he called after her, smiling. She was giving him the perfect opportunity to propose, and she didn't even know it yet. He headed back to the coffee table, topped their glasses up with more wine and continued eating.

Asha was back within five minutes, carrying three thick, fluffy blankets. She was also wearing a jersey, and had changed into flannel pyjama pants. She fussed around him for a bit until they were cosily leaning against the couch while eating.

Konstantinos couldn't remember ever feeling at ease with someone he was this attracted to.

"Do you always take care of others?" he asked.

"I guess, because I'm the eldest, I've got a bit of a mother hen complex."

"Have you thought about kids?"

She looked horrified for a couple of seconds. "Not really. Maybe when I'm older, you know? I've got too much to prove to myself first."

"We're in agreement." He bumped his shoulder against hers. "We're different, and yet we have things fundamental things common."

"It makes things easier," she said, kissing his cheek.

"I'd say." He finished his third box and patted his stomach. "This was probably the best idea you've had since baking that chocolate cake. Thank you for a lovely dinner."

She beamed at him. "You're welcome. Did you have enough to eat?"

"For now." He mentally prepared himself for what was to come and turned to her. She seemed confused by his serious facial expression, so he leaned over and kissed her until she was breathless. "I need your attention for roughly two minutes."

"What's up?"

"Asha, we've both admitted that we wouldn't have hooked up in the real world, but I want to tell you why I wouldn't have pursued you." He was glad that she didn't take offence. She really has come a long way. "You've already noticed this about me, but I hardly take anything seriously. I was raised with more money and luxury than most and I got cocky. I didn't want to settle down with anyone. If rich guys like Hugh Hefner could have multiple girlfriends at age eighty, why couldn't I, you know? My parents were getting annoyed because I wasn't growing up, but I figured they'd get over it if my brother married and gave them the heirs they so desperately want." He took her left hand in his, peering into her light green eyes. "I feel incredibly lucky that we're here, though. I wouldn't change a thing that's happened over the last three weeks. This has shown me that I *do* want a steadfast relationship, and I want one with *you*."

She blinked to lessen the moisture that had formed in her eyes.

"I can't imagine myself with anyone else. You've made such a big shift in my life that I'll never go back to being the boy I once was." He quirked a smile. "You turned me into a man, and we didn't even have to have sex for you to do so. Anyway, the point I'm getting to…" He pulled the ring box out of his pocket with his free hand and flipped it open. "I know we're engaged because our parents decided it, but I want to be engaged because you've accepted me as the man you want to spend the rest of your life with."

Her jaw dropped at the sight of the ring.

"Asha Dewali, will you marry me?"

"Yes, oh my God, yes!" She climbed on his lap and embraced him happily. "Of course I'll marry you! But first, tell me: where the hell did you get this ring?"

"Three options were waiting in my closet," he replied, slipping the ring on her finger. "This one reminded me of the things I love most about you."

She stared at the yellow-golden stone, set in a platinum band. "And what's that?"

"Your skin," he whispered, kissing the spot below her ear. "Your scent. Your aura."

"Teeny Sarantos, how on earth didn't you have girlfriends before?" She kissed him until he saw stars, pressing her upper body to his firmly. "You're so romantic!"

"I only want to be this way for you," he confessed. "I love you, Bigfoot."

"This…" She was panting while her eyes darted between his face and the ring. "You… I…" Giving up on verbalizing her thoughts, her mouth connected with his once more. "Screw your stupid rule! We're having sex tonight!"

He chuckled as she started pulling at his shirt and held

her wrists to still her hands. "You only need to wait a few more weeks until the wedding. Can you do that, for me?"

"Fine," she answered grumpily, resting her forehead on his. "But you better make it spectacular."

"Knowing us, it will be."

* * * * *

IN THE HEART of London, Marietta was next to a man she'd picked up at a bar. He was already fast asleep, but she stared at the ceiling while she mentally ran over her plan to pay Asha back for the lies.

Life just wasn't fair.

If anyone had the right to tame a man like Konstantinos Sarantos, it was *Marietta*, not some Indian heiress that didn't know her ass from her elbow when it came to relationships! If that Greek billionaire got his kicks by having inexperienced women in his bed, Marietta would be more than happy to play the part. She'll even get dressed in a Catholic schoolgirl's uniform and allow him to spank her because she's been a naughty, nasty girl.

There was no way that she's going to allow Asha Dewali to win again. That woman was already set to inherit billions of dollars; she had the talent to become one of the hottest fashion designers; she had the business acumen to ensure that her family's name will last for generations to come; and she was beautiful, on top of it all. It wasn't fair for her to have a man like Konstantinos.

It has never bothered Marietta before, because Asha's love life used to be a joke. Marietta used to praise herself for finding happiness in places that her best friend couldn't, but that has changed now. If Asha was getting married, then she had to be happy, and that simply would not do.

She smiled smugly in the darkness of the bedroom. Asha would rue the day she stepped into the lane destined for Marietta Angelotti.

CHAPTER 24

ASHA COULDN'T STOP staring at her ring. It's been nearly a week since the proposal—with a few days left to go before they were released back into society, if emails from her parents were to be believed—and she still wasn't over it. Konstantinos couldn't have chosen a better way to ask her to marry him.

"You're acting like such a cliché," he chuckled from across the room.

She stuck her tongue out at him. "Believe me, you would've done the same if you were the one wearing this." She closed her portfolio and wiggled the mouse of her computer to activate the screen. "Girls go crazy for bling."

"And here I thought you said yes because you actually want to get married to me."

"You're not all that great, Teeny. It's only ever been about the ring," she teased.

She logged into Dewali Enterprises' staff interweb to

check on the latest sales reports, happily noting that everyone was looking forward to her showcase at next year's Paris Fashion Week. She only hoped that nobody would be disappointed by what she's presenting.

Deciding to have a look at the automotive division, she realized that Konstantinos wasn't participating in their usual banter. "Teeny? Are you at a loss for words?" she quipped, eyes glued to the screen. She was stunned once she saw one of her brother's flamboyant vehicle designs was being considered as a prototype. She never imagined that Kash would get serious about his position at the company, yet here he was, proving that he could do it.

And still, not a word from Konstantinos.

She lifted her head and frowned, since he wasn't in the room anymore. Had she offended him? "Teeny?" She rose to her feet and headed for the door. "Where are you?"

As she reached the doorway, a tanned arm slipped around the wall to dim the lights. "Sit down on the chair behind you," Konstantinos' rich voice demanded from the hallway.

"Uh, what's going on?" she asked nervously.

"Do as you're told, Bigfoot."

"There better be a good reason for this." She turned around and was surprised to see a solitary chair beckoning to her. How hadn't she noticed that before? "Uhm, there's a remote on it."

"Press play once you're seated."

She got comfortable on the chair and pressed play, scepticism dripping off her aura. Her eyes widened when the familiar piano intro of Enrique Iglesias' *Heartbeat* filled the study. She was positively gaping in astonishment as Konstantinos stepped into the room wearing loose-fitting jeans and a white button-up shirt, mostly because he was wearing a shirt in the first place.

When Enrique's sultry voice joined the music, her fiancé's body began moving to the beat.

"Teeny, what the hell are you doing?" she asked shakily, unable to look away.

He raised his finger to his lips with a naughty glint in his dark gaze, swaying his hips. He kept eye contact as he began dancing like a professional stripper. She couldn't believe that he could use his body so languidly, as if he was wading through water. He had the muscles of a boxer, and yet he moved like the male version of Shakira? How on earth was that possible? Did his ballet background have something to do with this?

She only noticed that she was holding her breath when he took a step closer to her and undid the buttons on his shirt. One. By. *One*. With a soft whoosh, the oxygen left her lungs. She was basically squirming in her seat, wishing he'd speed up the process: she missed his shirtless torso.

Slowly, devastatingly slowly, he let the shirt slide off his skin. It fell to the floor seconds later. He took another step closer, twirling his hips in erotic ways, making her wonder what it would be like to feel him move against her. In bed.

Get your mind out the gutter, Asha Dewali! she chided herself mentally, but it didn't seem as if she had any control over her traitorous mind or body anymore.

The muscles of his eight-pack bulged as he performed a sensuous dance for her, and she wasn't imagining the delectable layer of sweat shining on his skin. He was within reach now but, when she made a grab for his jeans, he playfully smacked her hand away.

All the while, the two singers were breathily begging that their hearts wouldn't be stolen by the other. Asha could relate.

He stood, straddling her, while his crotch rocked dangerously close to her face. She licked her lips, unable to look away from the bulge behind his zipper. Her response to the visual feast in front of her was obviously turning him on, too. His jeans hung in such a way that it wouldn't take much to pull it off.

Oh, she was burning to. Her grip on her chair made her knuckles go white. She couldn't feel the tips of her fingers anymore.

And then, finally, the torture was over.

Konstantinos lowered himself onto her lap, careful not to crush her under his weight. He leaned forward to nibble on her ear. "Are you sure I'm not 'all that great'?" he murmured huskily.

It took a long time for her brain to figure out what he meant by that. "Did you do this to prove a point?" she countered with a quivering voice.

"I guess that depends whether I proved my point or not."

She lifted her head to stare into his eyes. "Point made, husband. You're better than butter or sliced bread, or butter *on* sliced bread. You're the best: everything I've secretly fantasized about but were too afraid to pursue.

You're *it*. I'm sorry if I offended you."

"You didn't," he assured her. He was beaming at her confession, knowing how difficult it was for her to admit her true feelings. "I wanted to have a little fun and give you a show anyway."

Reaching around him to squeeze his butt, she asked: "Have you done this for other girls before?"

"Just one," he admitted, "but I didn't love her."

"I guess I can live with that," she sighed, happy that he chuckled at her theatrics. "Will this be a one-time only event? I'd love to have this kind of thing happen on a weekly basis."

"You'll start taking it for granted." His mouth moved down her neck. "I want to see you dance."

"I'm not nearly that good, so I'm going to pass, thanks very much."

"Let's see, shall we?"

She wanted to protest as he got to his feet, but felt better once he pulled her into his arms. "You do that as if I weigh nothing," she laughed, placing her hands on his bare chest. Whoa! She sure was going to love her future husband for the rest of her life. Who wouldn't? His body was amazing.

"You're very light, Asha," he whispered. "I can't wait to see how your body changes over the years, especially once you're a mother."

Her face heated. "So, uh, what're we doing?"

"Getting that stick out of your butt," he joked, sliding his hands down to her hips. "If you're going to use 'lack of sensuality' as an excuse why you won't do a striptease for me one day, then I have to make sure that you're telling the truth."

"I'll be embarrassed."

"If you're not happy with the way you look, how do you expect me to be?"

"It's not that about that."

He tilted her chin up while they swayed to an imaginary beat. "Talk to me, Bigfoot."

"I just... I think about the other women that you've had. It's intimidating. I mean, they were obviously sexier, more confident than I'll ever be. I won't be able to dance for you, because you've been with women who're better."

He sighed. "You know, I hate Praven Kahn."

Taken aback, she asked: "Why?"

"He made a beautiful woman question her sexiness, for one. She's smart, kind, funny and ambitious, all packed into a body that most women envy. She wears clothes like others can only dream to do. She has stunning silky, waist-length hair and gorgeous green eyes. She's the one person that I want to change for so that I'll be the husband she deserves." He touched her cheek, intensely peering at her. "And yet, she doesn't see any of that, because one asshole didn't take the time to appreciate what he had." He wiped her tears away. "Asha, please don't let him ruin you. I wouldn't have wanted to spend the rest of my life with you if I didn't think that you're the only one who can match me physically, emotionally, mentally and sexually."

She closed her eyes, hoping that he didn't think she was being pathetic. "I'm really trying, Konstantinos. I don't want to be insecure, because you deserve someone who's sure of herself. But I'm trying to change something that was said to me for seven years. It's difficult."

"I'll be here to help with that. Whenever you feel like you're not good enough, I want you to tell me. I'll remind you every day if I have to, until you believe it." He tucked her hair behind her ears. "I want you to dance for me because it's a celebration of your femininity, just like my dance was a celebration of my masculinity. That's what makes it sexy." The corners of his mouth tilted up into a wry smile. "Besides, I made a lot of mistakes while I did it."

"Sure you did," she said disbelievingly.

"I didn't let it affect my confidence, which is why you couldn't see it," he insisted. "I missed a couple of beats. I was afraid that you were going to ask me to stop."

Her mouth popped open. "Why would I do that?"

"I knew that I'm the first man to do that for you, and I wasn't sure how you were going to react."

Asha was ashamed that her insecurities were affecting him. He had no right to question the raw, sexual power he possessed in spades. How could she allow him to second-guess himself? If she had to push aside her own fears to be sexy for him, she'd do it in a heartbeat.

"I promise I'll keep you in the loop of what's happening in my head," she vowed, giving him a soft, adoring kiss.

"I can live with that," he said cheerfully. "Now, are you ready to loosen up a little?"

"Teach me, wise one."

"It's really weird that an Indian woman doesn't move

like she's belly-danced all her life."

She rolled her eyes at him. "I'm not surprised that you're making assumptions. Everyone automatically thinks, just because I'm Indian, that I can move like an expert."

"I'll make you a pro in no time." He wiggled his eyebrows. "Trust me."

"You're the first man I trust," she informed him. "You better take good care of me."

"I'll do my best, Bigfoot. You have my word. Now," he said, grinding his hips against hers, "follow my lead."

Taking deep breaths, she obeyed every instruction he gave, even when it made her feel like she could crawl under the desk and never face anyone again. Soon, she was too out of breath to think. Her body lost its usual rigid posture. He alternated between dancing an impromptu salsa, twirling them around the room, and making her do a few sultry moves.

At some point, he even asked her to play with her hair while she danced.

She raked her fingers through the silky strands, swivelling on her heels and dropping to her hunches with her back to him. Then, still clutching her head, she slowly bent forward and lifted her butt until it rubbed his crotch.

He groaned and grabbed her hips, pressing closer to her. "How can you deny that you're the sexiest woman on earth when you feel that?"

He didn't have to clarify: she couldn't miss the hardness pressed to her behind. She turned around and jumped into his arms to kiss him. "I'm starting to believe," she gasped as she briefly pulled back, only to attack him again.

"Good," he growled.

She trembled once she felt a wall behind her. "Are we finally going to have sex?" With that question out in the open, he stilled and rested his forehead on hers. She instantly regretted opening her mouth. "Please?"

"I can't wait to get married to you, Asha Dewali." He stared at her. "I'm going to enjoy paying you back for the last couple of weeks of sexual torture."

"Don't think you're the only one," she giggled, stroking her lower body against his.

He bit her neck, hard. "I can't wait," he said again.

"Neither can I, Teeny, but I guess we'll have the rest of our lives to catch up."

Chapter 25

"How did you know about this place, *mon cher?*" Denise asked, her eyes nearly popping out of her head. She was dressed as if she was about to attend some swanky event—on Loikanos' request, of course—and yet the other people in this restaurant were donned casually.

The restaurant, on the other hand, was decorated with silky fabrics hanging from the ceiling, golden chandeliers and heavy wooden furniture.

"It's my favourite," he answered with a smile. He took her elbow to steer her past the tables, to a cushioned sitting area.

"Everyone's looking at us!" she whispered self-consciously.

"Good," he chuckled. "I want them to see how lucky I am to have you."

She could sense their eyes on her back as he pulled her down on one of the oversized cushions next to him.

She yelped in surprise, careful to keep her legs closed, since she was wearing an above-the-knee, tight-fitting pencil skirt. Her sleeveless white shirt had a low neckline, drawing attention to her full breasts.

"What if someone saw my underwear?" she blushed, tugging at her skirt.

Loikanos stilled her hands. "*Mon amour,* I wish you would stop worrying what they think. We're here to enjoy ourselves. Nothing else matters."

She calmed down instantly. "I'm sorry, *mon cher.* I had a rough day at the office."

"You're forgiven. Tell me what happened."

Sighing, she said: "With your brother and Asha coming out of the apartment tomorrow, it feels like a circus. We have a little over two weeks to go until the wedding and there are several catering issues I must sort out. I am worried that I won't be done in time."

"You will," he said, kissing her cheek. "My brother is in capable hands. I only hope that you will be this excited to plan our wedding, *mon amour.*"

Her heart fluttered in her chest. "We're talking about marriage?"

"Well, I'd love to spend the rest of my life with you, but if you don't want to put labels on our relationship then I won't ask."

"Loikanos—"

"No," he interrupted firmly, picking his menu up. "I'm not going to listen to the reasons why you think we shouldn't be together, Denise. I thought we've already talked about why we're good for each other."

"You're right," she admitted, feeling like an idiot for

repeatedly denying what they were. She pulled his face to hers for a seductive kiss. "Will you forgive me? I'd love to marry you, *mon cher.*"

"There's nothing to forgive, *mon amour,*" he murmured, nibbling on the corner of her mouth. It didn't look like he cared that her red lipstick was staining his own lips. "As for the second comment… I'm glad you said that, because I got you this."

She watched, stunned, as he nonchalantly placed a dark purple velvet box on the table. And then, as if he hadn't just take her off guard, he continued perusing the menu.

"Uhm, what is this?"

"Open it and see for yourself. Are you in the mood for red or white wine?"

"Red," she replied absently, staring at the box. Her fingers itched to open it, to feel the soft velvet sliding over her skin before revealing the mystery that was inside, but she was baffled. This was not how men normally proposed, and it certainly wasn't how Remi had. Where was the champagne? The red roses? The violinists? The public display that resulted in utter embarrassment on the woman's part?

Maybe she was a fool for comparing the two men even after Loikanos has proven, time and time again, that he wasn't like any man she's ever known before.

"Good choice," he said. "Ooh, they've got a good Pinot Noir, does that sound okay?"

"Sounds delicious, *mon cher.* What kind of food do they serve here?"

"Turkish, Greek and Mediterranean," he replied,

winking at her. "Why do you think I love it so much? I want you to enjoy my culture." He noticed the box was still on the table and rolled his dark eyes at her. "It's not going to bite you, Denise."

"I'm… nervous."

"Would you rather have me—"

"No!" she exclaimed, blushing again. "Give me time. I will do it."

"So brave, *mon amour.*" His eyes twinkled in the dim lighting. She knew what that grin meant even before he elaborated. "Why do you think I love you so much?"

She relaxed on the cushion, kicking her heels off and curling her legs under her. "I think it's because you know I am the best woman you will ever have."

"Isn't that the truth! Why else?"

"Because I make you laugh whenever you want to put it in the wrong hole," she teased playfully.

He glared at her. "That only happened once."

"I already told you I won't mind," she said, looking at him with faux innocent eyes. "You can use my body as you see fit, *mon cher.*"

"You're not too old for a spanking, *mon amour.*"

She tilted her head back and burst out laughing. "Neither are you!"

"You enjoy making fun of my age, don't you?" He leaned forward and licked his way into her cleavage. "Tell me, lover: did any of your other men know your body as well as I do?"

She arched her back when he nipped at the soft globes of her breasts with his teeth. "No," she managed to answer.

"Did they know that if they do this," he murmured, flicking his tongue dangerously close to the edge of her shirt, "that you get so aroused that you beg me for more?"

She clutched his head. "N-no!"

"And did they—"

Someone noisily cleared their throat, interrupting him.

Loikanos let out an annoyed breath that tingled along her skin before he lifted his head. The lust in his gaze cleared once he recognized their waiter. "Ah, there you are. We're ready to order."

Denise's face felt like it was on fire. She pulled at her shirt, trying to cover herself, but Loikanos—without looking—slapped her hands away. "Uhm, I'm going to the ladies'," she mumbled. Her body has come alive, wishing that he could finish what he'd started. "Order for me?"

"That was the plan," he commented dryly.

She hurriedly put her shoes on, grabbed her small handbag and rushed to the restroom. She couldn't shake the feeling that she was being watched, but dismissed her paranoia and flicked her thick blonde hair over her shoulder. Stifling a giggle at her risqué move, she pushed the door of the ladies' room open and went to stand at the basin.

There was a stunning girl in her early-twenties next to her, but Denise suddenly realized why Loikanos wanted *her*. The girl might have a glorious figure, yet she didn't have the rounded curves of a woman. Yes, the girl was probably a hit with younger men, but Loikanos was far

too mature and would easily get bored talking about...
whatever the topics were that kept a young crowd busy.

Denise finally knew what to say to Loikanos when she
opened that tempting velvet box.

Fixing her makeup and scrunching her hair, she
couldn't help her self-assured swagger as she exited the
restroom. She collided with a man in the hallway
between and froze once she recognized her ex-
husband.

This was the stare that had been locked on her every
move, the one she'd sensed earlier. The judgemental
one.

"I see you think you're good enough for that infant
outside," Remi said, addressing her in French while
crossing his arms over his chest.

She knew that move well. In the beginning of their
tumultuous relationship, she'd thought it was a
masculine gesture and she had fallen at his feet in
misplaced desire. As they had progressed through the
years, he'd started intimidating her and she would fear
him whenever he stood like that.

Now, she pitied him.

"I know I am," she countered haughtily, purposefully
jutting her hip out. She wanted to laugh when she saw
the look of hunger in his eyes, knowing that he's never
seen her this confident.

"You're old, Denise," he sneered. "That boy won't
love you a year from now! You don't know how to have
fun! Do you think, because you wear your hair loose
like a whore, he'll still be interested when he's
surrounded by stunning, young girls?"

"I don't think, Remi, I know." She took a seductive step forward and lifted a hand to his chest. "Unlike you, Loikanos knows how to handle a woman. He doesn't have to mingle with *girls* to feel better about himself." She lightly slapped his cheek, all hints of humour gone from her tone as she said: "You're a sad, sad little man, Remi. Don't contact me again, or I will go to the authorities. You have nothing to offer me."

She strutted back to Loikanos without another word, relishing in the glances men of all ages were giving her. She giggled like someone who was eighteen years old as she plopped down on the cushion and pulled her lover closer for a kiss that left him gasping.

"I love you," she told him. His eyebrows just about disappeared into his hairline at her sudden change in attitude. She pecked him on the cheek, let go, and picked up the ring box. "Let's see what you got me." Once she opened it, her jaw hit the floor. It was the platinum band with glittering diamonds and a large Tanzanite, one of the three she'd picked out for Asha.

The same one she'd imagined Loikanos using to propose to her!

"How?"

"I called Jacob and asked if he had any ideas," he answered. "He told me he knew exactly what to get you and, after I saw it, I knew it was the one." He lifted it out of the box and held it up to her face. "It matches your eyes."

If she'd still had doubts about his intentions, they would've shattered to the ground after that.

"I've already had it resized. Do you want to see if it

fits?"

"I'm sure it does," she laughed, holding her left hand out. "You think of everything."

He smiled as he pushed the ring onto her finger. "Maybe we're not so different, after all."

"I will marry you whenever you want," she whispered, kissing him with everything she had.

"Denise, do you want me to take you right here?" he groaned hoarsely.

"Anywhere. I'm yours, *mon cher.*"

"What if I want to get married first thing tomorrow morning?"

"Then I won't object." She reluctantly detached her limbs from his gorgeous body. "But I think we should tell your parents first."

He hugged her happily. "I'll arrange for it, *ma femme.*"

"I love that you call me your wife." She held him close. "I'll be yours forever."

CHAPTER 26

TODAY WAS THE day that Asha and her fiancé were coming back from wherever they've been. For weeks, Marietta has pondered the various ways she exact revenge and she's finally settled on a plan. It was perfect in its simplicity. She could hardly wait to start playing her role.

One thing was certain: for the first time, she was going to join the ranks of other people who have pretended to be Asha's friends, but for an entirely different reason. Where they had faked their affection for the Indian heiress to obtain a portion of her fortune and fame, Marietta would cut ties with Asha due to deceit.

If Asha didn't feel any remorse, Marietta wouldn't either. This was going to be fun!

"What time did they say they're going to get here?" she queried conversationally.

Kashinath, like everyone else in the room, was

unaware of the plans brewing beneath the surface of her smile. "In about half an hour. You've missed her, huh? You guys used to be joined at the hip!"

Until she lied to me about her relationship with Konstantinos.

"I can't wait to see her!" Marietta gushed. "We have so much to catch up on!"

"This is very exciting, yeah."

"Did you see her new designs on the website?" Farida asked her.

"I flipped through them earlier this morning," Marietta replied, barely keeping the raging jealousy from entering her tone. As if she needed to be reminded of Asha's talent. "This is going to be a great year for her, I can tell. Aren't you starting your studies soon?"

Farida pulled a face. "I'm not looking forward to it. I've always wanted to design cars, like Kash, but my family has this habit of forcing—" She broke off when Kashinath slapped her arm. "Ow! Was that necessary?"

"Yes," he said, giving her a pointed look.

"Oh, right, sorry," Farida muttered.

There was something else going on in the room, between these families. She's noticed it for weeks, but Marietta couldn't make herself care. It was unimportant, of no consequence. If she got distracted by the smallest things, she was never going to wreak havoc on Asha's life.

"What're you going to study instead, then?" she asked the youngest Dewali.

"Management," Farida sighed.

"That's not so bad! My dad asked me to do a course

in management, too, and it's worked out great. I get to help around the family business."

"Yeah, it's great for people who want to be in the family business to begin with," Kashinath mumbled.

Farida glared at him. "Says the guy who's designing a new car!"

"Everyone buckles under pressure at some point," Mariette said.

"I guess." Kashinath eyed her. "Who're you taking to the wedding?"

Who says there'll be a wedding to attend?

"I'm going alone, actually. Why do you ask?"

"We should go together. My parents don't want me to take any of the girls I want to take, but I know they approve of you."

"I'm the last resort, then?"

His eyes widened. "No, that's not what I meant at all!"

"It's okay, Kash." She forced her smile, pretending she wasn't hurt. "I get it, but I'd rather go alone. There are going to be so many people there, who knows what'll happen?"

"True."

Farida clapped her hands together. "Did you hear that Denise is getting married to Konstantinos' brother?"

Marietta asked: "Who's Denise?"

"She, uh, is kind of like the wedding planner," Kashinath responded slowly.

"Why is it scandalous? Have they dated for long?"

"That's the funny thing." Farida's voice dropped to a conspirator's whisper. "They've only known each other for, like, a month! Plus, she's about ten years older than him!"

"Nice," Kashinath chuckled.

"Is she pregnant?" Marietta blurted out.

Farida looked thoughtful. "Can she get pregnant?"

At that very moment a beautiful blonde woman walked into the room on the arm of a younger, skinnier version of Konstantinos. "Is that her?" Marietta asked, gaping. "She doesn't look older than thirty!"

"His parents aren't too happy with the pairing, but she makes him happy, so they're letting it slide," Farida finished her story.

The latest arrivals walked over to the three of them. "Yo, Kash! What's up, man?" the young Greek man asked.

Kashinath laughed and pulled him into a hug. "Not much, not much. How about you, Louis? Can't believe we're going to be brothers soon!"

"Yeah, especially because I won't be living my wild-child lifestyle anymore," the Greek man said, wrapping an arm around his date's waist. "Not that I was ever into that kind of thing to start off with, but now it's definitely off limits!"

"Loikanos, aren't you too young to get married?" Farida asked.

The blonde woman laughed. "He is dead serious about doing it, as soon as possible, too," she crooned in a French-accented voice. "He says he wants to knock me up, but that's not going to happen."

"Not through lack of trying," Loikanos teased, wagging his eyebrows.

Marietta couldn't wait for Asha to show up, since her

friend wouldn't be so lovey-dovey with Konstantinos. Loikanos and his fiancée's public displays of affection was making Marietta sick to her stomach.

"Ooh, they're here!" Anushka announced excitedly as she rushed into the room. "Places, everyone!"

With a grin, Marietta hid along with the rest of the guests in the restaurant, ready to get the ball rolling. This was going to be so much fun.

* * * * *

"I HAVE NOTHING to wear!"

Konstantinos laughed under his breath and walked to Asha's closet. She was sitting on a bench, clothes strewn all over the floor, while she stared at the few items that remained on the rack. "Are you sure?" he teased, buttoning his shirt up.

She glanced at him, her green eyes frantic. "You don't get to make comments, Teeny."

"What's the problem? Maybe I can help."

"Well, it's the first time we're going out." She gnawed on her bottom lip. "What do I wear? My parents said that we're having dinner with them tonight, but where? Do I need to look formal? Casual? I don't know the parameters!"

He stepped up to her and began hanging everything back in its place. It took longer than expected, but he was patient. He knew why she was nervous, and it wouldn't be prudent to add fuel to her already out-of-control fire.

"Okay, let's see." Tapping his finger on his chin, he

gazed at her wardrobe. "It's freezing outside, so you should definitely take a coat." He removed a dark green one from its hanger and placed it next her. "But we'll be inside, so you can go with something sleeveless."

"You don't have to pick my outfit for me."

He raised his eyebrow and gave her a look. "Yeah, 'cause *you* were having such a good time of it before I got here."

She sighed and rose to her feet. She was currently wearing something that had him hardening the instant she straightened out: a black, silky chemise with a low neckline and a slit from her thighs up to her hips on each side.

"Look, I know you're right," she said, unaware of his new mood, "but I just… Hey, should we match?"

He coughed to clear his throat. "I don't think that's necessary."

"Dark colours look really great on you, by the way," she complimented him, smiling as she touched his chest. "I love burgundy against your skin."

"It's one of my favourite colours."

She tilted her head to the side at his rough tone. "What's wrong?"

"Asha, you're my fiancée, one that I'm not having sex with until we're married, and you're standing in front of me wearing nothing but lingerie."

"Oh!" She tucked her styled hair behind her ears self-consciously. "I'm sorry, I completely forgot."

"I don't mind the view, Bigfoot." His gaze slithered down, from her head to her toes, and back up again. "All that's missing is a garter belt."

She lifted the front of her chemise slightly to show him the rest. "I'm already wearing one, but I'm still deciding if I should wear stockings or not."

He mentally counted backwards from ten, though it only further incensed his desire for her. "Do you want to wear a dress? I'd love to see green on you."

"That's a colour I know how to wear," she said proudly. Rummaging through the row of dresses she had at her disposal, she selected one and held it in front of her. "What do you think?"

It wouldn't show any cleavage, since it had high neckline, but it also had an oval cut-out between her shoulder blades. Fitted around the waist, it flared out over her hips and ended above her knees. The olive tone of the dress suited her hair, skin and eyes perfectly.

"That's the one," he declared. "Oh, and wear stockings. Will you be okay now?"

"It's funny: when I didn't have anyone in my life, I had more style than I knew what to do with, but now that I'm engaged I'm hopeless." She kissed his cheek. "Thanks for your help, Teeny."

"My pleasure." He ran his thumb over her lips. "We're going to be late if you don't hurry up. I'll wait in the living room." He quickly strode out of her closet before he did something stupid, like make love to her before she was Mrs. Konstantinos Sarantos.

"I won't be long!" she called after him.

Deciding to keep the top buttons of his shirt open instead of wearing a tie, he picked up the black jacket of the suit he was wearing, as well as a scarf and knee-length trench coat. It was going to be weird to see the outside world again. He wasn't really looking forward to it: if he could stay here the rest of his life, with Asha, wrapped in their own little planet… That would be the most ideal situation.

Reality, though, waited for no one.

He went to stand at one of the floor-to-ceiling windows in the living room and stared at the city below. A part of him was excited to attend the meeting with the other engineers on the Dubai project tomorrow. He was positive that his father would approve his designs, but it was going to be interesting to see how everyone else reacted. He was, after all, attempting it on a professional level for the first time.

"I'm ready!"

He glanced over his shoulder and held his breath. Her black heels rounded the picture off perfectly, but it didn't help that he knew what was going on under her dress. Her hair cascaded down to her waist in soft waves, and the only indications that she was wearing makeup were her soft red lips and darkened lashes.

The best part of her outfit, though, was the ring on her left hand. *His* ring.

"You look beautiful."

She smiled. "Thanks."

He moved forward to help her into her coat, before shrugging into his own. Together, they took step after step in the direction of the elevator. It felt like forever before they got there and, when they pressed the button this time, the doors immediately opened.

"Lockdown is officially over," she murmured.

He took her hand in his and gave it a squeeze. "We'll

be back."

"I'm assuming because our clothes are in the main bedroom that my parents won't be staying here when they're in London for business anymore," she remarked. "I wonder if they found a new place. They know I've always loved this penthouse."

"Are you going to be based here from now on?"

She nodded and glanced at him. In her heels, she was nearly as tall as him. "I think London's a good base. Would you want to live here?"

"Bigfoot, I want to be where you are."

Sliding her hand up to the fold of his elbow, she leaned into him when the elevator arrived on the ground floor. "Home is where the heart is."

"Exactly."

It felt strange to interact with other people after being in Asha's company for weeks. He loved her more than anything and thoroughly enjoyed their banter, but he didn't realize until now how much he's missed the world.

"Hmm, it's quite nice to talk to other people," she commented.

He chuckled. "I was thinking the same thing, though you still have to work on your vocabulary."

"Oh, shush."

He waited for her to get into the awaiting car before sliding onto the backseat. "It doesn't compare, so I'll let 'nice' slide this time around."

"How gracious of you," she teased.

He automatically draped an arm over her shoulders, gathering her to him. "Who're you looking forward to seeing most?"

"As much as they annoy me, my siblings. What about you?"

"Loikanos. Apparently, he's also engaged. We have a lot to talk about."

"Oh, wow! You've started a trend, Teeny."

"I'm all for marriage these days."

"Aw, such a sweetheart, you are."

He chuckled. "Thank you, Yoda."

They chatted about London for the rest of the drive, both feeling the nerves set in once the car halted at a swanky restaurant. The lights were off inside. For a moment, they weren't sure they were at the right place, but the chauffeur insisted that this was the address he'd been given.

"Ready or not, here we go," Konstantinos mumbled, holding her hand in his. He loved how she secured her other hand on his arm. She probably hadn't been this way with Praven, and knowing that did wonders for Konstantinos' ego.

The moment they stepped over the threshold, the lights went on, and a large portion of their friends and family—plus a couple of people he didn't recognize—jumped up from behind the furniture and shouted: "Surprise!"

Asha held a hand over her heart. "Wow, was that entirely necessary?"

They laughed, and Asha's parents moved forward along with Konstantinos' to greet their children.

"How're you feeling, son?" Kolina asked in Greek. "Are you happy and in love?"

"Yes, mama," he answered honestly. "I can't wait to be married."

"May the gods have mercy on an old woman's soul!" she exclaimed, laughing. To everyone except the Sarantos family, she appeared to be speaking in tongues. "My son is ready to settle down!"

Nikos grunted. "Yes, that's quite unexpected."

"I knew you could do it, bro!" Loikanos chuckled, pulling his older brother into a big hug. "You're going to make a lovely groom!"

"You guys are acting as if I was a soulless buffoon before," Konstantinos snorted. He was aware of Asha ogling him with interest, mostly because she couldn't follow the conversation. He pulled her closer and switched to English. "Mama, papa: I'd like to introduce you to Asha. In case you didn't know, we're getting married."

Kolina laughed and pulled Asha into an impromptu hug. "It is so good to meet you, darling! I have always wanted a daughter!"

Asha, obviously uncomfortable when physical contact came from anyone except Konstantinos, tentatively patted his mother on the back. "Thank you, Mrs. Sara—"

"No, please! Call me 'mama'!"

"Mama," Asha conceded.

"This is my husband," the Greek woman gushed, gesturing to the stoic Nikos. "Do not be deterred by his exterior, *i kóri mou*—"

Asha frowned at the foreign words.

"'My daughter'," Konstantinos translated.

"—he pretends to be unaffected by everything, but my Nikos cares very, very much," Kolina finished in a rush, beaming.

Asha held out her hand to Nikos. "Hi, Mr.—oomph!" She was abruptly pulled into a quick, slightly forceful hug, shocking everyone in the room.

"Look after my boy," the normally unemotional Nikos said tearfully.

"I'll do my best, sir," Asha promised, softening her stance and patting his shoulder.

The two Sarantos brothers exchanged worried glances, both thinking the same thing: *since when does papa initiate hugs?*

"And this," Konstantinos said once Asha was back at his side, "is Loikanos, my idiot little brother."

Asha laughed and kissed Loikanos on the cheek. "Don't worry, he has nothing but kind words behind your back."

"I'm surprised by that, to be honest," Loikanos grinned. He pulled a blonde woman forward. "I don't think you've met Denise, but she's the mastermind behind... well, everything."

"You're the one to blame, then?" Konstantinos asked, pretending to be outraged.

Denise rolled her blue eyes. "You better be nice to me, *chéri*, because I will soon be your sister-in-law."

"Right, I keep forgetting about that."

"Well, it's lovely to meet you, Denise, despite what you've put us through," Asha smiled. "Good job on the wedding arrangements, too. It's going to be better than I could've envisioned."

"*Merci*," Denise nodded, pleased.

Asha's family stepped forward and she introduced Konstantinos. He liked the look of them and could see that Christmas was going to be very interesting from now on. Both the Dewali and Sarantos family trees were vast: they obviously didn't know what the term 'contraception' meant.

He wondered what their kids would look like. He hoped they'd get Asha's skin tone and eyes, and that they would all be girls. He wouldn't know how to handle a boy.

"Hi, Konstantinos," a voice purred, shaking him out of his thoughts.

Blinking at the brunette woman in front of him, he frowned. "And you are?"

"Marietta," she replied, holding her hand out to him.

He smiled broadly. "Right, you're Asha's best friend! It's so good to meet you! Asha couldn't stop talking about you the whole time we were… uh, away."

A strange emotion flickered over Marietta's face before she composed herself again. "Yeah, we've always been close. It's good to have you back! You must be looking forward to the wedding?"

"Definitely," he agreed, turning his head to look at Asha, who was busy taking off her coat. That dress looked amazing on her. He couldn't seem to remove his gaze from her body for longer than five seconds. "I can't believe she's going to be my wife, you know? How does a woman like her—smart, sassy and incredibly beautiful—end up with a brute like me?"

He didn't catch Marietta's response because, like a

moth drawn to a flame, his feet started moving until he could take Asha in his arms and kiss her on her neck. He loved how she giggled and leaned into him.

He loved *her.*

* * * * *

MARIETTA WAS BEFUDDLED while she watched Asha and Konstantinos introducing each other to their respective families. The exchange raised so many questions. How hadn't they got around to that before? Why did this engagement look like a rushed job? Was Asha pregnant?

Now's not the time to get a tender heart, she argued with herself. *Remember why you're here.*

But then, distracted by the couple, Marietta found herself staring in astonishment. Since when was Asha a woman who enjoyed receiving—or giving, for that matter—unexpected kisses and cuddles? She never used to be like that with Praven, and those two had been together for seven years! How long has Asha been dating Konstantinos?

Why did they look like the perfect couple? It was damn unacceptable!

All she longed for was recognition, for someone to say: "Yes, Asha might have had him first, but Marietta is the one he really belongs to!" Or to say that Marietta was every bit as brilliant and beautiful as her Indian friend. Why couldn't she catch a break?

Because everyone was having fun without her, she remained in the shadows and watched how effortlessly the families mingled with each other, despite the cultural differences. Asha was the star of the show, socialising with everyone that approached her. She had this glow about her, as if she was content with her lot and approved of the life she'll start leading once she said: "I do".

Marietta couldn't allow that to happen. If she did, Asha would win again.

"There you are!" Asha exclaimed, pulling Marietta away from the bar. "I've been looking everywhere for you!" She embraced Marietta. "I've missed you so much!"

"I missed you too," Marietta said neutrally. "You've been quite busy tonight."

"I know, right?" Asha gushed. "I kept wanting to come to you, but then someone else popped up out of nowhere. I didn't realize that Teeny had such a big family!"

Marietta frowned. "Teeny?"

"Right, that's my nickname for Konstantinos. He calls me 'Bigfoot'."

"I'm assuming it's an inside joke?"

Asha stared at her hunk of a fiancé, smiling like she's won the lottery. "Yeah, something like that."

"When did this happen, Ash? A month ago, you were saying that he's a womanizing idiot."

Asha's facial expression fell. Avoiding eye contact, she responded: "It's complicated, M. I wish I could tell you everything… Just know that I'm so, so happy, and that I literally can't wait to be married to him. He's not who I thought he was. He's so much more."

"That's great," Marietta muttered insincerely. She had to get out of this conversation before her resolve crumbled. "Oh, look! He needs you."

Asha's green gaze found hers. "Are you sure you're okay? I'm sorry that we're not spending much time together tonight."

"Don't worry about it, Ash. We'll catch up soon."

"You're the best!" Asha proclaimed, hugging Marietta again. "Can I call you tomorrow? Oh, wait, I think I have back-to-back meetings—"

"We'll figure something out," Marietta interjected firmly. "Go to your fiancé! You can't keep a man like that waiting."

Asha giggled and skipped off to jump into Konstantinos' arms. He caught her and twirled her around before kissing her thoroughly, making everyone in the restaurant cheer as if their favourite damn soccer team won the World Cup.

It's probably criminal to want to ruin all of this, but Marietta has seen enough. Draining the rest of her drink, she collected her things and left the restaurant, ready for a long night of precision planning to derail Asha's perfect life.

CHAPTER 27

"As you can see, I'm trying to keep the integrity of the concept without compromising the design," Konstantinos declared, pointing to the large screen that displayed his ideas to the boardroom full of executives. "The problem with most solar panels is that they're not pleasing to the eye, and a building like yours would need hundreds of panels to run at fifty percent capacity as you're intending. I tried to make it as aesthetic as possible, though."

"Konstantinos, I am pleasantly surprised," the Sheikh said with a dip of his head. "This design will look magnificent in the Dubai skyline."

As if they were too afraid to voice their opinions before the Sheikh had, the other men and women around the table flung more compliments Konstantinos' way, some even clapping.

"This is my son," Nikos announced proudly. He walked to Konstantinos and slapped him on the back.

"We saved your presentation for last and, if I may say so myself, yours is the best. By show of hands, please indicate whether you are happy to continue with this design."

Every single person raised their hands. Konstantinos felt simultaneously relieved, proud and overwhelmed. This was merely the start of a long project.

"I only have one request." He waited until he had their attention. "Instead of calling it 'Sarantos Towers', as originally suggested, I'd like for it to be named 'Life Towers International'." He shrugged when everyone gave him a questioning stare. They didn't need to know the reason for that condition.

Late last night, with Asha in bed next to him, he'd used his iPad to research the origins of her name. He had been fascinated to find out that it was also an ancient African name that meant "life". It had struck him like a lightning bolt, and he had known he wanted to dedicate his first successful project to her. Without her, he never would have stepped up to the plate to begin taking over his father's empire.

Without her, he wouldn't know the true meaning of life.

"It will be as you asked, son," Nikos assured him after taking another vote. "I think I speak for all of us when I say that you should lead the project. Construction starts in four months, so you'll have to bring your wife along. You will be stationed in Dubai for a while."

Konstantinos suppressed his groan, giving everyone a polite handshake as he made his way around the table. "Of course, papa. I understand what I have to do."

"Good." Nikos switched over to Greek. "Let's go to my office: we have things to discuss."

They exited the boardroom and walked to his father's large, opulent office together. Konstantinos wasn't sure if he'd want something this pretentious. Maybe Asha's simplistic interior decorating style was already rubbing off on him.

"How are you feeling about the wedding, son? Don't sugar-coat it for me: I want the truth."

"I wouldn't have agreed if I didn't want to do it, papa," he insisted, taking a seat opposite his old man. "I would've gladly faced your wrath. The truth is that I love her, papa, and I want to spend the rest of my life with her."

"I ask because she wasn't my first choice. She doesn't cook and she's not housewife material."

Konstantinos raised an eyebrow. "We hardly live in those times anymore, papa. I don't care about that. I love that she's ambitious and independent."

Staring out of the window, Nikos nodded to himself. "When I met her, I could instantly see that she's more than your mother and I would've chosen for you. She's going to be very good for you. I like her." Here, he looked back at his eldest son. "I want to make sure that you're going to look after her. I don't want your past indiscretions ruining your marriage."

"You've only just met her and you're already on her side?" Konstantinos barely suppressed his eye-roll, crossing his arms over his chest. "Why am I not surprised?"

"This isn't personal, son. I know your reputation, and

I don't want it to affect her in any way."

"I'm planning to keep it in my pants, papa," he said bitingly. He hated it when his father shed a light on Konstantinos' inadequacies, which happened far too often. "Will you calm down? I'd rather jump off Life Towers International than hurt Asha intentionally."

Nikos chuckled. "I hope that doesn't come to pass, Konstantinos, because that will be a really tall building."

Konstantinos could only stare. "Since when do you laugh, papa?"

"Since my son has found that love is not so bad. Loikanos has always been a bit more emotionally tuned in than you. I wish he would find a younger woman, but I can't prescribe who he falls in love with."

"Instead, you stick people in an apartment for a month and hope for the best!"

"I was wondering if you're angry about that."

Konstantinos let out a long breath. "I was in the beginning, and I had all these things in my head that I wanted to say to you once I'm out, but it doesn't matter anymore. Your plan worked, congratulations. I'm willingly getting married. I want to be a good husband."

His father nodded thoughtfully, fighting a smile. "If you keep that in mind, you will be, son. I wish you all the happiness you deserve with this union." He clapped his hands together. "Now, let's discuss your next project!"

CHAPTER 28

"YOU KNOW, IT'S a little freaky to see how efficient you are," Asha told Denise with wide eyes. "You got my measurements right, as well as the fabric I wanted for my dress; you got all of my friends and family to participate and make this wedding happen as quickly as possible; and you're having no problems whatsoever with the catering."

Denise laughed softly. "If that's how it appears, Asha, then I am doing my job well. Truthfully, it's not always easy, especially with…" She blushed and tucked her blonde hair behind her ears.

"The Sarantos men are quite addictive, huh?"

"You can say that."

Asha sat down opposite the French woman. "Thanks for the ring, by the way. Teeny said that there were three options waiting for him. I'm happy that he chose the least expensive one: it's the prettiest."

"That's what I told Jacob. He doesn't always believe

in my methods."

Asha nodded to herself, deep in thought while she gazed at her ring finger. She wondered if she could ask what was on her mind. "I have a question, though. Why do you do this?" When Denise gave her a quizzical look, Asha elaborated: "Arrange marriages."

Denise sipped on her latte, eyeing Asha over the rim of the mug. "I was approached to do this when the trouble in my marriage started, about three years ago, for Yerik and Jun's wedding. I found it ironic that I was planning someone else's happiness if I couldn't even manage my own, but I welcomed the distraction. It's highly gripping once you get the hang of it." She lifted a shoulder. "When I was told of the possibility of another wedding, I immediately started doing research on the two of you. That's how I knew that I loved this side of my job more than planning events. In fact, when this is over, I do believe I'll be focussing on matchmaking, going forward."

"What made you think that I'd be a good fit for Konstantinos?"

"Because, *chérie*, no other man would have got under your skin so quickly," Denise grinned. "I knew he would be good for you, because he brings you out of your shell. He presses your buttons, but in a good way."

Asha smiled to herself. "Does it feel good, knowing you're right?"

"As it would to any woman, yes."

"So, how did you meet Loikanos? Do you love him?"

Denise turned her ring round and round her finger, a content look on her face. "He took me completely by surprise, when I least expected to meet someone. I fought hard in the beginning, mostly because I was afraid of getting hurt, but he's warm and approachable… We have a connection, one I'm not willing to let go of. One I'm willing to fight for until my dying day." She lifted her blue gaze to Asha's. "Tell me, do I love him?"

Asha inclined her head. "Yes, Denise, you definitely do. I feel the same about Teeny. Sometimes, when I think about it too hard, I'm convinced I'm the biggest idiot for going through with this, but he makes me this brave person and I love him for it. I'm not scared anymore."

"I'm quite the matchmaker!"

"Yes, you are." She reached over and gave Denise's hand a squeeze. "I'd love to be friends, if you have the time, especially because we'll soon be family."

"Of course, *chérie*, I would love that, too."

Asha clasped her hands together. "Okay, what do you need me to do? I don't like feeling as if I'm not contributing to my own wedding."

"All you have to do is show up," Denise chuckled. She took her tablet device from her handbag and tapped the screen a couple of times before sliding it over the table. "Here's your schedule. As you can see, we will host a joint bachelor/bachelorette party. It will be a classy event, so you don't have to worry about anything vulgar or inappropriate. I have arranged for a popular burlesque group to perform a fifteen-minute set."

Asha's eyes bulged as she read the names of her

favourite artists on the list of performers. "Uhm, are they really all going to be there?"

"Yes."

"Jeez, Denise, you really don't play around, do you?"

Denise smiled proudly. "I definitely do not, *chérie*. When I do something, I do it properly." She raised her left hand to show off her gorgeous ring. "As you can see."

"Damn, I'm going to love having a butt-kicking sister-in-law like you!" Asha got a sudden idea. "Hey, I invited my brother and sister over for dinner tonight so they can bond with Teeny. Why don't you join us, and bring Loikanos along? I promise I won't cook. Much."

Denise burst out laughing. "That is very good to know. Would you like for me to bring anything?"

"No, you should relax for once." Asha winked. "I think I know enough about restaurants and caterers in the area to put together something special. Is there anything you don't enjoy eating?"

"I am relaxed when it comes to food. Please, don't go out of your way."

"Oh, I shall," Asha commented cheerfully, "just watch!"

Chapter 29

"HONEY, I'M HOME!" he called once he stepped out of the elevator. He grinned from ear to ear. "Man, I've always wondered what it feels like to say that! You know when you're watching a movie and they—" He came to an abrupt halt once he saw Asha in the kitchen with an apron wrapped around her waist. "Hi, Bigfoot."

She turned and smiled happily. "You're home!"

"Yes, didn't you hear me talk all the way over here?" he chuckled, catching her when she jumped in his direction.

"Sorry, I'm a bit distracted because of tonight's dinner."

"Loikanos called me about that, yes."

"He's not cancelling, is he?"

Konstantinos leaned forward to nibble on her bottom lip. "No, he's looking forward to it. Apparently, you're getting along well with Denise?"

"She's such a great woman, Teeny. I don't know your brother well, but I think they're good for each other."

"I'm glad, because it's all happening so fast. Weren't you going to meet with Marietta, too?" he asked as he removed his coat.

Asha sighed. "I don't know what's wrong, but she's seriously avoiding me. Every time I call, I'm sent to voicemail, and she doesn't reply to any of my texts. I don't know what I did wrong."

"Maybe she's feeling the pressure of being the maid of honour," he soothed, embracing his dainty fiancée. She made him feel like a big bear protecting a small, fragile creature. "Weddings affect people differently."

"I guess you're right." She kissed him softly. "How'd the presentation go?"

"Very well," he answered. He let her go to walk around the kitchen, sampling each of the dishes until she slapped his hand. Laughing, he said: "They're going ahead with my design. Kick-off is four months from now." He eyed her seriously. "What do you say about living in Dubai during the first stage of construction?"

She pretended to mull that one over. "Hmm, where you go, I go, Teeny."

"Fantastic. Although, I'm going to miss you in skirts during that time."

"I think I can give you a little show behind closed doors," she teased.

"You drive a hard bargain, Bigfoot."

She rushed over to prevent him from opening a plastic container. "Don't touch that!"

"What's in there?" he complained. "You can't expect

me to lose interest, especially after you made such a big scene."

"I, uhm, called your mom to find out about your favourite dishes."

He raised an eyebrow. "You didn't think to ask *me*?"

"That's not the point," she muttered, pushing him out of the kitchen. "Anyway, she gave me a few family recipes. I spent the whole afternoon perfecting it, and you're not allowed to see it until it's time for dessert!"

He had a suspicion about what she could've baked. His mouth watered in anticipation. "You didn't have to go to the trouble."

"I'm almost your wife." She shrugged and turned on her heel to walk back to the stove. "There's every need!"

He grabbed her hand and pulled her into his arms. Peering into her eyes, he whispered: "I've got a surprise of my own."

"What's that?"

"I'm naming the building after you."

"You mean, it's going to have 'Asha' in the title?"

"Indirectly. I did some research into your name last night. You know that I struggle to fall asleep and, as beautiful as you are, I creep myself out when I stare at you for too long." He chuckled at her eye roll. "Anyway, I found out that one version of Asha means 'life'. The building is going to be called 'Life Towers International'."

She sniffed tearfully. "Why do you have to be romantic all the time?"

"Because I love you?"

Pulling his face down to hers, she kissed him lovingly, keeping a firm grip on the front of his jacket. She stepped away with a giggle when the doorbell buzzed, reminding her of their guests. "Can you get that? I have a snack platter to dolly up."

"Anything for you, Bigfoot," he said honestly. "I'm assuming I'm on entertainment duty?"

"Do you think you can manage that?"

"I'll be fine as long as I have my supporting act."

"Ha! Good luck getting me to participate!"

He laughed naughtily. "Oh, I will, Asha. Mark my words."

* * * * *

"I THOUGHT IT was a myth!"

Loikanos burst out laughing and handed another photograph over. "Nope, he really did take ballet."

"Teeny!" Asha exclaimed as she watched a younger version of her fiancé posing for *The Nutcracker*. His legs looked incredible in tights. It was everything she had imagined and more. "I'm changing your outfit for the wedding! Instead of pants, you're going to wear tights!"

"Hell no," Konstantinos argued, draining his glass of wine. "I'm never talking to you again, brother."

"Oh, please! If I had a million dollars every time I heard you say that—"

"Then you'd be richer than you are now?" Farida interrupted sweetly, fluttering her eyelashes.

Everyone laughed at the looks on the Sarantos brothers' faces: one was annoyed for literally having his history laid out on the table, while the other was doing the Math.

"You know, sis, I think you're right," Loikanos admitted finally.

"I like that the manly, rugged, sexy Konstantinos Sarantos has a softer side," Asha teased, lifting her glass to her fiancé.

"I don't," he grumbled.

"Why didn't you take ballet, *mon cher*?" Denise asked Loikanos.

"I saw my brother in tights and knew, with absolute certainty, that I never wanted to look that way."

Kashinath threw his head back and cackled. "Damn, dude! You're really looking for trouble, aren't you?"

"Come on, he's a tame little kitty cat!" Asha said, deliberately baiting Konstantinos, mostly because she loved his form of punishment.

As she expected, he rose to his feet and made his way to her end of the table. "Tame little kitty cat?" he asked as he pulled her into his arms. "I'll show you a tame little kitty cat."

"Teeny, we—"

He interrupted her with a thorough kiss. She sagged in his embrace, fireworks exploding all over her skin from the possessive, aggressive way he was conquering her mouth. Whoa, if she'd known this side of him sooner, they wouldn't have made it anywhere *close* to the altar without breaking his rule. She wished he would give in.

"Hoo boy," she heard Farida say, "you don't have another brother stashed away for me, do you?"

Loikanos chuckled. "Unless my father wasn't as faithful as he claims to be, I don't think so."

"Damn."

As quickly as Konstantinos had sexily accosted Asha, he stopped. It left her breathless. Her hands were shaking as she lifted them to tuck her hair behind her ears. The look in his dark brown eyes was going to cause her undoing.

"Tame little kitty cat?" he smirked.

"Hot, nasty, sexy jungle cat," she amended.

"That's better," he approved. He turned to their guests, who had entertained themselves in the meantime, and announced: "Anyone hungry? I think it's time for the main course."

"God, what is it with men and food?" Farida questioned. "I'm full already!"

"Believe me, it scares me to watch Teeny eat," Asha giggled. "I don't know about Loikanos, but I've never seen anyone consume so much food before, not even Kash."

"Yeah, they're on a whole different level," her brother agreed.

Loikanos shrugged and kissed his fiancée's cheek. "Like everything else, we simply enjoy our food. What's for dinner, Ash?"

She clapped her hands together excitedly. "Just wait till you see it! It's a feast!"

"I'll help," Farida said, jumping up before Asha could stop her.

Asha linked arms with her baby sister as they walked to the kitchen. "So, what do you think? Do we love him or hate him?"

"Ash, we adore him," Farida laughed. "I've never seen you this way! Praven never kissed you in front of other people. I'm so happy for you!"

"Thanks." Asha hugged her sister briefly. "If you want, I'll ask Denise to hook you up, too? She's very good at it."

"That's okay. I want to meet my future husband the old-fashioned way."

"You're braver than I am!" She handed two large bowls over. "Are you going to be okay carrying that? It's a cold salad. I'll wheel the warm stuff in."

Farida stared, as if she couldn't believe her ears. "I never thought I'd live to see the day *you*, Asha Dewali, become the perfect hostess. You never used to care about hosting parties!"

"Maybe there's a bit of Greek in me, after all." She leered at her sister. "Well, technically not yet."

Farida burst out laughing. "And now you're making sexual jokes? Seriously, what have you done to my sister?"

They kept joking around while taking the main course to the dining room, where Asha made a big show of unloading the meal trolley. She lifted the covers and loved that everyone licked their lips at the large marinated chicken, roasted vegetables, mashed potatoes and gravy in response.

She mentally made a promise that in a year's time she'll be able to cook a dinner like this, instead of buying it from a catering company.

Konstantinos topped up everyone's glasses and

entertained them with stories about his and Loikanos' childhood, carefully sidestepping the ballet jibes that were still fresh in his guests' minds. While they ate, the conversation flowed, despite no one being able to leave their mouths empty for too long. Asha used to think that socializing was an unnecessary thing that people did to pass the time but, now that she was a part of something bigger than her own boxed view of the world, she really enjoyed it.

She couldn't wait to see her future husband's face when she announced what was for dessert. Prompted by Kolina's quick acceptance of her, Asha had made a phone call to her mother-in-law to get a feel for Konstantinos' favourite things. She might've been able to observe him during their month together, but it was always better to get a man's mother's opinions.

"Are you ready for the next round, Teeny?" Asha asked as she removed the last dirty dishes from the table.

His eyes twinkled at her. "I can't wait to see what you pull out of your hat, Bigfoot."

"You two are so weird with those nicknames," Kashinath muttered to himself. "I thought you were supposed to give each other something sexy?"

"He wouldn't know sexy if it bit him in the ass," Asha giggled.

"'Aah-s'," Konstantinos mocked with a chuckle. "That never gets old."

She made a quick roundtrip to the kitchen to get dessert, glad that Farida had already taken care of small side plates. Placing the platter in front of Konstantinos,

Asha lifted the lid and said: "Ta-dah!"

"Holy smokes, bro, is that what I think it is?" Loikanos asked as he jumped to his feet to get a closer look.

Konstantinos stared with a smile on his face. Then, pulling her onto his lap, he pressed his nose into her hair and whispered: "Thank you, Asha."

"You're welcome. I'm not guaranteeing that it's as good as your mother's, but she talked me through the whole process. It was the longest conversation I've ever had over the phone."

"Let's try it, then. Will you dish for me?"

She eyed him cheekily. "Just this once, but you've got to start doing things yourself at some point." She yelped in surprise when he spanked her as soon as she was back on her feet, feeling her face heat up while everyone laughed. Lifting a piece of *galaktoboureko*, which was essentially the Greek version of a normal custard slice, onto a plate, she told everyone to pass it along to the next person, leaving Konstantinos for last.

"Aren't you having some?" he asked her, getting his fork.

"I've already had far too much of that," she replied while patting her stomach. She went to sit down at the other end of the table again, watching him curiously.

"It's as if mama made it herself," Loikanos groaned, shovelling another large bite into his mouth.

Konstantinos chewed thoughtfully, eyes closed. "Hmm, Bigfoot, this is really good! It's like being home!"

She beamed at him, accepting the praise. She'd

worked her little butt off to make it, so he'd better appreciate her efforts! At the same time, it felt good knowing that she could do something so special for him. Perhaps there was a chef in her, after all.

They finished off the evening with a nightcap but, after seeing that it was nearly twelve o'clock, she insisted that everyone spend the night. The penthouse had enough room, especially since she's moved into the main bedroom with her fiancé. She quickly double-checked that each bed had enough blankets before wishing them all a good night.

She took a bath, slipped into comfortable cotton briefs and a tank top, and walked to bed. Konstantinos looked glorious, shirtless as always, while he typed something on his laptop. "Ready for bed, Teeny?"

"I think I can sleep for an hour or two," he responded, glancing up. "You look beautiful."

She unclipped her hair and shook it out before getting into bed. "I feel so stuffed, I can hardly move."

"I'm pretty sure you're going to wish my brother feels the same in a moment," he chuckled. Closing his laptop, he put it on the large nightstand next to him and got under the covers. "You had to give them the room closest to ours, didn't you? He can't keep his hands off Denise."

"That doesn't sound familiar at all, huh?" she joked. She loved how he pulled her into his embrace so they were spooning, and rested her arms on his when he nuzzled her neck. "Why doesn't he share your sentiments about sex before marriage, though?"

"Who knows?" He kissed her shoulder. "Thank you

for a wonderful evening, Asha. I had so much fun."

She sighed with relief. "I'm glad." She froze once she heard muffled moaning sounds coming from the room next to theirs, and was that...? She swore she could identify the soft thumping noise of a headboard bouncing off a wall, but that's not possible, right? "Uhm..."

Konstantinos laughed softly, shifting closer to her. "Yup, it is what you think it is."

"Damn, is that what I've got to look forward to? I mean, I don't mind that you're a beast in bed, but what if we're in a public hotel or staying at your parents' place?"

"Then I guess I'll have to take you against a wall, but I can't promise that you won't get a concussion."

She giggled. "On second thought, maybe it's better to make noise. I don't want to be brain dead by age thirty."

"Are you planning on having sex with me that often, Bigfoot?"

"How many concussions can one sustain before being declared brain dead?"

He laughed into her hair. "I think five a week is conservative enough to please most doctors."

They were silent for a while, listening to Loikanos and Denise having sex. She tried her best not to laugh but, after holding it in for about five minutes, her body started shaking. Konstantinos let out a loud guffaw, which set off her giggles.

"What do you think they're saying now?" she sniggered.

"I don't think they're doing much talking."

"People don't talk during sex?"

He turned her around and got on top of her, his eyes sparkling with humour. "Unless someone's doing something wrong, they shouldn't be talking."

"Well then, aren't you in for a surprise."

Kissing her softly, he murmured: "If I can't make you shut up for at least fifteen minutes, then maybe we shouldn't get married."

"Game on, Teeny," she moaned, locking her arms around his neck and fusing her mouth to his. It turned out that he could prevent her from talking for half an hour, even while fully clothed. Somehow, he had the ability to make her feel desired and sexy, without getting inappropriately grabby. She was experiencing so many firsts with him.

When they finally cuddled up to each other and fell asleep, Loikanos and Denise were still at it, and Asha thought how tiring it must be to make love that long. She was sure, though, that Konstantinos was going to change her mind about that, just like he did everything else.

She couldn't wait.

CHAPTER 30

THERE WERE ONLY seven days to go until the wedding. Asha, contrary to her personality up to this point, wasn't nervous. In fact, she could hardly contain her excitement. She badly wanted to be Mrs. Sarantos!

"Do you have any idea what Denise planned for tonight?"

"It looks like there might be a burlesque element, and some entertainers," Asha told Marietta, securing a thin gold band around her head. A big, red flower was pinned to one side of her head, and reminded her of the style most women wore in the 1920s. "Thank you for the ideas you've given her, M. Who knows what they would've dreamed up without you?"

"Well, I remembered how much you loved that show we saw."

"That was such a cool evening! I swear I should've been born in that era."

"Yeah, you look so good in those clothes," her best

friend muttered.

Asha frowned and turned to the Italian woman. "Is everything okay? I feel like I did or said something wrong."

Marietta seemed horrified. "Not at all, Ash! I'm just nervous. Everything's happening so fast." She smiled wryly. "I always assumed that I would be the first to get married out of the two of us, you know?"

Wishing that she could come clean about her situation, Asha sighed and nodded. "Believe me, the proposal caught me off guard. I didn't want to get married to anyone, but it's hard to say no to someone like Konstantinos."

"I can tell he makes you very happy."

"He does, every day. I can't believe I ever doubted him." Asha wondered if she was imagining the hint of resentment in her friend's facial expression. "How about you? I know you've always enjoyed the single life, but are you going to the wedding with anyone?"

"Nah, I'm going on my own."

"Wait until you see some of my cousins." She winked and turned back to the mirror to apply her makeup. "I'm sure they're your type, and most of them are still single."

"I don't know if I have a type anymore."

Before Asha could ask Marietta to clarify, the rest of her bridesmaids streamed into the room with lively babbling. They gushed over each other's outfits while they finished their looks. Denise showed up and ushered them out of the penthouse suite.

"I'm really sorry about the other night, *chérie*," Denise

apologized yet again, pulling Asha to one side. If the blush on her cheeks was anything to go by, she was mortified. "I give you my oath that I never—"

"It's okay," Asha interrupted with a smile. "I think it's great that you're passionate about each other. Don't let what Teeny said influence an otherwise good night: he can't sleep anyway."

"I know that." The French woman sighed. "Loikanos might be very mature in some ways, but he doesn't always know what is socially acceptable."

"Oh, please! It's good that someone's having sex. It shouldn't matter where you do it."

Denise linked her arm with Asha's. "I am assuming that Konstantinos is still, uh, holding out on that front?"

"That's the damn understatement of the year," Asha mumbled.

"I'm sure it will be worth the wait, *chérie*."

Asha secretly hoped so. Considering the build-up of anticipation, it would be disappointing if it's over in two minutes.

They kept the conversation light as they rushed into the awaiting limousine. The thing that was becoming increasingly stranger to Asha was that she felt more comfortable in Denise's company than her best friend's. Something about Marietta triggered alarm bells. It's almost as if Marietta has taken on a rough, conniving energy, reminding Asha of the months leading up to Marietta's psychological break.

For the life of her, Asha couldn't understand what's wrong. They've always talked about anything—that was simply the nature of their relationship—so why was Marietta emotionally shutting down? Has something happened during Asha's absence that Marietta was too embarrassed to confess?

Could so much have changed during lockdown that Marietta was reconsidering their friendship? Was she hurt by the engagement, because she believed Asha deliberately kept it from her? And if so, why wasn't she saying anything?

Asha suppressed a sigh as the limo pulled over at the venue of her bachelorette party. She would like to believe that she could have a husband, a successful career and a best friend, but it was beginning to look like something had to give. In her current state of mind, she wasn't sure which one she was willing to give up.

The women all looked glamorous in their twenties-inspired outfits, gushing animatedly as they walked into the building. Asha trailed behind them, next to Denise. Maybe she was becoming more mature now that she was on her way to being a wife.

They entered a large conference area that could've been a set for *The Great Gatsby*. Asha was awed by the amount of detail Denise has brought to life. From the lighting to the tables, to the stage, to the overall decor, everything screamed the early era of Hollywood.

"This is amazing," she murmured appreciatively, pulling Denise into a hug. "Thank you so much."

"Wait until you see your fiancé, *chérie*," Denise giggled. "He's right over there."

Asha lifted her gaze and forgot how to breathe. Standing with his brother and friends, Konstantinos looked mouth-wateringly handsome. His pinstriped jacket was open, revealing a matching waistcoat and dark red shirt with the top three buttons undone. There was a gold chain dangling from the fitted waistcoat. The fedora was stylishly tipped forward on his head.

At that moment, she decided that she would be adding a male portfolio to her next fashion line. She was going to use Konstantinos, the embodiment of male perfection, as her inspiration.

He glanced up as if he'd been eavesdropping on her thoughts, and smiled warmly once they made eye contact. He excused himself from his group and strode to her. "You are so gorgeous," he whispered, taking her in his arms. "I can't believe you're going to be my wife."

"Only if you behave," she teased. There was no doubt in her mind that he would be satisfied with a monogamous lifestyle. "How great is this place?"

"Stunning," he agreed. "Denise did a great job, as always."

"Why don't you tell her that yourself?" She pulled out of his embrace and turned around, blinking in confusion when the French go-to woman was nowhere to be seen. "She was right here a minute ago!"

"She gave us some time together." Konstantinos took her hand in his. "Come on, I want you to meet my friends."

"Are these the ones who are just as raunchy as you used to be?"

He burst out laughing. "Yes, and believe me: you're not the only one who's noticed the change in my behaviour. They're still harassing me for turning into an honest man."

"Lies and deceit can probably be sexy, in a way, but I prefer integrity."

Winking at her, he cleared his throat as they arrived at the group of men who, like their leader, were incredibly good-looking and, damn, did they know it! Konstantinos introduced her, tucking her body into his side whenever she felt uncomfortable from the string of compliments heading her way.

The old Asha would never have fallen for their one-liners, and would've shrugged them off as womanizing bastards, because she had secretly been insecure about herself. The new Asha, though, quite enjoyed the attention, although she didn't want to get too appreciative of the things they said. She didn't want to develop a big ego.

The MC for the evening was a popular British comedian and called everyone to order. Once they were at their designated tables, with the engaged couple stationed in the middle of the room, he started his set. He had people in stitches in no time.

"Now, I believe that the parents have made a montage to show everyone just how far these two come," he said, gesturing to the large screen that was being lowered to the stage. "I'm sure we'd all love to see embarrassing pictures from their childhood, so let's get to it!"

Konstantinos groaned and whispered into her ear: "I swear, if mama put those ballet pictures up…"

Resisting her giggle, Asha kept her eyes on the screen, dismayed to see that her story was on display first.

The infamously deep voice of Louis Armstrong started singing in the background about a wonderful world, igniting giggles from the crowd once they saw a topless baby Asha standing in a small plastic, portable swimming pool.

"Oh, for the love of God!" she protested softly, burying her face in Konstantinos' rumbling chest. She smacked his arm. "Don't laugh!"

"But you're cute, Bigfoot," he chuckled.

She wondered why her parents had to be so damn embarrassing while she reluctantly pulled her gaze back to the screen. The rest of the presentation wasn't much better. Pictures of her as a bubbly toddler slowly faded, one over the other, as the years of her life progressed. By the time she was ten, the only time she appeared on a picture was if someone noticed the girl sitting in the corner of the room with a book on her lap.

"So serious," her fiancé murmured.

The next part of the montage showed her teenage years and the multiple awards she had received, both in school and during her short-lived career as a show-jumper. She'd given up horse-riding at age eighteen, mostly due to Praven.

When she thought about it, she realized that she had let go of many of her life's passions to please him and, in the end, they hadn't even pleased each other. Retrospect was 20/20 vision, as they say. She was happy her relationship with Konstantinos was different. So far, he only inspired her to achieve greater heights in her career.

"Thank God that's over," Asha muttered once the

slideshow stopped. She poked her fiancé in the stomach. "Your turn, Teeny!"

James Brown's *I Feel Good* blared out of the speakers as the baby version of Konstantinos appeared on the screen with dark, thick hair that was styled in a Mohawk. His overeager grin was infectious, and Asha found herself wishing that their kids would look that happy one day.

"You're adorable," she teased, nibbling on his ear.

"Mama's going to pay for this."

Slide by slide, the presentation depicted Konstantinos' life as a young boy and teenager. Though none of those dreaded ballet photographs ever showed, there was still plenty of proof that he hadn't always been the naughty boy that she had assumed. In fact, she was stunned to learn that he'd done very well, academically.

All too soon, the montage changed the focus to them as a couple, with India.Arie's *Ready For Love* as the theme song. Somehow, Denise had got a hold of the photographs Asha and Konstantinos had taken together during their confinement. They were pulling all sorts of funny faces and laughing out loud in most of them. If they'd been able to post on social media, these were the kind of pictures they would've put up on Instagram.

There were photos of the engagement party on the day they had been set free, as well as the other night's sibling-get-together.

Until now, Asha hadn't realized what a perfect couple they were on face-value. Thanks to their genetics, they looked like they were meant to be: they both had dark hair and naturally bronze skin, but there were enough differences to keep things interesting.

Everyone cheered once the presentation was over, clapping and whistling approvingly. The MC skipped back onto the stage, grinning at the audience.

"Before we start the sexy part of the evening, we have a surprise for Asha from her hubby-to-be," he announced, waggling his eyebrows. "Please help me give a warm welcome to the one, the only... John Legend!"

Asha's mouth fell open and she looked at Konstantinos in surprise. "You didn't!"

"I did," he confirmed, smiling broadly.

"Oh my God! Have I ever told you I love you?"

"I don't think so," he quipped.

She gave him a big smacker of a kiss on the mouth. "I love you, Teeny!"

He laughed happily. "You better keep your eye on the prize, Bigfoot, or you're going to miss him."

Doing as she was told, she applauded louder than anyone else when the enigmatic entertainer sauntered over to the black grand piano on the centre of the stage. He waved at her with his signature dimply smile before taking his seat.

He played three of her favourite tracks. She loved how cheeky he could be at times, giving the crowd a knowing look before falling into another pun-filled lyric, and wondered for the millionth time why the man wasn't more famous. He played piano like a modern-day Mozart; he could clearly hold a note; and he was sexy to boot. Who wouldn't want those characteristics in their favourite artists?

"I'm starting to think this was a mistake," Konstantinos joked once the performer finished his set. "You couldn't take your eyes off him."

"Are you surprised?" She laughed breathlessly. "Wow, Teeny, I didn't know you were going to outdo me tonight!"

"I wanted to show you that I pay attention to what you say every once in a while."

"I knew my tone-deaf singing in the shower was working on your nerves!"

"I'm glad you enjoyed that."

She jumped on his lap and hugged him tightly. "Best fiancé ever," she whispered, feeling close to tears because she was so happy. She only hoped that these random chivalrous acts were going to continue over the course of their partnership.

* * * * *

KONSTANTINOS WAS HAVING a blast.

From the burlesque show, to the various musical performances, to the crazy dancing with his fiancée… It was all perfect. His friends and family were enjoying themselves. Life really couldn't get better than this.

"Gosh, I'm so thirsty," Asha shouted over the loud music. "I'm going to get a bottle of water; do you want some?"

"Please," he answered, his eyes following her as she moved through the crowd to the bar in the far corner.

It wasn't long before one of his friends fell into step with her. Konstantinos smiled, happy that she was fitting into his life so well.

He nearly had a heart attack when Marietta appeared in front of him with a smile that looked devilishly wicked, especially in the strobe-lighting of the room. Her dark hair was styled in unruly curls, and her outfit was much more revealing than everyone else's.

"Care to dance?" she asked.

"Sure." He kept his hands on acceptable places as he led her into a jive. The live band was incredible and, even though most people couldn't dance the different styles perfectly, they were doing a damn good job trying. Sometimes, attitude made up for lack of skill, as was apparent tonight.

"I can't seem to get Asha alone for more than five seconds," Marietta told him.

"Things will probably calm down once the wedding's out of the way. You know how it goes with these events."

"It's very frustrating! I really want to set up a coffee date with her."

He frowned slightly. "She said that she couldn't get a hold of you."

"Yeah, I was out of town for a bit." She smiled deceptively sweetly, but Konstantinos' frown merely deepened. "Do you know what her schedule's like tomorrow? I was thinking of popping in to say hi and spending some time with her."

"As far as I know, she's going to Westminster Abbey with Denise for some last-minute arrangements in the decorations."

"Oh? What time?"

He was uncomfortable discussing this with her. Wasn't she Asha's maid of honour? Didn't they share everything? At the same time, though, he didn't want to upset the applecart. If Asha could slip into his friendship circles with ease, then he should try to do the same.

"I think from ten to twelve," he answered. "It's always difficult to say. Women are weird about weddings."

"How about you? How's life treating you now that you're back?"

"Not too badly. I have leave from work until after the honeymoon's finished. Denise is making sure we're both relaxed before saying 'I do'," he said, chuckling to himself.

Marietta grinned. "Asha's very lucky to have a guy like you. Not only are you a lot of fun, but you also take your responsibilities very seriously. I heard about the Dubai project. You must be excited!"

"Yeah, Asha and I will spend a few months there." He couldn't explain it, but a dark look flitted over her otherwise pretty face. It was gone before he could interpret it, making him wonder if he'd imagined it. "We're lucky that our business isn't focused in one particular city, and that we can travel to stay together."

"Very lucky," Marietta muttered, dropping her gaze from his.

"Oh, hey!" Asha exclaimed cheerfully as she approached them. She tugged her best friend away from him and gave Marietta a firm hug. "I've been looking for you!"

"She was just asking me about your schedule tomorrow," Konstantinos told his fiancée. He accepted the water bottle from Asha, dropping a kiss on her head. "You two should discuss it while I catch my breath."

Walking away from the dance floor, he wondered why he felt so dirty. Sure, he's been dancing non-stop for a very large part of the evening, but sweat wasn't the kind of filth that made his skin crawl. It's almost as if some slick, sticky substance had latched onto him at some point, ruining his good mood completely.

Looking back on it, he had begun feeling it during and after dancing with Marietta.

He rolled the sleeves of his collared shirt up and turned his gaze to the two best friends, who were conversing in the middle of the dance floor. Asha looked happy while she gestured wildly but, whenever she glanced away to wave at someone who tried to get her attention, he noticed those dark shadows hanging over Marietta's head. He couldn't figure out why she was being such a drip.

"Everything okay?" Loikanos asked in Greek.

"I don't know," the older Sarantos brother replied slowly. "Have you spoken to Marietta yet?"

"Asha's friend? No, she keeps to herself."

"Well, give me an outsider's point of view." Konstantinos pointed to the two women. "What do you see, bro?"

Loikanos regarded the Italian woman seriously. "I see

someone who's hurt and trying hard not to show it. She's also got a lot of anger in her, huh? Look how tense she is. It's almost as if she doesn't want anything to do with Asha anymore." Here, he glanced at his brother. "She looks like trouble."

Nodding, Konstantinos said: "That's what I thought."

"Isn't this something you should discuss with Asha?"

"I don't want her to feel like I'm dictating who she can and can't spend her time with. She's a grown woman, and I'm going to treat her like one."

"I think you should mention it. Asha doesn't come across as unreasonable."

He hesitated. "I'll talk to her about it later tonight."

"Tomorrow's your last night together before you get married." Loikanos eyed him, grinning. "Are you finally going to have sex with her?"

"Unlike you, I can keep it in my pants."

"I swear our roles have reversed."

"It's true! You're a man-whore now."

Loikanos' gaze found Denise, who was laughing with Asha's parents. "Only for her, hey. I've always believed in true love, and she's it."

"I'm happy for you, bro," Konstantinos said, slapping his brother on the back. "Now, are you ready to have some shots to celebrate the last few days of my so-called freedom?"

"Why do you think I walked over here in the first place?" Loikanos looked pretty damn pleased with himself as he gestured to their group of friends. "They've already set everything up. Are you ready for a hangover that you're not likely to forget?"

Konstantinos rolled his eyes. "Let's see what you've got, baby brother."

* * * * *

MARIETTA WAS MAD as hell. Her bubbly facade was beginning to falter, too: she could feel it sliding from her face the longer Asha gushed about her perfect life. Marietta knew she wasn't acting like a friend, but she just didn't care anymore. Asha might believe differently, but Marietta hasn't been her best friend for the last five weeks.

She's become her worst enemy.

She still couldn't believe that Konstantinos hadn't reacted to her advances. She had assumed that it would be easy for him to respond to her, but the man was obviously so far up Asha's ass that he hasn't seen the light of day in a long time. He had absolutely no idea what he was missing.

Marietta wasn't going to give up. The first part of her plan might not have unfolded the way she had anticipated, but she's never been the type of girl who rolled over and played dead just because of one little setback. The rest of her scheme was going forward, full steam ahead.

She will *not* fail.

"M, are you okay? You've got the strangest look on your face."

Snapping out of her reverie, she told Asha: "Sorry, I've got the worst period cramps."

Asha nodded empathetically. "I had bad ones this month, too. I'm surprised that didn't break up my engagement, actually."

I don't need your stupid cramps to jeopardize your wedding. I have bigger, better things waiting in the pipeline.

"I think I'm going to sit down," Marietta mumbled, turning on the theatrics. "It was a bad idea to dance."

"Okay, but let me know about tomorrow, in case I don't see you again? I'd love to go for coffee."

"I'll give you a ring when I'm on my way over!" she called over her shoulder. Rushing to the table she shared with the rest of the bridesmaids, she quickly got her phone out of her pocket, suspecting that she might have received an important message.

Is everything set up?

She hurriedly typed her response, adrenaline flowing through her veins.

Yes. Tomorrow. Will stay in touch.

Putting her phone away, she lifted her flute of champagne to her mouth and sipped at the deliciously expensive bubbly. Her gaze shifted across the room, watching everyone having fun. Her eyes locked on the happy couple.

"Soon, Asha," she whispered to herself, "soon you'll wish that you could've stayed in this moment forever."

CHAPTER 31

"HOLY CRAP, THIS place gives me the creeps."

Denise giggled softly. "This isn't something I decided, *chérie*. Your parents insisted on following the tradition to the T."

Staring at the delicate and incredibly intricate designs on the walls and ceiling of Westminster Abbey, Asha suddenly understood why Konstantinos didn't want to get married here. No one was really allowed to make a sound while inside and the building was so old… Plus, there were actual tombs in here!

"Teeny told me it would be like this, but I was thinking about something else at the time," Asha murmured softly. "Are you sure we can't get married in a normal church?"

"It's too late for that now, Asha. Everything is set in stone, so to speak."

"No pressure, huh?" She took a couple of steps toward the altar, trying to imagine what she will feel when she said her vows, but it was almost as if this place messed with her ability to visualize. She kneeled on the stage and let out a sigh. "Denise, I'm scared."

"Why, *chérie?*"

"What if it's not what I think it's going to be? I mean, it's great that this tradition exists—you know, locking two people in an apartment to make them fall in love— but I think it actually does more damage than good in this day and age."

Denise dropped to her hunches with a frown. "I'm not sure I follow."

"Well, we've been removed from the real world for so long. Even now that we're out, it's this big, fun celebration, but it won't always be like that. Once I'm officially back at work and he starts on that Dubai project…" Asha looked at her hands on her lap. "When we're a normal couple, who's to say that we won't fall apart?"

"Unfortunately, relationships are difficult to predict." Denise's expression was solemn. "I have my doubts about Loikanos. Everything's happened so fast, and I think that is why you and I are getting along as well as we do. We can relate to one another. At the end of the day, *chérie*, nothing is certain. Change is inevitable. And if it doesn't work out, at least you tried, right? Why look down that endless abyss of negativity if it might not even materialize?" She smiled kindly. "You will only miss out on all the good things, Asha."

Wiping her tears, Asha attempted to smile back. "I should just take it day by day, huh?"

"What else can you do? Live in the moment, Asha,

and in your heart… Ignore your head as far as you can." Denise laughed wryly. "You don't want to become a thirty-five-year-old woman filled with regrets, believe me."

Asha appreciated the advice. "When is your wedding, by the way? I've been so wrapped up in my stupid issues that I keep forgetting to ask."

"We haven't set a date yet. Loikanos wants to get married as quickly as possible, but I don't want a rushed job." She gestured to their surroundings. "Not on this scale either, though. I want to wear a white dress and have a couple of witnesses."

Asha grinned. "You shouldn't back down on that, Denise. If he gives you any trouble, send him to me: I'll show him what it's like to have an Indian sister."

"I have a more effective form of punishment, *chérie*," the French woman teased with a wink, "but I will keep that in mind. He can be quite stubborn at times." She slapped her knees and rose to her feet. "Do you want to practice walking down the aisle?"

"Uhm, our wedding isn't going to be broadcasted to the rest of the world, right?" Asha gulped nervously. "I don't think I could stomach that."

"Do not worry, Asha. It will be private, despite the extensive guest list."

"Yeah, about that," she muttered. "Did you have to invite my whole family? They're a bunch of hooligans!"

Denise laughed. "I have learnt that, yes. Although I was in charge of sending the invitations, I was only doing as I was told by your mother and Kolina."

"I'm seriously starting to doubt their taste in people."

"As am I, Asha," Denise giggled. "As am I."

* * * * *

KONSTANTINOS GOT THE last slice of his favourite dessert from the fridge, not caring that there were more calories in *it* than in a large pizza. He was planning on exercising within the hour, and decided that he could always put some extra effort in to ensure it didn't go directly to his waist.

If he didn't watch himself, Asha was going to fatten him up in no time. It's no small feat to cook as well as Kolina Sarantos but, because his mother adored his fiancée, he had this nasty suspicion that Asha's skills will go from strength to strength. Maybe that's why his father had such a nice collection of fat around his abdominal area.

It seems the way to a man's heart was through his stomach, after all.

Trudging over to the study, he plopped down on his chair while he ate the delicious slice of custard. He started his computer to check his emails. Since winning the Dubai project, he's been in constant contact with the construction part of his father's empire. He's never been on Skype as much as recent days, but he was enjoying himself. It was good feeling like a man, like someone that could provide for Asha.

Sure, she had more than enough money in a trust fund to take care of herself, but he was determined to make sure she wouldn't need a penny of it.

He smiled once he saw an email from his brother and

clicked to open it.

From: Loikanos Sarantos
To: Konstantinos Sarantos
Subject: Weddings & Funerals

*Hi, bro, whaddup? :-) I know, I know, I really should learn
to phone you, but what can I say? This has become a habit.
Anyway, I'm thinking of where I can get married to Denise...
Any ideas? And don't say West-Spinster Abbey! :P Get it?*

His brother was, for lack of a better word, a
blubbering idiot at times. He quickly typed a response
with the normal suggestions—a beach somewhere, in
front of a judge, Vegas—and got back to work. There
were a couple of reports on the ground testing that had
been done on location in Dubai. He was satisfied to see
that the foundation would support the weight of his
building.

A bit depressed now that his last bit of desert was
finished, he took his plate to the kitchen and hurried to
the main bedroom to get changed into more
comfortable clothes to exercise in. He wore a loose-
fitting shirt, mostly because Asha wasn't home to
admire his toned torso. He loved how her eyes always
stayed glued to his stomach whenever he waltzed
around half-naked.

He got hard thinking about the way she'll stare once
they became sexual. He couldn't wait to see what she'll
be like. Has he improved her confidence enough for
her to be a wild cat, or will she still be submissive?

Either way, he looked forward to finding out.

As he made his way downstairs to the gym, he heard a beep coming from the study. Curiosity made him walk to his computer to read the latest email.

From: Loikanos Sarantos
To: Konstantinos Sarantos
Subject: RE: Weddings & Funerals

Thanks for the sarcastic reply, it's greatly appreciated. If I go all the way to Vegas, will you still be my best man? PS: I found the perfect song for your first dance with Asha! Sure, some of the older folks won't like it, but maybe you can get an acoustic version? LOL! :-)

Curious, he opened the link and pressed play. He was familiar with some of Papa Roach's songs, but this one didn't ring a bell. The moment the guy started singing, though, Konstantinos was sold on *No Matter What.*

He quickly added the song to his Apple Music playlist and synced his iPhone before heading to the gym. He sighed with frustration when the doorbell rang as he was about to step over the threshold.

Grumbling under his breath, he marched to the intercom and pressed the button. "What?" he barked.

"I-I'm sorry to disturb you, Mr. Sarantos," the guard at reception stammered. "There is a Marietta Angelotti here to see Miss Dewali?"

Konstantinos sighed. "Send her up."

Great, now he had to entertain one of Asha's friends. He didn't even like Marietta, especially after last night's party. If Loikanos, his sometimes-intellectually-challenged baby brother, could sense that something was off about the Italian heiress, then there should be a big danger sign to accompany her wherever she went. Something like: "Befriend at own risk. The manufacturer will not be liable for any damage sustained during use".

He chuckled at his mental joke but dropped the smile as soon as the elevator doors parted. He gave an internal groan once he saw her revealing outfit. Did she draw inspiration from the lady-of-the-night theme? Her skirt was too short, especially considering the raging snowstorm outside, and her jacket was unzipped to show off her ample bosom.

In the past, he might've seen her as an easy, quick lay, but he was a monogamous man now.

"Asha's not back yet," he informed her. "You can wait in the living room, though. I'm going to exercise for a few hours."

She pouted at him, her red-tinted lips holding none of the magnetism of his fiancée's. "Aw, I was hoping you'd keep me company until she gets back."

"Sorry, no can do," he said, clenching his jaw in irritation. "I have a strict schedule and, if I don't hit the gym right now, I'm going to get fat from Asha's cooking."

Marietta blinked in surprise. "Asha cooks? Since when?"

"Her and mama are two peas in a pod. She's getting all of the family recipes, and mama doesn't give anyone the family recipes, not even to those of us who are biologically related."

Taking off her puffy jacket to reveal a skimpy top underneath, Marietta smirked. "It seems that absolutely no one can resist Asha."

He had no idea where this venom was coming from and no desire whatsoever to find out. "Well, I'm going to lift some weights. Make yourself at home."

"Oh, I will," she vowed in a syrupy tone.

He shuddered as soon as he was out of her presence. He hoped that Asha would come home soon because, if she took her time today, he might forget about his mental promises and force her to end this friendship with Marietta.

* * * * *

THE MAN WAS infuriating!

Here she was, dressed in barely anything at all, and the notorious playboy was keeping his hands to himself! What was it going to take for him to notice her, to realize that he was seriously missing out?

Marietta calmed her breathing before she shrieked her frustration to the heavens. No man has ever been able to resist her in this kind of outfit: she had incredible legs, a tiny waist and breasts out to *here*, for heaven's sake! What the hell was his problem? He couldn't be *that* in love with Asha, could he? The man was a womanizer! A leopard never changed its spots!

Her phone vibrated, bringing her back to the present. A cold chill went down her spine as she read the text message.

Left W/A. Will be there in 30min. Is everything ready?

What the hell? She glanced at her watch and fumed in silence for a moment. Asha was early! Why couldn't the stupid woman take her time?

Minor complication. Everything WILL be ready.

She put her phone down after sending her reply and raked her fingers through her hair. Okay, she'll have to improvise. This is a small setback, but it doesn't have to ruin the plan. In fact, the time limit could be the best thing that's happened to her in weeks.

Reading the next text that came through, she bristled at her contact's abrupt tone.

It better be. Hurry.

"Don't tell me what to do," she muttered angrily, her fingers nearly pressing her fingers right through the screen.

Stay on them. She'll come running.

Stuffing her phone back into her handbag, she left it on the chaise in the entryway and stormed over to the gym, where she could hear some pathetic man singing that no matter what happened, he'll always love his sweetheart.

Asha's turned Konstantinos Sarantos into a shell of his former self. He wasn't the type of man to sell his soul to monogamy. Why even entertain the notion?

Her steps slowed into a swaying walk as she entered the gym. She twirled her hair around a finger and placed her free hand on her hip. He was running on the treadmill, facing her way. She winked and smiled.

"My, it's always a thrill watching a man exercise," she

purred.

His dark eyes narrowed to slits. "Can I help you?"

"I'm bored, darling," she replied, licking her lips in invitation. "Can you talk and run at the same time?"

"I don't want to."

Red-hot rage pulsed through her. She barely kept it in check. "Fine, fine, then I'll look around for a sex toy and help myself," she said dramatically. "Can I bring you a bottle of water? You'll need it in a few minutes."

He glanced around and his face softened once he realized that he didn't have one already. "If it's not too much trouble," he conceded, keeping his voice level.

She grinned. "Of course not, darling. Be right back."

Excitement was steadily overriding the anger. She grabbed a small, Ziploc bag of pills from her handbag and went into the kitchen. She opened the fridge to get a bottle of water, emptied three tablets into the water and shook the bottle once it was closed. Eventually, the formula settled enough so it didn't look suspicious.

She took him the bottle with a smile. "There you go, darling."

"Thanks," he mumbled, taking a huge swig before putting it in the cradle.

Looking around the gym, she only had to wait for a few minutes before the dose began affecting him. She bit on the inside of her cheeks to prevent herself from laughing. It was like taking candy from a baby.

"Whoa!" he gasped.

She glanced over her shoulder. "Is everything okay?"

"I feel…" He switched the treadmill off and rubbed his forehead.

"You look like you're going to pass out!" she cried out dramatically.

"I need to… lie down."

She hurried to him to support some of his weight. "Come on, I'll get you to bed before you hurt yourself."

"Just give… me—"

"Shh, darling, don't try to talk."

She barely managed to guide him up the stairs. The man was much taller than her, and his body was ninety percent muscle. She sighed with relief once he collapsed on the bed, smiling to herself.

Finally.

She pulled his clothes and shoes from his body, her eyes nearly popping out of her skull once she glimpsed the spot between his muscular thighs. That little bitch! Not only did Asha have the hottest man as her fiancé, but she also had access to the best package? The man was not even erect! Life was too unfair.

Running downstairs once he was naked, she hurriedly checked her phone, her heart beating wildly when she read the text.

THREE BLOCKS AWAY.

"Showtime," she whispered excitedly, making her way back to the main bedroom. She dropped pieces of clothing along the way until she was naked, too. Then, feeling alive for the first time in a while, she climbed onto Konstantinos' unconscious form.

* * * * *

ASHA COULDN'T WAIT to get home. She loved

spending time with Denise, but she had to warn Konstantinos what he was up against. She still got chills whenever she thought about the eerie atmosphere in Westminster Abbey. It was, in short, hauntingly beautiful.

"Thanks, Pierce," she said as her bodyguard opened her door for her. She paused and turned to him, fixing him with a solid stare. "You know, that was a really good show you put on the other day."

He paused. "I beg your pardon, Miss Dewali?"

"Don't pretend you don't know! Asking for my phone like that?" She grinned. "I think you should move to Hollywood, 'cause your talents are being wasted under my father's employment."

He burst out laughing while she opened the door and went inside. She was giggling to herself as she entered the private elevator. She couldn't wait to tell this story to Konstantinos: he would find it hilarious.

The lift pinged once it arrived on the top floor, and the doors opened.

"Teeny?" she called, taking off her coat and gloves and stashing her handbag on chaise. She frowned at the Guess bag on it. "Do we have guests? Teeny?"

She only became aware of the noises once she was in the living room. Her frown deepened as she followed it up the stairs, wondering what the hell was going on. Was he watching a movie? That would explain why he hadn't heard her call. "Teeny?" she exclaimed. "Where are you?"

She came to an abrupt halt at the top of the stairs, staring at the piece of woman's clothing in confusion.

Her head whipped up in the direction of her bedroom when someone shouted out in joy.

"Oh my God!" the woman squealed.

Turn around and walk away. You don't need to see this.

She's never been very good at listening to something trying to save her sanity, whether it be an actual person or a random thought. She was a sucker for punishment. She had to see this for herself.

Slowly, she moved down the hallway, sliding her hand along the wall for support in case she stumbled. With every step, she could see a bit more of the big bed she's been sharing with Konstantinos for nearly two weeks.

Then she was in the doorway, gazing in horror at the betrayal in front of her.

Her fiancé.

In bed.

With another woman.

He was out cold already. The woman was tucked into his side—a cuddle that he frequently shared with Asha—and smiling sleepily. They were naked, with the duvet covering up to their waists. They were also very sweaty.

This isn't what it looks like!

She shook her head once. Her fiancé was in bed with another woman, naked. They had their arms around each other, and they had obviously been up to some kind of physical activity if the glistening drops of perspiration were anything to go by.

Let him explain!

What was there to explain? The only thing she found a little suspicious was the timing. Why would he call his lover over if he knew that Asha would be home soon?

With a start, she recognized Marietta, her supposed best friend.

How many times had Asha looked at the two of them dancing last night, thinking how glad she was that they were getting along? It seemed like such a long time ago. Was that why he had arranged for John Legend to sing at their party? A guilty conscience?

She had to admit, for a two-timing bastard, he sure made her feel like he didn't want anyone but *her*. He must have years of experience. She should've known better than to trust a man whose reputation preceded him.

As she was about to turn around, Marietta's eyes flipped open.

Asha suddenly saw something that's been staring her in the face the last few weeks: her friend has changed drastically. Her warm, bubbly nature has been replaced by someone calculating and cynical, as if she'd been wronged by a lover. It was something Asha's witnessed before, when Marietta had had that psychological meltdown.

Don't jump to conclusions!

Asha cleared her throat. "I want you gone by the time I'm back. You're can attend the wedding, but you won't be my maid of honour, nor will you be a bridesmaid. Goodbye, Marietta."

Swivelling on her heel, Asha strode downstairs. She collected the items she'd discarded no more than five minutes ago, and pressed the button for the elevator. As the doors closed her off inside the steel box, she felt absolutely nothing, as if she was back in Westminster Abbey. She will still marry Konstantinos, but not for love. Not anymore.

Their union will merely symbolize the upcoming merger between Dewali Enterprises and Sarantos International.

* * * * *

MARIETTA WAS CONFUSED.

Where was the anger she'd anticipated? Where were the tears? The mumbled apologies from Konstantinos? Why hadn't Asha thrown her toys out the cot the second she saw Marietta in bed with her fiancé?

Chucking the covers aside, Marietta quickly got dressed again. She hadn't had sex with him, of course— she wasn't desperate enough to do that to an unconscious man—but she suddenly felt dirty. Why was *she* the one getting emotional? She was supposed to have enjoyed this, to watch Asha's world crumble to the ground with satisfaction!

"I'm so sorry," she blurted to Konstantinos' sleeping form. She should never have embarked on this journey of vengeance: not only didn't it have the desired effect, but she's also lost the best friend she's ever had, someone who's been there through thick and thin.

And what had she, Marietta Angelotti, done in return? She had stabbed that poor, unsuspecting woman right in the back.

As she walked downstairs to get the rest of her things, she remembered something she'd learned in school about vengeance. "While seeking revenge, dig two graves—one for yourself," Douglas Horton had theorized.

She should've known better.

Silently weeping, Marietta exited Asha's penthouse suite, never to return again. Despite her friend saying that she could be at the wedding, Marietta wouldn't be able to face all those lovely people. She had to work on her vindictive personality before it killed her, or someone she loved.

She was going to disappear: it's the least she could do for Asha Dewali.

CHAPTER 32

THE LIGHT SEEMED harsher than before.

Asha blinked up at the snow clouds above London. She felt as if she was moving through water. Her senses were dulled. She hardly noticed Pierce calling out to her until he touched her shoulder.

"Miss Dewali, do you need to be taken somewhere?" he asked, concerned.

"No, Pierce," she replied hoarsely. "I just... I need some air."

"Is everything alright, Miss?"

"No, Pierce, it most definitely is not."

The man seemed to understand that she shouldn't be left alone. "Come on, we'll take a drive until you feel better. How does that sound?"

Wordlessly, she allowed him to lead her to the car, settling on the comfortable seat as if in a daze. She heard Pierce instruct the driver to do a scenic route of the Thames River and relaxed slightly. She closed her eyes once tears threatened to pour down her cheeks.

She could still remember every detail of the moment Konstantinos had asked her to marry him: how sincere he'd been, as if he had truly believed his own words. How could a man be romantic one minute, and inconsiderate the next? How could he help her build her confidence, telling her how beautiful and amazing she was, only to betray her in the one way that would shatter her self-esteem again? Was he a narcissist?

But then she remembered how kind he had been to their families. The man was clearly capable of love, so why had he insisted that they should wait until their wedding night to consummate their relationship if he was going to chase tail behind her back until then?

Talk to him, that annoying voice urged her. *Get his side of the story.*

What good would that do? She'll only end up hurting herself when he admitted that he'd found Marietta attractive from the start.

There are at least two sides to every story, Asha. Don't be rash.

She recognized a popular pub up ahead. "Please stop here. I'd like to get out."

The car pulled over and Pierce opened her door. "Are you sure you want to be here, Miss Dewali?"

"Don't judge me," she growled in response, shoving past him. "You can stick around, but I can't promise that I won't be a while!"

She headed straight to the bar, lifting her butt onto a stool and glaring at the barman until he noticed her. "Three shots of tequila," she ordered. She winced slightly as she recalled that night Konstantinos had taught her how to drink and kissed her for the first time. Her lips tingled. How could she find him attractive after he's broken her trust?

The drinks were deposited in front of her. She downed all three of them, ignoring the salt shaker and slices of lemon. "Keep them coming," she told the barman. Her tongue already felt numb. She knew she would regret this later, but she needed to forget.

Forget the way Konstantinos felt pressed to her body.

Forget the way he got her to open up like no man had before.

Forget the way he could make her laugh at the silliest things.

But, most importantly, forget the happiness in his eyes when she'd accepted his proposal, or thanked him for booking John Legend, or told him she loved him.

She couldn't taste the tequila anymore. She'd placed several quid on the counter and, every time she had a certain number of shots, the barman would take one to cover her tab. For all she knew, he could be taking more than he needed, but she didn't give a damn. She was a billionaire. Plenty more where that came from.

The world was a blur of sounds and images. Simmering beneath those flashes of colour were Marietta's eyes, staring at Asha with defiance. How had their friendship deteriorated so spectacularly?

"Asha?"

She rubbed her drooping eyelids before blinking at the person who had addressed her. Great, not only was she hallucinating Marietta's eyes, but also the smug face of her ex-boyfriend. Only when he took her hand in his did she realize that he wasn't an apparition.

Praven Kahn was sitting next to her, and she was too smashed to be bothered.

"What're you doing here?"

"I could ashk you the shame thing," she slurred.

"I was in the neighbourhood. I always come here for a midday beer. I saw you and… Well, I've been thinking about you a lot lately. I want to talk."

She nodded with faux enthusiasm. "Shure."

"Don't mock me, Asha." He ordered himself a drink. "I hear you're getting married?"

"Yesh."

"Is that why you're drinking?"

"What doesh that matter?"

"It matters because I saw Pierce outside, and I wanted to know if I should ask him to take you home."

She frowned. Since when did Praven care about her wellbeing? "Why did you shay I'm shit in bed?" she demanded, rounding on him. She regretted it an instance later, since her vision was lagging. Her stomach heaved at the motion.

Praven sighed. "Listen, Ash, I'm really sorry about that. I didn't mean to hurt you… It was just all too much, you know?"

"No, I don't. That'sh why I ashked."

"We were getting so serious. I wanted a break."

He thought, after seven years together, that they were only *getting* serious? Hadn't they been serious after a year, like she'd thought? The bloody cheek of this man! Konstantinos might be a lot of vile things to her right now, but at least the man was mostly honest!

"I should go," she muttered, slowly getting to her feet. She stumbled a bit and gave Pierce a thankful glance when he rescued her. She hadn't even realized that he had been waiting in the wings, so to speak.

"Asha, wait! I'm ready for commitment now!"

She looked at Praven, seeing the coward that he was for the first time. "I have nothing to shay to you. Let'sh go, Piersh."

As she was escorted outside, the freezing wind stabbed into her skull like daggers. She couldn't help but wonder if Praven and Marietta had been seeing each other on the side. Just because she never found out about it, didn't mean it never happened.

The thought of Marietta's recent betrayal made her sick. She lunged for a nearby trashcan and vomited until she had nothing in her body but sadness and regret. Her legs were shaking too badly to walk, so Pierce lifted her into his arms and carried her to the car.

"Take me home," she sobbed, curling up on the backseat. She cried for a love, shiny and new, that will never be the same again. She cried for the hundreds of people who would attend a farcical wedding, under the impression that the groom and bride were enamoured with each other. She cried for her own foolishness, believing she was the exception.

She'll never make that mistake again.

* * * * *

MARIETTA WAS AT the airport, waiting for her flight. Her father had been unable to send his private jet, so she had to be satisfied with first class tickets back home. She wandered around the Duty-Free section of Heathrow Airport.

Whenever she saw a happy couple holding hands, she felt worse. She really was a sad, sad little girl who needed therapy. She couldn't remember when she had become jealous of others, but it probably had something to do with her younger brother. It had taken her parents years to conceive again and, once they found out they were having a baby boy, they promptly forgot about her existence.

That led to her first psychotic break.

She started when her phone beeped, secretly hoping it was message from Asha. She rolled her eyes once she saw Praven's profile instead.

She didn't want me. What now?

She dumped the phone in the closest bin, ready to be done with everything.

She mentally formulated the apologetic email she was going to send to Asha the second she was back on Italian soil. She was too much of a coward to admit her questionable actions face-to-face. She would set things right on her own terms. She didn't want to die with regrets.

Her flight began boarding. She grabbed her hand luggage and made her way to the gate. She ignored the looks she received from men—even covered from head to toe, she grabbed attention, much to her annoyance—and greeted the crew with a smile once she eventually stepped onto the plane.

Don't wait until it's too late!

Marietta shook her head at that thought. Asha will have her happy ending, regardless of Marietta's actions.

You drugged that man. He won't remember anything! It's going to cause so much shit for them!

They could hang tight for a couple of hours while she went back to Italy, though.

Type up the damn email!

"Okay!" she exclaimed, startling her fellow VIP—she thought she recognized a politician or two—passengers. She rummaged through her hand luggage for her laptop and powered it up. She opened her email application, her fingers flying over the keys.

From: Marietta Angelotti
To: Asha Dewali
Subject: I'm Sorry

Asha,

I hope you don't delete this just because it's from me. Konstantinos didn't do anything wrong. I'm so sorry for what I've done!

I feel like I did when I was sixteen. I don't know when it came back, but knowing that you lied to me about your relationship with him didn't help. It's no excuse. I'm not trying to justify my behaviour, but why didn't you tell me the truth? What is going on? I feel as if everyone's in on a joke I don't understand!

I'm not proud of what I did today. I need you to know that he didn't do anything to me, I just made it look like he did. I hope he's okay. I hope the two of you will be okay.

I'm not coming to the wedding. I need help, so I'm going to my dad's. I hope I get to talk to you soon.

Love, M

"Miss? We're taking off soon," a flight attendant informed her, gesturing to the laptop.

"Alright." Marietta waited patiently for the email to send before she put the device away. She breathed deeply, feeling lighter. No regrets.

Unlike others, she paid attention to the safety briefing and made sure that her seatbelt was fastened properly. Her guilty conscience reminded her that, no matter how cruelly she's behaved, she had to look out for herself.

As the plane taxied to the runway, the co-pilot chatted to the passengers about the kind of weather they could expect on the flight and after they landed. Marietta read an article about Asha's rising star as a fashion designer. She should be counting her lucky stars that she knew a woman of Asha's calibre in the first place.

The plane's nose lifted. She had no idea that this would be the last flight of her short life and that she would, indeed, be dying with regrets.

CHAPTER 33

WHEN ASHA GOT back to the penthouse, Konstantinos was still asleep.

Pain sliced through her at the memory of why he was so tired. Would she be able to lock this part of her away during their marriage? If he wanted children, would she be emotionally ready to get pregnant, knowing that he would be screwing other women behind her back?

She took a long shower in her old bedroom's en-suite, got dressed and made herself an omelette. She already had a hangover and she felt stupid for going to a bar to drown her sorrows. Was Pierce ever going to take her seriously again?

She hoped he wouldn't tattle to her parents. She didn't feel like explaining what's going on. She just... wanted to be alone.

She knew from her research that most couples got cold feet before their weddings, but she wondered how many went through with the ceremony once they found out their partner was unfaithful. Her situation was different, since her marriage to Konstantinos was bridging the cultural gap between their families' businesses. She pondered the fate of those that got engaged for the right reasons, though, only to be disappointed this close to the finish line.

Did they cancel the wedding or, to save cost, go through with it anyway? Were they sleeping in separate beds, staying together for the kids?

Tears spilled out of her eyes as she took her plate to the study. She kept herself busy with work, craving a distraction. It had taken four weeks to fall in love with Konstantinos, but only one second to bring her back to earth.

"You managed without Praven," she whispered to herself. "You can do it again."

The only problem was, she'd never felt anything deep or irrational for Praven. Things had made sense with him: they'd spoken about settling down and having a bunch of kids. There had been no excitement; therefore, no room for heartbreak.

That didn't apply to her life with Konstantinos. He had found a way to get under her skin, and he wasn't relinquishing the hold he had on her battered heart, even after she'd found him in bed with Marietta. Whenever she thought about living without him, her soul cried out a little bit more.

As much as she hated him, she could set it aside for their families' sake. She would take whatever affection he gave her and pretend that it was enough to sustain her for life.

"You are so pathetic." Her voice was husky with emotion. "Walk away, Asha. Call it off and never look back. That would be better, right?"

She couldn't say for sure. The only thing she knew was that she wanted to spend the days leading up to the wedding alone.

Pulling a piece of paper closer, she scribbled a note addressed to Konstantinos. She turned the computer on while she finished her omelette, frowning once she saw she had an email from Marietta.

"I'm sorry," read the subject.

She couldn't do this, not so soon after… Her finger hovered over the DELETE button while she weighed her options. With a sigh, she closed the application and went upstairs to get another coat.

She would visit her siblings to give Konstantinos time to follow the instructions in her note, which she placed on the pillow beside his head. When she got back, she'll have the place to herself.

Then she'll burn the bed that had smashed her hopeful dreams to smithereens.

* * * * *

KONSTANTINOS HAD A pounding headache when he woke up.

Groaning, he turned on his side, only to drop to the carpet. Pain exploded in his skull. He gritted his teeth as he rolled around to clamber to his knees, reaching out for the support of his nightstand to raise him to his feet.

Why am I naked?

He couldn't remember anything that would qualify as a valid reason. He's always laughed at people who got hangovers, but he finally understood how it felt. He must be dying.

Stumbling to the bathroom, he splashed his face with water, hissing as the contact made tiny bombs explode behind his eyes. He clutched the glass he normally used to rinse his mouth and gulped down the water.

He walked back to the bedroom, frowning at the folded note on a pillow on the bed. He picked it up, his confusion growing while he read Asha's words.

Please go to your hotel a day earlier. I need to be alone. I'm with Kash and Farida, so text me when you're gone. Asha

What was this about? She might not have told him in person, but he sensed the anger vibrating off the page. And was that a tear stain on the one corner? Had he done something he couldn't remember? Had he been drinking to forget?

He picked up his phone to call her, but there was no answer. He didn't give up, though: Kashinath was next on the list. Luckily, the call connected after four rings.

"Hey, man, what's up?" Asha's brother answered.

"Can I speak to Asha?"

There was a short silence. "She's not here, man."

Konstantinos sighed. "If she's only asking you to say that—"

"Dude, I won't lie to you. She's not here. Is

everything okay?"

"She left a note saying she was going to be with you and Farida."

"Maybe she's still on her way?"

"Thanks, Kash. It's probably nothing, but will you call me if she turns up?"

"Sure, is it something you want to talk about?"

"Not until I've spoken to her, no."

"Understood. Good luck!"

"Thanks." He ended the call and rubbed his thumping temples. His headache was growing worse now that he was using brain power to think. Deciding to honour Asha's wishes—for now, at least—he rang his brother, hoping that Loikanos wouldn't be too busy with his own fiancé to help. He didn't feel like dealing with one of the many drivers at his disposal.

"This better be important."

Konstantinos could hear Denise giggling in the background. "Can you please come get me and take me to the hotel? I feel like shit. You know I wouldn't have asked if I was physically able to drive myself."

"Fine," Loikanos sighed. "I can be there in fifteen minutes, but you're going to have a lot of apologizing to do to my fiancée for this."

"Yeah, I'm sure." He found a pen and wrote an answering message on the back of Asha's note. "So, fifteen minutes?"

"That's it."

"Thanks," he said, hanging up. Then, all the while hoping that Asha wasn't having second thoughts about their marriage, he packed a bag and locked up. He remembered to text her just as Loikanos showed up in a sleek black Maserati. "Thanks for coming, bro."

"Trouble in paradise?" his younger brother asked.

Konstantinos remained quiet for a while. "I really hope not."

* * * * *

DENISE WAS SECRETLY grateful that Loikanos was off doing his brother's bidding: it gave her a few minutes to catch up on the work she would've missed, had they continued to deliciously arouse each other. What was it about the man? She couldn't get enough of him.

Her eyebrows furrowed once she saw Jacob's incoming call, checking the time. It was too late for a professional conversation, and her assistant hardly ever involved her in his personal life. What was so urgent?

"Sorry to bother you," Jacob said after she answered. "I need to make you aware of something."

"Tell me, *chéri*."

"Marietta Angelotti booked a one-way flight to Rome a few hours ago."

Denise digested that at her own pace. "What are you saying, Jacob?"

"She's not coming back." He took a couple of steadying breaths. "A plane went down shortly after take-off, the one she was on. It's making headline news."

She jumped to her feet and sprinted to her living room to switch her TV on. "Which channel?"

"BBC. It's bad, Denise."

She stared, in horror, as an onsite journalist indicated to the burning wreckage of the airplane behind him. "*Mon Dieu!*" she exclaimed. "Are you sure she boarded?"

"She was on the manifest. They released it about five minutes ago."

"This is not good. Asha will be crushed! Why did Marietta want to leave the country?"

"I have no idea," Jacob replied. "Maybe there was a family emergency?"

"See if you can find out, *chéri*, but be mindful. Her family must be grieving."

"I'll call them in the morning."

"Thank you, *chéri*. I'll wait until tomorrow to tell Asha, too."

"See you at the office on Monday?"

"Yes, you will. Have a good night."

Once she cut the call, Denise watched the rest of the report on the news. She was saddened by this event and could only hope that it wouldn't dampen the wedding's planned festivities. There was no way that she could postpone it, not even in light of the maid of honour's demise.

"May you rest in peace," she whispered under her breath, wiping tears from her eyes.

* * * * *

ASHA COULD SENSE the emptiness the second she stepped inside the apartment. It was colder, too, as if Konstantinos was the sole reason for any warmth she experienced. She cupped her elbows and walked to the room that had changed everything.

The bed was made, with a note perched on top of it. She opened it carefully, not sure what to expect. His words had tears filling her eyes.

Bigfoot, I don't know what this is about, but I respect your need for me-time: neither of us has really had any since lockdown started. I will see you next Saturday, wearing that suit you designed for me. I can't wait until we're married. I'm 100% committed to you. Love, Teeny

PS: call if you need me.

Her body was physically exhausted from crying, but why stop now?

How could he not to know what he's done? Was he faking his good manners, his concern, now that things were falling apart?

She didn't want to think anymore.

Switching her phone on silent—her brother and sister have been trying to get a hold of her—she headed to the bar to pour herself a glass of white wine. She took a blanket to one of the windows, making herself comfortable as she leaned against it to watch the city below. Emotionally drained, she soon fell asleep, but not without worrying about what the future held.

Chapter 34

Asha was freezing, and her neck had a cramp. She was also aware of the elevator's ping, informing her that she had visitors. But why would she be able to hear that from her bedroom? And where was all that light coming from?

She squinted as she opened her eyes, baffled to find that she was next to a window. She slowly lifted her cheek from the ice-cold glass, scared that she was going to stick to it. She finally straightened her posture, groaning at the jolts of awareness this sent to her immobile limbs.

"Ash, thank God!"

Looking up, she was further confused to find her sister running up to her, closely followed by the rest of her family, and Konstantinos. Loikanos and Denise came in last. She had no idea what was going on. Why did they seem so anxious?

"I was so worried about you when I heard the news!"

Farida exclaimed, helping Asha to her feet before enveloping her in a tight hug. There was a clinking sound as Asha's empty wine glass fell to the floor. "Oh my gosh, you're upset… I'm so sorry, Ash!"

Asha made eye contact with her fiancé. Had he told her family about his indiscretion? Was that why they were all here, to make sure that she wasn't going to cancel the wedding?

"I'm so sorry for your loss, sis," Kashinath murmured as he joined the hug.

Her loss? Was Konstantinos ending the engagement, then? But why bring his brother and the wedding planner here? "What's going on?" she asked croakily.

Denise stepped forward and gently took her out of her siblings' embrace. Placing her hands on Asha's shoulders, she peered into her eyes and announced: "*Chérie*, there is no easy way to say this. Marietta is dead."

"Great going, bird brain," Kashinath muttered to their little sister. "She didn't even know!"

Blinking in shock, Asha's frown deepened. "What're you talking about?"

"She left London yesterday," Denise explained. "Her plane went down right after take-off. There were no survivors."

She deserved it.

Asha was horrified by her own thoughts, but she couldn't deny she was relieved. She hadn't been looking forward to seeing Marietta at the wedding, not after the rift she's caused between Asha and Konstantinos.

"That's terrible," she heard herself say, surprised that

she could still produce tears. "Are you sure?"

"Yes, *chérie*," Denise nodded, "she boarded the plane. She was on the manifest. Though it will still take a day or two for them to work through the remains, I'm sure they will find her, mostly to put her family at ease."

Asha shook her head as tears pooled in her eyes. "That's terrible," she repeated numbly. She might not have felt close to Marietta these past couple of days, but that didn't take away the numerous happy memories of their decade-long friendship. Marietta was someone's daughter and sister. She didn't deserve such a grisly end.

Nobody did.

She burst into tears when she was taken into strong, familiar arms. Here was the man she was going to marry, and his recent conquest has died in a plane crash. Surely he had to be broken up about it, too? She felt immense grief for the whole situation.

"Are you okay, Bigfoot?" he whispered in her ear.

His voice used to sound seductive to her. Now, she couldn't help but think how women like Marietta had felt when he spoke to them in this soft, caring tone. Special, no doubt, like they were the only women in the world.

"I'm fine," she sniffed, stepping out of his arms before she lost sight of what he had done. "What happens now?"

"Everything will go forward as planned, Asha," her mother answered seriously. "But you will need a new maid of honour."

Life never gives free passes, Asha thought miserably. She reached out to take Denise's hand. "Will you take over that duty, if it's not going to be too much added pressure for you? I'd really like to have you up there with me."

Denise seemed stunned. "O-of course, *chérie*," she stammered. "It will be my honour."

"When will her funeral be, though?"

"Probably as soon as they have positively identified the body," Konstantinos informed her. For someone who's heard of the death of a woman he had recently slept with, he didn't seem too concerned, the bastard. He probably thought that he's getting away with his illicit affair.

Asha clenched her teeth before she started spewing insults at him. She wasn't going to be that kind of wife. If he wanted to have sex with random women, that's okay, as long as he didn't come home bearing diseases, or the news of illegitimate children.

She had to talk to her lawyer about a prenuptial agreement. Although her family's empire would be safe irrespective of how her relationship with him ended, she wanted to make sure that she protected herself.

"We can postpone the honeymoon," he suggested, bringing her back to the present moment.

Why, because you've already had your fill of sex?

"The show must go on," she mumbled. She rubbed her forehead and headed for the kitchen. "I need tea. Any takers?"

A chorus of affirmatives followed her.

She took deep breaths once she was alone, leaning against one of the counters to gather herself. Not only had she fallen asleep in an agonizing position, but her head was still pounding from the drinking she had done yesterday. She felt like she was running on empty. This time, though, there was no more fuel to keep her going.

"Asha, talk to me."

She spared her fiancé a glance before preparing a big pot of tea. "What about?"

"Why did you ask me to move out yesterday, and why did you do it in a letter? That's not like you."

"You were going to be out by today, anyway," she said, bitterness dripping from her tone. She really had to work on composing herself. "Besides, you were sleeping. I didn't want to bother you."

He came to stand next to her. "Where were you? When I called Kash, he said you weren't there."

Her hand fumbled over the box of tea. "You called Kash?"

"You said you were going to visit them."

She found it peculiar that *she* was the one feeling guilty, when *he* was the one who'd been unfaithful. "That was the plan, but I didn't feel like seeing them after I left the building," she said truthfully. "You know how siblings can get."

"Which brings me back to my original statement... Talk to me," he pleaded, turning her around to face him. He tilted her chin up. "What's wrong? And don't tell me it's nothing: you're not a very good liar."

Unlike you.

"I'm tired and nervous. I found out my best friend died no less than five minutes ago. And besides, you agreed with me in your own letter!"

"Asha, you promised that you'll always keep me in the

loop."

"And you…" She trailed off and pulled away from him once more. They couldn't get into this right now, not with their loved ones in the other room. She got a silver tray and a tea set out of one of the overhead cupboards. "I was thinking we should see our lawyers this week."

"What? Why?"

"To sort out the odds and ends of our relationship."

"If that's what you want to do, then we should rather go for couple's counselling," he grumbled. "I told you once and I'll say it again: I'm not signing a prenup, so if that's what you were getting at, forget about it."

"I won't marry you without one."

He gaped at her. "Asha, what the hell is going on? Why do you look at me as if I disgust you? Why are you talking like you don't want to marry me anymore?"

'Cause you do, and I don't.

"I'm sorry if I'm coming across less than pleasant, Konstantinos, but if you haven't heard, my best friend is dead!" She looked around once she heard she was shouting. They had an audience on the other side of the wall. Her family were notorious snoops. "We have a huge, and I mean *huge*, upcoming audit at Dewali Enterprises, thanks to the merger! To top it off, I'm getting married in a week to a man I really only got to know a little more than a month ago! I'm sorry if I'm not still as swept up by all of this as you want me to be! I can only take so much until I crack!"

His facial expression smoothed out. "You're right. I'm sorry for being inconsiderate." He took the tray once she'd placed everything on top of it. "But I'm still not signing a prenup, so get that idea right out of your head. Got it?"

"If you don't want to do that, then I want us both to go for blood tests every month," she blurted out. Her eyes widened at the fierce look in his gaze. Why did she have to go and say that so callously?

Gently, he put the tray back down and crossed his arms over his chest. "Blood-tests? Why would we need those?"

Oh, he was spectacular at playing the innocent fiancé. "For our health, why else?" she snapped.

"The only reason someone would have to have their blood tested so often is if they have some sort of health issue, like cholesterol, or if they want to make sure they're free of STD's." He glared at her. "Now, I know you didn't just imply that you want to see if I'm still on the straight and narrow."

"Guilty conscience?"

"What? Asha, have you been present at all during the last few weeks? Haven't I made it abundantly clear that *you're* the only woman I'm interested in?" He breathed in deeply. "I know you act like a fool when you're stressed, but this is ridiculous."

Sukesh peeked into the kitchen. "Is everything alright in here?" he asked, startled, once he took in the atmosphere between his daughter and her groom-to-be.

"Yes, daddy," she replied tightly. "We'll be right out, okay?"

"Asha—"

"Daddy, please," she interrupted, waiting until he was gone before she met Konstantinos' dark gaze again. This was the moment of truth, to prove to herself that she could turn the other cheek and move forward, instead of lingering on the past. "I'm being a fool, you're right. I'm sorry for starting a fight. I guess I have a funny way of dealing with stress."

"Tell me why you're doing all of this now. You seemed perfectly content while we were still living together."

"I don't know," she lied. "Can you help me take this to the living room, then? There are people waiting for us."

"Asha, we—"

"We're fine." She kissed his cheek, ignoring the thrill his coarse stubble sent down her spine. How could she be attracted to a cheater? "I'm sorry, okay?"

He sighed, defeated. "Apology accepted, Bigfoot."

When he spanked her butt before carrying the tray out of the kitchen, she was amazed at the automatic giggle that slipped past her lips. She followed him and noticed that her parents seemed greatly relieved at the smile on her face. She hated worrying people unnecessarily, but sometimes she simply couldn't keep her emotions in control.

Soon, she would master them.

Chapter 35

Denise kicked her shoes off once she was in Loikanos' trendy apartment, sighing as she sank onto the nearest couch. Her back ached, her feet were swollen, and there was a newly-bloomed headache pulsing at her temples. "What a day!"

"You're telling me," Loikanos muttered. He raked his fingers through his long hair and pulled his jacket off. "I never thought that one person could create so much drama."

She frowned at him. "What do you mean? She died, *mon cher*. I don't believe she did it on purpose."

"Konstantinos asked me what I think about her about two nights ago." He was thoughtful for a moment. "Yeah, it was at the bachelor party. She didn't look like a very sincere human being, and I wondered why Asha was friends with her."

"Did they have a disagreement, *mon cher*? That would explain why Marietta wanted to get out of the country."

"Not as far as I'm aware," he answered slowly. "Asha was very bubbly that night, but Marietta looked like she was ready to murder someone. I'm surprised Asha didn't notice."

"Curious."

He raised his eyebrows at her, grinning from ear to ear. "Are you playing detective, *mon amour*?"

"Aren't you interested to know why she left so abruptly? She wasn't planning on coming back," she reminded him. "Her ticket was booked one-way, so she was going to miss the wedding of the decade. Her *best friend's* wedding."

"Who knows why people act the way they do?" He got on top of her, slowly unbuttoning her thick jersey while he trailed kisses down her neck. "But I quite enjoy that you're so adamant to uncover the truth, *mon amour*. It's incredibly sexy. I can imagine you wearing those cute glasses female detectives always have at the ready."

She started laughing. "Will you ever tire of me?"

"I hope not. You're more than enough woman to last me for life."

"You know you're not getting anything from me tonight, Loikanos Sarantos," she purred, licking his earlobe. She knew he loved it when she did that, and suppressed a perceptive giggle once he shuddered in pleasure. "My womanly parts are otherwise occupied for the following three days."

He lifted his head to stare into her eyes. "There's a very simple way to solve that problem, *mon amour*. I can make you pregnant."

"I'll have you know that Remi and I tried to have a

baby for *years*."

"He was shooting blanks," Loikanos mumbled dismissively, his mouth working its way into her cleavage. "If a baby's what you want, Denise, then I will make it happen. *That's* a guarantee."

Her heart warmed. "Are you saying we can throw caution to the wind?"

"Yes, I think it's time we stop using condoms, and you're going off the Pill."

"And you're ready to be a father?"

"I'm ready to be the father to *our* children, Denise. If you're not pregnant in three months, I'm going to be very upset."

She burst out laughing. "I assume that you will want to practice every day?"

"Multiple times a day, for weeks, until you tell me you've skipped your period," he answered seriously. "If I have my way, which I usually do, this is the last month you'll give me the cold shoulder for four long, lonely days in a row."

"Then I'll have to reward your dedication," she murmured. His enthusiasm was contagious. She rolled him around and helped him out of his shirt, marvelling at the sight of his lean torso. "We should celebrate my last period. When was the last time I sucked you until you saw stars?"

His Adam's apple bobbed when he swallowed. "Last night?"

"Oh, I was merely warming up, *mon cher*," she teased, unzipped his jeans. Her mouth watered every time she saw him in fitted clothing, and without anything on.

She was completely comfortable with her *Madame Cougouar* role these days. "I will give you something to remember me by, so when I become so fat that you will no longer want me, you at least won't leave me."

"Denise, I doubt that I—"

She was happy that what she did next cut him off, already knowing deep in her soul that his love for her transcended the physical. She firmly believed they were soul mates, and she couldn't wait to have his child growing inside her womb.

* * * * *

KONSTANTINOS SIGHED ONCE he was back in his hotel room. He was, in short, exhausted. He couldn't believe how much energy it had taken to be there for Asha, especially taking her current mood into account. He was hurt by the strange things she'd been saying.

Hopefully, it really was due to stress, and not because she didn't want to marry him anymore. She would tell him if that was the case, right?

"Women," he muttered to the empty room around him. He strode to the fully stocked bar and opened a beer. It felt strange not to be in the penthouse apartment with Asha. Strangely enough, he saw that as *their* home, even before her parents had made it clear it was their wedding gift.

Switching the television on, he hoped for some sort of entertaining show or movie to be on. Instead, he ended up watching the coverage of Marietta's accident. Something was niggling at the back of his mind about her but, for the life of him, he had no idea what or why.

He remembered considering telling Asha that she should find a new best friend, someone loyal like Denise, but that's where it stopped. It's almost as if his mind had an invisible layer wrapped around it, preventing him from accessing his memories. He wondered if that was why he had felt crap the day before? Maybe he was coming down with something.

"It is speculated that the pilots lost control of the plane after both engines caught fire," the news anchor was saying. "The cause of the fire is still a mystery. Some of the passengers include the President of Ghana, British diplomats, as well as Marietta Angelotti, the only daughter of Italian millionaire Marco Angelotti. This has caused numerous rumours on conspiracy websites about a planned attack, mostly due to the President of Ghana's hate-speech at a recent United Nations assembly. At this point, however, the theories are inconsequential until the inspectors have uncovered the context of the black box. And onto other news—"

Konstantinos changed the channel before he had to sit through the mind-numbing celebrity news section. It seemed typical that Marietta would be involved in trouble that had been targeted at someone else entirely. It made that annoying voice at the back of his head insist that he was forgetting a crucial piece of the puzzle, but he couldn't trying to find answers only worsened his headache.

Besides, he was consumed with worry about whether or not Asha still loved him.

He found it funny that she'd been the one to fret over

the possibility of them drifting apart once they were reintroduced back into the real world. It's almost as if she was fulfilling her own doomed prophecy. She had tremendous trust issues.

Pulling his phone closer, he decided to call her, not expecting that she'll answer if recent events were anything to go by.

"Hey," she murmured as the line connected, surprising him.

"Hi," he said. Sitting up, he cleared his throat and asked: "Are you alone?"

"Yes, my parents just left, so I've finally got the place to myself." She sighed. "I never realized how big it is until now."

"Is that a hint of longing I detect?"

She was silent for a while before she quietly admitted: "Yes, the bed is cold without you."

"Soon, we'll never be apart again." He smiled, happy that the tension between them has dissipated. "I don't know if I'll be able to sleep at night, so don't blame me if I look like a train wreck by the time you walk down the aisle."

"Why would I blame you?"

There was a hint of something—trepidation? Blame? Resentment?—in her voice that he hasn't heard since they met. Maybe it was because her voice was coming through the airwaves, and he was chasing his own tail. Since he'd woken up in a daze the day before, he's been more than a little paranoid. It had exploded in his face in the worst way possible when he'd argued with Asha over nothing.

"How are you really feeling about Marietta, Bigfoot?"

"I'm a little... relieved."

He blinked in confusion. "How so?"

"Things haven't been the same between us, and I don't know why."

"You noticed that, did you? I wanted to mention something, but I didn't want to offend you."

"Mention what?"

"She didn't seem like a very good friend. I remember you telling me how close you were while we were alone, but I didn't see it when she was around you. She looked almost... *jealous* of you."

"I can't understand why. I mean, it's not like I—"

"You're not going to say things that aren't true, are you?" he interrupted with a chuckle. "I thought we've talked about this."

"I guess it's still difficult for me to understand why we're getting married. We're so different."

"Well, yes: I'm male and you're female. That's about as different as we can get."

"You're impossible, do you know that?"

"I think you've mentioned it to me once or twice before. And I'll probably get to hear it for years to come."

"Yeah, probably."

"I just wanted to make sure things are cool between us?" He hated that it came out sounding like a question. Where has his self-confidence gone?

"We'll be fine once this is behind us."

"Good, I'm glad. I'll let you get to bed, then. I don't want you to tire yourself out unnecessarily, and I could see that today was a bit too much for you."

"I'll cope, thanks Teeny. Get some sleep: you might be hot, but even *you* won't look good with rings under your eyes."

He grinned. "I'll definitely do that, but take your own advice, Asha. You won't be getting much sleep during our honeymoon."

With that sultry promise, he hung up. He knew that he's put her on edge, the way he used to do while it had just been the two of them. He was really looking forward to spending two weeks with her at his three-bedroom villa in Maui.

Until then, he will be counting down the days until they were husband and wife.

* * * * *

HE WAS INFURIATING.

Here she was, staring at the phone in her hand, with her mouth gaping open. How could she be attracted to him when he was blatantly attracted to every other female out there? She was shocked that her feelings for him hadn't ceased like she'd hoped, but only seemed to grow more every day. She really was turning out to be a masochist of note. Feminists everywhere would stone her to death for giving in to his every whim.

She pulled her laptop closer and checked her emails, carefully avoiding the one from her deceased best friend. There were so many messages of condolences from her friends and family. She filed them away to read at a later stage, when she had enough time and willpower. Her family had been so persistently concerned today, that she felt ready to pass out at any moment.

When she saw an email from Marietta's father, her blood ran cold.

From: Marco Angelotti
To: Asha Dewali
Subject: Marietta

Dear Asha,

I am sure that you have heard about Marietta's accident. I was very surprised when she told me she's flying home, as you can imagine, since your wedding is next week. This has led me to suspect that something must have happened between you.

I know that you have always looked out for her, even when she was admitted to hospital and after her numerous dalliances with unknown (to me, at least) men. Please tell me that you didn't part on bad terms with my daughter, Asha. Your father raised you better than that.

I look forward to your response, and for this old man's heart to be set at ease.

Sincerely,
Marco Angelotti, CEO
Angelotti Incorporated

She couldn't believe her eyes. Was he implying that *she* was the reason Marietta had died on that plane?

How could she be? *Marietta* was the one fooling around with an engaged man! Besides, Asha had told her that she could still attend the wedding, despite what she'd done!

Her fingers aggressively tapped on the keyboard. She could've been vindictive and told him everything: the numerous men Marietta had seduced, including Asha's fiancé, and the other crap the Italian heiress got up to whenever her father wasn't looking. In fact, Asha burned to set the record straight.

But she didn't.

She assured Marco that she hadn't argued with Marietta—this was true, at least—and that she had been looking forward to having Marietta at the wedding. She went on to state that she'd been under the impression that Marietta only wanted to go home to say hello to him and the rest of her family, before returning on Thursday.

She sent the email without checking for spelling mistakes, and stared at the one from Marietta. "I'm sorry", it taunted her. What could Marietta possible have to say, anyway, that would change anything?

With a sigh, she shut her laptop and climbed under the covers. Her childhood room was smaller than the main one, but she refused to sleep in *that* bed until it's been fumigated. Letting out a deep breath, she finally fell asleep, happy that her conscience was clear.

That was more than Marietta could say.

CHAPTER 36

THIS WAS IT: the moment they've steadily been heading towards for the last six weeks.

Konstantinos slowly blew the air out of his lungs, wishing he could take another shower. Considering that he's already done that twice, he figured that it wouldn't be such a good idea. He was looking forward to getting married, but damn, it was incredibly nerve-wrecking at the same time!

"You've got to calm down," Loikanos muttered in Greek. "I'm nervous for your part!"

"That's only because you've turned into a woman since getting engaged," Konstantinos chuckled.

"Have not!" Loikanos stared at himself in the mirror before redoing his hair, which had been slicked back. He ruffled it and pulled a face. "I can't get this to look right!"

"Like I said: you're a woman now."

"I can't wait until you're in Hawaii—"

"So that you can make babies with Denise? As if you haven't been practicing enough already."

"You're just jealous because you're suffering from blue balls."

"That may be true, but I still think you're too young to be a dad."

Loikanos snorted. "I know we've always had a sibling rivalry but, instead of focussing on whose wife gives birth first, why don't we focus on who raises their child the best?"

"She's not your wife yet, so your point is moot."

"Neither is Asha!" Loikanos seemed pleased by his appearance, at long last. "I'm happy you're only going to get married once, because you're impossible when you're like this."

"Look who's talking!" Konstantinos laughed, glancing over his shoulder at the knock on the door. His father peeked in. "Papa?"

"It's time," Nikos said gruffly. "Stop fooling around."

Konstantinos straightened his plain white tie for the millionth time and adjusted his posture. The white of his suit contrasted amazingly with his naturally tanned skin, like Asha had intended, and he was happy that the gold waistcoat didn't look like it hailed from the disco era. It was stylish and fashionable.

"Let's go get married," he told his reflection softly, following his groomsmen out of the room.

He got goosebumps as they entered a dark hallway that led to the main part of Westminster Abbey. The place was going to give him nightmares for weeks to come, he just knew it. For once, he could see the positives of having insomnia.

Loikanos began chatting to his friends, leaving Konstantinos to greet every family member that called out to him from the pews. He moved forward to shake the men's hands and accept the women's kisses, switching between Greek to English so quickly that he felt like he was talking gibberish. Eventually, when the priest made an impatient sound into the microphone, they let him go.

Konstantinos held his breath once he was standing where he should, trying to avoid eye contact with the guests and haunting decor of the church. This was easier said than done, since the interior of Westminster Abbey was packed to the rafters.

"All rise!" the priest announced, lifting his hands up.

This is it, Konstantinos thought anxiously, shifting from one foot to the other. *Oh my God, this is it!*

He heard the guests get to their feet, a soft murmur around him. He sensed every heartbeat, every breath, for the following couple of seconds and waited impatiently for the bridal march to begin. He hoped the ceremony wouldn't get dragged out for too long: he was going to need a few glasses of alcohol once this part of the day was over.

When he felt about ready to burst from excitement, the intro notes played on a harp. It sounded soft, sweet and melodic: representing Asha perfectly.

Turning on his heels, he watched as, one by one, the bridesmaids sashayed down the aisle. Their white dresses suited their different body shapes perfectly: they looked like Greek goddesses. Denise was last, and he had to wonder how she'd managed to get her dress tailored on such short notice. The woman worked magic, he was certain of it.

People gasped once Asha came into view. He couldn't blame them.

She was a vision.

The gold of her dress seemed to shimmer as it wrapped around her body, but not so much that it looked tacky. It was almost as if she was glowing, from head to toe, as she nervously sashayed towards him. Her hair was delicately bundled up on her head, held together by tiny little sparkles of gold. She was too far away for him to see what those splashes of gold were.

Her red bouquet of roses popped brightly against the rest of her outfit, matching the rose he had tucked in his jacket.

She lifted her gaze to his about halfway down the aisle, one corner of her mouth tilting up in a half-smile. Her grip on her father's bicep tightened slightly. Konstantinos knew that she had to be twice as edgy as he was. He had no idea why, but the pressure on the bride to be wonderful was traditionally nearly too much to bear.

His hands itched to hold hers, and he longed to see her from up close. He wanted to smell her womanly, floral scent, to drink her in front head to toe. He's never been in love with anyone else before, and he never will be again.

There was only her, from this day until his demise.

* * * * *

ASHA COMPOSED HERSELF as the harp started playing.

"Are you ready, darling?" her father smiled.

"I'm ready," she confirmed.

"I'll be with you every step of the way." Sukesh Dewali winked. "Literally."

She rolled her eyes at him. "Please stop talking. You're not helping."

Lifting her hand to his mouth, he gave her a soft kiss on her fingers. "It's not every day a father gets to walk his firstborn daughter down the aisle, Asha," he told her seriously. "I will not stop talking."

She giggled. "Fine, I'll stop judging you." Her blood ran cold when she realized that her bridesmaids were all gone. "Oh, shit, it's time."

"Come on, Mrs. Sarantos."

"Very funny," she muttered under her breath, falling into step with him. Her heart was beating wildly, as if she was exercising instead of taking a leisurely stroll towards her groom, but she couldn't help it. This was the climax point of a hectic couple of weeks.

Whoa, Konstantinos looked better than she had imagined! His suit was tailored to his sculpted body, accentuating his broad shoulders and tapered waist. She quickly glanced away, before her knees buckled. About halfway to the altar, though, her traitorous eyes wouldn't listen anymore. This time, her gaze locked on his, refusing to budge.

She felt as if she was wading through a marsh. Was she ever going to be by his side? It felt like an eternity before her father placed her left hand on top of

Konstantinos' outstretched right. Her skin tingled and she exhaled slowly, savouring this moment.

She could honestly say that in this moment, with them looking at each other like they were the only two people in the universe, she didn't care what had happened last week. She didn't care if he was going to find a new side piece five days, five weeks or five years from now. The look in his eyes told her one thing, and it's something that delighted her to her core.

He wanted *her* as his wife.

His thumb stroked the back of her hand and when he smiled, she almost melted. "Hi, Bigfoot," he whispered softly.

She bit the inside of her cheeks to keep from laughing. "Hi, Teeny."

"Dearly beloved," the priest began, "we are all gathered here today to witness the union of Asha and Konstantinos, who, from this day forth, will enter the kingdom of holy matrimony."

Konstantinos, whose gaze was still fixed on hers, widened his eyes theatrically. "Kingdom?" he quoted under his breath.

She tried her best not to snigger while she pinched the soft pad of his thumb.

"Marriage is a sacred union of the masculine and feminine," the priest droned on. "They come together in perfect harmony to create one living, breathing being and vow to always support one another, and never falter in their love."

"Come together?" her husband-to-be asked softly, waggling his eyebrows.

Her body was shaking as she continued to struggle holding her laughter in. His whispered jibes went on until they had to exchange their vows. It took a while for her face to neutralize. She was beginning to believe that him not taking anything seriously was his best trait.

"Asha, you are my Bigfoot," Konstantinos declared with unintentional dramatic flair. They both ignored the chuckles from the other people in the church, who were no doubt curious to know the size of Asha's feet. "Since day one, you were elusive and mysterious, only giving me hints of the person that lay beneath the surface of your professional mask. That all changed once I got to know you. Slowly, day by day, you drew me further into your magic."

Damn him. She blinked a few times to clear the tears that were forming in her eyes.

"I am your willing partner in this marriage," he continued. "I vow to honour and obey you, through sickness and in health, for richer or for poorer, for as long as we both shall live. You are my better half, and my loyalty to you knows no bounds. With this ring," he murmured, sliding a plain gold band onto her finger to join her sparkling engagement ring, "I solemnly swear to cherish you until the end of my days."

The priest motioned for her to start.

She took a few deep breaths first. "Konstantinos, from the beginning there was a *Teeny* tiny part of me that couldn't resist you." She grinned when he burst out laughing, startling the entire Westminster Abbey. "You have a childlike quality about you that brought out the woman in me. Everything about us is a contradiction, and I love it. You took the time to cut through the protective layers I had around me, and made me feel safe enough to show you the *real* Asha." With a trembling hand, she pushed his ring on, happily noting that his first knuckle would prevent it from sliding off. Perhaps it'll serve as a reminder that he should keep it in his pants. "From this moment onward, I will honour and obey you, through sickness and in health, for richer or for poorer, for as long as we both shall live. Today, with this ring, I solemnly swear to cherish you until the end of my days."

"Asha, Konstantinos," the priest addressed them both, "I now pronounce you husband and wife. You may kiss the bride."

Her eyelids fluttered closed as soon as her husband's mouth pressed to hers. The kiss was tender and without any tongue, but she wouldn't have wanted it any other way. She almost protested when he lifted his lips, clearing her throat before the thought was verbalised.

The twinkle in his eyes promised that they would get plenty of opportunities to pick up where they left off, later.

"Ladies and gentlemen: Mr. and Mrs. Konstantinos Sarantos!"

Konstantinos tucked her arm into the crook of his and grinned as they made their way to the front of the cathedral, ducking under the assault of small white flowers that were thrown their way. Soon, they were both laughing as they burst through the doors to the awaiting vehicle. He took over from the driver, holding the door open while she climbed into the car.

She watched him follow suit, wishing she could stop smiling. She was supposed to hate him. He had *cheated* on her no less than a week ago, for heaven's sake! Why was she so damn happy?

"Finally," he mumbled. He pulled her onto his lap, his face millimetres from hers. "Thank God you're mine."

She was sure that he could see the erratic pulse in her neck. In slow motion, his lips claimed her with a kiss that melted her steely resolve. She threw her arms around his neck, holding him closer to her as their tongues duelled. They were absolutely starved for each other. The sexual tension between them was ready to explode.

"Asha," he moaned as his hand trailed between her knees, upwards, and dangerously close to the apex of her thighs. "I want you so much."

She shifted on his lap and pulled her dress up so she could straddle him more comfortably. "Let's do this."

He returned her hunger when she resumed their kissing but, much to her dismay, he didn't do anything else. "Let's not rush this," he whispered huskily, peering into her eyes. "We'll have days to explore each other, Bigfoot. You deserve more than a quick romp in the back of a limousine."

"You're right," she sighed, pressing her forehead to his. "But we're husband and wife now."

"Isn't it great?"

His beaming smile disarmed her. "Yes." She gave him another swift kiss. She hoped that her walls would slowly rise around her again, or she was going to be in trouble. She didn't want to be distracted from what he really was, and the only way to prevent that from happening was to keep reminding herself that she married a man-whore.

* * * * *

"LADIES AND GENTLEMEN, the bride and groom will now share their first dance!"

While people applauded, Konstantinos took his jacket off and held his hand out to Asha. She rolled her eyes at everyone's enthusiasm but accompanied him to the dance floor anyway. He was secretly relieved that he'd taken the time to get her to loosen up while they were locked in the penthouse suite.

"I've got another surprise for you," he informed her, nodding towards the band.

Her mouth popped open once she saw whom he was referring to. "Again? Teeny, you're spoiling me."

"I do what I can to keep you happy." He winked and pulled her into his arms. "I know how much you love him, and I couldn't let him fly back to the States after I saw how much you enjoyed his performance last week."

She rested her cheek on his chest. "If I become a snob, it's because of you. I want that to be noted."

He chuckled and began leading her across the floor, guided by the familiar piano intro of *Ordinary People*. John Legend's smooth, emotive voice joined the melody shortly after. "I want to dedicate this song to you, to remind you that things won't always be moonlight and roses, but that I'm committed to you nonetheless."

"It's beautiful," she said, though her posture stiffened slightly.

Asha's body lost its tension as he twirled her around. He noticed that her eyes were closed: she was giving her full trust to him. He didn't want to let her down, and he didn't want to break her trust. He knew it didn't come easily.

The lyrics perfectly resonated with their relationship. Although they haven't had many fights, this entire experience has happened incredibly swiftly. From now on, they should relax more, live and breathe in the moments that will eventually scatter during the length of their union.

"I love you," he whispered into her ear, nibbling on that soft spot below her ear.

She sighed. "I love you too, Teeny."

John was taking their dance to new heights when he geared up for the bridge. Konstantinos held her closer, shutting his eyes to zone out the rest of the world. Her golden aura surrounded him, changing his life forever. He was so in love with her, he could hardly believe how much his attitude has adapted to be the partner she needed.

She hummed along to the song, sliding her hands from his forearms to his shoulders, wrapping him in a loving embrace.

She was the most beautiful woman in the world, but this moment was too pure for him to spoil it by becoming aroused. He pictured them swaying to a piano's beat ten, forty, *fifty* years from now. She was going to hold him like this until they were old and grey, watching their grandchildren getting married.

He would make sure of it.

The guests clapped and cheered once the dance ended. Konstantinos took Asha's face in his hands, wiping the tears from her cheek. Unable to help himself, he kissed her passionately, wordlessly assuring her of his intentions. Has a man ever loved a woman more?

"Let's pick it up a little, shall we?" Loikanos announced, bursting into the newlyweds' world. "I'd like to dedicate this song to my big brother, who was stupid enough to get married before I did. We're not very good singers, but this will be good."

Konstantinos groaned dramatically. "Don't let that man near a microphone!" he yelled.

Asha giggled along with the rest of the guests, watching the brothers' standoff with interest.

"Come on, bro, you know you want to!" Loikanos cooed. He smiled broadly and grabbed an extra microphone. "We've practiced this song too many times *not* to perform it in front of your wife and her innocent family!"

Konstantinos strode over to the raised platform that served as the band's stage. He stood next to his brother and decided to hype the crowd up even more. "I can't believe you're making me do this here," he told Loikanos.

"You're totally right, the stage isn't big enough." Loikanos motioned for Asha to move. "Be a doll and give us some room to dance in, sis." He glanced over his shoulder at the band. "Are you ready?"

The drummer, clicking his sticks together, shouted: "One, two, one, two, three, four!"

Konstantinos grinned when his brother wiggled his legs to the base intro of Bruno Mars' *Runaway Baby*. "I don't think you're ready!" he sang into the microphone. "Take it away, bro."

Loikanos followed their well-rehearsed choreography easily while he chanted the song, to the surprised enjoyment of the guests. Konstantinos did every dance step with precision, pointing to the audience at the right moments and making suggestive movements where appropriate. Pretty soon, the crowd was clapping and swaying along to the beat, and he spotted Asha nearly rolling on the floor from laughter.

He was having so much fun, he immediately forgave his brother for putting him on the spot. The band seemed to be enjoying this rendition too, but Konstantinos imagined that Denise would receive a long, strict letter from The Orangery about the lack of decent conduct during this event. The upper-crust of London had a stick up their butts, yet they'd never stood a chance against the Sarantos brothers.

They finished on a flourish, throwing their hands in the air.

"And *that*, bro, is how you get people to loosen the hell up," Loikanos declared with a laugh.

Konstantinos pulled his brother into a big hug. "I love you, man."

* * * * *

ASHA HAS NEVER had so much fun at a wedding before.

After the Sarantos brothers stole the show with their choreographed number, people of all ages raced to the dance floor to show off their own moves. She was laughing so hard that she was considering taking it up as a new form exercise to replace her morning yoga routine. Whenever she thought she's seen it all, someone else would do something hilarious. Once, her usually prim-and-proper aunt did a move so risqué that Asha nearly choked on champagne.

"You're so lucky, Ash!" Farida sighed, sitting down next to her. "Your husband is dreamy."

Asha stiffened. "Considering that every female in this place is in love with him, I guess you're right."

"Oh, come on! Any fool can see that he's crazy about *you*. No one else stands a chance."

Appearances can be deceiving.

She swallowed the remainder of her champagne. "Any cute boys you fancy?"

Farida rolled her eyes. "Oh, please! Don't make me laugh."

"You're a beautiful young woman, sis," Asha insisted, tucking her sister's dark hair behind her ears. "Don't be scared to put yourself out there. Don't be like *me*, in other words."

"You mean, married to a hottie of note?"

"You know what I mean."

Farida's brows furrowed. "You're too hard on yourself. I'm surprised you haven't had an emotional breakdown by now."

"I'm closer to one than you think."

"Why, are you nervous about the honeymoon?" Farida asked, leaning forward so they could talk more privately.

"Extremely," Asha admitted. "He's nothing like Praven and I'm... scared."

"It's a good thing they're different, Ash. *Praven* never got you to the aisle." Her little sister laughed. "He didn't get you close to one, actually."

"I saw him the other day."

Farida's eyes bulged. "What? Where?"

"I, uh, wasn't feeling well, so I went to a pub. He was in the neighbourhood." Asha shrugged as if it meant nothing. "He told me he wanted a second chance."

"You're here, so I'm assuming you said no."

"He was a little pathetic," Asha admitted. "I couldn't believe that he told me that. I mean, if he wanted me to take him seriously, surely he would've contacted me at any point during the last year? Instead, he waited until he accidently ran into me."

"Wait a minute. Do you want him back?"

Asha's eyes found her husband's body. He was dancing with his grandmother. She refused to let the scene charm her. "Praven's safe."

"Who wants safe? Ash, you just told me to live my life, but you can't even take your own advice!"

"Maybe I've been burnt too many times."

"Uhm, as far as I remember, *Praven* was the one doing the burning!" Farida slapped her older sister's arm. "What the hell's the matter with you? It's the night of your wedding, and you're thinking about your ex! You should be ashamed."

"You're right, I'm—"

"You should be going to Konstananana *right now* and owning him for the rest of the evening!" Farida interrupted.

Asha eyed her sister. "'Konstananana'? Really?"

"Go!"

"You know, you're way too immature for your age," Asha muttered, slipping her heels on and getting to her feet. "I don't know how we're family."

"I love you too!" Farida shouted after her.

Like a magnet, Konstantinos' dark gaze found hers. She saw him tell his gran something and hand her over to his grandfather. Then, smiling like the cat that got all the cream, he met Asha halfway. He pulled her into his arms and nuzzled her neck.

"I've come to monopolise you for the rest of the evening on Farida's demand," she informed him.

"I'll remember to thank her later."

Her guard was quickly dropping again. She closed her eyes and savoured his warmth, letting it soak into her bones. They danced together for hours, until the MC announced that it was time for their honeymoon.

* * * * *

LOIKANOS WRAPPED HIS arms around Denise, embracing her from behind while his hands spread over her stomach. "Do you think we have a baby in there yet?"

She laughed. "I'm not ovulating, *chéri*, so I doubt it."

"They look good together," he commented as they watched the newlywed couple exit the room. "Do you think we'll ever be that happy?"

"Aren't we already?" she countered, turning her head to kiss his cheek. "I thought we were."

"That's also true. We've perfected love, and they're only getting started."

"You are so cheeky. I'm surprised that you don't get into trouble more often."

He eyed her teasingly. "Are you saying you would scold *this* face?"

"Sadly, no," she said, sighing theatrically. "That's how you keep me young. Besides, that performance you put on earlier… You never told me you could dance like that."

"If I did, I wouldn't have surprised you, *mon amour*."

"What else have you been hiding?"

He grinned. "Wouldn't you like to know?"

Turning in his embrace, she kissed him softly. "You might be the cuter one in this relationship, *chéri*, but I can also be mysterious."

"Oh, I know." His hands slipped down to cup her butt. "That's all you've been ever since I met you. Making love to you is just one more way that I get to know you."

"If that were true, then you should know me better than I know myself."

"That would mean that I've arrived." He kissed her softly. "And if I've arrived, it means that there is nothing left to learn. But you, my sweet Denise, are an enigma that I'll take my time deciphering. I'll take off layer," he murmured, kissing one side of her neck, "by layer." He nipped at the other side.

She locked her arms around him. How did she get this lucky? "Good."

CHAPTER 37

ASHA HAD FALLEN asleep during the drive to Heathrow, so Konstantinos carried her into the awaiting private jet as soon as the car pulled over on the tarmac. He found it fitting that he would be carrying her over every single threshold. Who knew he was such a closeted traditionalist?

He put her down on one of the luxurious leather seats. He knew she would be more comfortable on the bed, but didn't want her to get hurt during take-off. Removing his jacket, he walked to the front of the plane and greeted the cockpit crew.

"Mr. Sarantos," the captain said, extending his hand with a smile. "Congratulations are in order, I believe. How does it feel to be a married man?"

"So far, so good," Konstantinos replied. "How's the weather looking in Hawaii?"

"It looks like the day after we arrive, there will be three days of severe thunderstorms, then it's sunny skies for the rest of your stay," the co-pilot informed him. "We'll have to stop in Las Vegas to refuel, so we're only expecting to arrive in Maui in twenty hours."

Konstantinos sighed. "There's no way that we can cut down on flight time, maybe get a more direct route?"

"Either way, we will need to refuel," the captain responded.

"When do we take off?"

"We're just waiting for the final cargo to be loaded, and then we'll start the engines."

"Thanks," he muttered as he made his way back to the cabin. He wanted to be on honeymoon already, for heaven's sake! He's waited for this moment for nearly two months! Granted, that was nothing compared to most engaged couples, but his relationship with Asha couldn't exactly be dubbed "normal".

"Can I get you *anything* while you wait, sir?"

He glanced up at the cabin crew member and frowned. He was a married man and she was hitting on him? Didn't she have any self-respect? "A bottle of still water, please," he responded levelly. The old Konstantinos would've shagged the living daylights out of her once they reached cruising altitude, but he wasn't that man anymore.

In fact, the way her outfit clung to her body revolted him. Didn't women know that they didn't have to show off every curve to be deemed sexy?

"Of course, sir," the flight attended purred, going to the galley and returning with his drink. "I'll be in front if you need *anything* else."

He grunted a noncommittal answer and took his iPad

out of the laptop bag one of his bodyguards had placed in the overhead locker. Then, getting comfortable on his seat next to Asha's sleeping form, he logged onto Facebook, suspecting that his brother has already uploaded photographs of the wedding.

The corners of his mouth slowly tilted upwards when he saw the first one. It had been snapped the moment Asha joined him at the altar. They were grinning at each other like two sappy romantics. The photos that followed showed how he'd joked around without the priest noticing. Konstantinos especially loved the one where his wife looked like she was about to burst with laughter.

He ignored the comments of congratulations and praise, flipping through the album at a leisurely pace. The next couple of pictures were of him and Asha rushing out of the church, and there was one where he had helped her into the car.

"Sir, we're about to taxi for take-off," the flight attendant murmured, appearing at his side. "Please help me get your wife buckled in and switch off your iPad until we're in the air."

"That's okay, I've got this," he told her. "We've already turned off our phones."

"I'll secure the rest of the cabin, then."

He put the iPad in the magazine rack attached to the side of his chair as the plane started moving. Leaning over the comfortable armrest to Asha's chair, he dug under her body for her straps and clicked them into place, careful not to wake her. She shifted in her sleep, unconsciously reaching for him. He stroked her cheek and let her use his shoulder as a temporary pillow. He'll take her to the bedroom once the seatbelt signs were switched off.

"Cabin crew, your seat for take-off," the first officer announced over the PA system.

Then, with the engine noise rising, they shot down the runway and into the air. Konstantinos looked out of the window as they ascended from Heathrow. He's always loved watching other planes in the sky, their lights blinking on and off proving that he wasn't alone. His eyes shifted back to Asha and he smiled.

I'll never be alone again.

"We've reached cruising altitude, Mr. Sarantos," the captain chuckled fifteen minutes later. "Feel free to join the mile-high club."

Konstantinos laughed softly, unbuckling both himself and his wife before lifting her into his arms. He strode to the bedroom, gaze on her face. She was knocked out cold, so there was no point to attempt what the captain had suggested. They'll have to knock that item off her to-do list later, or on the flight back.

He put her on the queen-size bed and took off her shoes. He got an extra blanket from the small closet on the other side of the room before draping it over her. She sighed and turned on her side, curling up into a tiny ball. He smiled, kissed her temple and walked back to the main part of the cabin. Now that they were officially on their honeymoon, he could finally get out of this restrictive suit.

"Did you see a hanger with my clothes on it?" he asked the flight attendant.

"Of course, sir," she answered, lunging for the closet and taking out a dry-cleaning bag. "Is Mrs. Sarantos up yet? Would she like to change, too?"

"She's still sleeping."

"Please let me know when I can prepare something for you to eat."

"I'm fine with a big bag of crisps and a biscuit or two for now, thanks. I tend to snack when I'm working."

Her perfectly tweezed eyebrows furrowed. "You're going to work?"

"No time like the present," he commented as he turned around and went to the bathroom. Instead of kicking his discarded clothes into a corner like he normally would, he got dressed first and smoothed his suit out over the hanger. He took it back to the front, hung it up himself and went to sit down again.

This time, he opened his laptop and worked through the reports he'd received earlier in the week on the Dubai project. There were some issues with the materials that will be used in the support beams of the building. He was liaising with a more experienced engineer to solve the problem, and took his time reading the last email Niall had sent. The man sure knew what he was talking about.

Soon, though, Konstantinos found himself staring at the screen of his iPad, having saved a couple of the pictures his brother had posted. He stopped as he found the one where he was dancing with his wife for the first time, zooming in until only their faces were in view. He stared at her beauty and happiness, wishing that he would always be able to make her look like that.

* * * * *

ASHA WOKE UP, blinking in confusion. Of all the places she's been, she was pretty sure that she's never slept on *this* bed before. There was a strange humming noise in the background, too. It took her a while to figure out that she was on an airplane.

Her heart thundered in her chest. She was a married woman, currently flying towards her honeymoon destination. Why wasn't her husband in bed with her?

She sat up and noted that she was still in her dress. No wonder she'd been so uncomfortable. She remembered Denise mentioning something about having an extra set of clothes to travel in. Where on earth would she find that?

Getting up, she stretched her limbs and wrapped the blanket around her. She walked out of the room, stopping in her tracks when she saw her husband staring intently at his tablet device. His hair was unruly, not the coiffed style it had been at the wedding. He was wearing a dark blue, loose-fitting T-shirt and equally comfortable jeans, and was barefoot.

She quietly made her way over to him, eyes widening once she saw what he was mesmerized by: a photograph of them, gazing lovingly at each other. It was moments like this that made her question her conviction that he was a womanizing man-whore.

"Hi," she whispered.

He gazed up and smiled. "Feeling more rested?"

"I couldn't get the sleep I wanted to. My dress isn't

made for bed."

"I'll go get your things." He pushed his devices away and got to his feet. "Be right back."

"Thanks."

A smile threatened to appear on her face as she picked his iPad up. How long had he been looking at this photograph? It was a beautiful one. She would want it on the entry wall in their apartment, as a visual reminder of their vows: for their benefit, as well as whoever came to visit. She might hate him sometimes, but women everywhere had to know that he was *hers*.

"Here you—" He broke off once he saw her with his iPad, his cheeks stained red. Since when did *he* blush? "Loikanos put them up," he told her, before she could ask. "He's a bit addicted to social media."

"I'm surprised he finds the time, since he's always trying to get Denise into bed," she teased, switching his iPad for her clothes. She clutched the hanger to her chest and looked at him, nervous.

"Normally he would upload nearly a thousand pictures after a wedding like ours, but he stopped after two hundred." Konstantinos chuckled and rubbed his hair. "I'm assuming that Denise threatened to kick him out if he didn't pay her some attention."

She nodded, smiling. "Those two are really insatiable, huh?"

"Yes," he said, his dark eyes glowing as they bore into hers.

Shifting from one foot to the other, she tucked the strands of hair that had escaped from her stylish bun behind her ears. "I'm, ah, going to get changed."

"I'll be here."

Her stomach was tied in knots once she shut the bedroom door behind her and stripped down to her underwear. There were two outfits on the hanger: one was a summery dress, while the other was something similar to what her husband was wearing. She decided on the latter, thinking that she'll change into the dress before they landed in Hawaii.

It took her a few minutes to take the golden clips out of her hair. She brushed her hair out carefully, loving the soft curls that framed her face. Her hair was naturally straight, so she enjoyed having waves cascading down her back for once.

She removed her makeup and earrings, took a deep breath, and exited the bedroom. Konstantinos was typing something on his laptop, looking nothing at all like the carefree man she'd known the first couple of days of their captivity. She was amazed by how much they've both changed, by letting down their guards to reveal the compatible personalities that had been hiding beneath.

"What're you busy with?" she asked, sitting down next to him and folding her legs under her.

"Give me one second." He squinted at the screen, switching to a window where he adjusted the design of something. He saved his work, shut the laptop and turned to her. "The building. Just when I thought that everything is as it should be, my colleague pointed out a problem."

"Is it a big one?" When he nodded, she smiled kindly. "You'll figure it out, Teeny."

He pushed his chair back to sit more comfortably. "I should probably thank you for showing up to our wedding," he teased.

For a second or two, I really considered ditching you at the altar.

"Likewise."

"I had a really good time."

"What was with that dance you and Loikanos did?"

He grinned sheepishly. "We saw a performance that Bruno Mars did on *X Factor*, and watched the video over and over again to learn the choreography. It's like our party trick. Every year, we find another cool song to dance to."

"You pulled out some James Brown moves there. I was impressed."

"I aim to please." He winked at her. "One day, maybe we could choreograph our own number."

"You're going to have to get me seriously wasted before I dance like *that* in front of random people."

Leering at her, he whispered: "Oh, I think I can get you to do it without having alcohol as the motivating factor."

She couldn't blink or move. She was overly aware that they were married, and alone. All that was left to do was consummate their union. She couldn't run away from it anymore: it was going to happen. Soon. Maybe even right *now*.

She really didn't want to hold back anymore.

She pulled his face to hers and kissed him hungrily. She felt the vibrations of his moan on her lips: it sent tingles down her spine. When he helped her onto his lap, she went willingly, straddling his hips while their mouths aroused each other even more.

"I've wanted you for so long," she whimpered, loving how his stubble was grazing her chin and cheeks.

"Asha," he growled possessively, his hands cupping her behind and pushing their crotches together.

Yes, yes, yes!

Finally, oh finally, she had a chance to experience the reason why women loved having him in their beds. A part of her hoped that he would be disappointingly premature. What if he was so good that they will never venture outside again?

"Wait," he panted. He closed his eyes and leaned his head back. "We shouldn't do it like this."

"What are you talking about?" she complained, trying to prod him into another kiss.

"Asha, there's a flight attendant on board," he pointed out. "Let's wait until we're in Maui, okay? It's only a day away. I don't want anyone to be aware of what's going on between us. It's a private moment, and it should stay that way."

He was making complete and total sense, but she was hearing something else entirely. Maybe he's slept with the flight attendant on a previous occasion and he didn't want to make things awkward? That seemed more likely than him denying her simply because they had an audience. *Loikanos* never considered an audience other people in his adoration for Denise!

She felt the muscles of her face clench as she attempted to hide her disappointment. She really was a terrible liar, but if he knew how much he affected her... She couldn't show any weakness. He should never have the upper hand.

"Fine," she grumbled, jumping off his lap and heading to the bathroom to splash her face with cold water. She stared at her reflection and sighed. "You had to go and fall in love with him, didn't you?"

* * * * *

THEIR STOP IN Las Vegas gave them three hours to do some sight-seeing, but she wasn't enjoying it. Ever since he had rejected her, she's constantly been on the brink of tears. When he opened his stupid mouth, she felt like she could scratch his eyes out for being such an asshole.

She wasn't exactly the most rational person on the planet but, if he noticed her mood swings, he wasn't showing it. His endless patience was more infuriating than anything else.

As they walked the streets of Vegas, she noticed the way women of all ages responded to his rugged sex appeal. He held her hand and walked closely to her, but every once in a while some bimbo would brush past him and murmured an even faker apology. Asha was fuming from the cheek of some people.

Her rage worsened when she realized that he wasn't doing anything to deter them. Either he was oblivious to the effect he had on the opposite sex—which seemed laughable, given his reputation—or he didn't care what they thought anymore. This last point made her chuckle. She doubted that married life was going to change him.

She ignored the voice that assured her that he already has.

When they boarded the plane again, she decided to sleep the rest of the way. Konstantinos had enough work to keep him busy. Besides, that damn flight attendant was ogling him like a cat on heat and, if Asha didn't watch herself, she was going to commit murder before they touched down in paradise.

She couldn't sleep for more than ten minutes at a time, and her foul mood worsened all the way to Maui. She was so infuriated that she imagined the volcanoes spontaneously catching fire from her presence alone. They were ushered into an awaiting car, and she seethed on the drive to Konstantinos' property.

"Don't you ever get jetlag?" she asked him bitingly.

He chuckled. "Ask me two days from now." He pointed to the sky. "Those clouds look ominous, don't they? The flight crew told me that we're in for some rough weather."

That perfectly matches my mood.

"I think I'm going to sleep until the sun eventually comes out."

"The weather's perfect for staying in bed, yes," he agreed, wagging his eyebrows.

She resisted rolling her eyes. "I'm finding it confusing that it's past sunset here. I hate you for being unaffected by time zones and climate changes."

He burst out laughing. "I guess that's better than hating me for other reasons."

I do that anyway, jerk.

"How long until we get there?"

"We're about five minutes away," he answered, gazing out the window. "You're going to love it. I don't come here nearly often enough, because it's so far to travel, but it's really worth the wait."

She saw why once the car came to a halt in front of a Japanese-style home. She could only imagine how beautiful the interior decorations were. Thanking her husband for holding the door open for her, she stepped out of the car and walked up the perfectly stoned pathway to the front of the house.

"Mrs. Sarantos," a maid nodded as she entered.

Asha nearly got a heart attack. She hadn't expected anyone else to already be here. "Hi."

"My daughter and I will be taking care of you," the woman said cheerfully, gesturing to the young girl standing next to her. "Should you need anything, don't hesitate to ask."

"I'm Asha," she introduced herself, holding her hand out.

The woman blinked in surprise and looked at Konstantinos for support.

He laughed softly. "She's not going to bite, Halina." He wrapped an arm around Asha's waist, explaining: "We took Halina and Kaila in about five years ago. They use the house as their own when we're not around. Because of mama and her... enthusiastic behaviour, Halina is a bit wary of women. She's not a fan of physical touch."

"But mama is harmless!" Asha argued lightly. "I was taken aback by her mannerisms at first, too, but I like it now. You get used to it."

"And Asha is not the type of person to make someone uncomfortable, Halina," he soothed. "Do you have everything you need in your cottage?"

Asha frowned. "I thought you said they stayed in the house."

"We do," Halina confirmed, "but it's your first night together as a married couple. We'll be out of your way during your honeymoon." She turned to Konstantinos. "There are some appetizers in the living room, sir. Call me if there's anything I've forgotten."

He kissed the middle-aged woman's forehead. "I'm sure you've thought of everything. We'll see you in the morning."

Asha's heart rate increased substantially when the last pieces of their luggage were taken to their bedroom and everyone moved out of the house, leaving her alone with her husband. He took her hand in his and led her to the living room, sliding doors open and revealing a stunning view from the patio.

"Wow, it's so beautiful," she murmured, watching the sandy pathway that disappeared into the jungle brush and the ocean below.

"You've never been to Hawaii before?"

"No," she replied. "I've been to the Caribbean, though."

He brought her a cup of tea, sipping on coffee. God, the amount of caffeine this insomniac ingested should be illegal! "I'm always calmer when I'm here." He stood behind her, his warm breath tickling her skin as he dropped kisses on her shoulder. "I wanted to take my time with you."

She shivered involuntarily and leaned against his chest. "Is that why you're drinking coffee?"

Chuckling softly, he replied: "Yes."

"Uhm, I should take a shower first," she said nervously, finishing her tea and grabbing a bunch of grapes from the fruit bowl on the coffee table. She avoided eye contact. "I feel really dirty."

"I'll do the same. I'll find you when I'm done."

She was afraid that her voice would sound too squeaky if she spoke, so she clamped her mouth shut and followed her instincts to the main bedroom. The four-poster bed was even bigger than the one in their London apartment. She hurriedly opened one of her bags, grabbed a light green chemise with a matching G-string and rushed into the bathroom.

The shower was between a few bamboo bushes and had no ceiling. She stared up at the sky while she cleaned a day's worth of sweat from her body, pulling her thoughts back into the present moment. She had to remember who she was married to, or she was easily going to lose track of her resolve.

She mentally ran through the reasons why she loathed him with such fiery intensity. They will be together as husband and wife tonight, but she wasn't going to respond the way she usually did when he got her riled up. She would keep her passion tightly locked up.

She lathered her skin with body lotion once she was done, twisting her damp, fresh-smelling hair into a bun on top of her head and donning the lingerie. She spent a few seconds brushing her teeth, feeling much better now that she was clean from head to toe. She sprayed perfume behind each ear, took deep breaths and walked into the bedroom.

Konstantinos had pushed the panel blinds in front of the floor-to-ceiling windows open and was staring at the ocean. His boxers hung loosely from his tapered waist, putting his muscular body on display. She licked her lips, nearly drooling at the sight of him.

What happened now? Should she get on the bed and call him to her? Should she announce her presence and wait for him to make the first move? Why did this feel like her first time? She's had sex before, but Praven had always got right down to business. Konstantinos, on the other hand, said that he wanted to take his time.

Good God, she was going to lose her mind before they even started.

Clearing her throat, she dug her toes into the thick carpet under her feet. She froze when he turned around, his gaze slithering down her body. Her arousal steadily ascended while his eyes darkened with lust.

"You look beautiful, Bigfoot," he murmured as he stepped up to her. His fingers found the clip that held her hair together and took it off. Cupping her face in his hands, he stared into her eyes. "I love you so much."

When he kissed her, she responded eagerly, but with the sting of betrayal still fresh in her mind, she waited for him to take the lead. She wasn't going to lift a finger tonight. He might own her body and make her hormones go haywire, but he wouldn't have her heart.

CHAPTER 38

SOMETHING WAS VERY, very wrong.

They'd finally had the opportunity to make love as a married couple, but Konstantinos couldn't shake the feeling that she was mad at him. Why, he had no clue, but she hasn't been her fun-loving self for a while. In fact, he'd go as far as to say that she's reverted to the ice princess she used to be, the one he'd known before they fell in love.

He had assumed that her attitude while they were travelling had largely been due to jetlag, but things were starting to add up. Something had happened a week ago to make her change the way she felt about him. It's almost as if she didn't trust him anymore. First insisting on a prenup; then that they should both go for blood tests each month? And now, with her stoic attitude in bed…

It had felt phenomenal to make love to her after the mounting sexual tension. She had made the right noises at the right times, but there was something missing. He couldn't put his finger on it. Their coupling hadn't been as explosive as he had predicted.

He glanced at her when his breathing calmed. "Asha, is something wrong?"

She was on her side with her back to him. "I'm fine."

"Don't give me that," he warned, not caring if he ruined their afterglow. He had to know what the hell was going on in that closed-off mind of hers. "Tell me."

"Is this the part where you say I'm shit in bed?"

He felt like he'd been slapped. Perhaps he was going about this the wrong way: he didn't want to remind her of Praven or what that bastard had done to her self-confidence. He reached out to turn her around, flinching at the blank look she gave him.

"You're not shit in bed," he insisted, "but I can tell something's bothering you. You're clearly stressed. Why won't you tell me?"

"Why do I have to tell you?" She pulled the sheet up to her chin while she searched for her discarded underwear. "You know what you did!"

"Obviously I've forgotten," he snapped, angry that she was brushing him off. "Why don't you remind me?"

"I need to go for a walk."

He jumped out of bed and stopped her before she could head out of the room. He didn't care that he was still naked. "What did I do to make you shut me out, Asha? I have no idea what you're talking about! You were so responsive when we were fooling around in the apartment, losing yourself the same way I was, but none of that happened a few minutes ago."

Her green eyes were downcast. "Please get out of my way."

"Where the hell are you going? It's eleven at night!"

"I don't ask you where *you've* been," she hissed through clenched teeth, her gaze meeting his. "I need to go for a walk, so *get out of my way!*"

He stepped aside, grabbed his briefs and followed her to the living room. "Is this how things are going to be, then?" he asked her furiously. "You promised me that we'll always talk about what's on our minds, but now that we're married you're going to run away?"

"Don't talk to me about promises, Konstantinos Sarantos!" she threw at him over her shoulder. "You don't know what the word even *means!*"

He grabbed her elbow and swung her around. "When did I ever break a promise to you?"

Tears were sliding down her cheeks, causing his heart to clench. She shoved his hand until he let go of her. "If you're asking that question, you're thicker than I thought! I'm going for a *walk*! Don't come after me!"

Speechless, he watched her run out of the house. What on earth was going on? He felt like he's slipped into an alternate universe, never to reunite with the *real* Asha Dewali again. He picked the closest vase up and threw it on the floor, screaming his frustrations to the gods.

Storming back to the bedroom, he switched his phone on and called his brother. He didn't give a damn what time it was in London: he needed to share what's happened, before he reached his wit's end.

"How do you have time for a phone call?" Loikanos asked by way of greeting, a grin in his tone. "You're on your honeymoon! You're supposed to be shagging each other senseless!"

"God, I wish that was the case," he growled.

"Okay, what the hell is going on?"

Konstantinos raked his fingers through his hair and laughed without humour. "I wish I knew."

"Start from the beginning."

"I don't know what to do. Asha seems to think that I broke a promise to her but, for the life of me, I have no idea what she's talking about! I think it has something to do with the reason she kicked me out of the apartment a day earlier than planned." He sighed, rubbing his eyes. "Ever since, she's acted like a nutcase, and I… Bro, the way I feel right now, I wouldn't mind an annulment."

"Shit," Loikanos muttered in surprise. "But you've waited so long for her!"

"I know," he groaned emotionally, sitting down on the edge of the couch. "I just… What can I do? I've been supportive, but she's not giving me a break!"

"Listen, let me talk to Denise. Maybe Asha let something slip. We'll figure this out, but you've got to give me a few minutes."

"Call me back, okay?"

"Keep your phone charged," Loikanos instructed, hanging up.

Konstantinos fell back on the couch and sighed deeply. He couldn't believe that he had to involve other people in his marriage so early on, but what choice did he have? Asha wasn't giving him an inch. He couldn't allow her to keep treating him this way.

Since when was *he* the monster in their fairy-tale?

* * * * *

DENISE'S EYES WIDENED while Loikanos divulged Asha and Konstantinos' problems. Normally, she wouldn't care what happened in other people's lives, but she felt responsible for their happiness. *She* had paired them up: it was only fair to make sure they were successful in every way.

"She didn't tell me anything, *mon cher*," she said once her fiancé finished. "As far as I'm aware, she's happy." She picked up her phone and scrolled through her contact list. "Why don't you call Kashinath or Farida, and I'll see what I can dig up on my end of things?"

"Good idea," Loikanos praised, giving her a peck on the cheek before doing as he was told.

Denise rang her assistant. Her fingers impatiently tapped on her knee while she waited for the call to connect. It wasn't so early in the morning that he wouldn't be awake.

"What can I do for you, boss?" Jacob asked brightly, moments before the call would have diverted to voicemail.

"We have a problem with the newlyweds, *chéri*." She frowned while she tried to think of what he could do. "Can you please go over the security footage of the Dewali apartment and look for anything suspicious? Start with, hmm, last week Sunday and work your way backwards. Are you writing this down?"

"Yup, I grabbed a pen when I saw it's you calling. What else?"

"I don't want to alert their parents, so try to keep this as quiet as possible. If I find out anything else on my side, I will let you know. This is our top priority, Jacob: forget whatever else you were doing."

"You've got it, boss."

She ended the call and turned to Loikanos, who was still talking to Farida. She felt like she was missing something, and had no idea why Marietta Angelotti kept coming to mind. What would Asha's best friend have to do with this?

"Thanks, sis," Loikanos sighed. "Please, don't tell your parents, or even your brother. Let's just sort this out quietly, okay? If we can't, we'll get more help." He nodded at her response. "Okay cool, chat to you soon."

"How bad is it?" Denise asked her future husband, knowing what that look on his face meant.

"It might be nothing, but Farida was telling me how Asha complained about other women hanging around my brother." He pushed his hair out of his eyes. "She also said that Asha mentioned Praven a lot."

She gasped, taken aback. "No, things are over between Praven and Asha!"

"Are you sure? Maybe she doesn't love my brother, after all."

"No one can act that well, *mon cher*, believe me. It has to be something else." She massaged her temples. "Maybe Asha thinks Konstantinos will be tempted by other women?"

"Are you kidding me?" He looked exasperated. "Any fool can see that he worships the ground she walks on! I've never seen him this way about a girl before. It's as if no one else exists but her! What the hell is wrong with women?"

"I can relate to—"

"What?" Loikanos glared at her. "When have I *ever* given you any kind of indication that I want someone else?"

Leaning over to kiss him, she smiled kindly. "In the beginning of our relationship, *mon cher*. You shouldn't interrupt a woman. My reason is simple: you're younger than I am. There will always be a part of me that wonders if you'll find a younger model. But, unlike Asha, I will talk to you about it so we can sort it out amongst ourselves. I suspect that she was incredibly hurt by Praven, and that she finds it difficult to express herself in a romantic relationship, even after all the work your brother has put in."

"I'm sorry I jumped to conclusions, but I'm worried for him. He's never loved like this before."

"I know, but we will…" She trailed off as her phone rang. Her eyebrows lifted when she recognized Jacob's number. "That was quick, *chéri*, even for you."

"You have a sixth sense about things, Denise, I swear." Jacob sounded tense. "I didn't have to look for very long. The problem started last Saturday."

"I'm putting you on speaker." She placed the phone between her and Loikanos, her frown returning with a vengeance. "What happened?"

"It's Marietta."

Loikanos exchanged a glance with her. "What about her?"

"While Asha and Denise were at Westminster Abbey, Marietta went over to their apartment. Konstantinos was alone. I'm watching it back as I'm talking to you and I still can't believe…" Jacob sighed. "She's dressed like some sleazy slut, boss. It looks like she keeps trying to make a pass at him, but he rejects her—"

"Of course he does," Loikanos muttered, "he's in love with *Asha*!"

"—and then he walks to the gym. She types something on her phone before following him. They exchange a few words and then she walks to the kitchen to get a bottle of water. She gets pills from her handbag, opens the bottle and drugs the water. Konstantinos takes a long sip when she gives him the bottle. A few minutes later, he becomes unsteady on his feet and she helps him upstairs to the bedroom, goes back down to check something, and then strips off her clothes when she's back with him. You know there's only that one camera in the hallway of the second floor, so I don't see what happens next, but Asha arrives within five minutes, finds them, and storms out."

By the time her assistant stopped talking, Denise felt like she was stuck in a movie. She could see Loikanos was experiencing something similar, although he was also understandably furious.

"Let me get this straight: Marietta *drugs* my brother, takes him to the bedroom and removes her clothes along the way, knowing that Asha was minutes away?"

"That's what it looks like, yes," Jacob confirmed.

"Did she rape him, too?"

Denise held up her hands. "Let's not get ahead of ourselves. Jake, I want you to take screenshots of the most important things that transpired during that video and email it to me. We'll forward it to Konstantinos after we've spoken to him. This explains why Marietta wanted to leave the country so quickly. Asha must have said something to her."

"But why would Asha marry him if she thought he cheated?" Jacob asked.

She smiled grimly. "Because she knew her family expected her to. I can look out for that email in five minutes then, *chéri*?"

"Make it three."

Sighing deeply when the call disconnected, she gazed at her lover. "Can you believe that one woman caused this much drama?"

"I believe I told you that very thing after she died." He couldn't hide that he was livid. "This is unbelievable! What if she raped him? And why, in heaven's name, would she do something like this to her best friend?"

"I get the feeling that we were all oblivious to Marietta's state of mind. She was obviously a very deranged girl." Denise shook her head sadly. "I remember reading she's been admitted to a mental institution before."

"How much do you have to hate someone to do this?"

"This wasn't hate, *mon cher*." She pulled her laptop closer once it pinged. "This was jealousy."

"I can't believe Asha fell for it! Why didn't she *do* something?"

"She is passive, especially when she is emotionally involved in the situation."

"No, she's just plain stupid! What kind of woman doesn't *talk* about things?"

Denise gave him a look. "Need I remind you how I behaved in the beginning of our relationship?"

"I need coffee," he mumbled, avoiding the subject by getting off their bed. "Would you like a cup?"

"Please, *mon cher.*"

When she was alone in the room, she checked the email, gaping at the screenshots. It would've been easy to dismiss Jacob's allegations as a work of fiction, but she was now staring at the hard evidence. Letting out a long breath, she reached for her phone to call Konstantinos.

* * * * *

KONSTANTINOS JUMPED WHEN his cell phone vibrated on the table. "Denise?" he answered.

"*Chéri*, it's bad," she sighed in reply.

He stiffened, foreboding dripping through his veins. "How bad?"

"I need to ask you something before I carry on. What can you remember about last Saturday?"

"Is that really important?"

"Frankly, yes."

His frown deepening, he searched his memory banks. "Hey, that was the day I woke up naked in bed, feeling like shit," he realized. "I had a terrible headache, as if I'd spent the day drinking. I don't remember much that happened before that. Why?"

"You're not helping us solve this mystery."

"Denise, put me out of my misery and *tell me* what you learned."

"I've sent you an email. Are you close to a computer?"

"Hold on." He pinched the phone between his shoulder and his ear, getting his laptop bag in the foyer and opening the device. He swore under his breath: it had no battery life left, so he rushed through the house looking for an adapter for his charger. He had sweat on his forehead by the time everything was set up. "Okay, give me a second to connect to the wireless internet in the house…"

"I've got all day, *chéri*," Denise soothed.

"I'm sorry for getting you involved."

"I'm glad you did, Konstantinos, and you will soon see why. Asha might have been able to explain some of her misplaced anger, but it still would not have made sense to you."

The email arrived in his inbox and he clicked it. His heart stopped beating. One by one, he went through the attachments, feeling ice cold. "What did she do to me?"

"We suspect that she drugged you."

"And then? She took me to the bedroom and stripped naked!"

Denise hesitated. "I don't know what happened then, *chéri*. I am so sorry."

"That bitch!" He dropped to his knees in defeat,

especially after he saw the photos of Asha walking towards the bedroom. "How am I supposed to fix things with my wife if I don't know what Marietta did to me? God, no *wonder* Asha was frigid! I should've told her about that sleazy friend of hers!"

"Why didn't you?"

"Because I don't want her to feel like I'm trying to control her life! It's like telling *me* to stop seeing my brother, merely because he can be such an idiot sometimes! Do you really think she would've listened?"

"We can speculate all we want, *chéri*, but it will change nothing. You should go to your wife and explain this. Show her these pictures if you have to."

He felt violated. How was he supposed to act like he wasn't affected by what Marietta had done? A woman had taken advantage of him.

Again.

Tears slipped down his cheeks as he remembered one night, six years ago, when more or less the same thing had happened. It had left an emotional scar so big that he hadn't wanted to get close to someone else again.

His first real girlfriend had been on a power trip one night, insisting that she take control of their lovemaking. He hadn't been against it, per se, but her attitude had made him wary. And then, when he'd least expected it, she had tied him to her wrought-iron headboard and done things that had him walking oddly for two days, bruises covering his body. Normally, he wouldn't have minded a bit of discomfort after sex, but she hadn't stopped when he'd begged her to.

Needless to say, they had broken up not long after

that.

"Konstantinos?"

He barely heard Denise. Marietta had drugged him, causing him to black out and forget why he had even allowed her to stay in the apartment while Asha wasn't there. She'd taken off her clothes... How was *he* supposed to know if she had taken it that one step too far?

"Bro, are you there?"

"I'm here," he answered hoarsely.

"Dude, are you crying?"

"It's like Lena all over again." Loikanos was the only person he'd ever told about that horrific night. Konstantinos wished he could erase the memories from his mind forever. "What do I do?"

"Ah, shit, I'm sorry for being insensitive. I completely forgot about that." His younger brother sighed. "We've done what we could to make you aware of this problem, bro. Go to Asha and sort it out. Like it or not, the two of you need each other now more than ever."

Konstantinos took a couple of moments to compose himself. That's when he realized that there was a violent thunderstorm raging outside, and Asha was only wearing that thin layer of lingerie. "Thank you for your help. Give Denise a kiss from me."

"Keep in contact, do you hear?"

"I'll do my best."

He chucked his phone aside, walked to the closest bedroom to get two blankets, and headed out of the house. He had no idea where to start looking, but assumed that she would be on the beach. Rain pelted his skin, like Lena's whip had, and drenched him in the memories of his less-than-perfect past. He could still remember the evil glint in her eyes when she'd hit him until he bled, before shoving a vibrator...

He shouted out a profanity to distract himself, picking up the pace. He wasn't cold yet, but he wrapped one of the blankets around him while keeping the other dry against his chest. Squinting through the spray, he saw a hunched shape on the beach and broke into a run.

It was time for them to step up to the plate.

CHAPTER 39

ASHA WAS SHIVERING with cold, yet it was preferable to being with Konstantinos. It had appeared as if he was truly baffled by her behaviour. How was it so easy for him to forget his sexual exploits, especially those he'd had right before getting married to her?

The tide was rising with every second she remained here—in the middle of the storm—but she wished that she could get swept up by the water. It would be much easier than living with all the lies; to see the disappointment in his eyes after they make love. She felt like she was back in Praven's bed.

She lifted her knees up, wrapped her arms around them and tucked her chin into the little warmth generated by her skin. She bit her bottom lip hard, forcing herself not to cry. The sky was already doing it for her, so why bother?

"You're not sexy when you try too hard, Ash," Praven had told her one night. "I feel sick every time you touch me."

Don't go there, she pleaded her stupid brain, but it had other plans. It wanted to hurt her the way her husband had.

"Why can't you be like other women? You should watch porn and learn a few things. You're like an ice princess."

She sobbed loudly, recalling Konstantinos accusing her of the same thing once. Why did she always fall for the pricks in this world? Why couldn't she find a good, honest man who loved her regardless of what she did, or didn't do, in bed?

"Asha!" someone shouted over the sound of clapping thunder.

Hesitantly looking up, she broke down completely when she realized that her husband was rushing to her as if the hounds of hell were on his tail. She told herself that, if he didn't care, he would've left her here to rot.

He fell to his knees next to her, wrapping a thick blanket around her shaking shoulders. "Are you out of your mind?" he yelled. After she was covered, he took her in his arms and enveloped her in his warmth, adding another blanketing layer around her. "You're going to get yourself killed!"

"How could you?" she cried. His hold was crushing her, but she welcomed it. If she was going to die out here, she might as well get peace.

"How could I *what*?"

"You slept with her!" She wasn't even angry anymore, simply unbelievably sad. "You told me that you wanted me, but then you slept with Marietta! How could you *do* that to me? You knew I was going to be home! Did you want me to see it?"

"Why didn't you tell me what's bothering you?" he snapped in her ear, his voice harsh. "Asha, you *promised* that you were always going to be honest with me!"

"What does that matter? You cheated on me, you son of a bitch!"

He exclaimed something in Greek and angrily launched her to her feet, keeping her tucked into his side. "Things aren't always what they seem! Did you ever consider that?"

She laughed bitterly, her teeth clattering. "What, are you trying to make me believe that you were taking a nap with her, *naked*? You must really think that I'm intellectually challenged, you disgusting brute! Let go of me!"

"Never," he declared ominously, basically dragging her back to the house.

They were both out of breath as he dumped the blankets in the laundry room. She hunched as she followed him to their bathroom, where he pulled a screen door shut to block off the cold air that was coming from the shower's open ceiling. He opened the taps of the bath, which was big enough to comfortably accommodate four people.

"Strip and get in," he demanded.

"No!"

"Asha, don't push me today. I might push back." He took his soaked briefs off and glared at her. "You'll hate me, I'll hate you, and we'll get a divorce and live miserably ever after."

Something in his eyes prompted her to do as he asked. She moaned at the sudden heat of the water on her icy skin, but clenched her jaw and kept dipping more of her body under the surface. She watched as he did the same, expecting an explanation. They were on opposite sides of the huge bath, eyes fixed on one another.

"Why do you think I slept with Marietta? Walk me through it."

She swallowed, inwardly happy that he wasn't shouting anymore. "Are you kidding me? I came back from Westminster Abbey. You were in bed, completely naked and sweaty, with Marietta cuddled up to you. She woke up as I was about to leave and I told her she wasn't my maid of honour anymore."

"Why didn't you talk to me? Chase her out of *your* apartment and confront your fiancé?"

"And what would that have helped, Konstantinos?" she sighed. "You would've admitted it, I would've been even more hurt and we would've postponed or cancelled the wedding. I couldn't do that to our families."

His eyes blazed. "Let me get this straight: you only married me to please our *families*?"

She winced at his fury. It sounded bad now that he's spelled it out like that. "Our companies are merging, or have you forgotten?"

"I thought we agreed that we'll get married because we want to be with *each other*! God, Asha, I'm so disappointed in you."

"You're kidding, right? You cheated on me, and you're talking to *me* about disappointment?"

"Yes," he answered, "because unlike *you*, I get my facts in order before I make my conclusions. I do *research*." He lifted a finger from below the water, glaring at her sarcastically. "For example, did you know that your *best friend*, Marietta, drugged me? That she dragged me through the apartment and did God-knows-what-else to me while I was *unconscious*?"

Those questions took her off guard. "What a convenient excuse!"

"For God's sake, Asha Dewali, it's not an excuse! I can show you the pictures that Denise sent me about fifteen minutes ago!"

"You spoke to Denise about us?"

"Yes, because *you* ran off!"

She couldn't believe her ears. They've been married for hardly two days, and she was already avoiding her responsibility in their relationship. This whole time, she's hated him for doing something he hadn't even participate in? He was right: she should've spoken to him, instead of leaving that note. What kind of woman was she?

Asha recalled the subject of Marietta's email: *I'm Sorry*. It was still in her inbox...

"I can't remember anything about that day," he confessed, rubbing his eyes. "I woke up on the bed feeling disoriented and hung over. I didn't know why I was naked. I got your note and tried to call you but, being the stubborn woman you are, you wouldn't answer. We could've settled everything right then, do you realize that?"

"Yes," she answered softly, sniffing her tears away.

"I'm so sorry. I didn't know."

"I'm so mad I can…" He sighed. "Asha, I don't care what you think about my past, but I told you: I keep my promises. Ever since we got close, I haven't been able to imagine caring about another woman, much less *having sex* with them. I didn't like Marietta, and I should've told you why the second I realized that there was something fishy about her, but I trusted you to make your own decisions."

"Why didn't you like her?"

"You mean to tell me that you didn't see the way she glared at you all the time? I don't know what you did to piss her off, but she wasn't a happy camper, Asha. To top it off, she kept making passes at me, even though I made it abundantly clear that I only want to be with *you*." He made eye contact again. "Speaking of, if I'd been this big man-whore that you made me out to be, why would I still have given you so much attention?"

"I thought it was due to a guilty conscience."

He shook his head and added more warm water to their bath. "Look, I don't want to play the blaming game anymore. We're both at fault. I'm taking full responsibility for my part in this, and I want you to do the same." He waited for her to nod in agreement before continuing. "I'm going to say this one last time, so I want you to listen carefully: *you* are the woman I wanted to marry. I want to spend the rest of my life with *you*. If I hadn't been in love with you, we would've parted ways the second we stepped out of that apartment building, because I don't base my happiness on pleasing other people. I'm never going to look at another woman in that way. You are *it* to me. I thought I made this clear in my vows."

"I'm so stupid," she bawled, holding her face in her hands. "Oh my God, I will never be able to say how sorry I am, Teeny."

The water sloshed over the edge of the bath as he moved to her side and embraced her. "Make it up to me by trusting me," he pleaded. "I'm worthy of your trust, Bigfoot. I'll never intentionally hurt you or mistreat you. I take my promises seriously."

She clung to him. "Thank you for not going easy on me."

He barked a laugh and said: "Jeez, that's the understatement of the year. You can be extremely difficult."

"I'm trying to change that. You're the only one who's ever helped with that."

He stared into her eyes, kissing her softly. "You're worth it."

Her breathing hitched at the compliment. She frowned as she noticed the underlying sadness in his demeanour. "Teeny, what's wrong?"

"Marietta's not the first woman that's taken advantage of me," he admitted, dropping his gaze to her collarbones.

"What do you mean?"

"Do you remember when we used to talk about bondage and how I insisted that I won't get tied down by anyone?"

She had a nasty suspicion about what was coming, but she nodded anyway.

"I had a girlfriend once before. Her name was Lena. We met in university and became serious." He sucked a breath through his teeth, purposefully avoiding eye contact, until Asha tilted his chin up. "One night, she wanted to do role playing. I'm usually up for anything, but my gut was telling me she was high or something. She was insistent, though, so I agreed to give it a shot. She got me tied up and…" He faltered, panic in his deep brown eyes. "The whips appeared out of nowhere. She beat the shit out of me, Asha, and she didn't stop when I asked her to. I was bleeding from gashes on my stomach."

She sat back as he rose, pointing to the sexy indentations his abdominal muscles made as they bulged. She narrowed her eyes, trying to see what he was talking about, and gasped once she saw the fine white lines on his skin. She'd never seen them before, because of his naturally tanned complexion and overall sexiness.

He turned around and she inspected his back. He shuddered when her fingers traced the lines she found there. She was livid that this Lena bitch had taken advantage of a young Konstantinos, forever ruining him for romantic relationships. At the same time, her heart expanded with unbearable sadness now that she knew the curse he carried around with him.

Yes, he was hot, and that could work in his favour… But there were sick men and women out there who would take advantage at the drop of a hat.

"Knowing that Marietta drugged me brings back that helplessness I'd felt with Lena," he whispered, glancing at her over his shoulder. "I don't remember anything, Asha. I should've gone to the doctor after waking up, but I didn't think it was important. What if she…?" He trailed off and bit his lip.

"Teeny," she murmured, getting in front of him and standing, like he was. She touched his face and peered into his eyes. "I'm right here. I'm not going anywhere."

His strong arms circled her waist, and he buried his face in her neck. "Asha, I'm scared."

She wasn't sure she'd heard him right, *that's* how quietly he had admitted that. She held him closer, not caring that she was basically giving him permission to squeeze her until she couldn't breathe. If she'd known then what she knew now…

But she realized that things had to unfold the way they had, otherwise she would've never married him. There was more depth to this man than anyone knew, and he wanted to reveal every light and dark corner to *her*.

"I love you so much," she murmured, vowing that she will never doubt him again.

* * * * *

KONSTANTINOS GROANED AND snuggled up to Asha. "I can't sleep with my stuffy nose," he mumbled pathetically. "I'm blaming you for this."

She giggled and turned in his arms. "I'm sorry, okay?" She didn't sound much better than him. "How many times do I have to say it?"

"We're on honeymoon in one of the most exotic places in the world, but I have a cold. Next time you want to go traipsing into a thunderstorm, please make sure we haven't argued before that. It saves me the trip."

Giving him a soft kiss, she pulled back with a gasp. "Damn it! I'll suffocate if we had sex right now."

"I'm glad you think I'm up for it."

"I bet you're wishing you hadn't made that stupid promise that we'll wait until we're married, huh?"

He got frustrated just thinking about it. It's been five days since they had arrived in Maui, and they haven't been outside since that stormy—in more ways than one—night. He was seriously regretting the statements he'd made while they were locked up in that apartment.

He was keen to have another shot at making love to her, but it simply wasn't happening. Fate was obviously against them and God was having a laugh at their predicament. At least they've both read Marietta's email and he could sleep soundly, knowing he hadn't been raped.

"Have you found that time machine yet, Bigfoot? I was almost sure that it's as elusive as you are, so you're bound to have stumbled over it at some point."

"No, sorry. I guess I'm not as mysterious as everyone assumes I am."

He glanced up when he heard the front door open. "Ah, that must be Halina and Kaila. I'm starving."

"I can't even think about eating."

"Come on," he said, gently rolling out of bed and pulling her along. "I told them to research some quick fixes, *that's* how horny I am."

She sniggered, sighed, and got a tissue to blow her

nose before she began sputtering snot. "I'm so unattractive."

"Strangely enough, I can still get hard by looking at your legs," he teased, smacking her butt. "Your voice, on the other hand…" He burst out laughing at the glare she sent his way. "Just kidding, Bigfoot." He grinned happily at his two housekeepers. "Morning, ladies. How're you feeling?"

"Much better than you," Kaila giggled as she assisted her mother in the kitchen. "I don't have a runny nose and itchy throat."

Asha laughed. "Lucky, aren't you? So, Teeny tells me you've got some home-grown medicine we can try out? I'd love to go to the beach without feeling like complete and utter crap."

"Man, don't you love her accent?" he chuckled, receiving a slap from Halina. "Come on, I was saying that with respect!"

"You better have," she warned him. "I will not allow you to talk down to your wife."

"It feels good to know I'm supported by my sisters," Asha sniggered.

"You know, I pray to the gods that we'll have loads of boys." He eyed his wife with a grin. "There's already too much oestrogen around me. A man can only take so much."

"I'm glad you think I want to have your babies," she said sweetly.

Raising an eyebrow, he asked: "Who would you prefer to father your children, Bigfoot?"

"John Legend, who else?"

He threw his head back and guffawed loudly. "I might arrange that, if it'll make you happy, but you will *not* be having sex with him."

"It's not like she's having sex with you," Kaila teased. When the married couple looked surprised, she shrugged. "What? I clean your room, and there's nothing—"

"Okay!" Asha exclaimed brightly. "I think I've heard enough of that. I'm going to sit outside and catch some sun!"

His gaze followed her body as she walked away, still chuckling. "You two, I swear," he murmured affectionately. "She's not as open about everything as we are."

"We'll sort her out," Kaila said proudly.

Halina rolled her eyes at her daughter. "Sometimes I think that I gave birth to a boy."

"That's because she hung around Loikanos as a child. Did you hear he's getting married?"

"To a French woman, right?" Kaila pouted. "I always thought he'd wait for me."

Konstantinos thought about that. "No, you're far too busy for him. Maybe I should introduce you to Asha's brother. He's a cool guy." He rummaged in the fridge, complaining when Halina chased him away. "Come on, I was this close to getting that tub of yoghurt!"

"Go spend time with your wife," she insisted. "We will prepare breakfast."

He sighed. "You better make it a big meal, 'cause it feels like I haven't eaten in days."

Kaila gave him an annoyed look. "We know all about

your appetite for food, Kay."

Smiling at the nickname, he traced Asha's steps and shouted: "I'll give you Kash's number, Kay-Kay!" He dropped a kiss on his wife's head and plopped down on the lounger next to hers. "Do you want to go down to the water today?"

"It's a private beach, right?" When he nodded, she eyed him seductively. "Want to get it on in the ocean?"

"I thought you were feeling like crap."

"I'm here to have so much sex that I can't walk."

His heart skipped a beat. Whenever she turned up her inner flirt, he felt like a fish out of water. "Right now? Before breakfast?"

"Let's work up an appetite."

She got to her feet, smiled smugly at the effect she had on him, and started walking towards the sandy pathway. Once she was under the shade of the plantation around her, she undid the drawstring on her halter-neck dress and dropped it to the ground.

She was naked underneath.

It further went to prove that he didn't notice things when he was sick: after showering together this morning, she'd gone off to get dressed and they had got back in bed. Even with her butt pressed to his crotch, he hadn't realized that she hadn't donned underwear.

He's never chased after a woman so fast, discarding his shirt and shorts as he ran. He didn't care that his housekeepers weren't far away. Once they spotted the clothes, they will leave the food on the table and go about their day. He had Asha all to himself for now, and he was going to enjoy every second of it.

When he caught up with her, he threw her over his shoulder with a laugh. "Think you can take control of me, do you?" he asked, spanking her bare butt.

She giggled and slapped *his* ass, which was in line with her face at the moment. "Put me down, Teeny!"

He loved how warm the water was as he entered the waves. Once he was deep enough, he let go of her. Only, she pulled him down with her, causing them both to get dunked under the waterline. "You're going to regret that," he informed her with a grin.

"Oh, I hope so." She stood up, revealing her stunning breasts, and smiled back. "Can you handle all of this?"

God, she was beautiful when she was this confident. Without further ado, he took her in his arms and kissed her until they both forgot about being sick. Their body temperatures soon matched that of their surroundings.

And, this time, they made love without holding back.

* * * * *

ASHA SIGHED HAPPILY. "I'm probably going get a nasty sunburn, but that was definitely worth it."

"That should've been our first time." He rolled her around on the wet sand, hovering on top of her to nibble his way down her throat. "After we've had breakfast, we're doing it again and again and *again*."

She clutched his head as his mouth moved to one of her breasts. "Oh?" she asked breathlessly.

"I'm going to make you bedridden, like you want to be."

"Not *forever*," she clarified, "only for a few days."

"Consider yourself tied to the headboard, 'cause we're not leaving the bedroom."

"That's if you can get me back to the bedroom," she teased.

His dark eyes found hers, twinkling in the sunlight. "We'll see. I really need to eat something first, or I'm going to pass out."

"Fine," she complained dramatically, allowing him to help her to her feet. Hand-in-hand, they walked back to the bungalow, collecting their clothes along the way. "Hey, is it just me, or do you feel better?"

"Bigfoot, I feel fantastic." He sat down at the table on the veranda. "I've always wanted it to be like that for us."

"That's not what I meant and you know it. Pervert."

He feigned offence. "In that case… Yeah, my nose has cleared up. Probably because you tried to drown me in the ocean, but who's counting?"

"Oh, please." She shook her head and uncovered her plate of food. "Wow, this looks delicious! I think I'm picking up weight while we're here, thanks to those two."

"Do I look like I'm complaining?" he grinned.

"There will only be more of me to fit into your hands," she agreed.

He stared at her in silence for a long time before he began wolfing down his breakfast. "Finish your food. I want to be in that bedroom within the next ten minutes."

It was official: she was back in love with her husband. She wasn't going to overanalyse their relationship anymore. They'll take it day by day, play it by ear and grow closer as time went on.

They were a team now.

CHAPTER 40

"WHAT A LUCKY bastard," Loikanos muttered as he read the latest email from his brother.

From: Konstantinos Sarantos
To: Loikanos Sarantos
Subject: Extended Honeymoon

Hi, bro.

I'm not sure what time it is over there, but I thought I'd let you know that Asha and I will be spending an extra week here in Maui. I've already told papa, and he's fine with it, provided I work extra hard in Dubai.

Please forward any emails that I'm not copied on that are relevant to the project. Hope you're doing well. Say hi to Denise for me.

Brotherly love, K

PS: I'll name our firstborn after one of you for what you did to save my marriage, I swear.

With a sigh, Loikanos got out of bed. So much for sleeping late: he'd hoped to make love to his fiancée once more before they went to work, but she was in such a deep state of unconsciousness that he couldn't find it in his heart to wake her. They'd been busy for hours the night before. He was really taking his role as her sperm donor seriously.

He took a quick shower and got dressed, padding to the kitchen to make breakfast. It was the most important meal of the day and, with the way he's feeling now, he was going to need the added energy to make it through. Because of Konstantinos' absence from head office, the responsibility fell on Loikanos' shoulders. For someone who'd been an innocent bystander during the merger and wedding, their father even expected him to actively participate in the family business. Who knew when he'll get a chance to eat again?

He checked the clock mounted on the wall and swallowed the rest of his coffee. Getting up from the breakfast nook, he made Denise a cup of tea and took it to her. He placed it on the nightstand, kneeled on the floor and kissed her forehead.

"Time to get up, *mon amour*," he murmured softly, stroking the side of her face. He still couldn't believe that someone so beautiful and kind wanted to be with *him*. His parents were finally warming up to her. No one could resist her charm for very long, anyway: she had this gentle nature that was addictive to be around.

Her eyelids fluttered open and her vibrant blue gaze found his. "What time is it?"

"Half past six."

"Why are you dressed already, *mon cher*?"

"I have an early morning." Denise rolled onto her back and raked her fingers through her blonde tresses. His fingers ached to do the same, knowing how those silky strands felt... He cleared his throat to fight his arousal. He truly didn't have time for that, as much as it pained him. "Would you like to go to lunch with me?"

"I can't," she replied. "I have a meeting with a celebrity couple." She looked at him with a faint smile. "This is the first morning we won't make love before work. Is it the start of a trend, *mon cher*?"

He snorted. "Don't get too comfortable, *mon amour*. This is once only."

"I knew you would tire of me eventually," she whispered dramatically.

He stared at her, jaw clenched. He understood that she was taunting him and, like countless times before, he didn't think he could resist. "Denise, I really can't afford to miss this meeting. If I'm late, it will be a bad reflection on my father. I'll make it up to you tonight, okay?"

Nodding, she smiled and answered: "Okay. You know I was only teasing."

"I love you," he told her, pressing a kiss to her lips. "Have a good day, *mon amour*."

"You too, *mon cher*. Thank you for waking me up so sweetly."

He went to the bathroom to brush his teeth and slap aftershave on his neck. Then, gathering his things, he exited his apartment and took the elevator down to the ground floor of the building. A car was already waiting, and he inclined his head at Christopher in greeting before sliding onto the backseat. He received an email from his assistant with the agenda of the meeting attached, and he quickly scanned through the list.

God, it really *was* going to be a long, hellish day. He was already regretting not taking Denise's offer.

This fusion between Dewali Enterprises and Sarantos International was a killer. One would assume, because the families had decided on Asha and Konstantinos' union months ago, they would've put the business cogs in motion, too. Surprisingly, they'd waited until the ink had dried on the marriage contract before moving forward with the merger.

"Days like these, I'm really happy I'm only a bodyguard," Christopher commented as he opened the door at their destination.

"Want to swap for a day?"

The man chuckled. "No, thank you, Mr. Sarantos. You may be the furthest thing from being unfit, but you're not exactly bodyguard material, either."

"You'd rather have my brother on your team, huh?"

"I knew you would understand, sir."

Loikanos rolled his eyes. "Come along then, beefcake. There's a chance that you will have to save me from myself."

"Sounds ominous."

Stepping into his father's office building, Loikanos

gave a curt nod. "Exactly." He walked through the security checkpoint, and traipsed over to the private elevators, one of which took him straight to the top floor. He was surprised to spot his new brother-in-law loitering outside the boardroom.

"Louis," Kashinath greeted warmly. "I'm assuming you heard about the honeymoon?"

"I did. It's enough to make me want to get married."

"Well, at least you're already halfway there."

"Denise doesn't think I know, but she's already working on the invitations," Loikanos said, laughing quietly. "I think we're getting married in Greece."

"You two are so adorable, I think I might puke."

He burst out laughing. "How about you? Are you ready to settle down?"

"I think it's contagious," Kashinath bitched. "Ever since seeing my sister walk down the aisle, I can't help but feel a little jealous." He cleared his throat and lowered his voice. "Uhm, what do you know about Kaila?"

The name rang a bell, but Loikanos didn't link it to a face immediately. "Who?"

"Your brother's housekeeper in Maui."

"Oh!" He smiled fondly as he remembered their childhood. They used to cause a lot of trouble on that island. "We grew up together. She's pretty cute, why do you ask?"

"Well, she called me out of the blue about a week ago, and we've been chatting ever since." Kashinath smiled wryly. "Apparently Teeny told her we'll make a cool couple."

"My God, is *everyone* going to start calling him Teeny?"

"Even you have to admit that his name is awfully long."

Loikanos laughed, not willing to put his neck on a block by agreeing. His brother would murder him. "As for Kaila… She'll never move away from her mother in Maui so, if you want to get serious about her, be aware of that. You don't look like the kind of guy who wants to be stationed in one place."

"Thanks, I'll keep that in mind."

They glanced up once their fathers arrived and strode into the boardroom. It took several minutes for everyone to get settled. Only the owners, upper management executives and board members of each company were present today. Loikanos was amazed that they managed to fit around the table.

Nikos nodded at Sukesh to start the proceedings.

"Morning everyone," Sukesh greeted. "I know it's an early one for most of you, so we'd like to start off by thanking you for being here. As you know, we've got a rough couple of weeks ahead of us. The sooner we get started, the better for us all."

"Your new joint CEO's will be here for Phase Two of the merger, beginning next week," Nikos added brusquely. "They have extensively studied the documents handed to them from each side of this venture. Our job now is to come to an accord regarding the processes, policies and procedures that will have to be amended, created or removed to successfully serve the new company."

Sukesh nodded. "It's important to keep the integrity

of the individual enterprises that make up the whole. As you're all aware, we're bringing everything—from construction to the automotive industry to fashion—together in one giant conglomerate. We decided against using external consultants, but once we've reached an accord, we will be audited on a quarterly basis to ensure that our plans are effective."

"Now we can start," Nikos said, sliding the first stack of files closer to him. There were identical packages in front of every person in the room. "Please turn to page six of Dewali Enterprises' Processes…"

Loikanos and Kashinath shared a look, both thinking the same thing: *Will I get out of here before I die?*

CHAPTER 41

"WE ABSOLUTELY ADORED what you did with the Sarantos wedding," the famous actress gushed from the opposite side of Denise's desk. She clutched her fiancé's hand. "Do you think there's any way for us to get married in Westminster Abbey, too?"

Denise smiled professionally. "Unfortunately not. We had to get the Queen's stamp of approval for Miss Dewali and Mr. Sarantos to have their ceremony there. There is a whole checklist of what you need to do and who you need to be to get married there. I hope you understand."

The actress nodded sadly, though her musician husband-to-be rolled his eyes.

"I can suggest many other lovely places, if you're looking for a fairy-tale wedding."

Denise took out a couple of photographs of the venues she had in mind, smiling triumphantly when she saw the look of excitement on the woman's face. She had a nasty suspicion that *this* union wasn't going to last long, but luckily their longevity wasn't any of her concern. They weren't here for her matchmaking skills.

She spent the next hour and a half going over the details in a mind-numbing fashion, sighing with relief once the musician insisted they'd had enough for one day.

"We haven't even touched on cakes!" the blonde bombshell complained.

He glared at her. "If you want me to continue being a man, you won't ask me to sit through *that*." He turned to Denise with a forced smile. "Miss Lemont, thank you for your time. We'll pick this up another time."

She didn't trust herself to speak, so she merely nodded.

The actress watched him storm out of the office and sighed deeply. "I'm really sorry about that, Denise. He's normally much more pleasant."

"Men deal with stress differently. I always say that's when their true colours show."

"You don't think I should get married to him, do you?"

"My opinion doesn't matter," Denise replied, carefully selecting her words. "I don't get to see the inner workings of your relationship. I am an objective party."

"Wow, you're very diplomatic," the woman remarked. She rose to her feet. "I'll have my agent arrange another meeting with you next week? I swear I'll come alone."

"Either way, I'm comfortable." Denise walked her to

the door. "Please don't hesitate to call if you need anything."

They exchanged another couple of pleasantries and then, mercifully, Denise was left alone. She let out a long breath, rubbed her forehead and retraced her steps. She heard Jacob come into the office and shut the door behind him, already dreading what he wanted to discuss.

"Man, sometimes I *hate* our confidentiality clause," he muttered. "Do you know how much money I'd make if the tabloids found out the truth about them?"

"It will be easy, quick money, *chéri*," Denise chuckled. "You'll be stuck with a drug addiction and living in poverty within a year."

Jacob lifted the back of his hand to his temple, acting as if he was offended. "Your faith in my ability to resist the temptation is heart-warming, boss. I'm assuming that your young piece of meat is still too tired to shag you at night?"

She flushed slightly. "He's never too tired for that, but yes, he is exhausted."

"And it's only the first week." Jacob shook his head sadly. "When young love comes crashing down."

"Oh, stop." Turning to her computer, she resumed the process of securing a venue for her own wedding. "It'll quiet down soon. Asha and Konstantinos are arriving from honeymoon tomorrow. That will relieve some of the pressure."

"So, when are you sending out the invitations?"

"After the merger. I doubt that anyone would be able to RSVP if they're neck-deep in paperwork."

He smiled teasingly. "I'm invited, right?"

"But of course, *chéri*. You're the ring bearer."

"Happy to hear it." He sashayed to the door. "Do you need anything from Starbucks? I'm slipping out for twenty minutes or so."

She wrinkled her nose. Thinking about coffee left a rancid taste at the back of her tongue. That didn't make any sense, since caffeine was—apart from Loikanos— her favourite indulgence. "No thank you, *chéri*. I'm not thirsty."

He raised his eyebrows but left without another word.

She sat back in her seat, thinking. It worried her that she was losing her appetite for espressos and lattes, though most health-conscious people would tell her how good it was that she didn't crave coffee anymore.

Frowning, she opened her internet application and did a Google search for pregnancy symptoms. She was probably chasing her own tail, since she's only been off the Pill for a little over three weeks, but the results on the screen made her do a double take.

It can't be, she thought to herself, eyes wide. It was impossible, at least not this quickly! *Remi* had never got her pregnant, not once during their decade of marriage! How on earth was this possible?

She picked her phone up and dialled Jacob's number. "I do need something," she informed him once he connected the call, "but you won't find it at Starbucks."

"Okay, hit me."

"Please buy a large bottle of apple juice—"

"You hate apple juice!"

"—and three different brands of pregnancy tests."

There was a long silence that followed.

"Oh my God, do you think you're pregnant?" Jacob squawked happily. "Denise! Oh my God!"

"Will you do it or not?"

"I'm on it, boss! Be back soon!"

She hung up and continued reading the online article on pregnancy cravings. She became entirely engrossed and, when Jacob returned, she didn't notice until he dumped items on her desk and held the two-litre bottle of apple juice out to her.

"Drink," he instructed enthusiastically.

She did as she was told, wincing at the terrible taste while she gulped down half of the bottle's contents. She used to loathe apple juice as a child because it always made her pee like a racehorse. Right now, that's exactly what she needed.

Feeling that familiar press on her bladder, she grabbed the pharmacy packet and darted to the bathroom. She didn't even read the instructions of each pregnancy test—Jacob had bought four instead of three—but simply pulled down her G-string and did her thing.

Her eyes stretched wide. Her period was meant to have started already.

It can't be!

Her heart was thudding wildly once she cleaned up and stuffed the sticks into the bag. She felt light-headed as she strode over to her office, where Jacob was impatiently keeping an eye on the clock on her wall.

"How long?" he demanded.

"Relax, *chéri*," she soothed. *Oh please, as impossible as it may sound,* please *let me be pregnant!* "Another three minutes or so. I want to make sure that I don't rush the tests."

"Denise, I'm going to *die!*"

She giggled at his mood, knowing that Loikanos would've been ten times worse. "Get that juice out of my sight. I'll check the sticks once you're back." She laughed as he sprinted out of the office, returning mere seconds later. "I'm so nervous!"

"Boss, you've got nothing on me! Open up already!"

Taking deep breaths, she took them out one by one, lining them up on the desk. She removed the leaflets from each package, aware that Jacob was hovering next to her, reading along. Her gaze alternated between each test and the instructions, tears forming in her blue eyes. She put the brochures down and turned to her assistant.

"I'm pregnant. Every test is positive!"

He hugged her tightly. "Get your ass over to your fiancé's office *right this second,* or I'll take you over my knee."

"But what about—"

"I'll happily take the heat for your absence and reshuffle your schedule," Jacob interrupted. He had moisture in his eyes as he kissed her forehead. "Congratulations, *Madame.*"

"Thank you, Jake," she breathed, patting his cheek affectionately. Giving him a wave, she basically flew out of the building and to the sidewalk below. She collided with someone there, groaning as she straightened herself. She would have apologized, had it not been Remi. "What are you doing here?" she shouted in

English.

"Denise, come back to France with me."

"Never," she seethed, purposefully making a big scene in case she needed to report this to the authorities at a later stage. Granted, this was London and no one gave a shit about each other, but people were staring and that's all she wanted: witnesses. "Get it through your thick skull: *I don't love you*! If you'll excuse me, I need to go to the father of my unborn child."

Remi paled. "You're pregnant?"

"Yes," she replied, not caring if she hurt him. She's had it with her ex-husband's manipulative ways. "It took him only one month to make me pregnant, further proving that he's much more of a man than you will ever be. Never come here again, Remi. We are divorced, like you wanted, so, as they say in England, *piss off*!"

She hailed a black cab while Remi was still sputtering an indignant response, got in and rattled off her destination. By the time the driver pulled away from the curb, she'd already forgotten about the incident, deciding to focus on her future husband instead.

The drive felt like it took forever. Lifetimes later, she was dropped off at Sarantos International.

"I'm here to see Loikanos," she told the receptionist after succumbing to a security search.

"I'm sorry, Miss, but—"

She showed off her ring and slid her ID across the counter. "I'm his fiancée, and I'd like to see him as soon as possible."

The woman gaped in surprise. "Of course, Miss

Lemont, please—"

"I know where to find him. May I use one of the private elevators?"

"Of course, Miss Lemont!" the woman repeated. "One of the guards will assist you."

Denise has only ever felt this confident after meeting Loikanos, and it wasn't something she was willing to let go of anytime soon. She wished that every woman in the world would find a man who made them blossom this way. Women deserved to be loved and cherished.

She stepped out on his floor and marched to the boardroom. Over the past four days, he's complained about how stuffy the place got and how he wished that he could take more breaks. Well, she was about to give him a good excuse to delegate his work to someone else for the rest of the afternoon.

"Pardon me, but I'd like to speak to Loikanos," she announced, knocking on the open door of the boardroom.

He gazed up from the opposite side of the room. "Denise?"

"It's urgent," she insisted.

"Excuse me, gentlemen," he muttered under his breath as he made his way over to her. He had bags under his eyes. "What's the matter, *mon amour*?"

Grinning, she took him in her arms, tilted her chin up and whispered her news.

He grabbed her elbow and steered her to the other side of the floor, where his office was located. He shut and locked the door after they were inside. "Say it again."

"I'm pregnant, *mon cher*," she purred, perching on the edge of the desk. She pushed her handbag aside and hitched her skirt up. "Will you ravish me now?"

His movements were predatory as he sauntered over and kissed her passionately. She melted against him. He was the kind of man that kept his promises—the baby growing in her belly was proof of that—and whatever fear she'd had left of loving him disappeared like mist before the sun.

"We're going to your gynaecologist after this," he growled as he removed every stitch of clothing from her body.

"Whatever you want," she moaned, helping him with his belt buckle. "Also, we're getting married in three months."

He groaned. "Thank the gods. The sooner, the better." He kissed her slowly. "Please shut up while I ravish you. Your every wish is my command."

CHAPTER 42

Asha let out a happy breath once they were back in the penthouse, thanking the bellboy for bringing their luggage up. "I'm really going to miss Maui, but there's no place like home."

Konstantinos grinned. "That's high praise, coming from someone who's jetlagged."

"Can you blame me? You couldn't keep your hands off me on the flight."

"You told me you wanted to join the mile-high club," he reminded her. "Do you have regrets?"

"No, except that we don't have much time to recover. We start working in two days." She pulled a face. "I don't know about you, but paperwork is not my favourite activity."

"Agreed."

She burst out laughing when he picked her up, taking her by surprise. "Teeny! I don't have the energy!"

"I obviously did a terrible job in Maui, 'cause you're

still walking," he teased, carrying her up the stairs. "Besides, we haven't properly christened this place yet. We'll start with our bed, but I fully intend to take you on every available…"

She didn't have to look to know why he had trailed off. He was standing at the threshold of the main bedroom, staring at the wreckage in front of him. His grip slowly loosened and she took the opportunity to get to her feet, biting her lip so she wouldn't laugh at his facial expression.

A part of her was relieved to realize no one's been in here since they've left, not even to clean up the mess. They finally had their privacy back!

"Bigfoot, I don't mean to sound like an idiot, but I'm pretty sure there used to be a bed here."

She shrugged nonchalantly. "I burned it."

"I can see that," he murmured, eyes wide. "You're an angry little thing when you think you're being wronged, huh?"

"Well, I wasn't going to sleep in the bed where you supposedly shagged my best friend."

"Damn, remind me never to make you mad."

"Oh, I will," she promised. "So, if we're *not* going to have sex, can you please leave me alone while I catch up on some much-needed sleep? If you recall, I didn't get a lot of that on our honeymoon, especially after we began feeling better."

His gaze saw right through her clothes. "I remember everything."

She bit her bottom lip to stifle a moan. With one heated look from this man, she wanted to strip naked and jump him without any consideration of the consequences. Her exhaustion faded, replaced by pure desire. In fact, remembering their latest antics in the private jet's bedroom was quickly making her hot and bothered.

"Hmm, I should probably thank you for fulfilling my mile-high fantasy," she said, taking his hand and dragging him to the next available bedroom, which happened to be hers.

"How are you going to do that?"

"By ticking another one off the list."

He raised an eyebrow, intrigued. "Go on."

Feeling braver than usual, she opened one of the drawers of the bedside table and extracted two pairs of silver, heavy-duty handcuffs, dangling them from her fingertips.

"Are those for me or you?" he asked, his voice hoarse.

"For you."

She bit her lip while she waited for him to say no, aware that he still had a fear of being at someone else's mercy thanks to the things his ex had done. The muscles in his jaw worked while he mulled her proposition over. She was about to apologize, to put his mind at ease and insist that they didn't have to go through with it, when he said something that amazed her.

"Okay, for me," he nodded, undressing. Once he was naked, he got on the bed and motioned for her to come closer. He held his hands in place and she cuffed him to the headboard. Staring into her eyes, he said: "I trust you, Asha."

She went to stand at the foot of the bed and pressed play on her iPod's docking station. "I think it's time for me to give you a show, Mr. Sarantos," she murmured seductively, swaying to the beat. "I promise you won't be disappointed."

"You tied me to the bed for *this*? A striptease?" His eyes went black with desire as her dress dropped to the carpet, and the cuffs rattled on the bedframe while he tried to get free. "Bigfoot, this is torture!"

She smiled broadly. "We'll see about torture, Teeny. Wait until I start your lap dance…"

CHAPTER 43

KONSTANTINOS WAS INDESCRIBABLY proud as he watched Asha's creations parade down the runway. He couldn't take his eyes off the models, but not because of the same reasons he had been used to: he was no longer hunting his next conquest. No, he was gazing at the way the outfits emphasised the curves of these women and appreciating Asha's talent.

Dubai was in for a real treat tonight.

His wife had insisted on breaking the size-zero-or-below trend, and it was paying off. The audience was enamoured with her work, as well as the shapely models. Konstantinos was basically vibrating with excitement, much to his brother's amusement.

"Calm down," Loikanos laughed, jabbing his older brother in the ribs with his elbow. "If you clap any harder, your hands are going to start bleeding."

"Are you kidding? This is the most spectacular thing Asha's ever done!"

Denise, rubbing her small six-month bump, nodded in agreement. She had a knowing smile on her face when she touched Loikanos' leg. "You can't fault a husband's pride, can you, *mon cher*?"

Loikanos lifted her hand to his mouth, kissing her knuckles and giving her stomach a meaningful look. "You're right, *mon amour*." He leered at his brother. "I'm sorry if I offended you, Teeny."

Konstantinos rolled his eyes. "It's only cool if my wife calls me that."

"She started a trend. You can't blame everyone for catching on."

"But you don't call *her* Bigfoot," he complained.

"We've been over this a million times, bro. Asha's name is shorter and easier to pronounce, even though I'm Greek and should be able to say your name in my sleep. Admittedly, that would be weird. I mean, why would I say your name in bed? Disgusting! And... God, *mon amour*, are you seeing this? He's ignoring me again!"

Konstantinos kept his smile in check, not alluding to the fact that he'd heard everything. His gaze was fixed on the show: male models were beginning to pour out to the delight of the photographers. His heart swelled with love, since he knew that *he* was the inspiration behind every design. Heck, he was currently dressed in a suit Asha had made with her own hands.

It was the most comfortable thing he's ever worn.

"I'm going to check up on her."

Loikanos gripped Konstantinos' forearm before he could move. "You'll only be in the way, bro. You have no idea what it's like backstage."

"He's right," Denise said, giving Konstantinos an apologetic look. "She'll be mad. The two of you don't exactly argue… quietly."

Konstantinos threw his head back and guffawed loudly. He couldn't argue with that. Less than a week ago, they'd had a fight about something that currently made no sense to him. Whenever this happened, she lost her cool mask and shouted at him until she was red in her face: an accomplishment for someone with her genetics. The argument escalated significantly whenever he answered in his mother tongue. This was why, to piss him off, she was learning Italian so that she could swear at him in a language *he* didn't understand.

It's a good thing they didn't have neighbours, because he could only imagine what it must sound like, hearing people from two different nationalities arguing in even stranger tongues.

Their fights never lasted longer than half an hour, leaving them laughing breathlessly at each other for being dramatic. He appreciated that she didn't keep quiet about what bothered her anymore. His culture was built on loud rows. Asha would make a very convincing Mediterranean woman.

She didn't know that he was aware yet, but he'd learned that she was busy studying Greek with his mother's help. The two of them were two peas in a pod. Heaven help his children one day, because they were going to be spoilt rotten. Kolina was crazy about her daughter-in-law.

"Are you kidding me?" Loikanos asked, bringing his brother back to the present. "That's the last time I ever invite you to my house for dinner. I can't believe you fought because of the salt and pepper shakers!"

"Don't be ridiculous!" Denise chided her husband. "You are welcome any time, *chéri*."

"Thanks, Denise." Konstantinos gave them a knowing look. "You can only imagine what we do to make up for those fights."

The French woman smiled smugly. "I knew, the second I was given this task, that things would be pretty explosive between the two of you."

Oh, were they ever!

"Can we please not talk about their sex-life?" Loikanos requested grumpily.

Konstantinos was already reminiscing about their bedroom antics, the rest of the world fading to a dull throb around him. Asha was not afraid to try new things. Sure, they weren't making love as often as they had on their honeymoon—mostly thanks to real life finally catching up to them—but when they did, they made it count.

He'd been terrified that other tenants would call Dubai's authorities now that they were temporarily living here. Asha could raise the roof off a place, good God. Gone was the shy, withdrawn woman that had initially captured his heart. She's blossomed into someone who drove him wild with one look: a real temptress.

"Get your mind out of the gutter, damn it!" Loikanos grumbled.

Konstantinos neatly dodged his brother's hand and stood up. "I'm going back there."

"We warned you!"

He grinned, rushing backstage. Yes, people certainly had warned him about marriage, stating that the first year was the hardest. Well, if this was supposed to be difficult, he looked forward to the wheel turning to the easier part. How much fun were they going to have *then?*

He spotted Asha in the middle of the room with three different models around her. He admired the view from afar. Her hair was pulled back in a fashionable high ponytail that ended in the middle of her back; her makeup was simple, though her lips were tainted with a soft red that complimented the slightly revealing green, sleeveless top she wore. Her black slacks were fitted to her curvier body.

He was still stunned that she hadn't minded the few pounds she's picked up. She's lost her almost-too-thin frame and looked like a woman now and, heaven above, her body was his favourite physical thing in the world.

She was frantically telling the stylists what to do, moving between the models while she made last-minute adjustments to their outfits. Her brows were furrowed in concentration. She flinched when she accidently pricked her finger with the sewing needle she was running through the back of a dress.

A split-second before he took a step forward, she glanced up at him, as if she's been aware of him standing there this whole time. He nearly melted on the spot, wishing that they were alone. He would like to relieve the tension in her rigid posture.

"I love you," he whispered, knowing she'd be able to read those words from his lips, given the amount of times he said it daily.

She beamed at him and winked. "You too."

Satisfied that she wasn't freaking out from, he made his way back to his seat for exactly the seventh time in the past hour. He loved that woman with an intensity that used to scare him, but he wouldn't have it any other way.

As far as he was concerned, his heart was on lockdown for Asha Sarantos.

* * * * *

SHE WOULD BE lying if she said that she didn't feel better every time her husband checked up on her. He had this innate ability to calm her whenever she was about to go over the edge. This was probably the most important show of her career, and she felt like everything was going wrong.

Five of her models had dropped out due to a delayed flight from the US, leaving her to scramble to get other women with similar shapes. Of course, she's had to tailor many pieces from scratch. She had numerous bruises on her fingers from stitching things together, but at least the show was going on.

And, at the centre of it all, was Konstantinos.

In the space of eight months, he's completely transformed her life from the bottom up. She couldn't imagine what she would do without his constant love and support. She even liked the way they argued; and especially adored what happened in the bedroom, or in the shower, or against a wall...

"Focus, Asha," she admonished herself softly. She glanced up to catch her stylist's eye, tapping the model in front of her on the shoulder to indicate that she was finished. "Can you get this one off to makeup? Who else except these two needs something altered?" she yelled.

"Over here!"

She heaved a mental sigh. "Well, come on, then! We don't have all night!" She carefully placed pins on the one model's shirt in a way that the audience wouldn't be able to detect before moving off to the next crisis. She felt like she was being pulled in a million different directions.

Asha sensed that someone was looking at her, but she it wasn't Konstantinos' familiar tingling. Tilting her head up, she nearly screamed once she recognized Praven. What the hell did he want? She didn't have the time or patience for this!

"Can I talk to you?" he asked, stepping forward now that she's acknowledged his presence.

"Sure, it's not like I'm busy or anything," she replied sarcastically. "There aren't hundreds of people in this room with me, and there certainly aren't millions watching outside."

He stared at his hands. "It's important, and it'll only take a second."

"And you can't wait until the show's finished? I *work* on seconds, Praven."

"I realize that, Ash."

"I'm not getting rid of you, am I?"

"Not tonight."

She rolled her eyes. "Give me five minutes. Go wait in the next room." She finished up with the models, made sure that everyone was ready to go, and walked to Praven. She crossed her arms over her chest. "Talk."

"Asha, you look beauti—"

"Stop wasting my time."

Fidgeting with his hands, he said: "I have to tell you something about Marietta."

She fell silent, a cold drop of sweat sliding down her spine. She hasn't heard that name in months. She's been avoiding that topic as far as she could, and for good reason: though that Italian slut had been her best friend, once upon a time, she'd also deepened Konstantinos' psychological scars. Asha refused to be sad when Marietta had nearly ruined everything.

Thank God for people like Loikanos and Denise.

"This better be good," she ground out, furious.

"I'm hoping it'll give you closure." Praven looked at her intently. "She texted me before orchestrating that entire event. I'm the reason why she knew when to do everything, because I had you followed."

She couldn't believe her ears. "You son of a—"

"She said she wanted to destroy your happiness because you never told her about the engagement, even though you guys were best friends. She also said that you always got everything you want and that she was sick of it. She said I should be there for you when you broke off the engagement, because *I'm* what you deserved." He forced a smile. "Was I really that terrible,

Ash?"

Her jaw dropped to the floor. "Are you kidding me with this shit? You have the nerve to tell me that you were a co-conspirator in what happened to my husband, and then you have the audacity to ask about our relationship? Praven, were you at all present during that time? You broke my self-esteem down to *nothing* with the things you said!"

He flinched. "I was a stupid boy—"

"Oh, you haven't changed," she sneered. "What kind of man agrees to sabotage a perfectly good relationship? Did you know that Marietta drugged my husband? Actually, don't answer that, 'cause I don't want to hear your soppy excuses. I guess I'm not altogether surprised that you just *happened* to show up at that pub after Marietta's plan worked." She shook her head. "You should leave, before I call Konstantinos to kick your ass. He really hates you for what you did to me, and if he finds out that you had a part in *this*... Oh, and he will, because I don't hide anything from him."

"Asha, I wanted to apologize. I should never have done that."

She turned on her heel. "Make like a tree, Praven. I never want to see you again."

"But Ash—"

"What's going on in here?" Konstantinos asked, appearing in the doorway. His dark eyes narrowed when he saw her ex. "They're calling for you, Bigfoot."

She checked her watch. "But the show shouldn't be finished yet."

"Some problem with one of the girls' heels. What's *he* doing here?"

"He was just telling me how he worked with Marietta to set up that wonderful incident that nearly annihilated our marriage before it began," she responded, folding her arms over her chest while she glared at the lowlife she used to date. She loved how a flash of fear crossed Praven's features when Konstantinos flexed his hands. "Apparently, the deal was this: Marietta gets you, and he gets *me*. Ambitious, right?"

"I'm really trying not to bash his face in right now," Konstantinos snarled, taking a menacing step forward, "but only because this is your night and I don't want to spoil it by killing this bastard."

"Look, man, I told Ash that—"

"Only close friends and family members are allowed to call her that," he interjected. He rolled his shoulders. "Since you are nothing of the sort, I think I should warn you that I'm incredibly possessive over things that are mine. You should've taken this story to your grave, Praven Kahn, because I'm not opposed to murder."

Asha did nothing when her husband wrapped a large hand around the Indian's throat. In fact, she was mildly jealous that Konstantinos got to do that. She would love to torture Praven for the twisted things he's done since she's known him.

"Leave," Konstantinos told Praven, his face inches away from the latter's. "If I hear that you've contacted her in any way, I'll be very upset. You won't like that at all. I am, after all, one of the most powerful men in the world." He cocked his head to the side. "Who the hell are *you*?"

Praven scampered to his feet and out of the room as soon as Konstantinos let go, not even bothering to greet Asha.

She, on the other hand, swooned at her husband's display of masculinity. "Thanks for showing up when you did," she murmured, dying to go to him. "I was about to kick him in the balls, but that was more satisfying."

He rubbed his hair, causing it to point in all directions, the way it did after sex. Whoa. "I can't believe people actually do the shit he does."

"He told me I look good, too, before he told me the whole story."

"I should've killed him," Konstantinos snapped. "*No one* gets to flirt with my wife and live to tell the tale."

His dangerous mood was thrilling her to her toes. She shivered as she put her arms around his shoulders. "Hulk angry," she teased, nipping at his earlobe. "Hulk need sex."

"Asha, don't play with me. I won't let you out of this room for at least twenty minutes."

"Since when has that been a problem?" she hummed on his neck. "Come on, Mr. Territorial: claim what's yours."

When he lifted her into his arms, she wrapped her legs around his waist. He slammed the door shut and pressed her against it. "You asked for it, Bigfoot." He kissed her hungrily, and their hands were everywhere, all at once. She welcomed him like only a happy wife could, moaning at every caressing touch and encouraging word.

The audience was calling for an appearance by the designer while Asha and Konstantinos reached completion.

CHAPTER 44

"WE REALLY DON'T have to be here."

Asha glanced at him and smiled reassuringly. "What better way to put this to bed, so to speak?"

He sighed, realizing he wasn't going to win, and got out of the car. He walked around to open his wife's door. "I hate cemeteries," he muttered, taking her hand in his. "I can't believe you dragged me all the way to Italy to do this."

"You can't say you didn't enjoy Rome."

"I did," he conceded, "but this isn't a tourist attraction. This is where that bitch is buried."

"We have to move on, Teeny," she soothed. "This is the only way I can put it behind me. What plot number did they say it was?"

"Hell, do you think I paid attention?"

"I think it's this one." She stopped in front of a headstone with a statue of an angel. "Ironic."

He couldn't look at the name on the gravestone. Just

being here sent shivers up and down his spine: not because they were in a place where corpses were decomposing, but because Marietta had caused him to relive the darkness of his past.

Asha was the only woman allowed to take control of him in bed. She's never broken his trust. She stopped when things got too much and held him whenever he broke down, though the latter had only happened in the beginning. His wife had healed him by using his fears against him, proving that he could be tied up and safe, at the same time.

He still had to decide which was better: being at her mercy, or restraining her while he gradually worked his way over her body. Currently, it was a tie.

"Teeny, hello? You here?"

He shook himself and smiled. "Yeah, I'm here."

"Okay, I'm going to talk to her now, so I don't think I'm weird," Asha stated, shuffling closer to the grave.

"I already know you are."

"Smartass." She kneeled and touched the gravestone. "Hey, M, it's me. You know, the woman you loved to hate. Towards the end, anyway. Uhm, Praven told me what you did, so I thought I'd come here with Teeny to come to terms with it. I guess I'll never know what went through your mind at the time. I wish you could've talked to me: I would've broken the rules and told you the truth about our engagement, because that's how much I loved you."

Konstantinos looked around, sussing out if there were eavesdroppers around. He had tears in his eyes, too, and didn't want his wife to see.

"That being said, what you did was wrong on so many levels. You were obviously a damaged girl. I know it's probably because of your family shunning you when your brother was born, but you should've dealt with it." Asha sniffed. "I miss you, especially now that I have at least four runway shows a year. I want to know what you think of my ideas. You used to be so trendy." She cleared her throat. "Anyway, even though it was a shitty time during my relationship with Teeny, I want to thank you for what you did."

He blinked in surprise. What?

"We're much closer than we ever thought we would be. If you hadn't done that, he would probably never have admitted what Lena had done to him. I guess your plan backfired. I'm sad that you weren't around to see it. I could tell by your email that you regretted it the second I left." She placed a white rose on the grave and stood up. "I forgive you and I love you. I hope you're in a better place."

Konstantinos silently admitted that Asha had a point. It might be such a tired cliché, but things really *did* happen for a reason.

"Are you going to say something?"

He shook his head. "I think you said it all. I feel better already."

"We're never coming back here again," she warned him. "This is your last chance."

"Fine," he mumbled. Fixing that deceptive angel with a cold stare, he declared: "I never liked you, but thanks for what you did. Asha's right. It was a blessing in disguise, actually. It doesn't mean that I'm suddenly going to think you're this awesome person, but it certainly helps to tolerate what you did. If you reincarnated somewhere, stay out of other people's happiness and create your own instead."

"Aw, that was beautiful!" Asha cheered, jumping into his arms. "You're adorable, Teeny. Is that a *tear* I see in your left eye? Are you crying?"

"No," he answered gruffly.

"Oh, please! I'm not an idiot! You know I love it when you show your softer side."

He carried her back to the car and dumped her on the passenger seat. "I don't have one," he said before he slammed her door shut. She was laughing when he started the car. "Shush, Bigfoot, or you're going to get it tonight."

"Sounds promising. Will I be on top?"

Giving her a sideways glance, he grinned. "Wouldn't you love to know?"

EPILOGUE

"I HATE YOU, do you know that?" Asha told Denise while she struggled to take her seat.

The French woman—and her best friend in the world—seemed offended. "Why, *chérie?* What have I done?"

"You make pregnancy look so good!" Asha was panting by the time she was finally comfortable on her favourite chair. Her hands automatically cupped her large belly. "You hardly pick up any weight, and you're much calmer than usual. *I*, on the other hand, am a raving bitch and look like a bus!"

"Konstantinos loves your curves," Denise soothed. "All he does is stare at your bosom when you're in the same room together."

"Pervert," Asha muttered.

"Besides, this is my third time." Denise patted her slightly rounded stomach. "I know what to expect by now."

"Can't you barf in front of me to make me feel better? I'm so bloated! You'd swear I'm carrying twins."

"I think you look beautiful, *chérie*," Denise said earnestly. "It will all be worth it when you have that boy in your arms."

Asha couldn't wait to meet her son. After five years of marriage and her beloved mother-in-law's incessant pleading, she'd finally decided to succumb to peer pressure and get knocked up. Konstantinos had required a bit of convincing, but he had agreed once she pointed out that their workloads weren't as excessive anymore. Or maybe they were simply getting used to their busy lives.

She was due in three weeks. She struggled climbing stairs—though she was inwardly pleased every time her husband carried her to bed—so she'd taken maternity leave from work earlier than she had to. She handled what she could during the day, but mostly kept her feet propped up while she stuffed her face. Eighteen kilograms later, she was beginning to worry that she'll be fat forever.

"It's harder for me, in a way," Denise went on. "I'm in my early forties."

Asha shook her head at the blonde woman. "And yet you don't have a grey hair on your head. Life is so unfair."

Denise laughed. "Come now, *chérie*! Stop putting yourself down, or I'll tell Teeny."

"Tell me what?" the man in question asked, carrying a tray of goodies into the living room. Her toes curled when his gaze landed on her tummy and lit up with pride. He dropped to his knees next to her chair and massaged her calves.

"She said she's a bus," Denise tattled gleefully.

"Traitor," Asha mumbled, shutting her eyes as her husband's lovely fingers caressed her skin and aching muscles.

"Crazy," Konstantinos growled before dropping a kiss on her protruding belly. "Can I get you anything?"

"You're such an enabler." Her eyes widened at the sight of those delicacies on the coffee table. "Give me a doughnut and a cup of tea, please."

He chuckled, pressing his lips to hers and doing as he was told. "Anything for you, Denise?"

"A cup of tea would be lovely, *chéri.*"

"Zoom!" Loikanos exclaimed, sprinting into the room with a giggling Charlotte—his four-year-old daughter—in his arms, Superman-style. "Zoom, zoom, zoom!" He twirled her while he came to a stop in front of the grown-ups in the room. "Look, mommy! Isn't she the mightiest little girl you've ever seen?"

"She has to be if she's making you behave like an idiot," Konstantinos laughed.

"Not so loud, bro!" Loikanos put his daughter down and rushed over to the pram next to Denise. "You're going to wake Adeleine!"

"Like it's any better that you're shouting at me?"

"Boys, please," Asha said around a mouthful of her chocolate doughnut. "Not again."

She had to admit that Loikanos was the cutest father she's ever seen. She already knew that Konstantinos would be stricter, yet still kind and loving, and she was grateful for that: Loikanos might be more whimsical than his older brother, but Asha would be exhausted from spending too much time around him.

She had no idea how Denise managed to stay this serene, what with that activity surrounding her.

"Mum, here," Charlotte said, giving Denise a pink flower.

A headache throbbed at Asha's temples: the little girl must've dug that out of her garden. Great. Why chase away rabbits when Charlotte was around? Those poor rabbits had nothing on Denise and Loikanos' eldest daughter. In fact, Charlotte might teach rabbits even worse manners!

Asha took another bite of the doughnut before she said anything mean. Damn pregnancy hormones!

Denise mouthed a meek apology to Asha, but told her daughter: "Ah, *chérie*, it's beautiful! Thank you."

Asha rested her hands on top of her stomach, wondering for the gazillionth time what her relationship with her son was going to be like. She hoped it would be playful and fun, but she got the feeling that she had a brooding soul snuggled in her belly.

"Addy, you're up!" Loikanos bolted to his two-year-old, lifting her out of the pram even though she hasn't started complaining yet. Adeleine was very good at letting people know when she's upset. "Aw, baby, daddy missed you! Do you want to play with uncle Teeny's pencils?"

Konstantinos groaned. "Please don't do that again!

Do you know how much they cost?"

His younger brother snorted. "As if you're living on a tight budget, Mr. Forbes' list."

"That's not the point! They're rare and—"

"Mum, what's rare?" Charlotte interrupted, ogling Denise with guileless blue eyes. Her dark locks were kept out of her face by a head band.

"One of a kind," Denise murmured, kissing the top of her eldest daughter's head. "Just like you."

Konstantinos sat down on the arm of Asha's chair, giving her a look. "I'm already regretting this. You know it's only going to get worse when mama and papa get here? Not to mention *your* family."

"It's a good thing we got a bigger house, then," Asha teased, leaning her head on his arm. "This family is huge. I need a list just to remember everyone's names!" She eyed him. "What's your name again?"

He moved closer to nibble on her bottom lip, murmuring: "You screamed it in pleasure only last night, Bigfoot."

Her body pulsed at that reminder. Damn pregnancy hormones! She wanted to jump him, all the time. That was difficult to do on the best of days, since she was as big as a mountain. Even though her body has filled out—hello, her breasts were out to *here*—he was still the muscled, eight-pack man she had fallen so madly in love with. He was adamant to keep his body the way it was, often exercising up to two hours a day. She loved to follow the sweat dripping down his skin with her eyes...

She could recall how careful he'd been with her the

night before. It was quite an accomplishment to make love this far into the pregnancy, yet he always found a way to take the edge off. She loved that about him: he worshipped her, and she returned that admiration tenfold.

"If you keep looking at me like that, we'll give these kids a show they didn't ask for," Konstantinos told her, jerking her back to the present.

"Hmm, you're right." Her nose twitched at a scent coming from the kitchen. "Oh God, help me up before the food burns!"

"What?" Loikanos glanced at her with confusion. Adeleine was cosily sitting on his lap and drooling over her doll. "I don't smell anything."

"You know she's got a sixth sense, like mama," Konstantinos reminded his brother.

"Here, I'll help," Denise said once Asha was on her feet. "You should have let me cook, *chérie*."

Asha smiled at her friend. "You know I love it too much. Who'd have thought I'd be a housewife, huh?"

"The role suits you."

Asha put her gloves on and opened the oven door, her eyes shutting in bliss at the aroma of the roast chicken and vegetables. The bird was crispy on the outside and juicy on the inside. If she had waited five minutes longer, it would've started turning to coal.

She switched the oven off and laughed as the doorbell rang. "Could you get that, Denise? Mama said she looks forward to seeing you again."

"Of course, *chérie*."

Asha checked on dessert, knowing that her husband

was basically going to wet himself once he found out she'd prepared those custard slices he loved. He begged her for it all the time, but she only made it on special occasions, in case he took it for granted.

Besides, *she* wanted him to remain fit and toned as much as he did.

She took out enough wine glasses for the adults, subconsciously rubbing her stomach at the thought of not being able to join them. They were going to have the best bottles of wine today. Her son kicked in response to her internal sulking and she chuckled softly. "Yes, baby boy, I know. I don't regret that I can't have wine, so why don't you lay off?"

"Stavros!"

Asha jumped and glanced over her shoulder, her eyebrows pulling together at Kolina's exclamation. "Stavros?" she echoed, giving her mother-in-law a fierce hug.

"My grandchild's name," Kolina explained in Greek. She touched Asha's stomach with a happy smile. "I know how you have struggled to find a strong, masculine name for him, so I took the liberty of asking around. All of my friends agree that Stavros is perfect."

"Hmm, it could work," Asha said thoughtfully. "It's Indian enough, too."

"Your Greek is beautiful, daughter. I am so proud of you."

Asha kissed Kolina's cheek. "Will you take a look at the food, mama? I can hear my parents, and you know how much papa hates it when he thinks I'm ignoring him."

"Of course! I can smell that everything is perfect, but I'm happy to help."

Exiting the industrial-sized kitchen, Asha caught up with the rest of her boisterous family in the living room. It's a good thing Adeleine had woken up by herself, or she would have been shrieking from the interruption. Asha hugged her father-in-law fondly. Even though he was a hard man, he seemed to have a soft spot for her and Denise. Then she moved on to her own family.

"You're huge!" Kashinath laughed, wincing when Kaila punched him on the shoulder.

"She's *beautiful*," the Hawaiian beauty insisted.

"I'm both?" Asha giggled. "Thanks for trying to make me feel better, but my brother's right. I'm huge."

Farida, who'd dyed her hair red a year ago, embraced her sister. "Ash, I'm so jealous! Can I watch while you give birth?"

"You mean, while another living being pushes its way out of one of the tiniest holes in my body? Sure, why not?"

Kashinath grimaced. "That's disgusting. I'll pass."

"You weren't invited," Farida said sweetly.

"Where's the boyfriend today?" Konstantinos asked, draping an arm around Asha's waist. His hand, as always, ended up touching her swollen stomach.

"We broke up," Farida mumbled dismissively. "So far, Denise's matchmaking skills suck."

"Oh, please!" Loikanos chuckled. "You never go out with the men she recommends!"

Anushka shook her head at her youngest daughter. "If you seriously want to find the man of your dreams, you should listen to Denise."

"I enjoy playing around."

"Just remember that no man wants a used bicycle," Sukesh muttered.

"Daddy!" Asha clamped her ears shut. "No, I can't listen to this! I think we should get dinner out of the way so you can go back to where you came from!"

Sukesh grinned. "I don't know about the rest of y'all, but *I* only came here for the food, anyway."

They shared a laugh and ushered the smaller children to the large dining area. Denise, Kolina, Farida and Anushka went to the kitchen to fetch the meals Asha had prepared earlier. Everybody gushed over the food once the lids came off.

Konstantinos pulled Asha's chair out for her and went to sit down on the opposite side of the table to stare at her, pure love in his gaze. She winked at him and began serving everyone a plate, telling them about his latest skyscraper, the one that had recently been unveiled in Melbourne. Their time in Australia had been one of the best experiences of her life.

She was happily married to the man who had named a building after her, made her forget about her insecurities, and fought for her when she'd been certain they were going to fall apart. Not only that, but she *adored* her new relatives: it was a healthy mix of fun-loving Indians and family-oriented Greeks, with a dash of French romance in the form of Denise Lemont and her offspring.

From her perspective, family traditions were there for a reason and, if given the chance, she wouldn't change anything in her life. Every bump in the road had led her to this moment, sitting across from her husband with their child inside of her. Her life was complicated, simple, busy and quiet, all wrapped into one.

She loved it.

The End.

Acknowledgements

ALTHOUGH I HAVE never met Kanye West, I'd like to give him a shout-out: *Love Lockdown* (the song, not this book) played on repeat when I penned the first draft of this novel way back in 2012. Hands down the best song he's ever created, in my humble opinion, of course.

This story has always been dear to my heart simply because it is the wholesome, happily-ever-after type of romantic fiction that I enjoy reading. I often smile when I read this, which I've done more times that I can count. I feel like 90% of an author's time is spent going over what they've written and, seeing as I edited and published this novel all by my lonesome, it's doubly true.

Lyn, in many ways, you are my spirit animal. You are vibrant and bubbly and brilliant. I don't know what I'd do without your enthusiastic, contagious support. Thank you for being such an uplifting friend! I can only hope that I return the favour.

Finally, to you, dear reader: thank you for choosing this book. I hope you enjoyed it. There might be surprises—in the form of a short novella from Marietta's perspective, and a novel from Stavros'—in store in future, so keep an eye on my website for more information!